THE COUNTRY OF THE POINTED FIRS
AND OTHER STORIES

HARDSCRABBLE BOOKS—Fiction of New England

Laurie Alberts, *The Price of Land in Shelby*

Thomas Bailey Aldrich, *The Story of a Bad Boy*

Anne Bernays, *Professor Romeo*

Chris Bohjalian, *Water Witches*

Sean Connolly, *A Great Place to Die*

Dorothy Canfield Fisher (Mark J. Madigan, ed.),
Seasoned Timber

Joseph Freda, *Suburban Guerrillas*

Ernest Hebert, *The Dogs of March*

Ernest Hebert, *Live Free or Die*

Sarah Orne Jewett (Sarah Way Sherman, ed.), *The Country
of the Pointed Firs and Other Stories*

Kit Reed, *J. Eden*

Rowland E. Robinson (David Budbill, ed.), *Danvis Tales:
Selected Stories*

Roxana Robinson, *Summer Light*

Rebecca Rule, *The Best Revenge: Short Stories*

Theodore Weesner, *Novemberfest*

W. D. Wetherell, *The Wisest Man in America*

Edith Wharton (Barbara A. White, ed.), *Wharton's New England:
Seven Stories and* Ethan Frome

Thomas Williams, *The Hair of Harold Roux*

THE COUNTRY
OF THE POINTED FIRS

AND OTHER STORIES

CENTENNIAL EDITION

SARAH ORNE JEWETT

Edited, with an introduction, by Sarah Way Sherman

University of New Hampshire

Published by University Press of New England

UNIVERSITY PRESS OF NEW ENGLAND
publishes books under its own imprint and is the publisher for Brandeis
University Press, Dartmouth College, Middlebury College Press, University
of New Hampshire, Tufts University, and Wesleyan University Press.

University of New Hampshire
Published by University Press of New England, Hanover, NH 03755

The Country of the Pointed Firs was originally published by Houghton Mifflin
and Company, Boston and New York, in 1896.

"A Dunnet Shepherdess" and "The Queen's Twin" were originally published in
The Atlantic Monthly (February and December 1899), then revised and collected
in The Queen's Twin and Other Stories (Boston and New York: Houghton Mifflin,
1899). The book edition is used here for both.

"The Foreigner" and "William's Wedding" were originally published in The Atlantic Monthly (August 1900 and August 1910).

Printed in the United States of America   5 4 3 2 1

Library of Congress Cataloging-in-Publication Data
Jewett, Sarah Orne, 1849–1909.
    The country of the pointed firs and other stories / Sarah Orne
Jewett ; edited, with an introduction, by Sarah Way Sherman. —
Centennial ed.
        p.   cm. — (Hardscrabble books)
    Contents: The country of the pointed firs — William's wedding —
The queen's twin — The foreigner — A Dunnet shepherdess.
    ISBN 0–87451–826–1 (pa : alk. paper)
    1. United States—Social life and customs—19th century—Fiction.
2. Maine—Social life and customs—Fiction. 3. Women—Maine—
Fiction. I. Sherman, Sarah Way. II. Title. III. Series.
PS2132.C64 1997b
813'.4—dc21   96–53845

CONTENTS

INTRODUCTION TO
THE COUNTRY OF THE
POINTED FIRS

This Hardscrabble book reproduces the 1896 first edition of Sarah Orne Jewett's *The Country of the Pointed Firs*. Its pages are taken directly from a text purchased at a used book store in Portsmouth, New Hampshire; the flyleaf still bears the inscription, "In memory of pleasant summer days C. H. M. from H. E. R. December 23, 1896." I don't know who C. H. M. and H. E. R. were, but I imagine that they were friends and that Jewett's book was exchanged as a kind of token, a symbol of a summer they shared, much as the narrator of this book and her landlady share the pieces of early apple pie at the Bowden Reunion. Jewett's readers still give this book as a gift. I am even occasionally asked to inscribe my own, rather scholarly, book about Jewett as a present from one friend to another or, as happened several times, from a daughter or son to a mother.

What makes *The Country of the Pointed Firs*, like the coastal village it describes, "so attaching" is hard to say. Its pleasures are so subtle and unassuming. But like a landscape one comes to admire gradually, walking it slowly and seeing it change over several seasons, or like an acquaintance who grows into an intimate friend, Jewett's book can enter into the fabric of daily life for the sympathetic reader. Its vision and the reader's can seem mysteriously to merge. Above her desk Jewett pinned this passage from Flaubert: "Ce n'est pas de faire rire, ni de faire pleurer, ni de vous mettre à fureur, mais d'agir à la façon de la nature, c'est à dire de faire rêver" ("It is not to inspire laughter, nor tears, nor rage, but to act as nature does, to inspire dreaming"). Hers was a kind of poetic realism, a restrained art of suggestion. These stories, as Willa Cather said, can evoke a sense of "living things caught in the open, with light and freedom and air-spaces about them." While Jewett's father once told her, "Don't try to write *about* people and things, tell them just as they are!" her greatest work shows that the meaning of "people and things" shifts with one's perspective. Landscapes, houses, and people reveal their being only to a perceiving eye, and perhaps their deepest being only to a loving eye. Hence Sarah Wyman Whitman's graceful design for the cover of this 1896 edition: three stylized wildflowers stamped in gold upon a green background, each flower blooming atop a sinuous solitary stem, each stem growing from a simple heart.

The ground of Jewett's art was in many ways her relation to the country life she described. Its people and their ways not only gave her literary material, but shaped her understanding and treatment of that material. Looking to the pastoral world that Jewett celebrated can give us insight into the power and endurance of her writing, and its possible limitations as well. Her relationship to this world, however, was not simple. She was in no way an unsophisticated writer. She once wrote that she hoped to die in the house where she was born in South Berwick, Maine, with the lilacs still green and all the chairs in their places. While these lines might give the impression she was an uncomplicated version of her own Mrs. Todd, firmly planted in her rustic cottage, a visit to Jewett's home quickly reveals the social distance between her rural characters and their author. A distinctive eighteenth-century Georgian, painted white in the classicizing taste of the colonial revival, the house still commands the center of South Berwick, a town on the Salmon Falls River, ten miles inland from the coast. Formal box hedges still line the walk to the broad front door and the lilacs still come into bloom every spring. In the front hallway, alongside the elegant moldings and cornices that supposedly took three ships' carpenters one hundred days to carve, you can see the wallpaper Jewett and her sister installed: a flamboyant floral in bright maroons, creams, and olives. Lush and vibrant in the style of William Morris and the height of fashionable nineteenth-century aestheticism, its design makes visible Jewett's taking possession of the past, linking inherited form to modern sensibility.

The seeming effortlessness of this style is deceptive, as is the apparent ease of Jewett's rural representations. The vision that produced *Pointed Firs* was the result of long looking and listening, a study of her chosen literary subjects informed as much by emotion as intellect. Like those works of American literature to which Cather once compared it, *Huckleberry Finn* and *The Scarlet Letter*, *The Country of the Pointed Firs* represents a moment of artistic self-realization, a writer's reaching beyond her customary limits and inhibitions to produce a work whose greatness even she cannot quite grasp. So Twain frequently underrated *Huckleberry Finn*, and Hawthorne seemed almost frightened by the passionate ambiguities of Hester Prynne's story. Jewett herself preferred *A Marsh Island*, a far more conventional novel. She had put more of herself, she thought, into *The Tory Lover*, a tepid historical romance now forgotten. Like the springs that fed Hawthorne's and Twain's best work, the sources of *Pointed Firs* run deep in Jewett's life and history.[1]

I

Jewett was seen by both her contemporaries and later critics as a regional writer, but, as she herself knew, before one can write about the parish one must know the world, and the world of later nineteenth-century America was one of immense and rapid change. In comparison to coastal Maine and New Hampshire, urban centers such as Boston, Chicago, and New York were virtually exploding. New York, for example, grew from 500,000 in 1850 to three and half million in 1900, roughly over the course of Jewett's lifetime. Only 40 percent of Americans could be described as truly rural by the century's end. By the close of the First World War, about a dozen cities were home to half the population. The United States, despite nostalgic images, had never been a racially or culturally homogeneous country, but now it became even more diverse. Immigration increased from five million between 1829 and

1860 to fourteen million between 1860 and 1900. Rather than the English, Scotch, Irish, and Germans of the earlier years, the post-bellum period saw arrivals from Central, Eastern, and Southern Europe—Austria, Poland, Russia, Greece, Italy, and Turkey—as well as the Far East. These new Americans brought great ethnic and religious differences, and cities like New York, Boston, and Chicago saw the rise of ethnic enclaves and ghettos: Chinatown and Little Italy, Jewish neighborhoods like New York's lower East Side. By 1900 the population of Boston was 30 percent foreign-born; 70 percent were of foreign parentage.[2]

These years also saw the consolidation of monopoly capitalism and the formation of the great industrial empires such as Rockefeller's Standard Oil and Carnegie's U.S. Steel. The robber barons amassed such enormous wealth that by 1890, 1 percent of Americans held 25 percent of the country's wealth. However, the country also experienced serious economic depressions, notably in the years before Jewett's two most pastoral and popular works. There was the Depression of 1873 and the Panic of 1893; the latter led to years of hardship and an unemployment rate as high as 20 percent. Such growing disparities also underlay the labor agitation of the period, culminating in violent confrontations such as the Homestead Strike of 1892 and the Chicago Pullman Strike of 1894. Further, class anxieties exacerbated by labor conflicts often focused on immigrants as a suspected source of "un-American" agitation and discontent. Chinese immigration, for example, was sharply curtailed by the Chinese Exclusion Acts of 1882, 1888, and 1891.

Racial antagonism and suspicion also extended to other groups. The policy of Indian Removal led to the eviction of the Poncas from Dakota Territory in 1877. In 1890 U.S. troops massacred Lakota Sioux at Wounded Knee. By the early 1890s there were between eight and nine million African Americans in the United States. Civil rights won after the Civil War were attacked and relentlessly rolled back by segregationist groups such as the Klu Klux Klan, founded in 1866. Between 1885 and 1910 there were 3500 lynchings. The steady enactment of "Jim Crow" laws established racial segregation in the South, a practice declared legal by the U.S. Supreme Court in its decision, *Plessy* v. *Ferguson* in 1896, the year that *Pointed Firs* was published—a coincidence that gives disturbing resonance to the narrator's apparently approving comment that "clannishness is an instinct of the heart."

However, at the same time that the United States seemed riven by internal differences and conflicts, the new railway systems knitted its cities, towns, and villages together into an immense national network. Similarly, mass circulation magazines and syndicated newspapers linked readers in a vast print community of readers. By 1890 the country had filled its continental borders, an achievement of its supposed destiny acknowledged officially when the United States Census declared the frontier closed in 1890. Thus the famous, and often studied, Columbian Exposition at Chicago in 1893 celebrated a continental, industrialized, and urbanized nation. With its transformed transportation and communication systems in place, its cities full of department stores, its magazines full of advertisements, the United States was poised for entrance into the twentieth century, an entrance also marked by its experiment in imperialist military action, the Spanish-American War of 1898.[3]

In retrospect, the pastoral image of coastal Maine seems very much a product of its contrast with this larger whole, a immense variegated nation in the throes of a vast and far reaching transformation. Of her own South Berwick, Jewett wrote: "From this inland town of mine there is no sea-faring any more, and shipwright's hammers are never heard now. It is only a station on the railway, and it has, after all these years, grown so little that is hardly worth while for the trains to stop."[4] South Berwick had been a flourishing town whose prosperity was based on shipbuilding and lumbering. Sea captains and ship owners like her grandfather, Theodore Furber Jewett, built their fortunes on trading produce and lumber in the West Indies for rum and molasses. Her great uncle Thomas Jewett ran the family's West India store in the center of South Berwick until 1870. It was a gathering spot for farmers from outlying districts and locals to meet and gossip, with perhaps a young Sarah Jewett sitting quietly, and attentively, by. The transatlantic trade, however, began its decline early in the nineteenth century with Jefferson's 1807 Embargo and the War of 1812. The arrival of the railroad before the Civil War further weakened the business. Lumbering also declined as well, as the great trees grew scarcer. On the coast itself, the once prosperous cities of Portsmouth and

Portland seemed seedy and stagnant compared to the metropolises booming to the south. Smaller coast towns like York and Wells, prototypes for Jewett's first regional sketches, seemed completely "out of fashion," backwaters of old times and ways. Jewett described them as almost bereft of young ambitious men, who had left for the opportunities of the industrialized cities or the rich farmland of the Midwest. Whether or not her portrait was entirely accurate, it demonstrates Jewett's own sense of the place where she was born and raised: a traditional society with vibrant memories of the shipping trade's glory days, with strong links to English culture and a still vital preindustrial community of fishing and farming families, a community that kept the bonds to an older agrarian America and its ways still alive.

However, it is now clear that Jewett downplayed or even erased evidence of modernization's effects on the coastal societies she portrayed. South Berwick after the Civil War, for example, was home to several mills. The Salmon Falls River, while longer busy with the gundalow traffic that had once served the shipping trade, provided power to the many thriving small factories along its banks. The textile mill in Rollingsford, New Hampshire, was just a short piece down the road from the Jewett house. Sarah may have heard its shift bells every day. Moreover, the apparent cultural and racial homogeneity of the region was complicated by an influx of immigrant workers, first Irish, then French-Canadian. Historians such as Hal S. Barron argue that rural New Englanders actually coped skillfully with the changes reshaping the nation; many found ways to take advantage of the new opportunities modernization brought.[5] Ironically, the most successful strategy was to capitalize on the rural image that modernization endangered. Tourism, as Dona Brown writes, became the second economic boom after the failure of shipping. Far from sleepy, "by the last quarter of the nineteenth century, the region of the Piscataqua had become a thoroughly modern place. From its textile mills to its vacation resorts it offered the latest in technology, business, and social arrangements. And yet its most 'modern' innovation may have been the recreation of its history."[6]

Of course, Jewett herself was central to this recreation, which drew its evocative power from its opposition to a complex urban present. However, the tourist industry in the Piscataqua region did not come into being through her; it was already in full swing when she began to write. In fact, Jewett attributed one of her strongest motivations as a young writer to her desire to turn the "new relationship" between the urban tourist and rural host into a chance for deeper understanding on both sides. However, here too she simplified the social reality of her material. Thus her first book, *Deephaven* (1877), describes a summer two young Bostonians, genteel and well connected, spend in a fictional community based on the coastal towns of York, Wells, and Kittery. They are virtually the only outsiders around, with the exception of a few shop girls on a day trip. The "ancient" towns are described as depopulated and decaying. Although the visitors arrive by train, no hotels and restaurants mar the historic landscape. The final lines conjure up a future vision of the wharves falling into sea. However, York was at that very moment beginning a thriving new career as a tourist destination, carefully stratified by class. Accommodations ranged from the working-class resort of York Beach to the grand Cliff House hotel (built in 1877) to the elegant new shingled mansions lining York Harbor. A visitor to Wells, Maine, would not have found rotting hulks and mossy docks, but a smart new train delivering hordes of vacationers directly to the beach.

What writers like Jewett offered, intentionally or not, to these eager visitors was the image of Maine as a respite, a visitable past with whose aristocratic history many of the more elite tourists sought to align themselves. Thus this period also saw the founding of local historical and preservation societies anxious to influence villagers "for their own good" and often headed and funded by wealthy summer visitors, some with family roots in the area. The efforts of these summer people, such as Barrett Wendell and Emily Tyson, to restore the seacoast's architecture and recover its "charm" had a decisive impact on the region's image and identity.

In addition to its antimodern bias, much of this motivation had a xenophobic and even racist cast. Jewett's colleague Thomas Bailey Aldrich, for example, grew up in Portsmouth and later become an editor of *The Atlantic Monthly*. An ardent preservationist and summer visitor, known for his kindliness (he even found writing rejection letters agonizing), Aldrich nevertheless made an unguarded plea in his 1892 poem "The Unguarded Gate" to close off immigration and preserve America for the "true" Americans. Similarly, author Thomas Nelson Page, a leader in the movement to restore historic homes and landmarks in York, celebrated his and the town's glorious Anglo-Saxon roots in York's tercentenary celebration in 1902. For many such preservationists, the image of a pastoral Maine was "the way life should be," as a sign still announces to tourists crossing the Piscataqua River on Interstate 95. But as critics have pointed out, this could also translate into a more sinister message, "the way *America* should be," not only rural and peaceful, but also white, Protestant, and preferably of Western European ancestry.[7]

According to some readers, then, Jewett and other regionalists constructed an image for consumption by a literate elite, an image that promised and affirmed their membership in a less diverse and troubled nation than the one encountered in their urban experience. Amy Kaplan and Richard Brodhead have argued, for example, that by focusing their stories on rural "others" who spoke in dialect, these writers catered to a demand not only for a reassuring sense of America's homogeneous cultural roots, but also effectively erased the more threatening presence of those foreign "others" who increasingly peopled not only the urban but also the rural landscape. That is, these stories satisfied an elite market's desire to appropriate the "primitive" to its own needs and to substitute less dangerous and more easily reconcilable differences for those that conflicted the nation.[8]

It is fair to say, as Jewett herself acknowledged, that she came to her literary genre and vocation within this new context of tourism and ethnographic acquisitiveness, as well as within its atmosphere of class and racial anxiety. Her own ideas on class often seem problematic. In *A Country Doctor*, for example, the narrator speculates on the heritability of traits associated with middle and upper class identity, such as "good taste" and professional talent. At times the implications here and in *Deephaven* sound almost feudal, as if "gentle" birth grants innate distinction. But Jewett in these texts also seems aware that such traits had nothing to do with a person's morality or intrinsic worth. There are, one character says, good gentlemen and bad gentlemen. Like the Puritan theologians who recognized intelligence without grace, but saw it as all the more

dangerous for being unenlightened, so Jewett discerns "aristocratic" qualities, yet emphasizes the necessity to direct their use by
democratic compassion and moral obligation. Older representatives
of the gentry, such as Captain Littlepage in *Pointed Firs*, Honora
Carew in *Deephaven*, or Aunt Prince in *A Country Doctor*, are often
represented as rigid and self-absorbed, isolated by their elitism. On
the other hand, *Deephaven*'s Kate Lancaster, Jewett's idealized version of a newly democratic gentry, never shows herself more of a
lady than when she treats the Kentucky Giantess, an enormous
woman who earns her living as a circus display, with "exquisite
courtesy."

A similar balancing act, also not always successful, appears in
Jewett's attempts to deal with ethnicity and race. Her stories
about the Old South, for example, are problematic for their nostalgic treatment, which bears an uncomfortable resemblance to
Thomas Nelson Page's more overtly racist work, and her 1887
work *The Story of the Normans*, written for young readers, cele-
brates the inherited quasi-racial traits of the Normans.[9] As Jewett
writes in *Pointed Firs*, "it is the Norman Englishman, not the
Saxon, who goes adventuring to a new world." Her narrator also
reflects on the "French" faces and traits of the Bowden family, who
may have inherited their instinctive good taste and refined ways
from an aristocratic ancestor in the medieval courts of France.
Jewett's sympathies draw her close to the more xenophobic, even
racist, theories of writers such as Matthew Arnold, whom she
knew and admired.

And yet according to her biographer Paula Blanchard, no pattern of overt xenophobia or racism has surfaced in Jewett's fiction
or letters. Architectural integrity engaged her passions far more
than ethnic homogeneity; she was more distressed by the incursion
of Victorian gingerbread than of immigrant populations.[10] When
Deephaven's Honora Carew expresses relief that no "disagreeable
foreign element" has sullied the local society, Kate Lancaster, rep-
resenting Jewett's new and more enlightened gentry responds, "but
wouldn't you some pleasant new acquaintances?" Hardly a fiery
defense, but in stories like "Between Mass and Vespers" (1893),
"Little French Mary" (1895), and "Where's Nora?" (1899) Jewett
treats recent Irish and French-Canadian arrivals with sympathy

and insight, and in the "The Gray Mills of Farley" (1898) she addresses the exploitation of workers by the capitalist mill owners with real passion. With ethnic differences, as with class identifications, there seems to be a constant struggle in Jewett's work to acknowledge the particular ground in which identity is rooted (to use her own Romantic metaphor) without asserting the superiority of that identity through invidious comparison to others.[11]

Among the many differences and contradictions striating the developing nation, the ones that captured Jewett's literary imagination were those between city and country, present and past, urban elite and preindustrial working class. She found some of her richest material in the conjunction of wealthy tourist and rural host, and the dangerous opportunities for invidious comparison their relationship presented. In a preface written in 1893 for a new edition of *Deephaven*, Jewett reflected that tourism "meant something more than the instinct for green fields and hills and the seashore; crowded towns and the open country were to brought together in a new association and dependence upon each other. . . . It appeared as if a second Harvey had discovered a new and national circulation of vitality along the fast-multiplying railroads that spun their webs to bind together men who had once lived far apart." As a young writer, Jewett confesses, she was at first afraid that this new association would destroy all that was best of the past. She was "possessed by a dark fear that townspeople and country people would never understand one another, nor learn to profit by their new relationship. It seemed not altogether reasonable when timid ladies mistook a selectman for a tramp, because he happened to be crossing a field in his shirtsleeves. At the same time, she was sensible of grave wrong and misunderstanding when these same timid ladies were regarded with suspicion, and their kindnesses were believed to come from pride and patronage."[12]

Jewett saw her task as the mediation of this national division; her role was to interpret, to smooth the way for mutual respect and understanding, to facilitate the healing work of circulation within the national "body." As she herself put it, "There is a noble saying of Plato that the best thing that can done be done for the people of a state is to make them acquainted with one another." For Jewett this acquaintance meant not the appropriating gaze of the condescending tourist nor the opportunistic pose of the rural entrepreneur, but the empathy and understanding of true dialogue. While Jewett certainly came to her literary material within the framework of the tourist economy, what she did within that framework, it seems to me, was to encourage her elite readers to venture beyond their role as spectators into more intimate, demanding, and compassionate relationships with those others whose state they shared. The result she figured as a kind of national exchange with each party receiving the benefit of the other's special wisdom: "Human nature is the same the world over, provincial and rustic influences must ever produce much the same effects upon character, and town life will ever have in its gift the spirit of the present, while it may take again from the quiet of hills and fields and the conservatism of country hearts a gift from the spirit of the past."[13]

However, some crucial questions remain. What exactly is the "gift of the past"? Was Jewett's portrayal of these people and their interrelationships an evasion of the more difficult differences confronting her countrymen and -women, or a preliminary sketch of the attitudes necessary to resolving them? While I will look at these questions more closely a little later, let me first acknowledge that Jewett's representation of coastal Maine was certainly a fiction. But if Jewett simplified and exaggerated the opposition between city visitor and country host, it was perhaps to render their reconciliation and discovery of their deeper similarity more dramatic. Further, while her work certainly acknowledged the "gifts of the present," its overwhelming emphasis was on the lessons to be learned from rural life, particularly the preindustrial past.

The pastoral was Jewett's genre, and assessing its evasiveness in the face of the nation's struggles, I am reminded of the critic Richard Chase's well-known study, *The American Novel and Its Tradition* (1957), which opens by arguing that "the imagination that has produced much of the best and most characteristic American fiction has been shaped by the contradictions and not by the unities and harmonies of our culture." When this fiction does try to resolve contradictions, it makes the attempt "in oblique, morally equivocal ways. As a general rule it does so either in melodramatic actions or in pastoral idyls, although intermixed with both one may find the stirring instabilities of 'American humor.'"[14] Whether or not one agrees with Chase's honor roll of authors or his principles of selection, returning to the two American novels with which Cather ranked *The Country of the Pointed Firs*, one can easily find these fragile moments of unity, the pastoral idyls in which Huck and Jim forge their alliance on the Mississippi River or in which Hester Prynne and Arthur Dimmsdale grasp emotional freedom in the Salem woods. So too the final moments of "William's Wedding," in which the unnamed narrator and Mrs. Todd climb the Dunnet Landing hill, holding hands. Here also there is a momentary stay against cultural confusion, a fragile unity, lasting only the length of a summer.

II

In a famous letter to Willa Cather, Jewett urged the younger writer to take stock of the literary material experience had given her: "I want you to be surer of your backgrounds—you have your Nebraska life,—a child's Virginia, and now an intimate knowledge of what we are pleased to call the 'Bohemia' of newspaper and magazine-office life. These are uncommon equipment, but you don't see them yet quite enough from the outside, you stand right in the middle of each of them when you write, without having the standpoint of the looker-on who takes them each in their relations to letters, to the world."[15] In Jewett's own case, the backgrounds she knew most surely were the diverse classes—the gentry, professionals, artisans, fishermen, farmers, and working women—of her home, as well as the literary elite and urbane vacationers she came to know through her friendships and literary success. Intimately connected to those inside the region and those without, Jewett's experience placed her in an usually advantageous position to "take them each in their relations to letters, to the world."

Jewett's own position in local society was high and her financial situation was always secure. Family members were well traveled and well read, cosmopolitan in their tastes. Sarah herself was born Theodora Sarah Jewett on September 3, 1849, the second of three daughters. Mary Jewett, two years older, remained one of Sarah's closest companions all her life. Caroline Jewett was born in 1855.

Despite the decline of shipping, Sarah's grandfather did well enough to purchase the grand house in the center of South Berwick. Her father, Theodore Herman Jewett, was a brilliant student who graduated from Berwick Academy, then attended Bowdoin College and finally Jefferson Medical College. An obstetrician and specialist in the diseases of women and children, he had to forego his desire for an ambitious medical career after a bout of tuberculosis. His parents, already grieving from the loss of another son at sea, begged him to remain in South Berwick. Apparently always a dutiful as well as an intelligent and engaging man, Theodore stayed on to become the town's physician.

Jewett's mother, Caroline Gilman Perry, came from an even more distinguished family, the Gilmans of Exeter, who counted among them a New Hampshire governor and several other high-ranking officials. Caroline's father, like her husband, was a well-known physician, in this case a surgeon, highly respected in the region. Of Scotch Covenanter background, this grandfather was one of the few uncompromising Puritans in Sarah Jewett's background (most took a more easy-going, liberal approach to their religion). Despite his stern calls to duty, she remembered her grandfather Perry as an enthusiastic believer in his grandchildren's abilities, whatever their gender.

These families, then, the Jewetts, Gilmans, and Perrys, represented some of the upper class and upper middle class ranks of the New Hampshire and Maine seacoast. Although Sarah was born in her grandfather Jewett's house, and spent much of her later life there (she and Mary eventually came into its possession), she actually grew up in the much more modest and newer Greek Revival house her father built next door. Like most women of her time, Jewett did not attend college, although she did attend Miss Olive Raynes's school and graduated from Berwick Academy, then one of the best preparatory schools in the region. However, as a young girl Jewett suffered a number of "childish illnesses." Seeing that she was given to "instant drooping" if shut in school, her father brought Sarah with him on his rounds. In her essay "Looking Back on Girlhood" she recalls driving with Dr. Jewett through the countryside and listening as he pointed out aspects of the landscape or reflected on the sometimes somber, sometimes amusing stories of the country people they visited. Through his example, she learned to treat the working men and women of her region with respect and courtesy, and to recognize the strength and dignity of their lives. In Theodore Jewett can be seen a strong professional self-respect and class awareness, balanced by an equally strong ethic of service and a democratic compassion for those he served. These traits were to mark his daughter's vocation as well.

Her father was also one of the first to encourage Jewett's literary talent, and his advice remained with her to the end: "He gave me my first and best knowledge of books by his own delight and dependence upon them, and ruled my early attempts at writing by the severity and simplicity of his own good taste."[16] Theodore Jewett's receptivity to his daughter's talent and his encouragement of her professional ambition shows the unconventionality of his thinking. In her 1884 novel, *A Country Doctor*, Sarah drew his portrait as the beloved Dr. Leslie who takes a "wild" young orphan and helps her realize her talent for medicine, ultimately mentoring her into the assumption of his own role as the region's "country doctor." Jewett later wrote to a friend that she had herself considered medicine, then still a highly unusual choice for a woman. However, she added that she had found in writing another way to offer the healing and wisdom she admired in her father.

While Jewett left a clear record of her relationship, often idealized, to her father, we know less about her feelings for her mother. Caroline Perry Jewett appears to have been an amiable, somewhat retiring and conventional woman of the upper-middle class. Domestic, literate, engaged in the rearing of her children and the maintenance of a large and lively social circle, she nevertheless seems to have also encouraged her talented second daughter and provided another kind of model to follow. As Jewett later wrote, "while I was too young and thoughtless to share [my father's] enthusiasm for Sterne, or Fielding, and Smollett or Don Quixote, my mother and grandmother were leading me into the pleasant ways of 'Pride and Prejudice' and 'The Scenes of Clerical Life,' and the delightful stories of Mrs. Oliphant."[17] In addition to the women writers Jewett mentions here, she admired Elizabeth Barrett Browning, especially her "Aurora Leigh," and found a crucial example in Harriet Beecher Stowe, whose *Pearl of Orr's Island* (1862) taught her "to see with new eyes, and to follow eagerly the old shore paths from one gray, weather-beaten house to another where Genius pointed the way."[18] Jewett reread Stowe's *Pearl*, one of the first novels to depict coastal Maine, over and over in the course of her career. Another important model, according to Paula Blanchard, was Margaret Fuller, whose transcendental feminism and vision of androgynous self-realization may have inspired Jewett's own resolution of the conflicts faced by the literary women of her time.

The particular nature of coastal society, in which preindustrial and postindustrial models of womanhood coexisted, may also have given Jewett a variety of options to choose from in resolving those issues. Numerous historians have pointed out the powerful effect industrialization had on gender roles. As the production of textiles, foodstuffs, soaps, and candles left the home for the factories, these crucial items became commodities, and many middle-class women became their consumers rather than their producers. Their most important role narrowed to child rearing, which was now done in a home perceived not as a workplace but as a "private sphere," a "haven in heartless world." The departure of many men to work in factories or offices redefined the home as a private space, a respite from the public world outside. Although historians have also recently shown that the split between public and private spheres was more perceived than real (and, further, that "private" mothering often reproduced values and behavior demanded by the larger social system), the perception was important. "Ladies" had their gentility defined by their leisure, by their freedom from labor in the fields and barns of the agrarian past or the factories and offices of industrial present.[19]

The Jewett, Perry, and Gilman women were, without a doubt, ladies. These were women who enjoyed a life freed from even the labor of preparing meals; they consistently had one or two women to "help" in the kitchen and with the housework (at first these servants were local farm women; later they were primarily Irish immigrant women, from whom Jewett gained a keen appreciation of Irish lore and culture). In their gentility and love of domestic ritual, and in their closely knit ties of friendship and affection, Caroline Perry Jewett and her daughters exemplify historian Carroll Smith-Rosenberg's description of nineteenth-century women's communities: a "female world of love and ritual" extending outward from a core relationship between mother and daughters through widening circles of female friends.[20]

This model, however, would seem to offer an aspiring young writer no place to practice her art. Although seacoast society gave Jewett the example of several strong independent widows of wealthy means, its aspirations for young women of her class were undeniably focused on marriage. In *A Country Doctor*, Jewett's alter ego, Nan Prince, is not so gently prodded toward this goal by her wealthy aunt, the rigid and conventional Aunt Prince. There was, of course, the example of the best-selling women authors such Stowe, yet Jewett later commented on the necessarily divided attention that she felt ultimately had weakened the writing of *Pearl of Orr's Island*. As Mary Kelley has shown, the early generation of "literary domestics" had been forced to disguise their artistic ambitions, sometimes even to themselves. The result, Jewett shrewdly noted, was an art that fell short of its author's best potential.[21]

However, the preindustrial world that still lingered in the region, flourishing alongside the new order coming into preeminence, offered another model of femininity. In the men and women who fished and farmed, spun wool, and gathered herbs for their living, Jewett saw people whose characters seemed less distorted by rigid notions of gender. In her sketch "An Autumn Holiday" (1881), Jewett described a visit with Miss Polly Marsh and her sister, Mrs. Snow. Polly Marsh had been a respected nurse in the region and had cared for Sarah during one of those childhood illnesses. The time was one of her happiest memories. Arriving at the house in the woods, Jewett encounters the two sisters "stepping back and forward together spinning yarn at a pair of big wheels. The wheels made such a noise with their whir and creak, and my friends were talking so fast as they twisted and turned the yarn, that they did not hear my footsteps, and I stood in the doorway watching them, it was such a quaint and pretty sight."[22] Such women offered the developing writer an example of how to integrate work and domestic life, companionship and productivity. These women were neither "masculinized" nor "tainted" by their labor, but strengthened and enriched by it. Here the home was a place for both productive work and family bonds.

Then there is Jewett's sly pun on "yarn," for as the sisters "turn and twist" the strands of wool they are also turning and twisting the threads of their stories, the colorful "yarns" of the region's oral literature that their young friend adapted so tellingly. Thus not only did this preindustrial, pastoral world become the central subject of Jewett's best writing, but its women became an important model for her own vocation. Just as Jewett's father showed her how "masculine" professionalism could be combined with sensitivity and compassion, so women like Polly Snow demonstrated how "feminine" caring could be integrated with independence and linguistic skill.

Equally significant, the yarn that the two sisters twist and turn deals directly gender roles and their transgression. A old militia captain, Daniel Gunn, comes to believe after a sunstroke that he is, in fact, his own sister. He dresses in the dead woman's clothes and attends the Sunday meeting and the parish women's sewing society in her place. While his behavior is clearly seen by his fellow townspeople as aberrant, the point of the story is that Daniel Gunn is also tolerated and treated with compassion. Thus this tale reveals another important theme of Jewett's work and of her appreciation for the values of the small communities she delineated. Here are the origins of Mrs. Todd's storytelling prowess and healing arts, as well as Dunnet Landing's tolerance of misfits like Captain Littlepage and Joanna Todd. Here there is a place for Elijah Tilley, the hardened fisherman who quietly knits his woolen stockings and brushes away tears for his lost wife.

III

While later in this introduction I will look more closely at the specific themes and narrative structure of *Pointed Firs*, for the moment I would like to turn to Jewett's treatment of the pastoral as a genre and as a way of life, even a way of seeing. In its classical versions, a poet of Athens or Rome journeys to the countryside in summertime, where he is mysteriously moved by the lives and voices of rural people. When the season ends, the poet returns to the city. As Jewett saw it, the pastoral was a story of exchange between urban and rural, center and margin, outsider and insider. The benefit of such an exchange was the special consciousness she recommended to Willa Cather, the ability to see the materials of one's life from the outside. In the unpublished notes for a sketch titled "A Modern Idyll," we see this consciousness in the making. An aging married couple returns to the country for a small holiday. As they leave the road and cross the fields on foot, they recall their courtship and married life together, their progress from simpler, poorer days to their present prosperity. At the house of an acquaintance they are "given bread & honey and fruit—and come home at night happy and tired and full of country pleasure but liking their home best." As in Jewett's finest sketches, the point is subtle, a matter of perspective rather than conflict and resolution. When the couple return home, "they have for once a consciousness of their life in general and seem to watch and *review* their course all the way, instead of being occupied and intent upon details." The notes conclude: "Do all this in the manner of Theocritus—"[23]

The last comment reveals Jewett's awareness of her work's place in a long tradition stemming from Theocritus, Hesiod, and Virgil to Wordsworth (both William and Dorothy) and George Sand. This genealogy is also linked to the strong Romantic element in her reverence for the pastoral landscape and its people. In a central chapter of *Deephaven*, the two summer visitors from Boston, Kate and Helen, meditate on the special powers, almost visionary gifts of their Deephaven friends: "They live so much nearer to nature than people in cities, and there is a soberness about country people oftentimes that one cannot help noticing." Helen connects this habitual style to the preindustrial way of life, so dependent upon natural forces and seasonal cycles: "I wonder if they are unconsciously awed by the strength and purpose in the world about them, and the mysterious creative power which is at work with them on their familiar farms." However, in the passage that follows, her respect for rural folk is undercut by her condescension: "Because they are so instinctive and unreasoning, they may have a more complete sympathy with Nature, and may hear her voices, when wiser ears are deaf. They have much in common, after all, with the plants which grow up out of the ground, and the wild creatures which depend upon their instincts wholly."[24] Although Helen's reflections have much in common with the thinking of many artists of the time (see, for example, Paul Gauguin's contemporary ideas about Breton peasants), its easy assumption of intellectual superiority is an unpleasant reminder of the class biases with which Jewett struggled as a young author. Significantly, her later work, such as *Pointed Firs*, represents country people not as primitives, but as peers.

The *Deephaven* passage is prefaced by Kate's retelling of "the old myth of Demeter and Persephone," a story that she once knew "almost all by heart" and in which she is "always finding a new meaning." Demeter was the Greek goddess of the grain and its harvest; her daughter Persephone was goddess of the spring and queen of the dead. The "Homeric Hymn to Demeter" told of the maiden Persephone's abduction from the Sicilian plain by Hades, lord of the underworld, and of her mother's grief, which rendered the earth barren. In the myth's resolution, Zeus allows Persephone to return to her mother each spring, only to descend once more to her husband with autumn. In this ancient story the cyclical death and rebirth of the natural world are figured, with the vegetation's annual blooming signified in Persephone's joyous reunion with her mother. Many Victorian writers were fascinated by this myth. The German historian J. J. Bachofen saw it as the survival of a lost matriarchal culture; Alfred Lord Tennyson saw it as an anticipation of Christ's death and resurrection; T. W. Higginson saw it as a potential symbol for modern women's lives and spirituality.[25] Jewett herself returned many times to this myth, adapting its plot and motifs in different ways throughout her career. Like Kate, she was always finding a new meaning in it.

Jewett's source for the *Deephaven* passage was probably Walter Pater's "The Myth of Demeter and Persephone," published in 1876, as she was revising the sketches for book publication. The essay describes these mythic figures as "the peculiar creation of countrypeople of high impressionability, dreaming over their work in spring or autumn, half consciously touched by a sense of its sacredness." Pater believed this special consciousness would always be with us wherever and whenever men and women lived close to the earth and in harmony with its forces: "The temper of a people engaged in occupations of the country, so permanent, so 'near to nature,' is at all times alike; and the habitual solemnity which Wordsworth found in the peasant of Cumberland, and Francois Millet in the peasant of Brittany may well have had its prototype in early Greece."[26]

If the characters of Dunnet Landing suggest the motifs of classical literature, then, it is not because the narrator inflates them with literary allusions, but because they have grown out of the same "ground" as their primeval prototypes. The same forces shaping the landscape animate its central figures, particularly its women, who also manifest a "mysterious creative power." For example, Mrs. Todd's intimacy with the natural world gives her wisdom, strength, and ultimately a numinous force. As the narrator's appreciation of this character grows, she describes her landlady and friend as a "sibyl," a "caryatid," as "Antigone on the Theban plain," and finally, as a personification of Nature herself, a "cousin to the ancient deities." In "The Queen's Twin," she writes that Mrs. Todd "might have walked the primeval fields of Sicily; her strong gingham skirts might at that very moment bend the slender stalks of asphodel . . . instead of the brown wind-brushed grass of New England."

As Sicily was to Athens, so Maine might be to Boston. In Dunnet Landing's rural festivals the urban visitor sees a twin to the ancient world's sacred rituals. Here, for example, is Pater's translation from Theocritus's *Idylls*, a description of two shepherds going to Demeter's "homely feast": "Many poplars and elm-trees were waving over our heads, and not far off the running of the sacred water from the cave of the nymphs warbled to us; in the shimmering branches the sun-burnt grasshoppers were busy with their talk, and afar the little owl cried softly . . . the bees flew round and round the fountains softly, the scent of late summer and of the fall of the year were everywhere."[27] And here is the narrator of *Pointed Firs*, describing the Bowden family's procession to its own "sacred grove": "There was a wide path mowed for us across the field, and, as we moved along, the birds flew out of the thick second crop of clover, and the bees hummed as if it still were June. There was a flashing of white gulls over the water where the fleet of boats rode the low waves together in the cove, swaying their small masts as if they kept time to our steps. The plash of the water could be heard faintly, yet still be heard; we might have been a company of ancient

Greeks going to celebrate a victory, or to worship the god of harvests in the grove above."

As she marches with the others in this scene, the narrator finds it "strangely moving to see this and to make a part of it. The sky, the sea, have watched poor humanity at its rites so long; we were no more a New England family celebrating its own existence and simple progress; we carried the tokens and inheritance of all such households from which this had descended, and were only the latest of our line. We possessed the instincts of a far forgotten childhood; I found myself thinking that we ought to be carrying green branches and singing as we went." One of the gifts of the past is this sense of rootedness, of belonging to a people and a place. "Clannishness," says the narrator, "is an instinct of the heart." The emphasis is on instinct, on the "ground" of identity in a common landscape, common "blood." And yet, there is a danger here, too, signaled in the use of the term "childhood."

Part of Dunnet Landing's original attraction for the narrator is what she imagines to be its "childish sense of being the centre of civilization." When William Blackett brings her to the heights of Green Island to view the circling sea and outer islands, he claims, proudly, "there ain't no such view in all the world." The more worldly narrator finds it "impossible not to feel as if an untraveled boy had spoken," and yet, she adds, "one loved to have him value his native heath." How to value one's own cultural center without becoming ethnocentric? There is a recognition in these sketches, and throughout Jewett's work, that this childish sense, if not balanced and informed by a greater knowledge, can too easily become provincialism and xenophobia. Here we see Jewett addressing a difficult problem: how to affirm cultural identification, figured as organic and chthonic (a Romantic folk rooted in the motherland), without jeopardizing other, more encompassing identifications.

However, many of Jewett's country people manage to negotiate multiple perspectives. Just as her urban visitors benefit from acquaintance with apparently simpler rural communities, so her rural folk gain broader views from their own encounters with the larger world outside. Historically, this broadening experience came through the region's shipping trade. As Captain Littlepage explains, "in the old days, a good part o' the best men here knew a hundred ports and something of the way folks lived in them. They saw the world for themselves, and like 's not their wives and children saw it with them. They may not have had the best of knowledge to carry with 'em sightseein', but they were some acquainted with foreign lands an' their laws, an' could see outside the battle for town clerk here in Dunnet; they got some sense o' proportion." In the opening of "The Queen's Twin," the narrator echoes Captain Littlepage's assessment: "More than this one cannot give to a young State for its enlightenment; the sea captains and the captains' wives of Maine knew something of the wide world, and never mistook their native parishes for the whole instead of a part thereof; they knew not only Thomaston and Castine and Portland, but London and Bristol and Bordeaux, and the strange-mannered harbors of the China Sea."[28]

And yet, Jewett also shows how this sense of proportion could be developed by the conditions of country life itself. If one of the gifts of the past was this sense of instinctive relationship to the natural world, equally important gifts were the qualities of tolerance and compassion fostered by the face-to-face relationships of small town and village life. While clannishness, or the need to belong, is presented as an instinct, the actual community is a product of human creativity and struggle. While the narrator may be retreating from the apparently greater complexity of urban life, Dunnet Landing does not so much offer a more "natural" community as a greater clarity about the means of its own achievement, a sharper view of its own production and the processes of maintaining itself. Without the larger world's "distractions," the work of creating and maintaining human connections can be seen more clearly.[29]

Thus, although she claims that life in Dunnet Landing is simpler, the narrator's own representation reveals that Dunnet's social relations do not become easier as they move down the scale from parish to village to clan to wedded couple. There are differences and difficulties at every level. In marriage, there is Almira Todd's loss of her first love to class prejudice; her union with Nathan Todd was never what she would have wished. In the nuclear family, there is reticence between Almira and William; neither can speak their deepest feelings before the other. In the extended family, there is Almira's struggle to accept her near relations; she can hardly bear "to own" a cousin by marriage. In the village, there are struggles over the town selectmen, or the feuding families who share an island but won't deign to pass on the news that the Civil War has ended. Finally, there is the parish's difficulty in accepting, let alone assimilating, Mrs. Captain Tolland, the French-speaking woman from Jamaica whose ways and religion differ from the population's norm.

Jewett's characters grapple with these issues throughout *Pointed Firs*, even during the Bowden Reunion, which seems so unequivocally to claim the "natural" identity of the clan. For example, there is the passage where "Sister" Caplin, "her face brightening with sudden illumination," says, "Somebody observed once that you could pick out the likeness of 'most every sort of foreigner when looked about you in our parish. . . . I did n't see the bearin' of it then quite so plain. I always did think Mari' Harris resembled a Chinee." As critic Sandra Zagarell points out, by stigmatizing Mari' Harris with an apparent ethnic slur, this comment sounds a sour note in the reunion's apparent harmonies.[30] And yet the comment also vividly figures the way in which the community can recapitulate global differences on a smaller scale. Moreover, the passage as a whole shows various strategies in managing such differences.

Most significantly, there is an immediate response to the possibly slighting tone of Sister Caplin's remark from Mrs. Blackett, who has joined the group "to see, as she insisted, that we were out of mischief." Judging that they are, in fact, up to no good, she attempts to turn the slur into a compliment: "Mari' Harris was pretty as a child, I remember." But Mrs. Todd won't let the problem be smoothed over: "Yes, Mari' was one o' them pretty little lambs that make dreadful homely old sheep. . . . Cap'n Littlepage never 'd look so disconsolate if she was any sort of a proper person to direct things. . . . 'T would n't hurt her to sit down an' hear his great stories once in a while." When Mrs. Todd winds up calling Mari' Harris "a sordid creatur," her mother makes one last try at keeping her "out of mischief": "'Live and let live,' said dear old Mrs. Blackett gently."

The source of the animosity toward Mari' Harris is only suggested in original *Pointed Firs* sketches. She is uncaring and unsympathetic. As Captain Littlepage's housekeeper, she is seen as remiss in that care. However, when Jewett returned to Dunnet Landing in the 1900 story "The Foreigner," she made Mari' Harris a pivotal figure in its tale of cultural misunderstanding. In the Bowden Reunion sketches, the narrator reflects on how many old feuds must have been overlooked to produce the spirit of the day, and Mrs. Blackett's interventions show how one might attempt such a truce. "The Foreigner" shows the other side of the social tapestry, the side where the threads hang out and the missed stitches show. Here the community fails in inclusiveness; the episode's legacy is a complicated mix of learning, loss, and regret.

This is the story of Mrs. Tolland, a French-speaking woman from Jamaica married to a Dunnet Landing ship's captain. He and his colleagues rescue her from destitution in Kingston, where she was singing for her living in public houses. Having lost her husband and children in an epidemic, she is alone in the world. Arriving in Dunnet Landing does not assuage that feeling. A feud in her new husband's family prevents any welcome there, and soon after, the captain leaves for a voyage from which he never returns. Able to speak English "no better than a child," she is Roman Catholic, emotionally expressive, and artistically creative. Invited to a church social, the foreigner reveals her difference. When she hears the discordant singing of Mari' Harris and one of the Caplin sisters, she does not restrain her criticism nor make a false show of approval. Instead she puts her hands over her ears when they sing flat, then offers to help them find the key. As Mrs. Todd recalls, "She was real willin' an' pleasant, but that did n't suit, an' she made faces when they got it wrong. An' then there fell a dead calm, an' we was all settin' round prim as dishes, an' my mother, that never expects ill feelin', asked her if she would n't sing somethin', an' up she got,—poor creatur', it all seems so different to me now,—an' sung a lovely little song standin' in the floor. . . ." Caught up in the lively rhythms of her song, the captain's wife begins a little dance and they all, Mrs. Todd remembers, enjoyed it, every one. She recalls her mother afterward, patting the Frenchwoman's hand.

"But next day there was an awful scandal goin' in the parish. . . ." When Mari' Harris, perhaps as revenge for her musical humiliation, protests the foreigner's heathenish dancing, Mrs. Todd argues that "Mis' Tolland did n't intend no impropriety,—I reminded her of

David's dancin' before the Lord; but she said such a man as David would never have thought o' dancin' right there in the Orthodox vestry, and she felt I spoke with irreverence." The rift widens until Mrs. Tolland walks out of a Sunday meeting. Isolated and ostracized, she has no one to turn to—except Mrs. Blackett. When Mrs. Blackett sees the stranger's distress, she chastises her own daughter. Mrs. Todd's memory of that conversation tells us much about tensions within Dunnet Landing parish:

"I want you to neighbor with that poor lonesome creatur'," says mother to me, lookin' reproachful. "She's a stranger in a strange land," says mother. "I want you to make her have a sense that somebody feels kind to her."

"Why, since that time she flaunted out o' meetin', folks have felt like she liked other ways better 'n our'n," says I. I was provoked because I'd had a nice supper ready, an' mother 'd let it wait so long 't was spoiled. "I hope you like your supper!" I told her. I was dreadful ashamed afterward of speakin' so to mother.

"What consequence is my supper?" says she to me; mother can be very stern,—"or your comfort or mine, beside letting a foreign person an' a stranger feel so desolate; she 's done the best a woman could do in her lonesome place, and she asks nothing of anybody except a little common kindness. Think if 't was you in a foreign land!"

The effect of Mrs. Blackett's sermon is that her daughter does extend herself to neighbor with Mrs. Tolland, "if 't was only for mother's sake." But although Mrs. Todd tries to find common ground with the foreigner she confesses to the narrator that "you could n't get to no affectionateness with her. I used to blame me sometimes; we used to be real good comrades, goin' off for an afternoon, but I never give her a kiss till the day she laid in her coffin and it come to my heart there wa'n't no one else to do it." And yet the other woman recognizes Mrs. Todd's attempt in the legacy she leaves her, a legacy not only of property but of her special knowledge of healing herbs and cookery. At the foreigner's death, Mrs. Todd remembers how "I wished I had her back again to do somethin' for, an' to make her know I felt sisterly to her more 'n I 'd ever showed, an' it come over me 't was all too late, an' I cried the more. . . ." Although Mrs. Tolland is of French "blood," that blood does not produce a natural bond between her and Mrs. Todd. While longing for intimacy may be "an instinct of the heart," intimacy itself is humanly constructed, through linguistic acts of communication and imaginative acts of interpretation and empathy. In the social continuum that marks Dunnet Landing we can see two poles of response to the foreigner, from the ethnocentrism and xenophobia of Mari' Harris, who cannot accept a tradition other than her own, to the tolerance and compassion of Mrs. Blackett, who recognizes the foreigner's religion and sends for a priest to give her solace and last rites. The belief that Dunnet Landing is the only center of civilization is a childish belief, but there are those in Dunnet who recognize the relativity of their ways and the validity of other centers. As Mrs. Todd recalls the lonely outsider's funeral, "'T was in Reverend Mr. Bascom's day, and he done very well in his prayer. . . . He spoke very feeling about her being a stranger and twice widowed, and all he said about her being reared among the heathen was to observe that there might be roads leadin' up to the New Jerusalem from various points. I says to myself that I guessed quite a number must ha' reached there that wa'n't able to set out from Dunnet Landin'!"

The valuing of "large-mindedness," despite its difficulties, is apparent even in Mrs. Todd's treatment of Mari' Harris. When she recounts the scandal over dancing in the vestry, Mrs. Todd remembers how "Mari' Harris reproached my mother to her face, an' I never wanted to see her since, but I've had to a good many times." Mari' Harris is not, like the Chinese immigrants whom she supposedly resembles, excluded. Mrs. Todd has to deal with her. She might criticize her, she might "pray her by" (as she does her Bowden cousin), but she cannot permanently turn away from her. In "William's Wedding" Mrs. Todd welcomes Mari' Harris into her home with the same civility she offers all her other neighbors. Her civility may be perfunctory in this case, but it is perfunctory to all.

Thus while Jewett shows us the darker side of Dunnet Landing's clannishness, she also reminds us that Mrs. Blackett is "always the queen." In Mrs. Blackett's plea for the "stranger in a strange land," we can perhaps hear Jewett's own values. But if Mrs. Blackett represents an idealized vision of the pastoral world's moral potential, Mrs. Todd represents its more troubled struggle to overcome personal and cultural limitations. And it is Mrs. Todd, with her worldly realism and forgiving humor, who holds this text's center stage, perhaps because her understanding of "poor human natur'" acknowledges the difficulty of meeting her mother's ideal. As the two women arrive home after the Bowden Reunion it is Mrs. Blackett who remembers with pleasure the harmonies of the day: "'T was pretty when they sang the hymn, was n't it? . . . There was such a plenty o' men's voices; where I sat it did sound beautiful. I had to stop and listen when they came to the last verse." But it is Mrs. Todd who gets the last word: "There was good singers there; yes, there was excellent singers . . . but I chanced to drift alongside Mis' Peter Bowden o' Great Bay, an' I could n't help thinkin' if she was as far out o' town as she was out o' tune, she would n't get back in a day."

Describing her own process of literary invention, Jewett once said, "the thing that teases the mind over and over for years, and at last gets itself put rightly down on paper—whether little or great, it belongs to Literature."[31] In stories like "The Foreigner" or "Poor Joanna," she shows the same process at work as members of the Dunnet Landing community use their narrative skills to make sense of behavior that "teases" or troubles the mind. In the case of Joanna Todd, Mrs. Todd and Mrs. Fosdick rework the tale of a "strayaway," and gain fresh insight into this woman whose feelings "hurt her more than she could bear." In "Miss Tempy's Watchers" (1888), another story from this period, two country women watch through the night over the body of a beloved and recently deceased friend, and forge their own friendship through reminiscences of her generosity and gift for living. Storytelling not only reveals new aspects of the tale's subject, but weaves connections between those who share the tale's telling. This dynamic is particularly important to our understanding of the relationship between the narrator and those whose stories she hears.[32]

In "The Foreigner," for example, there is a curious, even ironic relationship between the frame and interior narratives. Unlike the frame story, which describes the companionable give-and-take between another "foreigner" and herself, Mrs. Todd's story represents the failure of two women to connect. And yet, the narrator's presence makes a difference. In telling the foreigner's history, Mrs.

Todd, like the couple who return from their pastoral visit, seems to review her own history, to see her "life in general" ("I was a sight younger than I be now"). The impetus for this perspective may be her audience. Whereas once Dunnet Landing natives gained their sense of proportion from journeying away from home, now perhaps that larger world comes to them, in the guise of visitors like the narrator. As an audience she represents a new perspective, a wider view, the standpoint of the "looker-on." Significantly, something like this was also bestowed by Mrs. Tolland, for as Mrs. Todd remembers, "she made me imagine new things, and I got interested watchin' her an' findin' out what she had to say." In that case, barriers of language and background proved too great for a deeper trust to form, and the tone of the Mrs. Todd's story is regret for a lost opportunity. However, the tone of the frame story is one of success and completion, for between Mrs. Todd and her guest the hoped-for intimacy has been achieved. The gift to each is their shared understanding of the story's significance, a significance not only for the narrow sphere of Dunnet Landing, but for the greater world of which Dunnet makes a part.

IV

Jewett initially had difficulty getting her work into the prestigious *Atlantic Monthly*, which, along with *Harper's* and *The Century*, represented the "highbrow" literary magazines of the period. Several efforts were rejected with encouraging letters before "Mr. Bruce" was accepted for the December 1869 issue by the magazine's then assistant editor, William Dean Howells, arguably the most influential editor and literary mentor of the period. Jewett's weakness, as she frankly confessed in an 1873 letter to another *Atlantic* editor, Horace Scudder, was plot: "I can furnish the theatre, and show the actors, and the scenery, and the audience, but there never is any play! I could write you some entertaining letters from some desirable house where I was in most charming company, but couldn't make a story about it."[33] Luckily, this weakness was less damaging in the regionalist genre where she eventually excelled. Her ability to bring the reader into an imagined setting, a kind of tour and later even initiation into the mysteries of country life, was well suited to this form, then enormously popular with American readers. So too was her close observation and ability to reproduce the flavor and exact pitch of rural talk. Her dialogue had the effect of bringing readers into the very midst of the "charming company" she described. Then there was her humor: sly and, as Cather put it, a little "arch." Finally, her love of the visual arts found expression in her lyrical landscapes, often evoking the serenity and power of artists like the American luminist John Frederick Kensett or the French Barbizon painter Jean-François Millet. All these came into play in her first real success, the sketches which were collected in *Deephaven*. The initial one, "The Shore House," appeared in the September 1873 *Atlantic*. Following the readers' enthusiastic response and Jewett's revisions, Houghton Mifflin brought the book out in 1877. An immediate hit, *Deephaven* eventually went through twenty-three editions in nineteen years. Critics noticed its lack of a conventional romantic plot, but found the book all the more intriguing for its absence. In many ways, this story of two young women summering in a Maine coast town prefigured the themes and even the imagery and situations of *Pointed Firs*.

Deephaven's success brought Jewett into Boston literary society. She came to know Howells and his family, who later bought a summer house in Kittery Point, as well as Thomas Bailey Aldrich and his wife Lilian. However, the most important friendship she formed in these years was with Annie Adams Fields. Annie was the wife of James T. Fields, editor of the *Atlantic* and cofounder of the famous publishing house Ticknor and Fields, which published Hawthorne, Whittier, and Longfellow. Seventeen years younger than her husband, Annie Fields, like Sarah Jewett, was the daughter of a well-known physician and offspring of a prominent New England family, in this case the presidential Adams family of Massachusetts. She was celebrated for her graciousness, intelligence, and tact. F. O. Matthiessen commented that her home at 148 Charles Street in Boston was the nearest America had come to a *salon*.[34] In its rooms overlooking the river and lined with books and paintings, the Fields entertained Thackeray, Hawthorne, and Dickens.

Significantly, Annie was an author in own right. Her poems on classical themes, including an 1877 adaptation of the Demeter-Persephone myth, appeared in several collections; she also published a few novels, although their reception was only lukewarm. However, Annie Fields's lasting contribution to her city was without doubt her charitable work. For many years, she headed the Associated Charities of Boston, which she had founded with Mary Lodge in 1876. Their organization set up a system of volunteer visiting social workers and established coffee houses as alternatives to taverns. Her book *How to Help the Poor* (1883) was especially influential, selling 22,000 copies in two years. In addition to her success as hostess, writer, and philanthropist, Annie Fields was also the center of a wide circle of intellectual and literary women. While Sarah Jewett may have found her way into this supportive and challenging group before meeting Annie, their deepening relationship placed her firmly in its midst. In addition to male colleagues such as Howells, Henry James, and Thomas Bailey Aldrich, their many friends included Celia Thaxter, Sara Norton, Alice Brown, and Sarah Wyman Whitman, an artist and founder of Radcliffe College.

From the early 1880s on, Jewett split her life between South Berwick and Annie Fields's homes in Boston and Manchester-by-the-Sea, on the North Shore. Attempting to describe the particular qualities of the Jewett and Fields relationship, their biographers and critics have stressed its richness and fluidity. Following the death of Theodore Jewett in 1878 and of James T. Fields in 1881, each woman seemed to fill a void in the other's life. Their letters reveal that Annie Fields became a new literary mentor for Sarah, as well as an older sister and quasi-maternal figure. At the same time there was a strong romantic element in their bond, and the correspondence often reads as love letters, full of passion and longing. Jewett had been intensely drawn to several other young women in her life; these early romantic friendships clearly were the model for the one between Kate and Helen in *Deephaven*. She also made it clear that she was never drawn to marriage. It is difficult to assess this relationship, however, from our own post-Freudian perspective. Carroll Smith-Rosenberg and Lillian Faderman have both discussed the greater tolerance for such romantic friendships in the nineteenth century. "Boston marriages" between single women were an accepted feature of Victorian social life, and Sarah's and

Annie's correspondence shows no anxiety about their attachment nor any effort at concealing it. While I might to hesitate to call their relationship lesbian in contemporary terms, I would not hesitate to say that their love for each other was central to their lives. They were, in the resonant genderless term Jewett used often in her work, "mates."[35]

In addition to her literary and artistic interests, much of Jewett's social life centered on the Episcopal Church, which she joined in 1871. The change reflected her adult criticism of the theological rigors of orthodox Congregationalism. In an unpublished essay entitled "The Decay of Churches," she wrote that the old-time ministers lost their congregations because they ignored parishioners' human needs, failed to offer compassion and comfort, instead of theory and judgment.[36] In her stories ministers such as Reverend Dimmick are often ineffectual. It is the wise older women such as Mrs. Blackett and Mrs. Todd who offer true spiritual counsel. Doctors like Theodore Jewett are also presented as spiritual and psychological healers. Another important strand in Jewett's switch was her love of tradition and her appreciation of the importance of ritual and sacrament in giving a form and body to spiritual faith. These needs were better met by the old Episcopal ways with their stress on gradual spiritual growth and the power of religious community, as opposed to the Puritan emphasis on sin and crisis conversion.

And yet there is also a strain of spiritualism, even mysticism, in Jewett's writing. In "A Winter Drive" (1881) she confessed to a faith in the "old doctrine" of Hylozoism, "the theory of the soul of the world, of a life residing in nature, and that all matter lives; the doctrine that life and matter are inseparable."[37] Thus trees and plants also have embodied souls—an idea that finds its way into stories like "A White Heron" or moments such as Mrs. Todd's communing with a young ash tree. Jewett's spiritualism was obviously influenced by her reading of English and American Romantic writers, but it was also fostered by her friendship as a young writer with Theophilus Parsons, a Harvard law professor who introduced her to the mystical ideas of the Swedish philosopher Emmanuel Swedenborg. Although Jewett's correspondence with Parsons, begun in 1872, dropped off after *Deephaven* was published, she later said that Swedenborg's idea of a mystical correspondence between the spiritual and the physical worlds remained with her throughout her career.[38]

It was friendship, however, that perhaps held the first place in Jewett's life—even more than writing, Willa Cather thought. In Jewett's fiction and her letters we can see how human intimacy and compassion came to be the heart of her faith. In 1897, she wrote to Sara Norton, "There is something transfiguring in the best of friendship. One remembers the story of the transfiguration in the New Testament, and sees over and over in life what the great shining hours can do, and how one goes down from the mountain where they are, into the fret of everyday life again, but strong in remembrance." In an 1898 letter to Sarah Wyman Whitman she begged her friend "to hold on fast to the only certainty in this world, which is the certainty of Love and Care. I can't help feeling that Mary Darmesteter speaks true, out of great pain and the deep places of life, when she ends that last book, 'The true importance of life is not misery or despair, however crushing, but that one good moment which outweighs it all.'. . . The only thing that really helps any of us is love and doing things for love's sake."[39] Jewett remained a practicing Christian all her life, but it was the Christianity of liberal theologians such as Philips Brooks, rector of Boston's Trinity Church which she often attended. At its core is the distinction the Transcendentalist Theodore Parker made between "the transient and the permanent" in Christianity. For Jewett, the permanent was love: love of God and love of neighbor. For her, transcendence was not found apart from the immanent, embodied world of nature and other people, but through one's relations to them. Here was her true communion, realized in those shining moments of silence and sharing that transfigure her characters and her fiction.

These years from *Deephaven* to the century's end were extraordinarily productive ones for Jewett. During the eighties alone she produced two novels, *A Country Doctor* (1884) and *A Marsh Island* (1885), and four collections of short stories. In addition, Charles Johanningsmeier has traced Jewett's many publications in syndicated newspapers, an important discovery that increases our understanding of the size and diversity of her audience.[40] Travel with Annie Fields significantly broadened Jewett's horizons as well; they made trips abroad in 1882, 1892, 1898, and 1900. In 1882 they went to England, France, Norway, Ireland, and Italy. In 1892 they stayed a month in Fountainbleu, where they visited sites painted by Jean-François Millet. In 1900 they traveled to Pompeii, Athens, and Constantinople, viewing the pastoral landscapes and classical art that had inspired them both. Meetings with literary figures were an important part of these pilgrimages. Jewett had two audiences with Tennyson, whom she admired as her literary "king." She also met the family of Charles Dickens, who had stayed with the Fields in America. In France she visited several times with Marie Thérèse Blanc-Bentzon, who had translated her work and written sensitively about it for French readers. The two became close friends. In 1898, Jewett and Fields had lunch with Henry James at Lamb House in Rye, England. He returned the favor by stopping at South Berwick during his tour of America in 1905.

At home Jewett's mother continued to suffer from an undisclosed but debilitating illness. Sarah and her sister Mary tried not to leave her unattended. While the patient caring for an invalid must have been frustrating and tedious at times, Jewett wrote of becoming closer to her mother during the long afternoons they shared in these last years. Her renewed appreciation for the bonds between mother and daughter and the subtle intimacy that connects both families and communities can be found in this period's strongest stories, such as "Miss Tempy's Watchers" (1888) and "The Town Poor" (1890), as well as *The Country of the Pointed Firs*. Also central to the later book, however, is the surprising sense of independence Jewett discovered after her mother's death in 1891. The event brought Jewett an understandable relief mingled with a sense of even deeper intimacy to her mother, now that all barriers of misunderstanding had been removed. It seems to have marked a new chapter in her life, much as the death of her father had in 1878. That death preceded the strong affirmation of Jewett's professional vocation in *A Country Doctor*. This one seems to have brought a new "sense of proportion." In an 1892 letter to Georgina Halliburton, who had also recently lost her mother, Jewett wrote that, with "all the loss and pain," her friend might find "something new and sweet." She emphasized the importance, "as one grows older and makes one's own decisions," of "standing on your own ground, and living your OWN life," for then, she explained, "one can

flow into [the lives of others] with all the stronger impulse."[41] It is
this balance of self-possession and self-transcendence that marks
Almira Todd, the central figure of *Pointed Firs* and perhaps Jewett's greatest character.

Other events in the early 1890s contributed to the making of
Pointed Firs. Houghton Mifflin brought out a new edition of *Deephaven*, illustrated by Charles and Martha Oakes Woodbury. Jewett's preface, written in 1893, led her back to the themes, imagery,
and even the narrative structure of that earlier work. The death of
Harriet Beecher Stowe in 1896 prompted a rereading of *The Pearl
of Orr's Island*, another influential text. Annie Fields's publication
of *The Singing Shepherd* in 1895 might have revived Jewett's interest in the classical mythology and pastoral motifs whose imagery
pervades *Pointed Firs*. Pater's essay on the Demeter and Persephone myth also reappeared, collected in his *Greek Studies* (1894);
Tennyson had offered his own adaptation of the myth in *Demeter
and Other Poems* in 1889. Finally, there was the death of Celia
Thaxter, Jewett's close friend and fellow author who had been
raised on the Isles of Shoals. Thaxter's father had opened one of the
very first resorts off Portsmouth and Kittery. Celia's close relationship with her mother, Eliza Laighton, her early life on this "tiny
continent" of Appledore Island, even her own deathbed vision of her
mother's ghost may have all contributed to the making of Jewett's
work.

The immediate inspiration, however, was the sense of place itself. Although, like Deephaven, Dunnet Landing is a fictitious
town, as much of the imagination as the map, nevertheless it is
clearly modeled on the coastal fishing villages of Martinsville and
Tenant's Harbor, Maine. Jewett first visited this area "down east" of
Portland in the summer of 1889 when she stayed with Alice Long-
fellow at Mouse Island, in Boothbay Harbor. In 1895 her friend
Mary Garrett took a house on Isleboro on Penobscot Bay. That July
Sarah and Annie Fields visited Lilian and Thomas Bailey Aldrich,
who had a summer house, The Crags, in Tenant's Harbor. Evidently
charmed with the setting, the two of them rented a cottage called
The Anchorage in Martinsville, near Port Clyde, for September.
They brought with them Annie Fields's own cook and housekeeper.
Unlike the narrator, Jewett did not come alone, nor was she the

only summer visitor in the vicinity. Nevertheless, if she did not have her own Mrs. Todd as resident landlady, she did become friends with a neighbor, Mrs. Rosilla Bachelder, who, according to Paula Blanchard, provided some of the inspiration for Jewett's central character. (Blanchard also locates the original of Elijah Tilley in Dan Butland, a fisherman from Wells, Maine.) Then there was the landscape itself, even closer to the pastoral world Jewett loved than her native parish. In a letter to Sarah Wyman Whitman, she wrote: "I sleep in a little back bedroom whose window gives on a lane and a stone wall and potato field where the figures of J. F. Millet work all day against the very un-French background of the pointed firs that belong to Maine, like the grey ledges they are rooted in."[42]

The first Dunnet Landing sketches were composed after Jewett left Martinsville and appeared in *The Atlantic* in four installments during 1896: January, March, July, and September. The magazine sketches ended with "The Bowden Reunion." For book publication, Jewett composed two new ones to round out the pastoral plot: "Along Shore" and "The Backward View." To refresh her memory, she went back that summer to Penobscot Bay on her friend Henry Pierce's steam yacht, the Hermoine. The book itself came in November, in time for the Christmas trade. As mentioned earlier, Jewett seems to have been so surprised by the praise heaped on what she called "the Pointed Firs papers" that Rudyard Kipling was moved to write her, "I don't believe even *you* know good that book is."[43] But many readers did. Through various literary fashions, these stories have remained in print. Sometimes seen as an American classic and masterpiece, sometimes as an enduring if minor work of regional literature, they continue to find and keep a community of readers.

In addition to new stories that appeared in the late 1890s, some of the same high quality as *Pointed Firs*, and the historical novel *The Tory Lover*, which received only mediocre reviews, Jewett returned to Dunnet Landing three more times. "The Queen's Twin" and "The Dunnet Shepherdess" were collected in *The Queen's Twin and Other Stories* (1899). "The Foreigner" came out in *The Atlantic* in August 1900. In 1901 she became the first woman awarded an honorary Litt.D. from Bowdoin College, her father's alma mater.

Then in 1902, at the height of her artistic power, Jewett suddenly suffered an accident that cut her career short. She was thrown from a carriage; the fall caused a concussion, injured her spine, and affected her balance and concentration. The following years were marked by weakness and difficulty working. Among their few bright spots was her friendship with Willa Cather, then managing editor of the popular *McClure's* magazine. Cather had a novel and some strong stories to show, but her talent, Jewett felt, was being wasted on the demands of magazine work. Jewett's encouragement and advice were a critical influence on Cather's ultimate decision to devote her life to fiction and turn her imagination to the materials of her own experience. Their friendship inspired some of Jewett's most searching reflections on her own artistic vocation.⁴⁴ Apparently on the mend, visiting Annie Fields in Boston, Jewett suffered a stroke in April of 1909. Brought home to South Berwick, she died that June, as she had wished, in the house where she was born.

V

After Jewett's death Cather paid tribute to her mentor first by dedicating the novel *O Pioneers!* to her, then by editing *The Best Stories of Sarah Orne Jewett* (1925). The collection included all the original Dunnet Landing stories, plus "The Queen's Twin," "A Dunnet Shepherdess," and "William's Wedding," the last still unpublished at Jewett's death and lacking, for that reason, the same finish as the others. ("The Foreigner" was not rediscovered until David Bonnell Green's 1962 *The World of Dunnet Landing*). Cather also included a selection of other stories she judged of the same caliber. Her preface remains one of the most insightful descriptions of Jewett's "beautiful and delicate work," in which Cather found "the perfection that endures."⁴⁵

However, given her admiration for Jewett's artistry, Cather's editing of *Pointed Firs* shows an almost inexplicable disrespect for the original text's integrity. Although Jewett at no time indicated any desire to insert the later Dunnet Landing stories into the original 1896 edition, Cather went ahead and did so.⁴⁶ There are several reasons why this was a bad idea. First, the later pieces, written to stand alone, are longer than the originals, and their more complex structure disturbs the balance and symmetries of the book. The opening of "The Queen's Twin" is also clearly addressed to a reader who may not have read the earlier sketches, and the introductory material is superfluous and jarring. Most disturbingly, the placement of "William's Wedding" before "The Backward View" destroys the narrative's seasonal structure and renders its internal chronology meaningless.

All of the sketches show Jewett's careful notation of the time, expressed through her exquisite descriptions of landscape and seasonal patterns, even the characteristic light and air of different times of year. As the narrator moves through her summer, we see the vegetation progress from fresh green pennyroyal to frost-bitten goldenrod. Internal cues in the later stories also show her imaginatively playing with the original time sequence. Thus "A Dunnet Shepherdess" is set in midsummer, during mosquito season; "The Foreigner" in August, during the time of heavy storms; "The Queen's Twin" in September, when there is "a cold freshness in the morning air." Significantly, "William's Wedding," the last to be composed, is the only one to move outside this span of a single summer. Here the narrator is returning after being away for a winter. Now we are in very early spring, and Mrs. Todd's leafless garden seems initially as "cold and sterile" as the narrator's own sense of displacement and loneliness.

Since "A Dunnet Shepherdess" and "The Queen's Twin" take place within the same summer as the original sketches, their presence in the book disturbed its stylistic integrity, but not its coherence. Putting "William's Wedding" before "The Backward Glance," however, disrupted the story violently. Suddenly it is spring and the narrator has been away all winter. We never saw her leave, and there are no transitions to make sense of the shift. Then, in the very next chapter, she is leaving (again?) and we are back to late summer (but didn't the narrator say in "William's Wedding" that she was going to spend *this* summer in France?). Given that Cather's version remained the primary one available for many years, it is hardly surprising that some readers thought *Pointed Firs* was just a collection of interchangeable sketches without any overarching plot or structure.

With the restoration of the 1896 edition, the tight construction and elegant harmonies of the original can once more be appreciated.[47] While there may not be a plot in the conventional sense, there is a subtle development and progress. Although it may appear that "nothing happens," in fact the book traces a different kind of event than readers are accustomed to. Like her contemporary, the French painter Edouard Vuillard, who defamiliarized domestic interiors by emphasizing their negative spaces—rendering the "empty" places with vivid color and excitement—Jewett focuses her art on often unremarked events of tea parties and visits, meals and storytelling. By foregrounding this social background she makes the often peripheral domestic world central, for it here that the drama of building friendships, families, and communities takes place and her story unfolds.

Fostered through these quiet social interactions, the narrator's growing intimacy with Dunnet Landing is the delicate link between the sketches. With Mrs. Todd as her guide she is initiated into this pastoral world and its values. The climax of this process is the Bowden Reunion, where the narrator comes "near to feeling like a true Bowden." But it makes a difference that she has been to Green Island before this celebration; the episodes are not interchangeable, for it is on Green Island that the narrator establishes a relationship with William and Mrs. Blackett. That visit makes her participation in the larger gathering not only possible, but meaningful. Here also a seasonal marker guides our awareness of the narrator's growth: the Bowden Reunion is dated August 15th, high summer, but close to its end.

If the sketches follow the season's inevitable progress, the narrator's own progress is not straightforward. The growth of her understanding accumulates through small instances of dialogue leading to moments of new understanding. Individual episodes seem to circle or spiral toward their climax, which is not usually an action, but an insight, marked not by speech but by silence, a gap in the text itself. These gaps are not empty but filled with feelings which narrator and reader must both intuit. There is the moment on Green Island when the narrator and Mrs. Blackett understand each other without speaking, the moment when Mrs. Martin cannot go on and her listeners cannot ask a question, the long afternoon when the narrator and Elijah Tilley and the narrator keep silent watch together. Some of these silences follow the expression of a remembered grief or loss; the narrative gap marks the place where the listener's empathy goes beyond speech. Others mark cryptic exchanges that the narrator must quietly puzzle out for herself. Others are "shining moments" of friendship and transfiguration. The latter are often celebrated with a silent, sacramental sharing. An early apple pie, a gingerbread house, a simple coral pin—all say what words cannot. They give outward and visible form to an inward and invisible grace.[48]

Domestic rituals and moments of emotional communion were central to the women's fiction Jewett loved as a child, but as an adult she criticized precursors like Stowe for letting "sentiment fall to sentimentality." In *Pointed Firs* and other stories, such as "Miss Tempy's Watchers" or "The Town Poor," she returned to these themes with the literary skill and sophistication she had learned from European writers like Flaubert, de Maupassant, and Turgenev. Her narrative restraint and powerful use of suggestion, as well as the polish and discipline of her style, anticipate modernist techniques in poetry as well as fiction.[49] These affinities explain the mutual respect between herself and Henry James, also an admirer of Flaubert. James in this period was also experimenting with psychological realism; in stories like "The Beast in the Jungle" (1903) or "The Birthplace" (1903) he too portrayed internal rather than external events. While James and Jewett may seem far apart, in fact both were fascinated by the drama of social interaction and shaped their fiction around narrative gaps whose ambiguities both characters and readers are forced to interpret.

This technique is most obvious in Jewett's treatment of the narrator in *Pointed Firs*. Here is a central character about whom we know almost nothing, not even a name. All we know must be gleaned from incidental clues, and from these we discover she is a professional writer, that she is no longer young, that she is wealthy enough to have been to Dunnet Landing once before, on a yachting cruise. She is well traveled, having been to London and France, and certainly highly literate, since her classical and other literary allusions establish her educational (and social) status. However, her more personal history, her family, friends, loves and losses, are hidden. The history that gave her the emotional resources to interpret the people she sees or the stories she hears is not disclosed.

Jewett's choice to leave this background hidden is one of this text's major innovations, one that anticipates Ernest Hemingway's technique in stories like "Big Two-Hearted River" (1925).[50] That piece, also a pastoral, describes Nick Adams's return from World War I to the Michigan woods where he camped and fished as a boy. In precisely calibrated details we see Nick reenacting his past, recovering as he does a lost sense of peace and order. This was a story, Hemingway said, about the war, and yet the war is never mentioned. A good story, he added, should be like an iceberg, seven-eighths submerged. Just so, *The Country of the Pointed Firs* is about the narrator's life in the larger world outside Dunnet Landing, yet that life is never described.

Jewett's treatment of character also anticipates modernist approaches, since individuals here are only known dialogically, through their relations with others. Lacking the narrator's history, for example, readers must intuit that past through her present responses to Dunnet Landing. We learn who she is through how she learns about others. We never see her directly, only through her vision of others. Similarly, we never see her characters except in relation to her, in the context of her coming to know them. Thus the creation of these sketches depends fundamentally on the narrator's ability to enter into dialogue. Faced with each person, she must bring herself into connection through an empathic leap. Moreover, the reader's appreciation of the sketches depends on making a similar leap. We are initiated into the community through the narrator, but to make her knowledge our own we must reenact her imaginative work; we must participate as invisible partners in these dialogues and draw on our own histories to read the silences with which they are punctuated.

However, while we must draw on our own experience to interpret another's, there is also the danger of appropriation: of filling the silence not with empathy but with the projection of our own desire. The risk the narrator runs in entering these people's lives is a kind of ethnographic acquisitiveness. She could easily turn them into quaint snapshots for the urban tourist's scrapbook, hers or ours. Significantly, Jewett's narrator is careful to preserve the subjectivity of her literary subjects. Moreover, they frequently assert their ownership of what they show her. Over and over, characters direct the narrator's attention to what is important to them: a special landscape, a family portrait, a treasured artifact. Anxious to guide her vision, they are also eager to seen by her, perhaps because she represents the larger world with its prestige and validating power. On the other hand, the narrator is equally anxious to let her vision be guided and struggles to put her imagination at the service of the other. The difficulty of her effort can be seen in the next-to-last episode, "Along Shore."

The sketch's placement is, as always, important. We are at the summer's end. The narrator has already been to the Bowden Reunion. Having begun her visit by seeking simplicity and solitude, she has found instead a social life as busy and rich as London's high season. Now she is venturing forth on her own. Her acquaintance with the old fisherman Elijah Tilley is initiated without the help of Mrs. Todd; his invitation marks a new chapter in her Dunnet Landing life. Approaching the old fisherman's place, the narrator is surprised to find "a neat sharp-edged little dwelling, which looked strangely modern for its owner. I should have much sooner believed that the smart young wholesale egg merchant of the Landing was its occupant than Mr. Tilley, since a man's house is really but his larger body, and expresses in a way his nature and character."

The tension between rural and urban is figured here in the tension between the handmade artifacts of the preindustrial era and the machine-made goods of the new consumer culture. Tilley's immaculate kitchen, however, initially displays a kind of William Morris integrity dear to the narrator's eye. Her genuine appreciation for its hand-made rugs and rustic furnishings encourages her host to talk about his lost wife, Sarah. It is her taste the house expresses; Tilley keeps it just as she wanted it, as a kind of shrine. The narrator's tactful questions and silences allow this dignified widower to open his feelings to her. Trusting her judgment, he offers to show her the best room, where his wife's most precious things are kept. As in other such moments of confidence, we see the rural native willing to be seen through the eyes of the urban outsider. Her appreciation can validate what he himself values: her approval, perhaps, stands for the world's.

And yet, the narrator's first response is far from approving: "The best room seemed to me a much sadder and more empty place than the kitchen; its conventionalities lacked the simple perfection of the humbler room and failed on the side of poor ambition." There is a strong class dynamic at work here, expressed in the distinctions of taste, a powerful status marker.[51] Curiously, what repels the narrator is not the room's difference from her own background, but the dead women's aspiration to modern middle-class gentility. The narrator admires the primitive kitchen with its evocative of a timeless, preindustrial world, separate from her own. Mrs. Tilley in her own place as rural other is one thing, but when the rural woman attempts to claim a distinction she herself possesses, the visitor's reception is chilly.

But then something happens. The narrator forces herself to stop and remember "what patient saving, and what high respect for society in the abstract go to such furnishing." She begins to try to see the room from its owners' point of view: "I could imagine the great day of certain purchases, the bewildering shops of the next large town, the aspiring anxious woman, the clumsy sea-tanned man in his best clothes, so eager to be pleased, but at ease only when they were safe back in the sail-boat again, going down the bay with their precious freight, the hoarded money all spent and nothing to think of but tiller and sail." This imaginative work accomplished, the narrator "looks at the unworn carpet, the glass vases on the mantelpiece with their prim bunches of bleached swamp grass and dusty marsh rosemary, and . . . could read the history of Mrs. Tilley's best room from its very beginning."

Above her writing desk, next to the passage from Flaubert quoted earlier, Jewett kept another passage, also by Flaubert, "Écrire la vie ordinaire comme on écrit l'histoire" ("Write about everyday life as you would write history"). Like the ideal historian described by R. G. Collingwood in his philosophical study *The Idea of History*, Jewett's narrator attempts to overcome her preconceptions and to see her subject in its own terms.[52] The core of this technique, as Collingwood asserted, is the interpreter's use of available evidence to reenact its human history, for it is through such imaginative reenactment that its informing ideas can be recovered. The result is a kind of dialogue with the past, whether evidenced in a statesman's document or a countrywoman's parlor.

Thus the best room's initial "emptiness" was produced by the narrator's own resistance to reading it; her effort to overcome this resistance is rewarded by her perception of its meaning: "The French cups with their gay sprigs of pink and blue, the best tumblers, an old flowered bowl and tea caddy, and a japanned waiter or two adorned the shelves. These, with a few daguerreotypes in a little square pile, had the closet to themselves, and I was conscious of much pleasure in seeing them." However, the strain of her effort still shows in the narrator's strangely neutral tone. She does not say that Mrs. Tilley's best room is beautiful in absolute terms, only that it is deeply interesting in relative ones: "One is shown over many a house in these days where the interest may be more complex, but not more definite."

By the sketch's end, the narrator has achieved new appreciation for Sarah Tilley, whose aspirations she comes to respect, even as she recognizes their thwarting by poverty and isolation. At the Bowden Reunion she had reflected that "More than one face among the Bowden showed that only opportunity and stimulus were lacking,—a narrow set of circumstances had caged a fine able character and held it captive. One sees exactly the same types in a country gathering as in the most brilliant city company. You are safe to be understood if the spirit of your speech is the same for one neighbor as for the other." Despite the apparent contrast between urban and rural, a deeper human similarity connects them. In a curious way this insight bridges, and thereby undoes, the gap that provoked the tourist's desire in the first place, but with luck it replaces an exotic spectacle with something more mundane and far more valuable: a friend.

This insight is nowhere more important than in the growing relationship between the narrator and Mrs. Todd. One of this book's many pleasures is watching their growing respect for each other's authority and unrecognized potential. Thus the narrator comes to value her landlady's literary judgment, revealed, for example, in Mrs. Todd's shrewd critique of the Bowden Reunion poetess, "When she speaks o' those that are gone, she feels it all, and so does everybody else, but she harps too much. I'd laid half of that away for next time, if I was Mary Anna." However, the narrator also has talents that have gone undeveloped in her urban setting. After her guest's initial effort at selling herbs, Mrs. Todd comments frankly, "I have never had nobody I could so trust. All you lack is a few qualities, but with time you 'd gain judgment an' experience, an' be very able in the business. I 'd stand right here an' say it to anybody." If Mrs. Todd, differently placed, might have become an author, the narrator, differently placed, might have become a healer. But then, perhaps each in her own way has.

And yet the narrator is not, after all, a true Bowden. Her stay in Dunnet Landing is only temporary. When the northern summer comes to its lovely end, like Persephone leaving a grief-stricken Demeter for the Underworld, she must return to the city from whence she came. As she prepares to leave, the gap between her and Mrs. Todd seems magnified: "It was as if we were on the verge of a quarrel. It seemed impossible to take my departure with anything like composure." Her landlady speaks in "an unusually loud and business-like voice," as if trying to restore the economic relationship with which they had begun the season, but then, the narrator writes, "I glanced at my friend's face, and saw a look that touched me to the heart. I had been sorry enough before to go away." When Mrs. Todd hurries off without a proper goodbye, the narrator runs after her, only to be waved aside. "When I went in again the little house had suddenly grown lonely, and my room looked empty as it had the day I came. I and all my belongings had died out of it, and I knew how it would seem when Mrs. Todd came back and found her lodger gone. So we die before our own eyes; so we see some chapters of our lives come to their natural end." Then, on the kitchen table she finds the gift that says all that Mrs. Todd could not.

As the narrator leaves by the small coastal steamer, she catches one last glimpse of Mrs. Todd. Scanning the bay she spots Elijah Tilley and wishes "he had waited for one of his mates, it was such hard work to row along shore through rough sea seas and tend the traps alone." Then, as her boat strikes out to sea, she looks back once more, only to find that the "islands and the headland had run together and Dunnet Landing and all its coasts were lost to sight."

Now the place itself seems to die before her eyes, but as Wallace Stevens knew, "Death is the mother of beauty." The narrator's return gift to her lost friends is to evoke their presence in language, to make Dunnet Landing rise again from her pages and share its gifts with the foreigners who read them.

VI

In response to an inquiring letter from a child, Jewett once wrote, "The people in books are apt to make us understand 'real' people better, and to know why they do things, and so we learn to have sympathy and patience and enthusiasm for those we live with, and can try to help them in what they are doing, instead of being half suspicious and finding fault."[53] Finally, the question of whether Jewett's fiction is an evasion of her country's problems or a contribution toward their solution is one that only readers can decide. In her optimism she has affinities with other American writers such as Emerson, Whitman, and Harriet Beecher Stowe, even Horatio Alger. Like theirs, hers was a faith that, in the end, psyche is superior to circumstance; feeling right is prerequisite to doing right. If her fiction is limited by its failure to grapple directly with the conflict and pain brought by an industrialized and capitalist economy, or with the depth of prejudice dividing a multicultural and multiracial society, its subtle plea for empathy and tolerance, for understanding which does not erase differences nor their difficulties, seems worth heeding. At its best, Jewett's Dunnet Landing is a smaller world that knows itself in relation to a larger, and can keep its sense of proportion. Inviting her readers to become temporary part of this community, her narratives call on the interpretive skills necessary for such membership. With their silences and mysterious gaps, they enlist the imagination in the delicate and uncertain task of understanding others. As *The Pearl of Orr's Island* led a young writer to see the gray, weather-beaten houses of her native Maine with fresh excitement, so Jewett dreamed her art would inspire its readers to see their fellow citizens and their common world with new and compassionate eyes.

Notes

1. With some important additions and reflections prompted by more recent scholarship, this introduction is based on my critical study, *Sarah Orne Jewett, an American Persephone* (Hanover and London: University Press of New England, 1989). As for major additional sources, the most recent and most thorough biography of Jewett is Paula Blanchard's *Sarah Orne Jewett: Her World and Her Work* (Reading, Mass.: Addison-Wesley, 1994). Collections of critical essays include: *Appreciation of Sarah Orne Jewett: Twenty-Nine Interpretive Essays*, edited by Richard Cary (Waterville, Maine: Colby College Press, 1973); *Critical Essays on Sarah Orne Jewett*, edited by Gwen Nagel (Boston: G. K. Hall, 1984); and *New Essays on The Country of the Pointed Firs*, edited by June Howard (New York: Cambridge University Press, 1994). Valuable critiques of Jewett scholarship are provided in two essays by June Howard, "Introduction: Sarah Orne Jewett and the Traffic in Words," in *New Essays on The Country of the Pointed Firs*," pp. 1–37, and "Unravelling Regions, Unsettling Periods: Sarah Orne Jewett and American Literary History," *American Literature* 68:2 (June 1996): 365–84; and by Marjorie Pryse, "Sex, Class, and 'Category Crisis': Jewett and the Postmodern Reader," Keynote Address delivered at "Sarah Orne Jewett and Her Contemporaries: The Centennial Conference," Westbrook College, Portland, Maine (22 June 1996). Willa Cather's comments are from her "Preface" to *The Best Stories of Sarah Orne Jewett* (Boston: Houghton Mifflin, 1925).

2. Richard Brodhead, "The Reading of Regions," in *Cultures of Letters: Scenes of Reading and Writing in Nineteenth-Century America* (Chicago and London: University of Chicago Press, 1993), p. 134. See also Brodhead's "Jewett, Regionalism, and Writing as Women's Work," in the same volume. Other important discussions of Jewett as a regionalist include: Josephine Donovan, *New England Local Color Literature: A Woman's Tradition* (New York: Frederick Ungar, 1983); Amy Kaplan, "Nation, Region, and Empire," in *The Columbia History of the American Novel*, edited by Emory Elliott (New York: Columbia University Press, 1991), pp. 240–66; as well as the provocative essays included in *New Essays on The Country of the Pointed Firs*, ed. Howard. For an overview of the critical issues see Judith Fetterley and Marjorie Pryse, "Introduction" to *American Women Regionalists, 1850–1910: A Norton Anthology* (New York: W. W. Norton, 1992), pp. xi–xx; and Howard, "Unravelling Regions, Unsettling Periods, Sarah Orne Jewett and American Literary History."

3. See Amy Kaplan on this cultural "moment"; also Benedict Anderson, *Imagined Communities: Reflections on the Spread and Origin of Nationalism* (London and New York: Verso, 1983, 1991).

4. Sarah Orne Jewett, "River Driftwood," in *Deephaven and Other*

Stories, edited by Richard Cary (New Haven, Conn.: College and University Press, 1966), p. 71.

5. Hal S. Barron, *Those Who Stayed Behind: Rural Society in Nineteenth-Century New England* (New York: Cambridge University Press, 1984). See also *The Countryside in the Age of Capitalist Transformation: Essays in the Social History of Rural America*, edited by Steven Hahn and Jonathan Prude (Chapel Hill: University of North Carolina Press, 1985).

6. Dona Brown, "Purchasing the Past: Summer People and the Transformation of the Piscataqua Region in the Nineteenth Century," in *A Noble and Dignified Stream: The Piscataqua Region in the Colonial Revival, 1860–1930*, edited by Sarah L. Giffen and Kevin D. Murphy (York, Maine: Old York Historical Society, 1992). My discussion in the following section is indebted to Brown's interesting and important analysis. See also Dona Brown, *Inventing New England: Regional Tourism in the Nineteenth Century* (Washington, D.C.: Smithsonian Institution Press, 1995). On antimodernism, see T. J. Jackson Lears, *No Place of Grace: Antimodernism and the Transformation of American Culture, 1880–1920* (Chicago and London: University of Chicago Press, 1981, 1983).

7. On this issue see Howard, *New Essays on The Country of the Pointed Firs*: Sandra Zagarell, "*Country*'s Portrayal of Community and the Exclusion of Difference," pp. 39–60; Elizabeth Ammons, "Material Culture, Empire, and Jewett's *The Country of the Pointed Firs*," pp. 81–99; and Susan Gillman, "Regionalism and Nationalism in Jewett's *The Country of the Pointed Firs*," pp. 101–117. Also: Karen Oakes [Kilcup], " 'Colossal in Sheet-Lead': The Native American and Piscataqua-Region Writers," in *A Noble and Dignified Stream*, eds. Giffen and Murphy, pp. 165–76.

8. Kaplan, "Nation, Region, and Empire," p. 251; Brodhead, "The Reading of Regions," pp. 134–37.

9. Sarah Orne Jewett, *The Story of the Normans, Told Chiefly in Relation to their Conquest of England* (New York: G. P. Putnam's Sons, 1887). For discussion, see Zagarell, "*Country*'s Portrayal of Community and the Exclusion of Difference"; Ammons, "Material Culture, Empire, and Jewett's *The Country of the Pointed Firs*"; and Gillman, "Regionalism and Nationalism in Jewett's *The Country of the Pointed Firs*." Also Blanchard, *Sarah Orne Jewett*, pp. 162–63; and Fermin Bishop, "Sarah Orne Jewett's Ideas of Race," *New England Quarterly* 30:2 (1957): 243–49.

10. Blanchard, *Sarah Orne Jewett*, pp. 198–99.

11. Jewett intended to publish a collection of her Irish-American stories under the title *Transplanted Shamrocks*. Happily, readers should have access to much of this work in a new collection, *The Irish Stories of Sarah Orne Jewett*, edited by Louis Renza and Jack Morgan (Carbondale, Ill.: Southern Illinois University Press, 1996).

12. Jewett, "Preface to the 1893 Edition," *Deephaven and Other Stories*, p. 32.

13. Jewett, "Preface to the 1893 Edition," *Deephaven and Other Stories*, p. 33.

14. Richard Chase, *The American Novel and Its Tradition* (Garden City, N.Y.: Doubleday-Anchor, 1957), p. 1.

15. Sarah Orne Jewett to Willa Cather, 13 December 1908, in *The Letters of Sarah Orne Jewett*, edited by Annie Fields (Boston: Houghton Mifflin, 1911), pp. 249–50.

16. Sarah Orne Jewett, "Looking Back on Girlhood," in *Sarah Orne Jewett: Novels and Stories*, edited by Michael Davitt Bell (New York: Library of America, 1994), pp. 758–59.

17. Jewett, "Looking Back on Girlhood," p. 759.

18. Jewett, "Preface to the 1893 Edition," *Deephaven and Other Stories*, p. 32.

19. There is now a wealth of scholarship on social structure, gender roles, and class identity. Three early influential works are: Ann D. Gorden and Mari Jo Buhle, "Sex and Class in Colonial and Nineteeth-Century American," in *Liberating Women's History*, edited by Bernice A. Carroll (Urbana: University of Illinois Press, 1976); Gerda Lerner, "The Lady and the Mill Girl: Changes in the Status of Women in the Age of Jackson, 1790–1840," in *A Heritage of Her Own*, edited by Nancy F. Cott and Elizabeth H. Pleck (New York: Simon and Schuster, 1979); and Nancy F. Cott, *The Bonds of Womanhood: "Woman's Sphere" in New England, 1780–1835* (New Haven, Conn.: Yale University Press, 1977). Newer work on these questions includes: Linda Kerber, "Separate Spheres, Female Worlds, Woman's Place," *Journal of American History* 75:9 (1988): 9–39; Kathy Peiss, "Going Public: Women in Nineteenth-Century Culture History," *American Literary History* 3:4 (1991): 817–28. Also Margaret Roman, *Sarah Orne Jewett: Reconstructing Gender* (Tuscaloosa: University of Alabama Press, 1992).

20. Carroll Smith-Rosenberg, "The Female World of Love and Ritual: Relations Between Women in Nineteeth-Century America," in Smith-Rosenberg, *Disorderly Conduct: Visions of Gender in Victorian America* (New York: Oxford University Press, 1985).

21. Mary Kelley, *Private Woman, Public Stage: Literary Domesticity in Nineteenth-Century America* (New York: Oxford University Press, 1984).

22. Sarah Orne Jewett, "An Autumn Holiday," in *Country By-Ways* (Boston: Houghton Mifflin, 1881), p. 146. For a discussion of sex, class, and the exchange between premodern, modern, and postmodern, see Pryse, "Sex, Class, and 'Category Crisis': Jewett and the Postmodern Reader."

23. Sarah Orne Jewett, "A Modern Idyll," MS. Am 1743.22 (70), Houghton Library, Harvard University, n.p. There have been several interesting studies of Jewett as a pastoral writer. Some of these are included in Cary's *Appreciation of Sarah Orne Jewett*: Robin Magowan, "Pastoral and the Art of Landscape in *The Country of the Pointed Firs*," pp. 187–95; David Stouck, "*The Country of the Pointed Firs*: A Pastoral

of Innocence," pp. 249–54; and Paul Eakin, "Sarah Orne Jewett and the Meaning of Country Life," pp. 203–22. See also Louis Renza, "'A White Heron' as a Rare Bird of Pastoral," in *"A White Heron" and the Question of Minor Literature* (Madison: University of Wisconsin Press, 1984). Raymond William's *The Country and the City* (New York: Oxford University Press, 1973) provides a valuable overview of pastoral themes in English literature, as well as an important analysis of the relationship of the rural and regional to the urban and national (or imperial).

24. Jewett, *Deephaven*, pp. 130–31.

25. Johann Jakob Bachofen, *Das Mutterrecht* (1861); reprinted in *Myth, Religion, and Mother Right*, trans. Ralph Manheim (Princeton, N.J.: Bollingen Foundation, Princeton University Press, 1967); Alfred (Lord) Tennyson, *Demeter and Other Poems* (New York and London: Macmillan, 1889); Thomas Wentworth Higginson, "The Greek Goddesses," *The Atlantic Monthly* 24 (July 1869): 97–108.

26. Walter Horatio Pater, "The Myth of Demeter and Persephone" (1876); reprinted in *Greek Studies: A Series of Essays* (New York: Macmillan, 1894), p. 104.

27. Pater, "The Myth of Demeter and Persephone," pp. 126–27.

28. Jewett's belief in the possibility of affirming differences without invidious distinctions depends upon a vision of cultural childhood, a developmental scheme in which ethnocentrism is continuous with egocentrism and awareness of the other ultimately contributes to enlightenment. The possibility that the world is prior to the parish or that encounter with the other produces the cultural self, does not figure in this scheme. Nor does the idea that the cultural ground may itself be socially constructed, an insight that this text holds at bay, as it does the "dark fear" that, given historical inequities of status and power, closer acquaintance between groups might tragically heighten their perceived differences and widen the psychic distances between them. When these possibilities are suggested in "The Foreigner," they are still, as we shall see, safely contained within the larger frame of the narrator's and Mrs. Todd's friendship.

29. On Jewett's representation of community see Sandra A. Zagarell, "Narrative of Community: The Identification of a Genre," in *Revising the Word and the World: Essays in Feminist Literary Criticism*, edited by VéVé A. Clark, Ruth-Ellen R. Joeres, and Madelon Sprengnether (Chicago: University of Chicago Press, 1993), pp. 249–78, and Zagarell's more recent *"Country's* Portrayal of Community and the Exclusion of Difference." My discussion in this section is indebted to both articles and the important questions they raise.

30. Zagarell, *"Country's* Portrayal of Community and the Exclusion of Difference," p. 39. See also Ammons, "Material Culture, Empire, and Jewett's *The Country of the Pointed Firs,"* and Gillman, "Regionalism and Nationalism in Jewett's *The Country of the Pointed Firs.*

31. Sarah Orne Jewett to Willa Cather, quoted in Cather, "Preface," I, p. ix.

32. For an excellent discussion of these processes and their significance, see Marilyn Sanders Mobley, *Folk Roots and Mythic Wings in Sarah Orne Jewett and Toni Morrison: The Cultural Function of Narrative* (Baton Rouge: Louisiana State University Press, 1991).

33. Sarah Orne Jewett to Horace Scudder, South Berwick, 13 July 1873, Colby College Library, quoted in Blanchard, *Sarah Orne Jewett*, p. 61.

34. Francis Otto Matthiessen, *Sarah Orne Jewett* (Boston: Houghton Mifflin, 1929), p. 70. See also Willa Cather, "148 Charles Street," *Not Under Forty* (New York: Knopf, 1936), and Judith Roman, *Annie Adams Fields: The Spirit of Charles Street* (Bloomington: Indiana University Press, 1990).

35. See Smith-Rosenberg, "The Female World of Love and Ritual," and Lillian Faderman, *Surpassing the Love of Men: Romantic Friendship and the Love Between Women from the Renaissance to the Present* (New York: Morrow, 1981). Also, Glenda Hobbes, "Pure and Passionate: Female Friendship in Sarah Orne Jewett's 'Martha's Lady,'" in *Critical Essays on Sarah Orne Jewett*, pp. 99–107; Josephine Donovan, "Nan Prince and the Golden Apples," *Colby Library Quarterly* 22:1 (March 1986): 17–27; Judith Fetterley, "Reading *Deephaven* as a Lesbian Text," in *Sexual Practice/Textual Theory: Lesbian Cultural Criticism*, edited by Susan J. Wolfe and Julia Penelope (Cambridge, Mass.: Blackwell, 1993), pp. 164–83; Marjorie Pryse, "Archives of Female Friendship and the 'Way' Jewett Wrote," *New England Quarterly* 66:1 (March 1993): 47–66; and Pryse, "Sex, Class, and 'Category Crisis': Jewett and the Postmodern Reader."

36. Sarah Orne Jewett, "The Decay of Churches," MS. Am 1743.22 (25), Houghton Library, Harvard University.

37. Sarah Orne Jewett, "A Winter Drive," *Country By-Ways* (Boston: Houghton Mifflin, 1881), p. 168.

38. See Josephine Donovan, "Jewett and Swedenborg," *American Literature* 65 (1993): 731–50.

39. Sarah Orne Jewett to Sara Norton, 3 September (1897), in *Letters*, ed. Fields, p. 126; Jewett to Sarah Wyman Whitman, South Berwick, Maine, n.d., in *Letters*, Fields, ed., pp. 129–30. The internal quotation is from Agnes Mary Frances Duclaux (Robinson), *The Life of Ernest Renan* (Boston: Houghton Mifflin, 1898). Annie Fields dates this letter to Whitman 1897, but the publication date of the internal quotation is 1898 and the letter itself is very similar to one Jewett wrote to Grace Norton in 1898.

40. Charles Johanningsmeier, "The 'Lost' Newspaper Writing of Sarah Orne Jewett," paper delivered at the "Nineteenth-Century Women Writers in the Twenty-First Century" Conference, Trinity College, Hartford, Conn., 31 May 1996.

41. Sarah Orne Jewett to Georgina Halliburton, London, 22 April [1892], Houghton Library, Harvard University.

42. Sarah Orne Jewett to Sarah Wyman Whitman, 8 September 1895, Houghton Library, Harvard University.

43. Rudyard Kipling to Sarah Orne Jewett (January 1897), Houghton Library, Harvard University.

44. For a thoughtful discussion of this relationship, see Sharon O'Brien, *Willa Cather: The Emerging Voice* (New York: Oxford University Press, 1987).

45. Willa Cather, Dedication, *O, Pioneers!* (Boston: Houghton Mifflin, 1913).

46. Cather, however, was not the first to interfere with the original. A posthumous 1909 edition of *Pointed Firs* added "A Dunnet Shepherdess" and "William's Wedding" after "A Backward Glance." A 1911 edition interpolated these two stories plus "The Queen's Twin" into the text before "A Backward Glance." Cather's 1925 version then reversed "William's Wedding" and "The Queen's Twin." See Marco A. Portales, "History of a Text: Jewett's *The Country of the Pointed Firs*," *New England Quarterly* 55:4 (December 1982): 586–92.

47. This Hardscrabble edition is not the first to return to the 1896 text, but it is the only facsimile of that text now widely available.

48. On genre and plot, see Elizabeth Ammons, "Finding Form: Narrative Geography and *The Country of the Pointed Firs*," in Ammons, *Conflicting Stories: American Women Writers at the Turn into the Twentieth Century* (New York: Oxford University Press, 1991), pp. 44–58; Joseph Allen Boone, *Tradition Counter Tradition: Love and the Form of Fiction* (Chicago: University of Chicago Press, 1987); Zagarell, "Narrative of Community"; and Karen Oakes [Kilcup], "'All that Lay Deepest in Her Heart': Reflections on Jewett, Gender, and Genre," *Colby Library Quarterly* 26 (1990): 152–60. On empathy, Marcia McClintock Folsom, "Tact Is a Kind of Mind-Reading: Empathic Style in Sarah Orne Jewett's *The Country of the Pointed Firs*" in *Critical Essays on Sarah Orne Jewett*, pp. 76–89; Pryse and Fetterley, "Introduction," *American Women Regionalists, 1850–1910*, pp. xi–xx. On domestic ritual, Ann Romines, *The Home Plot: Women, Writing, and Domestic Ritual* (Amherst: University of Massachusetts Press, 1992), esp. pp. 19–90.

49. On Jewett's literary influences and use of suggestion, see, in *Critical Essays on Sarah Orne Jewett*: Richard Cary, "The Literary Rubrics of Sarah Orne Jewett," pp. 198–211; and Josephine Donovan, "Sarah Orne Jewett's Critical Theory: Notes Toward a Feminine Literary Mode," pp. 212–25. On Jewett's "realism" see Marjorie Pryse, "Women 'at Sea': Feminist Realism in Sarah Orne Jewett's 'The Foreigner,'" in *Critical Essays on Sarah Orne Jewett*; and Michael Davitt Bell, "Gender and American Realism in *The Country of the Pointed Firs*," in *New Essays on The Country of the Pointed Firs*, pp. 61–80.

50. Ernest Hemingway, "Big Two-Hearted River," *In Our Time* (New York: Scribner's, 1925).

51. On taste, see Pierre Bourdieu, *Distinction: A Social Critique of*

the Judgement of Taste, trans. Richard Nice (Cambridge, Mass.: Harvard University Press, 1984). Also Karen Halttunen, "From Parlor to Living Room: Domestic Space, Interior Decoration, and the Culture of Personality," in *Consuming Visions: Accumulation and Display of Goods in America, 1880–1920*, edited by Simon Bronner (New York: W. W. Norton), pp. 157–89.
52. R. G. Collingwood, *The Idea of History* (London, Oxford, New York: Oxford University Press, 1946).
53. Sarah Orne Jewett to Mary E. Mulholland, 23 January 1899, Colby Library; quoted in Blanchard, *Sarah Orne Jewett*, p. 230.

I would like to thank Melody Graulich and Marjorie Pryse for their thoughtful readings of this introduction in manuscript. My thanks also to The Book Guild of Portsmouth, New Hampshire, for locating the 1896 edition of *The Country of the Pointed Firs*. This facsimile preserves the original small size of its pages. Readers may also notice the distinctive spacing in dialect passages. Unusual according to today's usage, such spacing was common when Jewett wrote. For stylistic continuity, it has been maintained in the additional Dunnett Landing stories.

THE COUNTRY
OF THE POINTED FIRS
BY SARAH ORNE
JEWETT

BOSTON AND NEW YORK
HOUGHTON MIFFLIN AND COMPANY
The Riverside Press Cambridge

CONTENTS.

THE COUNTRY OF THE POINTED FIRS.

I.

THE RETURN.

THERE was something about the coast town of Dunnet which made it seem more attractive than other maritime villages of eastern Maine. Perhaps it was the simple fact of acquaintance with that neighborhood which made it so attaching, and gave such interest to the rocky shore and dark woods, and the few houses which seemed to be securely wedged and tree-nailed in among the ledges by the Landing. These houses made the most of their seaward view, and there was a gayety and determined flower-iness in their bits of garden ground; the small-paned high windows in the peaks of their steep gables were like knowing eyes that watched the harbor and the far sea-line beyond, or looked northward all along the

shore and its background of spruces and
balsam firs.   When one really knows a village like this and its surroundings, it is like
becoming acquainted with a single person.
The process of falling in love at first sight
is as final as it is swift in such a case, but
the growth of true friendship may be a life-
long affair.

After a first brief visit made two or three
summers before in the course of a yachting
cruise, a lover of Dunnet Landing returned
to find the unchanged shores of the pointed
firs, the same quaintness of the village with
its elaborate conventionalities; all that mix-
ture of remoteness, and childish certainty of
being the centre of civilization of which her
affectionate dreams had told. One evening in June, a single passenger landed upon
the steamboat wharf. The tide was high,
there was a fine crowd of spectators, and
the younger portion of the company followed
her with subdued excitement up the narrow
street of the salt-aired, white-clapboarded
little town.

II.

MRS. TODD.

LATER, there was only one fault to find with this choice of a summer lodging-place, and that was its complete lack of seclusion. At first the tiny house of Mrs. Almira Todd, which stood with its end to the street, appeared to be retired and sheltered enough from the busy world, behind its bushy bit of a green garden, in which all the blooming things, two or three gay hollyhocks and some London-pride, were pushed back against the gray-shingled wall. It was a queer little garden and puzzling to a stranger, the few flowers being put at a disadvantage by so much greenery; but the discovery was soon made that Mrs. Todd was an ardent lover of herbs, both wild and tame, and the sea-breezes blew into the low end-window of the house laden with not only sweet-brier and sweet-mary, but balm and sage and borage and mint, wormwood

and southernwood. If Mrs. Todd had occasion to step into the far corner of her
herb plot, she trod heavily upon thyme, and
made its fragrant presence known with all
the rest. Being a very large person, her
full skirts brushed and bent almost every
slender stalk that her feet missed. You
could always tell when she was stepping
about there, even when you were half awake
in the morning, and learned to know, in the
course of a few weeks' experience, in exactly which corner of the garden she might
be.

At one side of this herb plot were other
growths of a rustic pharmacopœia, great
treasures and rarities among the commoner
herbs. There were some strange and pungent odors that roused a dim sense and remembrance of something in the forgotten
past. Some of these might once have belonged to sacred and mystic rites, and have
had some occult knowledge handed with
them down the centuries ; but now they per-
tained only to humble compounds brewed at
intervals with molasses or vinegar or spirits
in a small caldron on Mrs. Todd's kitchen
stove. They were dispensed to suffering
neighbors, who usually came at night as if

by stealth, bringing their own ancient-looking vials to be filled. One nostrum was called the Indian remedy, and its price was but fifteen cents ; the whispered directions could be heard as customers passed the windows. With most remedies the purchaser was allowed to depart unadmonished from the kitchen, Mrs. Todd being a wise saver of steps ; but with certain vials she gave cautions, standing in the doorway, and there were other doses which had to be accompanied on their healing way as far as the gate, while she muttered long chapters of directions, and kept up an air of secrecy and importance to the last. It may not have been only the common ails of humanity with which she tried to cope ; it seemed sometimes as if love and hate and jealousy and adverse winds at sea might also find their proper remedies among the curious wild-looking plants in Mrs. Todd's garden.

The village doctor and this learned herbalist were upon the best of terms. The good man may have counted upon the unfavorable effect of certain potions which he should find his opportunity in counteracting ; at any rate, he now and then stopped and exchanged greetings with Mrs. Todd over the picket fence. The conversation became at once professional after the briefest preliminaries, and he would stand twirling a sweet-scented sprig in his fingers, and make suggestive jokes, perhaps about her faith in a too persistent course of thoroughwort elixir, in which my landlady professed such firm belief as sometimes to endanger the life and usefulness of worthy neighbors.

To arrive at this quietest of seaside villages late in June, when the busy herb-gathering season was just beginning, was also to arrive in the early prime of Mrs. Todd's activity in the brewing of old-fashioned spruce beer. This cooling and refreshing drink had been brought to wonderful perfection through a long series of experiments; it had won immense local fame, and the supplies for its manufacture were always giving out and having to be replenished. For various reasons, the seclusion and uninterrupted days which had been looked forward to proved to be very rare in this otherwise delightful corner of the world. My hostess and I had made our shrewd business agreement on the basis of a simple cold luncheon at noon, and liberal restitution in the matter of hot suppers, to

provide for which the lodger might sometimes be seen hurrying down the road, late
in the day, with cunner line in hand. It
was soon found that this arrangement made
large allowance for Mrs. Todd's slow herb-
gathering progresses through woods and
pastures. The spruce-beer customers were
pretty steady in hot weather, and there were
many demands for different soothing syrups
and elixirs with which the unwise curiosity of my early residence had made me
acquainted. Knowing Mrs. Todd to be a
widow, who had little beside this slender
business and the income from one hungry
lodger to maintain her, one's energies and
even interest were quickly bestowed, until it
became a matter of course that she should
go afield every pleasant day, and that the
lodger should answer all peremptory knocks
at the side door.

In taking an occasional wisdom-giving
stroll in Mrs. Todd's company, and in act-
ing as business partner during her frequent
absences, I found the July days fly fast, and
it was not until I felt myself confronted
with too great pride and pleasure in the display, one night, of two dollars and twenty-
seven cents which I had taken in during

the day, that I remembered a long piece
of writing, sadly belated now, which I was
bound to do. To have been patted kindly
on the shoulder and called " darlin'," to
have been offered a surprise of early mushrooms for supper, to have had all the glory
of making two dollars and twenty - seven
cents in a single day, and then to renounce
it all and withdraw from these pleasant suc-
cesses, needed much resolution. Literary
employments are so vexed with uncertainties at best, and it was not until the voice of
conscience sounded louder in my ears than
the sea on the nearest pebble beach that I
said unkind words of withdrawal to Mrs.
Todd. She only became more wistfully affectionate than ever in her expressions, and
looked as disappointed as I expected when I
frankly told her that I could no longer enjoy the pleasure of what we called " seein'
folks."   I felt that I was cruel to a whole
neighborhood in curtailing her liberty in
this most important season for harvesting
the different wild herbs that were so much
counted upon to ease their winter ails.

   " Well, dear," she said sorrowfully, " I 've
took great advantage o' your bein' here. I
ain't had such a season for years, but I have

never had nobody I could so trust. All you lack is a few qualities, but with time you'd gain judgment an' experience, an' be very able in the business. I'd stand right here an' say it to anybody."

Mrs. Todd and I were not separated or estranged by the change in our business relations; on the contrary, a deeper intimacy seemed to begin. I do not know what herb of the night it was that used sometimes to send out a penetrating odor late in the evening, after the dew had fallen, and the moon was high, and the cool air came up from the sea. Then Mrs. Todd would feel that she must talk to somebody, and I was only too glad to listen. We both fell under the spell, and she either stood outside the window, or made an errand to my sitting-room, and told, it might be very commonplace news of the day, or, as happened one misty summer night, all that lay deepest in her heart. It was in this way that I came to know that she had loved one who was far above her.

"No, dear, him I speak of could never think of me," she said. "When we was young together his mother did n't favor the match, an' done everything she could to part us; and folks thought we both married well, but 't wa'n't what either one of us wanted most; an' now we 're left alone again, an' might have had each other all the time. He was above bein' a seafarin' man, an' prospered more than most; he come of a high family, an' my lot was plain an' hard-workin'. I ain't seen him for some years; he 's forgot our youthful feelin's, I expect, but a woman's heart is different; them feel-in's comes back when you think you've done with 'em, as sure as spring comes with the year. An' I 've always had ways of hearin' about him."

She stood in the centre of a braided rug, and its rings of black and gray seemed to circle about her feet in the dim light. Her height and massiveness in the low room gave her the look of a huge sibyl, while the strange fragrance of the mysterious herb blew in from the little garden.

III.

THE SCHOOLHOUSE.

FOR some days after this, Mrs. Todd's customers came and went past my windows, and, haying-time being nearly over, strangers began to arrive from the inland country, such was her widespread reputation. Sometimes I saw a pale young creature like a white windflower left over into midsummer, upon whose face consumption had set its bright and wistful mark; but oftener two stout, hard-worked women from the farms came together, and detailed their symptoms to Mrs. Todd in loud and cheerful voices, combining the satisfactions of a friendly gossip with the medical opportunity. They seemed to give much from their own store of therapeutic learning. I became aware of the school in which my landlady had strengthened her natural gift; but hers was always the governing mind, and the final command, "Take of hy'sop one handful" (or whatever herb it was), was received in respectful silence. One afternoon, when I had listened, — it was impossible not to listen, with cottonless ears, — and then laughed and listened again, with an idle pen in my hand, during a particularly spirited and personal conversation, I reached for my hat, and, taking blotting-book and all under my arm, I resolutely fled further temptation, and walked out past the fragrant green garden and up the dusty road. The way went straight uphill, and presently I stopped and turned to look back.

The tide was in, the wide harbor was surrounded by its dark woods, and the small wooden houses stood as near as they could get to the landing. Mrs. Todd's was the last house on the way inland. The gray ledges of the rocky shore were well covered with sod in most places, and the pasture bayberry and wild roses grew thick among them. I could see the higher inland country and the scattered farms. On the brink of the hill stood a little white schoolhouse, much wind-blown and weather-beaten, which was a landmark to seagoing folk; from its door there was a most beautiful view of sea and shore. The summer vacation now prevailed, and after finding the door unfastened, and taking a long look through one of the seaward windows, and reflecting afterward for some time in a shady place near by among the bayberry bushes, I returned to the chief place of business in the village, and, to the amusement of two of the selectmen, brothers and autocrats of Dunnet Landing, I hired the schoolhouse for the rest of the vacation for fifty cents a week.

Selfish as it may appear, the retired situation seemed to possess great advantages, and I spent many days there quite undisturbed, with the sea-breeze blowing through the small, high windows and swaying the heavy outside shutters to and fro. I hung my hat and luncheon-basket on an entry nail as if I were a small scholar, but I sat at the teacher's desk as if I were that great authority, with all the timid empty benches in rows before me. Now and then an idle sheep came and stood for a long time looking in at the door. At sundown I went back, feeling most businesslike, down toward the village again, and usually met the flavor, not of the herb garden, but of Mrs. Todd's hot supper, halfway up the hill. On the nights when there were evening meetings or other public exercises that demanded her presence we had tea very early, and I was welcomed back as if from a long absence.

Once or twice I feigned excuses for staying at home, while Mrs. Todd made distant excursions, and came home late, with both hands full and a heavily laden apron. This was in pennyroyal time, and when the rare lobelia was in its prime and the elecampane was coming on. One day she appeared at the schoolhouse itself, partly out of amused curiosity about my industries; but she explained that there was no tansy in the neighborhood with such snap to it as some that grew about the schoolhouse lot. Being scuffed down all the spring made it grow so much the better, like some folks that had it hard in their youth, and were bound to make the most of themselves before they died.

IV.

AT THE SCHOOLHOUSE WINDOW.

ONE day I reached the schoolhouse very late, owing to attendance upon the funeral of an acquaintance and neighbor, with whose sad decline in health I had been familiar, and whose last days both the doctor and Mrs. Todd had tried in vain to ease. The services had taken place at one o'clock, and now, at quarter past two, I stood at the schoolhouse window, looking down at the procession as it went along the lower road close to the shore. It was a walking funeral, and even at that distance I could recognize most of the mourners as they went their solemn way. Mrs. Begg had been very much respected, and there was a large company of friends following to her grave. She had been brought up on one of the neighboring farms, and each of the few times that I had seen her she professed great dissatisfaction with town life. The people lived too close together for her liking, at the Landing, and she could not get used to the constant sound of the sea.   She had lived to lament three seafaring husbands, and her house was decorated with West Indian curiosities, specimens of conch shells and fine coral which they had brought home from their voyages in lumber-laden ships.   Mrs. Todd had told me all our neighbor's history.   They had been girls together, and, to use her own phrase, had " both seen trouble till they knew the best and worst on 't."   I could see the sorrowful, large figure of Mrs. Todd as I stood at the window.   She made a break in the procession by walking slowly and keeping the after-part of it back.   She held a handkerchief to her eyes, and I knew, with a pang of sympathy, that hers was not affected grief.

Beside her, after much difficulty, I recognized the one strange and unrelated person in all the company, an old man who had always been mysterious to me.   I could see his thin, bending figure.   He wore a narrow, long-tailed coat and walked with a stick, and had the same " cant to leeward " as the wind-bent trees on the height above.

This was Captain Littlepage, whom I had

seen only once or twice before, sitting pale
and old behind a closed window; never out
of doors until now. Mrs. Todd always
shook her head gravely when I asked a question, and said that he was n't what he had
been once, and seemed to class him with
her other secrets. He might have belonged
with a simple which grew in a certain slug-
haunted corner of the garden, whose use
she could never be betrayed into telling me,
though I saw her cutting the tops by moonlight once, as if it were a charm, and not a
medicine, like the great fading bloodroot
leaves.

I could see that she was trying to keep
pace with the old captain's lighter steps.
He looked like an aged grasshopper of some
strange human variety. Behind this pair
was a short, impatient, little person, who
kept the captain's house, and gave it what
Mrs. Todd and others believed to be no
proper sort of care. She was usually called
"that Mari' Harris" in subdued conversation between intimates, but they treated her
with anxious civility when they met her face
to face.

The bay-sheltered islands and the great
sea beyond stretched away to the far horizon

southward and eastward; the little procession in the foreground looked futile and
helpless on the edge of the rocky shore. It
was a glorious day early in July, with a clear,
high sky; there were no clouds, there was
no noise of the sea. The song sparrows
sang and sang, as if with joyous knowledge
of immortality, and contempt for those who
could so pettily concern themselves with
death. I stood watching until the funeral
procession had crept round a shoulder of the
slope below and disappeared from the great
landscape as if it had gone into a cave.

An hour later I was busy at my work.
Now and then a bee blundered in and took
me for an enemy; but there was a useful
stick upon the teacher's desk, and I rapped
to call the bees to order as if they were
unruly scholars, or waved them away from
their riots over the ink, which I had bought
at the Landing store, and discovered too
late to be scented with bergamot, as if to
refresh the labors of anxious scribes. One
anxious scribe felt very dull that day; a
sheep-bell tinkled near by, and called her
wandering wits after it. The sentences
failed to catch these lovely summer cadences.
For the first time I began to wish for a com-

panion and for news from the outer world, which had been, half unconsciously, forgotten. Watching the funeral gave one a sort of pain. I began to wonder if I ought not to have walked with the rest, instead of hurrying away at the end of the services. Perhaps the Sunday gown I had put on for the occasion was making this disastrous change of feeling, but I had now made myself and my friends remember that I did not really belong to Dunnet Landing.

I sighed, and turned to the half-written page again.

V.

CAPTAIN LITTLEPAGE.

It was a long time after this; an hour was very long in that coast town where nothing stole away the shortest minute. I had lost myself completely in work, when I heard footsteps outside. There was a steep footpath between the upper and the lower road, which I climbed to shorten the way, as the children had taught me, but I believed that Mrs. Todd would find it inaccessible, unless she had occasion to seek me in great haste. I wrote on, feeling like a besieged miser of time, while the footsteps came nearer, and the sheep-bell tinkled away in haste as if some one had shaken a stick in its wearer's face. Then I looked, and saw Captain Littlepage passing the nearest window; the next moment he tapped politely at the door.

"Come in, sir," I said, rising to meet him; and he entered, bowing with much courtesy. I stepped down from the desk

and offered him a chair by the window,
where he seated himself at once, being
sadly spent by his climb. I returned to my
fixed seat behind the teacher's desk, which
gave him the lower place of a scholar.

"You ought to have the place of honor,
Captain Littlepage," I said.

"A happy, rural seat of various views,"

he quoted, as he gazed out into the sunshine
and up the long wooded shore. Then he
glanced at me, and looked all about him as
pleased as a child.

"My quotation was from Paradise Lost :
the greatest of poems, I suppose you
know?" and I nodded. "There's nothing
that ranks, to my mind, with Paradise Lost ;
it's all lofty, all lofty," he continued.
"Shakespeare was a great poet ; he copied
life, but you have to put up with a great
deal of low talk."

I now remembered that Mrs. Todd had
told me one day that Captain Littlepage
had overset his mind with too much reading ; she had also made dark reference to
his having "spells" of some unexplainable
nature. I could not help wondering what
errand had brought him out in search of

me. There was something quite charming
in his appearance : it was a face thin and
delicate with refinement, but worn into appealing lines, as if he had suffered from
loneliness and misapprehension. He looked,
with his careful precision of dress, as if he
were the object of cherishing care on the
part of elderly unmarried sisters, but I
knew Mari' Harris to be a very commonplace, inelegant person, who would have no
such standards ; it was plain that the captain was his own attentive valet. He sat
looking at me expectantly. I could not
help thinking that, with his queer head and
length of thinness, he was made to hop
along the road of life rather than to walk.
The captain was very grave indeed, and I
bade my inward spirit keep close to dis-
cretion.

"Poor Mrs. Begg has gone," I ventured
to say. I still wore my Sunday gown by
way of showing respect.

"She has gone," said the captain,—
"very easy at the last, I was informed ; she
slipped away as if she were glad of the opportunity."

I thought of the Countess of Carberry,
and felt that history repeated itself.

" She was one of the old stock," continued Captain Littlepage, with touching sincerity. " She was very much looked up to in this town, and will be missed."

I wondered, as I looked at him, if he had sprung from a line of ministers; he had the refinement of look and air of command which are the heritage of the old ecclesiastical families of New England. But as Darwin says in his autobiography, " there is no such king as a sea-captain; he is greater even than a king or a schoolmaster! "

Captain Littlepage moved his chair out of the wake of the sunshine, and still sat looking at me. I began to be very eager to know upon what errand he had come.

" It may be found out some o' these days," he said earnestly. " We may know it all, the next step; where Mrs. Begg is now, for instance. Certainty, not conjecture, is what we all desire."

" I suppose we shall know it all some day," said I.

" We shall know it while yet below," insisted the captain, with a flush of impatience on his thin cheeks. " We have not looked for truth in the right direction. I know what I speak of; those who have laughed at me little know how much reason my ideas are based upon." He waved his hand toward the village below. " In that handful of houses they fancy that they comprehend the universe."

I smiled, and waited for him to go on.

" I am an old man, as you can see," he continued, "and I have been a shipmaster the greater part of my life, — forty-three years in all. You may not think it, but I am above eighty years of age."

He did not look so old, and I hastened to say so.

" You must have left the sea a good many years ago, then, Captain Littlepage? " I said.

" I should have been serviceable at least five or six years more," he answered. " My acquaintance with certain — my experience upon a certain occasion, I might say, gave rise to prejudice. I do not mind telling you that I chanced to learn of one of the greatest discoveries that man has ever made."

Now we were approaching dangerous ground, but a sudden sense of his sufferings at the hands of the ignorant came to my help, and I asked to hear more with all the deference I really felt. A swallow flew

into the schoolhouse at this moment as if
a kingbird were after it, and beat itself
against the walls for a minute, and escaped
again to the open air; but Captain Littlepage took no notice whatever of the
flurry.

"I had a valuable cargo of general mer-
chandise from the London docks to Fort
Churchill, a station of the old company on
Hudson's Bay," said the captain earnestly.
"We were delayed in lading, and baffled by
head winds and a heavy tumbling sea all the
way north-about and across. Then the fog
kept us off the coast; and when I made
port at last, it was too late to delay in those
northern waters with such a vessel and such
a crew as I had. They cared for nothing,
and idled me into a fit of sickness; but my
first mate was a good, excellent man, with
no more idea of being frozen in there until
spring than I had, so we made what speed
we could to get clear of Hudson's Bay and
off the coast. I owned an eighth of the
vessel, and he owned a sixteenth of her.
She was a full-rigged ship, called the Minerva, but she was getting old and leaky.
I meant it should be my last v'y'ge in her,
and so it proved. She had been an excel-

lent vessel in her day. Of the cowards aboard her I can't say so much."

" Then you were wrecked?" I asked, as he made a long pause.

" I wa'n't caught astern o' the lighter by any fault of mine," said the captain gloomily. " We left Fort Churchill and run out into the Bay with a light pair o' heels; but I had been vexed to death with their redtape rigging at the company's office, and chilled with stayin' on deck an' tryin' to hurry up things, and when we were well out o' sight o' land, headin' for Hudson's Straits, I had a bad turn o' some sort o' fever, and had to stay below. The days were getting short, and we made good runs, all well on board but me, and the crew done their work by dint of hard driving."

I began to find this unexpected narrative a little dull. Captain Littlepage spoke with a kind of slow correctness that lacked the longshore high flavor to which I had grown used; but I listened respectfully while he explained the winds having become contrary, and talked on in a dreary sort of way about his voyage, the bad weather, and the disadvantages he was under in the lightness of his ship, which bounced about like a chip in a bucket, and would not answer the rudder or properly respond to the most careful setting of sails.

"So there we were blowin' along anyways," he complained; but looking at me at this moment, and seeing that my thoughts were unkindly wandering, he ceased to speak.

"It was a hard life at sea in those days, I am sure," said I, with redoubled interest.

"It was a dog's life," said the poor old gentleman, quite reassured, "but it made men of those who followed it. I see a change for the worse even in our own town here; full of loafers now, small and poor as 't is, who once would have followed the sea, every lazy soul of 'em. There is no occupation so fit for just that class o' men who never get beyond the fo'cas'le. I view it, in addition, that a community narrows down and grows dreadful ignorant when it is shut up to its own affairs, and gets no knowledge of the outside world except from a cheap, unprincipled newspaper. In the old days, a good part o' the best men here knew a hundred ports and something of the way folks lived in them. They saw the world for themselves, and like 's not their wives

and children saw it with them. They may
not have had the best of knowledge to carry
with 'em sight-seein', but they were some
acquainted with foreign lands an' their laws,
an' could see outside the battle for town
clerk here in Dunnet; they got some sense
o' proportion. Yes, they lived more dignified, and their houses were better within an'
without. Shipping 's a terrible loss to this
part o' New England from a social point o'
view, ma'am."

"I have thought of that myself," I returned, with my interest quite awakened.
" It accounts for the change in a great many
things, — the sad disappearance of sea-cap-
tains,— does n't it ? "

" A shipmaster was apt to get the habit
of reading," said my companion, brightening
still more, and taking on a most touching air
of unreserve.   " A captain is not expected
to be familiar with his crew, and for company's sake in dull days and nights he turns
to his book. Most of us old shipmasters
came to know 'most everything about something ; one would take to readin' on farming
topics, and some were great on medicine, —
but Lord help their poor crews ! — or some
were all for history, and now and then there 'd

be one like me that gave his time to the poets. I was well acquainted with a shipmaster that was all for bees an' bee-keepin'; and if you met him in port and went aboard, he'd sit and talk a terrible while about their havin' so much information, and the money that could be made out of keepin' 'em. He was one of the smartest captains that ever sailed the seas, but they used to call the Newcastle, a great bark he commanded for many years, Tuttle's beehive. There was old Cap'n Jameson : he had notions of Solomon's Temple, and made a very handsome little model of the same, right from the Scripture measurements, same 's other sailors make little ships and design new tricks of rigging and all that. No, there 's nothing to take the place of shipping in a place like ours. These bicycles offend me dreadfully; they don't afford no real opportunities of experience such as a man gained on a voyage. No : when folks left home in the old days they left it to some purpose, and when they got home they stayed there and had some pride in it. There 's no large-minded way of thinking now : the worst have got to be best and rule everything; we 're all turned upside down and going back year by year."

"Oh no, Captain Littlepage, I hope not," said I, trying to soothe his feelings.

There was a silence in the schoolhouse, but we could hear the noise of the water on a beach below. It sounded like the strange warning wave that gives notice of the turn of the tide. A late golden robin, with the most joyful and eager of voices, was singing close by in a thicket of wild roses.

VI.

THE WAITING PLACE.

"How did you manage with the rest of that rough voyage on the Minerva?" I asked.

"I shall be glad to explain to you," said Captain Littlepage, forgetting his grievances for the moment. "If I had a map at hand I could explain better. We were driven to and fro 'way up toward what we used to call Parry's Discoveries, and lost our bearings. It was thick and foggy, and at last I lost my ship; she drove on a rock, and we managed to get ashore on what I took to be a barren island, the few of us that were left alive. When she first struck, the sea was somewhat calmer than it had been, and most of the crew, against orders, manned the long-boat and put off in a hurry, and were never heard of more. Our own boat upset, but the carpenter kept himself and me above water, and we drifted in. I had no strength to call

upon after my recent fever, and laid down
to die; but he found the tracks of a man
and dog the second day, and got along the
shore to one of those far missionary stations
that the Moravians support. They were
very poor themselves, and in distress; 't was
a useless place. There were but few Esqui-
maux left in that region. There we remained
for some time, and I became acquainted
with strange events."

The captain lifted his head and gave me
a questioning glance. I could not help noticing that the dulled look in his eyes had
gone, and there was instead a clear intent-
ness that made them seem dark and piercing.

"There was a supply ship expected, and
the pastor, an excellent Christian man, made
no doubt that we should get passage in her.
He was hoping that orders would come to
break up the station; but everything was
uncertain, and we got on the best we could
for a while. We fished, and helped the
people in other ways; there was no other
way of paying our debts. I was taken to
the pastor's house until I got better; but
they were crowded, and I felt myself in the
way, and made excuse to join with an old
seaman, a Scotchman, who had built him a

warm cabin, and had room in it for another.
He was looked upon with regard, and had
stood by the pastor in some troubles with
the people. He had been on one of those
English exploring parties that found one
end of the road to the north pole, but never
could find the other. We lived like dogs in
a kennel, or so you'd thought if you had
seen the hut from the outside; but the main
thing was to keep warm; there were piles
of birdskins to lie on, and he'd made him a
good bunk, and there was another for me.
'T was dreadful dreary waitin' there; we
begun to think the supply steamer was lost,
and my poor ship broke up and strewed herself all along the shore. We got to watching on the headlands; my men and me knew
the people were short of supplies and had to
pinch themselves. It ought to read in the
Bible, 'Man cannot live by fish alone,' if
they'd told the truth of things; 't aint bread
that wears the worst on you! First part
of the time, old Gaffett, that I lived with,
seemed speechless, and I didn't know what
to make of him, nor he of me, I dare say;
but as we got acquainted, I found he'd been
through more disasters than I had, and had
troubles that wa'n't going to let him live a

great while. It used to ease his mind to
talk to an understanding person, so we used
to sit and talk together all day, if it rained
or blew so that we could n't get out. I 'd got
a bad blow on the back of my head at the
time we came ashore, and it pained me at
times, and my strength was broken, anyway ;
I 've never been so able since."

Captain Littlepage fell into a reverie.

" Then I had the good of my reading,"
he explained presently. " I had no books ;
the pastor spoke but little English, and all
his books were foreign ; but I used to say
over all I could remember. The old poets
little knew what comfort they could be to a
man. I was well acquainted with the works
of Milton, but up there it did seem to me
as if Shakespeare was the king ; he has his
sea terms very accurate, and some beautiful
passages were calming to the mind. I could
say them over until I shed tears ; there was
nothing beautiful to me in that place but the
stars above and those passages of verse.

" Gaffett was always brooding and brooding, and talking to himself ; he was afraid
he should never get away, and it preyed upon
his mind. He thought when I got home I
could interest the scientific men in his dis-

covery : but they 're all taken up with their
own notions; some did n't even take pains
to answer the letters I wrote. You observe
that I said this crippled man Gaffett had
been shipped on a voyage of discovery. I
now tell you that the ship was lost on its return, and only Gaffett and two officers were
saved off the Greenland coast, and he had
knowledge later that those men never got
back to England; the brig they shipped on
was run down in the night. So no other
living soul had the facts, and he gave them
to me. There is a strange sort of a country
'way up north beyond the ice, and strange
folks living in it. Gaffett believed it was
the next world to this."

"What do you mean, Captain Littlepage?" I exclaimed. The old man was
bending forward and whispering; he looked
over his shoulder before he spoke the last
sentence.

"To hear old Gaffett tell about it was
something awful," he said, going on with his
story quite steadily after the moment of excitement had passed. " 'T was first a tale
of dogs and sledges, and cold and wind and
snow. Then they begun to find the ice grow
rotten; they had been frozen in, and got

into a current flowing north, far up beyond
Fox Channel, and they took to their boats
when the ship got crushed, and this warm
current took them out of sight of the ice,
and into a great open sea; and they still followed it due north, just the very way they
had planned to go. Then they struck a
coast that was n't laid down or charted, but
the cliffs were such that no boat could land
until they found a bay and struck across
under sail to the other side where the shore
looked lower; they were scant of provisions
and out of water, but they got sight of something that looked like a great town. 'For
God's sake, Gaffett!' said I, the first time
he told me. 'You don't mean a town two
degrees farther north than ships had ever
been?' for he 'd got their course marked on
an old chart that he 'd pieced out at the top;
but he insisted upon it, and told it over and
over again, to be sure I had it straight to
carry to those who would be interested.
There was no snow and ice, he said, after
they had sailed some days with that warm
current, which seemed to come right from
under the ice that they 'd been pinched
up in and had been crossing on foot for
weeks."

" But what about the town ? " I asked.
" Did they get to the town ? "

" They did," said the captain, " and found
inhabitants; 't was an awful condition of
things. It appeared, as near as Gaffett could
express it, like a place where there was
neither living nor dead. They could see
the place when they were approaching it by
sea pretty near like any town, and thick with
habitations ; but all at once they lost sight
of it altogether, and when they got close inshore they could see the shapes of folks,
but they never could get near them, — all
blowing gray figures that would pass along
alone, or sometimes gathered in companies
as if they were watching. The men were
frightened at first, but the shapes never came
near them, — it was as if they blew back ;
and at last they all got bold and went ashore,
and found birds' eggs and sea fowl, like any
wild northern spot where creatures were
tame and folks had never been, and there
was good water. Gaffett said that he and
another man came near one o' the fog-shaped
men that was going along slow with the look
of a pack on his back, among the rocks, an'
they chased him; but, Lord ! he flittered
away out o' sight like a leaf the wind takes

with it, or a piece of cobweb. They would
make as if they talked together, but there
was no sound of voices, and 'they acted as if
they did n't see us, but only felt us coming
towards them,' says Gaffett one day, trying to tell the particulars. They could n't
see the town when they were ashore. One
day the captain and the doctor were gone
till night up across the high land where the
town had seemed to be, and they came back
at night beat out and white as ashes, and
wrote and wrote all next day in their note-
books, and whispered together full of excitement, and they were sharp-spoken with the
men when they offered to ask any questions.

" Then there came a day," said Captain
Littlepage, leaning toward me with a strange
look in his eyes, and whispering quickly.
" The men all swore they would n't stay any
longer; the man on watch early in the morning gave the alarm, and they all put off in
the boat and got a little way out to sea.
Those folks, or whatever they were, come
about 'em like bats; all at once they raised
incessant armies, and come as if to drive 'em
back to sea. They stood thick at the edge
o' the water like the ridges o' grim war; no
thought o' flight, none of retreat. Some-

times a standing fight, then soaring on main wing tormented all the air. And when they'd got the boat out o' reach o' danger, Gaffett said they looked back, and there was the town again, standing up just as they'd seen it first, comin' on the coast. Say what you might, they all believed 't was a kind of waiting-place between this world an' the next."

The captain had sprung to his feet in his excitement, and made excited gestures, but he still whispered huskily.

" Sit down, sir," I said as quietly as I could, and he sank into his chair quite spent.

" Gaffett thought the officers were hurrying home to report and to fit out a new expedition when they were all lost. At the time, the men got orders not to talk over what they had seen," the old man explained presently in a more natural tone.

" Were n't they all starving, and was n't it a mirage or something of that sort?" I ventured to ask. But he looked at me blankly.

"Gaffett had got so that his mind ran on nothing else," he went on. "The ship's surgeon let fall an opinion to the captain, one day, that 't was some condition o' the light and the magnetic currents that let

them see those folks. 'T wa'n't a right-feel-
ing part of the world, anyway; they had
to battle with the compass to make it serve,
an' everything seemed to go wrong. Gaffett
had worked it out in his own mind that they
was all common ghosts, but the conditions
were unusual favorable for seeing them.
He was always talking about the Ge'graphi-
cal Society, but he never took proper steps,
as I view it now, and stayed right there at
the mission. He was a good deal crippled,
and thought they 'd confine him in some jail
of a hospital. He said he was waiting to
find the right men to tell, somebody bound
north. Once in a while they stopped there
to leave a mail or something. He was set
in his notions, and let two or three proper
explorin' expeditions go by him because he
did n't like their looks; but when I was
there he had got restless, fearin' he might
be taken away or something. He had all
his directions written out straight as a string
to give the right ones. I wanted him to
trust 'em to me, so I might have something
to show, but he would n't. I suppose he 's
dead now. I wrote to him, an' I done all I
could. 'T will be a great exploit some o'
these days."

I assented absent-mindedly, thinking more just then of my companion's alert, determined look and the seafaring, ready aspect that had come to his face; but at this moment there fell a sudden change, and the old, pathetic, scholarly look returned. Behind me hung a map of North America, and I saw, as I turned a little, that his eyes were fixed upon the northernmost regions and their careful recent outlines with a look of bewilderment.

VII.

THE OUTER ISLAND.

GAFFETT with his good bunk and the bird-skins, the story of the wreck of the Minerva, the human-shaped creatures of fog and cobweb, the great words of Milton with which he described their onslaught upon the crew, all this moving tale had such an air of truth that I could not argue with Captain Littlepage. The old man looked away from the map as if it had vaguely troubled him, and regarded me appealingly.

"We were just speaking of" — and he stopped. I saw that he had suddenly forgotten his subject.

"There were a great many persons at the funeral," I hastened to say.

"Oh yes," the captain answered, with satisfaction. "All showed respect who could. The sad circumstances had for a moment slipped my mind. Yes, Mrs. Begg will be very much missed. She was a capital manager for her husband when he was at sea. Oh yes, shipping is a very great loss." And he sighed heavily. " There was hardly a man of any standing who did n't interest himself in some way in navigation. It always gave credit to a town. I call it low-water mark now here in Dunnet."

He rose with dignity to take leave, a d asked me to stop at his house some day, when he would show me some outlandish things that he had brought home from sea. I was familiar with the subject of the deca-dence of shipping interests in all its affect-ing branches, having been already some time in Dunnet, and I felt sure that Cap-tain Littlepage's mind had now returned to a safe level.

As we came down the hill toward the vil-lage our ways divided, and when I had seen the old captain well started on a smooth piece of sidewalk which would lead him to his own door, we parted, the best of friends. " Step in some afternoon," he said, as affec-tionately as if I were a fellow-shipmaster wrecked on the lee shore of age like him-se .. I turned toward home, and presently met Mrs. Todd coming toward me with an anxious expression.

"I see you sleevin' the old gentleman down the hill," she suggested.

"Yes. I 've had a very interesting afternoon with him," I answered; and her face brightened.

"Oh, then he's all right. I was afraid 't was one o' his flighty spells, an' Mari' Harris would n't " —

"Yes," I returned, smiling, "he has been telling me some old stories, but we talked about Mrs. Begg and the funeral beside, and Paradise Lost."

"I expect he got tellin' of you some o' his great narratives," she answered, looking at me shrewdly. "Funerals always sets him goin'. Some o' them tales hangs together toler'ble well," she added, with a sharper look than before. "An' he 's been a great reader all his seafarin' days. Some thinks he overdid, and affected his head, but for a man o' his years he 's amazin' now when he 's at his best. Oh, he used to be a beautiful man!"

We were standing where there was a fine view of the harbor and its long stretches of shore all covered by the great army of the pointed firs, darkly cloaked and standing as if they waited to embark. As we looked far seaward among the outer islands, the trees seemed to march seaward still, going steadily over the heights and down to the water's edge.

It had been growing gray and cloudy, like the first evening of autumn, and a shadow had fallen on the darkening shore. Suddenly, as we looked, a gleam of golden sunshine struck the outer islands, and one of them shone out clear in the light, and revealed itself in a compelling way to our eyes. Mrs. Todd was looking off across the bay with a face full of affection and interest. The sunburst upon that outermost island made it seem like a sudden revelation of the world beyond this which some believe to be so near.

"That 's where mother lives," said Mrs. Todd. "Can't we see it plain? I was brought up out there on Green Island. I know every rock an' bush on it."

"Your mother!" I exclaimed, with great interest.

"Yes, dear, cert'in; I 've got her yet, old 's I be. She 's one of them spry, light-footed little women; always was, an' light-hearted, too," answered Mrs. Todd, with satisfaction. "She's seen all the trouble folks can see, without it's her last sickness; an' she's got a word of courage for everybody. Life ain't spoilt her a mite. She's eighty-six an' I'm sixty-seven, and I've seen the time I've felt a good sight the oldest 'Land sakes alive!' says she, last time I was out to see her. 'How you do lurch about steppin' into a bo't!' I laughed so I liked to have gone right over into the water; an' we pushed off, an' left her laughin' there on the shore."

The light had faded as we watched. Mrs. Todd had mounted a gray rock, and stood there grand and architectural, like a *caryatide*. Presently she stepped down, and we continued our way homeward.

"You an' me, we'll take a bo't an' go out some day and see mother," she promised me. "'T would please her very much, an' there's one or two sca'ce herbs grows better on the island than anywheres else. I ain't seen their like nowheres here on the main."

"Now I'm goin' right down to get us each a mug o' my beer," she announced as we entered the house, "an' I believe I'll sneak in a little mite o' camomile. Goin' to the funeral an' all, I feel to have had a very wearin' afternoon."

I heard her going down into the cool little cellar, and then there was considerable delay. When she returned, mug in hand, I noticed the taste of camomile, in spite of my protest; but its flavor was disguised by some other herb that I did not know, and she stood over me until I drank it all and said that I liked it.

"I don't give that to everybody," said Mrs. Todd kindly; and I felt for a moment as if it were part of a spell and incantation, and as if my enchantress would now begin to look like the cobweb shapes of the arctic town. Nothing happened but a quiet evening and some delightful plans that we made about going to Green Island, and on the morrow there was the clear sunshine and blue sky of another day.

VIII.

GREEN ISLAND.

ONE morning, very early, I heard Mrs.
Todd in the garden outside my window. By
the unusual loudness of her remarks to a
passer-by, and the notes of a familiar hymn
which she sang as she worked among the
herbs, and which came as if directed pur-
posely to the sleepy ears of my consciousness, I knew that she wished I would wake
up and come and speak to her.

In a few minutes she responded to a morning voice from behind the blinds. " I expect you 're goin' up to your schoolhouse
to pass all this pleasant day ; yes, I expect
you 're goin' to be dreadful busy," she said
despairingly.

"Perhaps not," said I. " Why, what 's
going to be the matter with you, Mrs.
Todd?" For I supposed that she was
tempted by the fine weather to take one of
her favorite expeditions along the shore pas-

tures to gather herbs and simples, and would like to have me keep the house.

" No, I don't want to go nowhere by land," she answered gayly, — " no, not by land; but I don't know 's we shall have a better day all the rest of the summer to go out to Green Island an' see mother. I waked up early thinkin' of her. The wind 's light northeast, — 't will take us right straight out ; an' this time o' year it 's liable to change round southwest an' fetch us home pretty, 'long late in the afternoon. Yes, it 's goin' to be a good day."

" Speak to the captain and the Bowden boy, if you see anybody going by toward the landing," said I. " We 'll take the big boat."

" Oh, my sakes ! now you let me do things my way," said Mrs. Todd scornfully. " No, dear, we won't take no big bo't. I 'll just git a handy dory, an' Johnny Bowden an' me, we 'll man her ourselves. I don't want no abler bo't than a good dory, an' a nice light breeze ain't goin' to make no sea ; an' Johnny 's my cousin's son, — mother 'll like to have him come ; an' he 'll be down to the herrin' weirs all the time we 're there, anyway ; we don't want to carry no men folks havin' to be considered every minute an' takin' up all our time. No, you let me do; we 'll just slip out an' see mother by ourselves. I guess what breakfast you 'll want 's about ready now."

I had become well acquainted with Mrs. Todd as landlady, herb-gatherer, and rustic philosopher; we had been discreet fellow-passengers once or twice when I had sailed up the coast to a larger town than Dunnet Landing to do some shopping; but I was yet to become acquainted with her as a mariner. An hour later we pushed off from the landing in the desired dory. The tide was just on the turn, beginning to fall, and several friends and acquaintances stood along the side of the dilapidated wharf and cheered us by their words and evident interest. Johnny Bowden and I were both rowing in haste to get out where we could catch the breeze and put up the small sail which lay clumsily furled along the gunwale. Mrs. Todd sat aft, a stern and unbending law-giver.

"You better let her drift; we 'll get there 'bout as quick; the tide 'll take her right out from under these old buildin's; there 's plenty wind outside."

"Your bo't ain't trimmed proper, Mis' Todd!" exclaimed a voice from shore. "You 're lo'ded so the bo't 'll drag; you can't git her before the wind, ma'am. You set 'midships, Mis' Todd, an' let the boy hold the sheet 'n' steer after he gits the sail up; you won't never git out to Green Island that way. She's lo'ded bad, your bo't is, — she's heavy behind 's she is now!"

Mrs. Todd turned with some difficulty and regarded the anxious adviser, my right oar flew out of water, and we seemed about to capsize. "That you, Asa? Good-mornin'," she said politely. "I al'ays liked the starn seat best. When 'd you git back from up country?"

This allusion to Asa's origin was not lost upon the rest of the company. We were some little distance from shore, but we could hear a chuckle of laughter, and Asa, a person who was too ready with his criticism and advice on every possible subject, turned and walked indignantly away.

When we caught the wind we were soon on our seaward course, and only stopped to underrun a trawl, for the floats of which Mrs. Todd looked earnestly, explaining that her

mother might not be prepared for three
extra to dinner; it was her brother's trawl,
and she meant to just run her eye along for
the right sort of a little haddock. I leaned
over the boat's side with great interest and
excitement, while she skillfully handled
the long line of hooks, and made scornful
remarks upon worthless, bait-consuming creatures of the sea as she reviewed them and
left them on the trawl or shook them off
into the waves. At last we came to what
she pronounced a proper haddock, and having taken him on board and ended his life
resolutely, we went our way.

As we sailed along I listened to an increasingly delightful commentary upon the
islands, some of them barren rocks, or at
best giving sparse pasturage for sheep in the
early summer. On one of these an eager little flock ran to the water's edge and bleated
at us so affectingly that I would willingly
have stopped; but Mrs. Todd steered away
from the rocks, and scolded at the sheep's
mean owner, an acquaintance of hers, who
grudged the little salt and still less care
which the patient creatures needed. The hot
midsummer sun makes prisons of these small
islands that are a paradise in early June,

with their cool springs and short thick-growing grass. On a larger island, farther out to sea, my entertaining companion showed me with glee the small houses of two farmers who shared the island between them, and declared that for three generations the people had not spoken to each other even in times of sickness or death or birth. " When the news come that the war was over, one of 'em knew it a week, and never stepped across his wall to tell the others," she said. " There, they enjoy it : they 've got to have somethin' to interest 'em in such a place ; 't is a good deal more tryin' to be tied to folks you don't like than 't is to be alone. Each of 'em tells the neighbors their wrongs ; plenty likes to hear and tell again ; them as fetch a bone 'll carry one, an' so they keep the fight a-goin'. I must say I like variety myself ; some folks washes Monday an' irons Tuesday the whole year round, even if the circus is goin' by ! "

A long time before we landed at Green Island we could see the small white house, standing high like a beacon, where Mrs. Todd was born and where her mother lived, on a green slope above the water, with dark spruce woods still higher. There were crops in the fields, which we presently distinguished from one another. Mrs. Todd examined them while we were still far at sea. "Mother's late potatoes looks backward; ain't had rain enough so far," she pronounced her opinion. "They look weedier than what they call Front Street down to Cowper Centre. I expect brother William is so occupied with his herrin' weirs an' servin' out bait to the schooners that he don't think once a day of the land."

"What 's the flag for, up above the spruces there behind the house?" I inquired, with eagerness.

"Oh, that 's the sign for herrin', " she explained kindly, while Johnny Bowden regarded me with contemptuous surprise. "When they get enough for schooners they raise that flag; an' when 't is a poor catch in the weir pocket they just fly a little signal down by the shore, an' then the small bo'ts comes and get enough an' over for their trawls. There, look! there she is: mother sees us; she 's wavin' somethin' out o' the fore door! She 'll be to the landin'-place quick 's we are."

I looked, and could see a tiny flutter in the doorway, but a quicker signal had made

its way from the heart on shore to the heart
on the sea.

"How do you suppose she knows it's
me?" said Mrs. Todd, with a tender smile
on her broad face. " There, you never get
over bein' a child long's you have a mother
to go to. Look at the chimney, now; she's
gone right in an' brightened up the fire.
Well, there, I'm glad mother's well; you'll
enjoy seein' her very much."

Mrs. Todd leaned back into her proper
position, and the boat trimmed again. She
took a firmer grasp of the sheet, and gave
an impatient look up at the gaff and the
leech of the little sail, and twitched the sheet
as if she urged the wind like a horse. There
came at once a fresh gust, and we seemed
to have doubled our speed. Soon we were
near enough to see a tiny figure with hand-
kerchiefed head come down across the field
and stand waiting for us at the cove above
a curve of pebble beach.

Presently the dory grated on the pebbles,
and Johnny Bowden, who had been kept in
abeyance during the voyage, sprang out and
used manful exertions to haul us up with the
next wave, so that Mrs. Todd could make a
dry landing.

"You done that very well," she said, mounting to her feet, and coming ashore somewhat stiffly, but with great dignity,, refusing our outstretched hands, and returning to possess herself of a bag which had lain at her feet.

"Well, mother, here I be!" she announced with indifference; but they stood and beamed in each other's faces.

"Lookin' pretty well for an old lady, ain't she?" said Mrs. Todd's mother, turning away from her daughter to speak to me. She was a delightful little person herself, with bright eyes and an affectionate air of expectation like a child on a holiday. You felt as if Mrs. Blackett were an old and dear friend before you let go her cordial hand. We all started together up the hill.

"Now don't you haste too fast, mother," said Mrs. Todd warningly; "'t is a far reach o' risin' ground to the fore door, and you won't set an' get your breath when you 're once there, but go trotting about. Now don't you go a mite faster than we proceed with this bag an' basket. Johnny, there, 'll fetch up the haddock. I just made one stop to underrun William's trawl .till I come to jes' such a fish 's I thought you 'd want to

make one o' your nice chowders of. I 've
brought an onion with me that was layin'
about on the window-sill at home."

"That 's just what I was wantin'," said
the hostess. " I give a sigh when you
spoke o' chowder, knowin' my onions was out.
William forgot to replenish us last time he
was to the Landin'. Don't you haste so
yourself, Almiry, up this risin' ground. I
hear you commencin' to wheeze a'ready."

This mild revenge seemed to afford great
pleasure to both giver and receiver. They
laughed a little, and looked at each other
affectionately, and then at me. Mrs. Todd
considerately paused, and faced about to regard the wide sea view. I was glad to stop,
being more out of breath than either of my
companions, and I prolonged the halt by
asking the names of the neighboring islands.
There was a fine breeze blowing, which we
felt more there on the high land than when
we were running before it in the dory.

" Why, this ain't that kitten I saw when
I was out last, the one that I said did n't appear likely? " exclaimed Mrs. Todd as we
went our way.

"That 's the one, Almiry," said her
mother. " She always had a likely look to

me, an' she's right after her business. I
never see such a mouser for one of her age.
If 't wan't for William, I never should have
housed that other dronin' old thing so long;
but he sets by her on account of her havin'
a bob tail. I don't deem it advisable to
maintain cats just on account of their havin' bob tails; they're like all other curiosities, good for them that wants to see 'em
twice. This kitten catches mice for both,
an' keeps me respectable as I ain't been for
a year. She's a real understandin' little
help, this kitten is. I picked her from
among five Miss Augusta Pennell had over
to Burnt Island," said the old woman, trudg-
ing along with the kitten close at her skirts.
"Augusta, she says to me, 'Why, Mis'
Blackett, you've took the homeliest;' an'
says I, 'I've got the smartest; I'm satisfied.'"

"I'd trust nobody sooner'n you to pick
out a kitten, mother," said the daughter
handsomely, and we went on in peace and
harmony.

The house was just before us now, on a
green level that looked as if a huge hand
had scooped it out of the long green field
we had been ascending. A little way above,

the dark spruce woods began to climb the top of the hill and cover the seaward slopes of the island. There was just room for the small farm and the forest; we looked down at the fish-house and its rough sheds, and the weirs stretching far out into the water. As we looked upward, the tops of the firs came sharp against the blue sky. There was a great stretch of rough pasture-land round the shoulder of the island to the eastward, and here were all the thick-scattered gray rocks that kept their places, and the gray backs of many sheep that forever wandered and fed on the thin sweet pasturage that fringed the ledges and made soft hollows and strips of green turf like growing velvet. I could see the rich green of bayberry bushes here and there, where the rocks made room. The air was very sweet; one could not help wishing to be a citizen of such a complete and tiny continent and home of fisherfolk.

The house was broad and clean, with a roof that looked heavy on its low walls. It was one of the houses that seem firm-rooted in the ground, as if they were two-thirds below the surface, like icebergs. The front door stood hospitably open in expectation of

company, and an orderly vine grew at each
side; but our path led to the kitchen door
at the house-end, and there grew a mass of
gay flowers and greenery, as if they had
been swept together by some diligent garden
broom into a tangled heap : there were portulacas all along under the lower step and
straggling off into the grass, and clustering
mallows that crept as near as they dared,
like poor relations.   I saw the bright eyes
and brainless little heads of two half-grown
chickens who were snuggled down among
the mallows as if they had been chased
away from the door more than once, and expected to be again.

"It seems kind o' formal comin' in this
way," said Mrs. Todd impulsively, as we
passed the flowers and came to the front
doorstep ; but she was mindful of the pro-
prieties, and walked before us into the best
room on the left.

"Why, mother, if you have n't gone an'
turned the carpet!" she exclaimed, with
something in her voice that spoke of awe
and admiration.   "When 'd you get to it?
I s'pose Mis' Addicks come over an' helped
you, from White Island Landing?"

"No, she did n't," answered the old woman, standing proudly erect, and making the most of a great moment. " I done it all myself with William's help. He had a spare day, an' took right holt with me; an' 't was all well beat on the grass, an' turned, an' put down again afore we went to bed. I ripped an' sewed over two o' them long breadths. I ain't had such a good night's sleep for two years."

" There, what do you think o' havin' such a mother as that for eighty-six year old?" said Mrs. Todd, standing before us like a large figure of Victory.

As for the mother, she took on a sudden look of youth; you felt as if she promised a great future, and was beginning, not ending, her summers and their happy toils.

" My, my!" exclaimed Mrs. Todd. " I could n't ha' done it myself, I 've got to own it."

" I was much pleased to have it off my mind," said Mrs. Blackett, humbly; " the more so because along at the first of the next week I was n't very well. I suppose it may have been the change of weather."

Mrs. Todd could not resist a significant glance at me, but, with charming sympathy, she forbore to point the lesson or to connect this illness with its apparent cause. She loomed larger than ever in the little old-fashioned best room, with its few pieces of good furniture and pictures of national interest. The green paper curtains were stamped with conventional landscapes of a foreign order, — castles on inaccessible crags, and lovely lakes with steep wooded shores; under-foot the treasured carpet was covered thick with home-made rugs. There were empty glass lamps and crystallized bouquets of grass and some fine shells on the narrow mantelpiece.

"I was married in this room," said Mrs. Todd unexpectedly; and I heard her give a sigh after she had spoken, as if she could not help the touch of regret that would forever come with all her thoughts of happiness.

"We stood right there between the windows," she added, "and the minister stood here. William would n't come in. He was always odd about seein' folks, just 's he is now. I run to meet 'em from a child, an' William, he 'd take an' run away."

"I 've been the gainer," said the old mother cheerfully. "William has been son an' daughter both since you was married off

the island. He's been 'most too satisfied to
stop at home 'long o' his old mother, but I
always tell 'em I'm the gainer.''

We were all moving toward the kitchen
as if by common instinct. The best room
was too suggestive of serious occasions, and
the shades were all pulled down to shut out
the summer light and air. It was indeed a
tribute to Society to find a room set apart
for her behests out there on so apparently
neighborless and remote an island. Afternoon visits and evening festivals must be
few in such a bleak situation at certain seasons of the year, but Mrs. Blackett was of
those who do not live to themselves, and who
have long since passed the line that divides
mere self-concern from a valued share in
whatever Society can give and take. There
were those of her neighbors who never had
taken the trouble to furnish a best room,
but Mrs. Blackett was one who knew the
uses of a parlor.

"Yes, do come right out into the old
kitchen; I shan't make any stranger of you,"
she invited us pleasantly, after we had been
properly received in the room appointed to
formality. "I expect Almiry, here, 'll be
driftin' out 'mongst the pasture-weeds quick's

she can find a good excuse. 'T is hot now. You 'd better content yourselves till you get nice an' rested, an' 'long after dinner the sea-breeze 'll spring up, an' then you can take your walks, an' go up an' see the prospect from the big ledge. Almiry 'll want to show off everything there is. Then I 'll get you a good cup o' tea before you start to go home. The days are plenty long now."

While we were talking in the best room the selected fish had been mysteriously brought up from the shore, and lay all cleaned and ready in an earthen crock on the table.

" I think William might have just stopped an' said a word," remarked Mrs. Todd, pouting with high affront as she caught sight of it. " He 's friendly enough when he comes ashore, an' was remarkable social the last time, for him."

" He ain't disposed to be very social with the ladies," explained William's mother, with a delightful glance at me, as if she counted upon my friendship and tolerance. " He 's very particular, and he 's all in his old fishin'-clothes to-day. He 'll want me to tell him everything you said and done, after you 've gone. William has very deep

affections. He 'll want to see you, Almiry.
Yes, I guess he 'll be in by an' by."

" I 'll search for him by 'n' by, if he
don't," proclaimed Mrs. Todd, with an air
of unalterable resolution. " I know all of
his burrows down 'long the shore. I 'll catch
him by hand 'fore he knows it. I 've got
some business with William, anyway. I
brought forty-two cents with me that was
due him for them last lobsters he brought
in."

" You can leave it with me," suggested
the little old mother, who was already stepping about among her pots and pans in the
pantry, and preparing to make the chowder.

I became possessed of a sudden unwonted
curiosity in regard to William, and felt that
half the pleasure of my visit would be lost
if I could not make his interesting acquaintance.

IX.

WILLIAM.

MRS. TODD had taken the onion out of her basket and laid it down upon the kitchen table. "There's Johnny Bowden come with us, you know," she reminded her mother. "He'll be hungry enough to eat his size."

"I've got new doughnuts, dear," said the little old lady. "You don't often catch William 'n' me out o' provisions. I expect you might have chose a somewhat larger fish, but I'll try an' make it do. I shall have to have a few extra potatoes, but there's a field full out there, an' the hoe's leanin' against the well-house, in 'mongst the climbin'-beans." She smiled, and gave her daughter a commanding nod.

"Land sakes alive! Le' 's blow the horn for William," insisted Mrs. Todd, with some excitement. "He need n't break his spirit so far's to come in. He'll know you need him for something particular, an' then we

can call to him as he comes up the path. I
won't put him to no pain."

Mrs. Blackett's old face, for the first time,
wore a look of trouble, and I found it necessary to counteract the teasing spirit of Almira. It was too pleasant to stay indoors
altogether, even in such rewarding companionship; besides, I might meet William;
and, straying out presently, I found the hoe
by the well-house and an old splint basket
at the woodshed door, and also found my
way down to the field where there was a
great square patch of rough, weedy potato-
tops and tall ragweed. One corner was
already dug, and I chose a fat-looking hill
where the tops were well withered. There is
all the pleasure that one can have in gold-
digging in finding one's hopes satisfied in
the riches of a good hill of potatoes. I
longed to go on; but it did not seem frugal
to dig any longer after my basket was full,
and at last I took my hoe by the middle
and lifted the basket to go back up the
hill. I was sure that Mrs. Blackett must be
waiting impatiently to slice the potatoes into
the chowder, layer after layer, with the
fish.

"You let me take holt o' that basket,

ma'am," said a pleasant, anxious voice
behind me.

I turned, startled in the silence of the
wide field, and saw an elderly man, bent
in the shoulders as fishermen often are,
gray-headed and clean-shaven, and with a
timid air. It was William. He looked just
like his mother, and I had been imagining
that he was large and stout like his sister,
Almira Todd ; and, strange to say, my fancy
had led me to picture him not far from
thirty and a little loutish. It was necessary
instead to pay William the respect due to
age.

I accustomed myself to plain facts on the
instant, and we said good-morning like old
friends. The basket was really heavy, and
I put the hoe through its handle and offered
him one end ; then we moved easily toward
the house together, speaking of the fine
weather and of mackerel which were re-
ported to be striking in all about the bay.
William had been out since three o'clock,
and had taken an extra fare of fish. I could
feel that Mrs. Todd's eyes were upon us as
we approached the house, and although I
fell behind in the narrow path, and let William take the basket alone and precede me

at some little distance the rest of the way, I
could plainly hear her greet him.

"Got round to comin' in, did n't you?"
she inquired, with amusement. " Well, now,
that 's clever. Did n't know 's I should see
you to-day, William, an' I wanted to settle
an account."

I felt somewhat disturbed and responsi-
ble, but when I joined them they were on
most simple and friendly terms. It became
evident that, with William, it was the first
step that cost, and that, having once joined
in social interests, he was able to pursue
them with more or less pleasure. He was
about sixty, and not young-looking for his
years, yet so undying is the spirit of youth,
and bashfulness has such a power of survival, that I felt all the time as if one must
try to make the occasion easy for some one
who was young and new to the affairs of social life. He asked politely if I would like
to go up to the great ledge while dinner was
getting ready; so, not without a deep sense
of pleasure, and a delighted look of surprise
from the two hostesses, we started, William
and I, as if both of us felt much younger
than we looked. Such was the innocence
and simplicity of the moment that when I

heard Mrs. Todd laughing behind us in the kitchen I laughed too, but William did not even blush. I think he was a little deaf, and he stepped along before me most businesslike and intent upon his errand.

We went from the upper edge of the field above the house into a smooth, brown path among the dark spruces. The hot sun brought out the fragrance of the pitchy bark, and the shade was pleasant as we climbed the hill. William stopped once or twice to show me a great wasps'-nest close by, or some fishhawks'-nests below in a bit of swamp. He picked a few sprigs of late-blooming linnæa as we came out upon an open bit of pasture at the top of the island, and gave them to me without speaking, but he knew as well as I that one could not say half he wished about linnæa. Through this piece of rough pasture ran a huge shape of stone like the great backbone of an enormous creature. At the end, near the woods, we could climb up on it and walk along to the highest point; there above the circle of pointed firs we could look down over all the island, and could see the ocean that circled this and a hundred other bits of island-ground, the mainland shore and all the far horizons. It gave a sudden sense of space, for nothing stopped the eye or hedged one in, — that sense of liberty in space and time which great prospects always give.

"There ain't no such view in the world, I expect," said William proudly, and I hastened to speak my heartfelt tribute of praise; it was impossible not to feel as if an untraveled boy had spoken, and yet one loved to have him value his native heath.

X.

WHERE PENNYROYAL GREW.

WE were a little late to dinner, but Mrs. Blackett and Mrs. Todd were lenient, and we all took our places after William had paused to wash his hands, like a pious Brahmin, at the well, and put on a neat blue coat which he took from a peg behind the kitchen door. Then he resolutely asked a blessing in words that I could not hear, and we ate the chowder and were thankful. The kitten went round and round the table, quite erect, and, holding on by her fierce young claws, she stopped to mew with pathos at each elbow, or darted off to the open door when a song sparrow forgot himself and lit in the grass too near. William did not talk much, but his sister Todd occupied the time and told all the news there was to tell of Dunnet Landing and its coasts, while the old mother listened with delight. Her hospitality was something exquisite; she had the gift which so many women lack, of being able to make themselves and their houses belong entirely to a guest's pleasure, — that charming surrender for the moment of themselves and whatever belongs to them, so that they make a part of one's own life that can never be forgotten. Tact is after all a kind of mind-reading, and my hostess held the golden gift. Sympathy is of the mind as well as the heart, and Mrs. Blackett's world and mine were one from the moment we met. Besides, she had that final, that highest gift of heaven, a perfect self-forgetfulness. Sometimes, as I watched her eager, sweet old face, I wondered why she had been set to shine on this lonely island of the northern coast. It must have been to keep the balance true, and make up to all her scattered and depending neighbors for other things which they may have lacked.

When we had finished clearing away the old blue plates, and the kitten had taken care of her share of the fresh haddock, just as we were putting back the kitchen chairs in their places, Mrs. Todd said briskly that she must go up into the pasture now to gather the desired herbs.

"You can stop here an' rest, or you can

accompany me," she announced. " Mother
ought to have her nap, and when we come
back she an' William 'll sing for you. She
admires music," said Mrs. Todd, turning to
speak to her mother.

But Mrs. Blackett tried to say that she
could n't sing as she used, and perhaps William would n't feel like it. She looked
tired, the good old soul, or I should have
liked to sit in the peaceful little house while
she slept; I had had much pleasant experience of pastures already in her daughter's
company. But it seemed best to go with
Mrs. Todd, and off we went.

Mrs. Todd carried the gingham bag which
she had brought from home, and a small
heavy burden in the bottom made it hang
straight and slender from her hand. The
way was steep, and she soon grew breathless,
so that we sat down to rest awhile on a convenient large stone among the bayberry.

" There, I wanted you to see this, — 't is
mother's picture," said Mrs. Todd; " 't was
taken once when she was up to Portland, soon
after she was married. That 's me," she
added, opening another worn case, and dis-
playing the full face of the cheerful child she
looked like still in spite of being past sixty.

" And here 's William an' father together.
I take after father, large and heavy, an'
William is like mother's folks, short an'
thin. He ought to have made something o'
himself, bein' a man an' so like mother; but
though he 's been very steady to work, an'
kept up the farm, an' done his fishin' too
right along, he never had mother's snap an'
power o' seein' things just as they be. He 's
got excellent judgment, too," meditated William's sister, but she could not arrive at
any satisfactory decision upon what she evidently thought his failure in life. " I think
it is well to see any one so happy an' makin'
the most of life just as it falls to hand," she
said as she began to put the daguerreotypes
away again ; but I reached out my hand to
see her mother's once more, a most flower-
like face of a lovely young woman in quaint
dress. There was in the eyes a look of anticipation and joy, a far-off look that sought
the horizon; one often sees it in seafaring
families, inherited by girls and boys alike
from men who spend their lives at sea, and
are always watching for distant sails or the
first loom of the land. At sea there is nothing to be seen close by, and this has its
counterpart in a sailor's character, in the

large and brave and patient traits that are developed, the hopeful pleasantness that one loves so in a seafarer.

When the family pictures were wrapped again in a big handkerchief, we set forward in a narrow footpath and made our way to a lonely place that faced northward, where there was more pasturage and fewer bushes, and we went down to the edge of short grass above some rocky cliffs where the deep sea broke with a great noise, though the wind was down and the water looked quiet a little way from shore. Among the grass grew such pennyroyal as the rest of the world could not provide. There was a fine fragrance in the air as we gathered it sprig by sprig and stepped along carefully, and Mrs. Todd pressed her aromatic nosegay between her hands and offered it to me again and again.

" There 's nothin' like it," she said ; " oh no, there 's no such pennyr'yal as this in the State of Maine. It 's the right pattern of the plant, and all the rest I ever see is but an imitation. Don't it do you good ? " And I answered with enthusiasm.

" There, dear, I never showed nobody else but mother where to find this place ; 't is

kind of sainted to me. Nathan, my husband, an' I used to love this place when we
was courtin', and " — she hesitated, and then
spoke softly — " when he was lost, 't was
just off shore tryin' to get in by the short
channel out there between Squaw Islands,
right in sight o' this headland where we 'd
set an' made our plans all summer long."

I had never heard her speak of her husband before, but I felt that we were friends
now since she had brought me to this place.

" 'T was but a dream with us," Mrs.
Todd said. " I knew it when he was gone.
I knew it " — and she whispered as if she
were at confession — " I knew it afore he
started to go to sea. My heart was gone
out o' my keepin' before I ever saw Nathan ;
but he loved me well, and he made me real
happy, and he died before he ever knew
what he 'd had to know if we 'd lived long together. 'T is very strange about love. No,
Nathan never found out, but my heart was
troubled when I knew him first. There 's
more women likes to be loved than there is
of those that loves. I spent some happy
hours right here. I always liked Nathan,
and he never knew. But this pennyr'yal
always reminded me, as I 'd sit and gather

it and hear him talkin' — it always would remind me of — the other one."

She looked away from me, and presently rose and went on by herself. There was something lonely and solitary about her great determined shape. She might have been Antigone alone on the Theban plain. It is not often given in a noisy world to come to the places of great grief and silence. An absolute, archaic grief possessed this country-woman; she seemed like a renewal of some historic soul, with her sorrows and the remoteness of a daily life busied with rustic simplicities and the scents of primeval herbs.

I was not incompetent at herb-gathering, and after a while, when I had sat long enough waking myself to new thoughts, and reading a page of remembrance with new pleasure, I gathered some bunches, as I was bound to do, and at last we met again higher up the shore, in the plain every-day world we had left behind when we went down to the pennyroyal plot. As we walked together along the high edge of the field we saw a hundred sails about the bay and farther seaward; it was mid-afternoon or after, and the day was coming to an end.

"Yes, they 're all makin' towards the shore, — the small craft an' the lobster smacks an' all," said my companion. "We must spend a little time with mother now, just to have our tea, an' then put for home."

"No matter if we lose the wind at sundown; I can row in with Johnny," said I; and Mrs. Todd nodded reassuringly and kept to her steady plod, not quickening her gait even when we saw William come round the corner of the house as if to look for us, and wave his hand and disappear.

"Why, William 's right on deck; I did n't know 's we should see any more of him!" exclaimed Mrs. Todd. "Now mother 'll put the kettle right on; she 's got a good fire goin'." I too could see the blue smoke thicken, and then we both walked a little faster, while Mrs. Todd groped in her full bag of herbs to find the daguerreotypes and be ready to put them in their places.

XI.

THE OLD SINGERS.

WILLIAM was sitting on the side door step, and the old mother was busy making her tea; she gave into my hand an old flowered-glass tea-caddy.

" William thought you 'd like to see this, when he was settin' the table. My father brought it to my mother from the island of Tobago; an' here 's a pair of beautiful mugs that came with it." She opened the glass door of a little cupboard beside the chimney. " These I call my best things, dear," she said. " You 'd laugh to see how we enjoy 'em Sunday nights in winter: we have a real company tea 'stead o' livin' right along just the same, an' I make somethin' good for a s'prise an' put on some o' my preserves, an' we get a-talkin' together an' have real pleasant times."

Mrs. Todd laughed indulgently, and looked to see what I thought of such childishness.

" I wish I could be here some Sunday evening," said I.

" William an' me 'll be talkin' about you an' thinkin' o' this nice day," said Mrs. Blackett affectionately, and she glanced at William, and he looked up bravely and nodded. I began to discover that he and his sister could not speak their deeper feelings before each other.

" Now I want you an' mother to sing," said Mrs. Todd abruptly, with an air of command, and I gave William much sympathy in his evident distress.

" After I 've had my cup o' tea, dear," answered the old hostess cheerfully; and so we sat down and took our cups and made merry while they lasted. It was impossible not to wish to stay on forever at Green Island, and I could not help saying so.

" I 'm very happy here, both winter an' summer," said old Mrs. Blackett. " William an' I never wish for any other home, do we, William? I 'm glad you find it pleasant; I wish you 'd come an' stay, dear, whenever you feel inclined. But here 's Almiry; I always think Providence was kind to plot an' have her husband leave her a good house where she really belonged. She 'd been very

restless if she'd had to continue here on
Green Island. You wanted more scope,
did n't you, Almiry, an' to live in a large
place where more things grew ? Sometimes
folks wonders that we don't live together ;
perhaps we shall some time," and a shadow
of sadness and apprehension flitted across
her face. "The time o' sickness an' failin'
has got to come to all. But Almiry's got an
herb that's good for everything." She smiled
as she spoke, and looked bright again.

"There's some herb that's good for
everybody, except for them that thinks
they 're sick when they ain't," announced
Mrs. Todd, with a truly professional air of
finality. "Come, William, let's have Sweet
Home, an' then mother'll sing Cupid an' the
Bee for us."

Then followed a most charming surprise.
William mastered his timidity and began to
sing. His voice was a little faint and frail,
like the family daguerreotypes, but it was a
tenor voice, and perfectly true and sweet. I
have never heard Home, Sweet Home sung
as touchingly and seriously as he sang it ;
he seemed to make it quite new ; and when
he paused for a moment at the end of the
first line and began the next, the old mother

joined him and they sang together, she missing only the higher notes, where he seemed to lend his voice to hers for the moment and carry on her very note and air. It was the silent man's real and only means of expression, and one could have listened forever, and have asked for more and more songs of old Scotch and English inheritance and the best that have lived from the ballad music of the war. Mrs. Todd kept time visibly, and sometimes audibly, with her ample foot. I saw the tears in her eyes sometimes, when I could see beyond the tears in mine. But at last the songs ended and the time came to say good-by; it was the end of a great pleasure.

Mrs. Blackett, the dear old lady, opened the door of her bedroom while Mrs. Todd was tying up the herb bag, and William had gone down to get the boat ready and to blow the horn for Johnny Bowden, who had joined a roving boat party who were off the shore lobstering.

I went to the door of the bedroom, and thought how pleasant it looked, with its pink-and-white patchwork quilt and the brown unpainted paneling of its woodwork:

" Come right in, dear," she said. " I want

you to set down in my old quilted rockin'-chair there by the window; you 'll say it 's the prettiest view in the house.   I set there a good deal to rest me and when I want to read."

There was a worn red Bible on the light-stand, and Mrs. Blackett's heavy silver-bowed glasses; her thimble was on the narrow window-ledge, and folded carefully on the table was a thick striped-cotton shirt that she was making for her son.   Those dear old fingers and their loving stitches, that heart which had made the most of everything that needed love!   Here was the real home, the heart of the old house on Green Island! I sat in the rocking-chair, and felt that it was a place of peace, the little brown bedroom, and the quiet outlook upon field and sea and sky.

I looked up, and we understood each other without speaking.   " I shall like to think o' your settin' here to-day," said Mrs. Blackett.   "I want you to come again.   It has been so pleasant for William."

The wind served us all the way home, and did not fall or let the sail slacken until we were close to the shore.   We had a generous freight of lobsters in the boat, and new potatoes which William had put aboard, and what Mrs. Todd proudly called a full "kag" of prime number one salted mackerel; and when we landed we had to make business arrangements to have these conveyed to her house in a wheelbarrow.

I never shall forget the day at Green Island. The town of Dunnet Landing seemed large and noisy and oppressive as we came ashore. Such is the power of contrast; for the village was so still that I could hear the shy whippoorwills singing that night as I lay awake in my downstairs bedroom, and the scent of Mrs. Todd's herb garden under the window blew in again and again with every gentle rising of the sea-breeze.

XII.

A STRANGE SAIL.

EXCEPT for a few stray guests, islanders or from the inland country, to whom Mrs. Todd offered the hospitalities of a single meal, we were quite by ourselves all summer; and when there were signs of invasion, late in July, and a certain Mrs. Fosdick appeared like a strange sail on the far horizon, I suffered much from apprehension. I had been living in the quaint little house with as much comfort and unconsciousness as if it were a larger body, or a double shell, in whose simple convolutions Mrs. Todd and I had secreted ourselves, until some wandering hermit crab of a visitor marked the little spare room for her own. Perhaps now and then a castaway on a lonely desert island dreads the thought of being rescued. I heard of Mrs. Fosdick for the first time with a selfish sense of objection; but after all, I was still vacation-tenant of the school-

house, where I could always be alone, and
it was impossible not to sympathize with
Mrs. Todd, who, in spite of some preliminary grumbling, was really delighted with
the prospect of entertaining an old friend.

For nearly a month we received occasional news of Mrs. Fosdick, who seemed to
be making a royal progress from house to
house in the inland neighborhood, after the
fashion of Queen Elizabeth. One Sunday
after another came and went, disappointing
Mrs. Todd in the hope of seeing her guest
at church and fixing the day for the great
visit to begin; but Mrs. Fosdick was not
ready to commit herself to a date. An as-
surance of " some time this week " was not
sufficiently definite from a free-footed housekeeper's point of view, and Mrs. Todd put
aside all herb-gathering plans, and went
through the various stages of expectation,
provocation, and despair. At last she was
ready to believe that Mrs. Fosdick must
have forgotten her promise and returned to
her home, which was vaguely said to be over
Thomaston way. But one evening, just as
the supper-table was cleared and "readied
up," and Mrs. Todd had put her large apron
over her head and stepped forth for an even-

ing stroll in the garden, the unexpected happened.   She heard the sound of wheels, and
gave an excited cry to me, as I sat by the
window, that Mrs. Fosdick was coming right
up the street.

"She may not be considerate, but she 's
dreadful good company," said Mrs. Todd
hastily, coming back a few steps from the
neighborhood of the gate. "No, she ain't
a mite considerate, but there 's a small lobster left over from your tea ; yes, it 's a real
mercy there 's a lobster. Susan Fosdick
might just as well have passed the compliment o' comin' an hour ago."

"Perhaps she has had her supper," I
ventured to suggest, sharing the housekeeper's anxiety, and meekly conscious of
an inconsiderate appetite for my own supper
after a long expedition up the bay.   There
were so few emergencies of any sort at
Dunnet Landing that this one appeared
overwhelming.

"No, she 's rode 'way over from Nahum
Brayton's place. I expect they were busy
on the farm, and could n't spare the horse
in proper season. You just sly out an' set
the teakittle on again, dear, an' drop in a
good han'ful o' chips; the fire 's all alive.

I 'll take her right up to lay off her things,
an' she 'll be occupied with explanations an'
gettin' her bunnit off, so you 'll have plenty
o' time.   She 's one I should n't like to have
find me unprepared."

Mrs. Fosdick was already at the gate, and
Mrs. Todd now turned with an air of complete surprise and delight to welcome her.

" Why, Susan Fosdick," I heard her ex-
claim in a fine unhindered voice, as if she
were calling across a field, " I come near giving of you up!   I was afraid you 'd gone
an' 'portioned out my visit to somebody else.
I s'pose you 've been to supper? "

" Lor', no, I ain't, Almiry Todd," said
Mrs. Fosdick cheerfully, as she turned, laden
with bags and bundles, from making her
adieux to the boy driver.   " I ain't had a
mite o' supper, dear.   I 've been lottin' all
the way on a cup o' that best tea o' yourn,
— some o' that Oolong you keep in the little
chist.   I don't want none o' your useful
herbs."

" I keep that tea for ministers' folks,"
gayly responded Mrs. Todd.   " Come right
along in, Susan Fosdick.   I declare if you
ain't the same old sixpence ! "

As they came up the walk together, laughing like girls, I fled, full of cares, to the kitchen, to brighten the fire and be sure that the lobster, sole dependence of a late supper, was well out of reach of the cat. There proved to be fine reserves of wild raspberries and bread and butter, so that I regained my composure, and waited impatiently for my own share of this illustrious visit to begin. There was an instant sense of high festivity in the evening air from the moment when our guest had so frankly demanded the Oolong tea.

The great moment arrived. I was formally presented at the stair-foot, and the two friends passed on to the kitchen, where I soon heard a hospitable clink of crockery and the brisk stirring of a tea-cup. I sat in my high-backed rocking-chair by the window in the front room with an unreasonable feeling of being left out, like the child who stood at the gate in Hans Andersen's story. Mrs. Fosdick did not look, at first sight, like a person of great social gifts. She was a serious-looking little bit of an old woman, with a birdlike nod of the head. I had often been told that she was the " best hand in the world to make a visit," — as if to visit were the highest of vocations ; that everybody wished for her, while few could get her; and I saw that Mrs. Todd felt a comfortable sense of distinction in being favored with the company of this eminent person who " knew just how." It was certainly true that Mrs. Fosdick gave both her hostess and me a warm feeling of enjoyment and expectation, as if she had the power of social suggestion to all neighboring minds.

The two friends did not reappear for at least an hour. I could hear their busy voices, loud and low by turns, as they ranged from public to confidential topics. At last Mrs. Todd kindly remembered me and returned, giving my door a ceremonious knock before she stepped in, with the small visitor in her wake. She reached behind her and took Mrs. Fosdick's hand as if she were young and bashful, and gave her a gentle pull forward.

" There, I don't know whether you 're goin' to take to each other or not; no, nobody can't tell whether you 'll suit each other, but I expect you 'll get along some way, both having seen the world," said our affectionate hostess. " You can inform Mis' Fosdick how we found the folks out to Green Island the other day. She 's always been well acquainted with mother. I 'll slip out now an' put away the supper things an' set my bread to rise, if you 'll both excuse me. You can come out an' keep me company when you get ready, either or both." And Mrs. Todd, large and amiable, disappeared and left us.

Being furnished not only with a subject of conversation, but with a safe refuge in the kitchen in case of incompatibility, Mrs. Fosdick and I sat down, prepared to make the best of each other. I soon discovered that she, like many of the elder women of that coast, had spent a part of her life at sea, and was full of a good traveler's curiosity and enlightenment. By the time we thought it discreet to join our hostess we were already sincere friends.

You may speak of a visit's setting in as well as a tide's, and it was impossible, as Mrs. Todd whispered to me, not to be pleased at the way this visit was setting in ; a new impulse and refreshing of the social currents and seldom visited bays of memory appeared to have begun. Mrs. Fosdick had been the mother of a large family of sons and daughters, — sailors and sailors' wives, — and most of them had died before her.

I soon grew more or less acquainted with
the histories of all their fortunes and mis-
fortunes, and subjects of an intimate nature
were no more withheld from my ears than if
I had been a shell on the mantelpiece. Mrs.
Fosdick was not without a touch of dignity
and elegance; she was fashionable in her
dress, but it was a curiously well-preserved
provincial fashion of some years back. In
a wider sphere one might have called her a
woman of the world, with her unexpected
bits of modern knowledge, but Mrs. Todd's
wisdom was an intimation of truth itself.
She might belong to any age, like an idyl of
Theocritus; but while she always understood
Mrs. Fosdick, that entertaining pilgrim could
not always understand Mrs. Todd.

That very first evening my friends plunged
into a borderless sea of reminiscences and
personal news. Mrs. Fosdick had been staying with a family who owned the farm
where she was born, and she had visited
every sunny knoll and shady field corner;
but when she said that it might be for the
last time, I detected in her tone something
expectant of the contradiction which Mrs.
Todd promptly offered.

" Almiry," said Mrs. Fosdick, with sadness, " you may say what you like, but I
am one of nine brothers and sisters brought
up on the old place, and we 're all dead but
me."

" Your sister Dailey ain't gone, is she ?
Why, no, Louisa ain't gone ! " exclaimed
Mrs. Todd, with surprise. " Why, I never
heard of that occurrence ! "

" Yes 'm ; she passed away last October,
in Lynn. She had made her distant home
in Vermont State, but she was making a
visit to her youngest daughter. Louisa was
the only one of my family whose funeral I
was n't able to attend, but 't was a mere
accident. All the rest of us were settled
right about home. I thought it was very
slack of 'em in Lynn not to fetch her to the
old place ; but when I came to hear about
it, I learned that they 'd recently put up a
very elegant monument, and my sister Dailey
was always great for show. She 'd just been
out to see the monument the week before she
was taken down, and admired it so much
that they felt sure of her wishes."

" So she 's really gone, and the funeral
was up to Lynn ! " repeated Mrs. Todd, as
if to impress the sad fact upon her mind.

" She was some years younger than we be,
too. I recollect the first day she ever came
to school ; 't was that first year mother sent
me inshore to stay with aunt Topham's folks
and get my schooling. You fetched little
Louisa to school one Monday mornin' in a
pink dress an' her long curls, and she set
between you an' me, and got cryin' after a
while, so the teacher sent us home with her
at recess."

" She was scared of seeing so many children about her ; there was only her and me
and brother John at home then ; the older
boys were to sea with father, an' the rest of
us wa'n't born," explained Mrs. Fosdick.
" That next fall we all went to sea together.
Mother was uncertain till the last minute, as
one may say. The ship was waiting orders,
but the baby that then was, was born just
in time, and there was a long spell of extra
bad weather, so mother got about again before they had to sail, an' we all went. I
remember my clothes were all left ashore
in the east chamber in a basket where
mother 'd took them out o' my chist o'
drawers an' left 'em ready to carry aboard.
She did n't have nothing aboard, of her own,
that she wanted to cut up for me, so when

my dress wore out she just put me into a spare suit o' John's, jacket and trousers. I was n't but eight years old an' he was most seven and large of his age. Quick as we made a port she went right ashore an' fitted me out pretty, but we was bound for the East Indies and did n't put in anywhere for a good while. So I had quite a spell o' freedom. Mother made my new skirt long because I was growing, and I poked about the deck after that, real discouraged, feeling the hem at my heels every minute, and as if youth was past and gone. I liked the trousers best; I used to climb the riggin' with 'em and frighten mother till she said an' vowed she 'd never take me to sea again.

I thought by the polite absent-minded smile on Mrs. Todd's face this was no new story.

"Little Louisa was a beautiful child ; yes, I always thought Louisa was very pretty," Mrs. Todd said. "She was a dear little girl in those days. She favored your mother; the rest of you took after your father's folks."

"We did certain," agreed Mrs. Fosdick, rocking steadily. "There, it does seem so pleasant to talk with an old acquaintance that knows what you know. I see so many of these new folks nowadays, that seem to have neither past nor future. Conversation 's got to have some root in the past, or else you 've got to explain every remark you make, an' it wears a person out."

Mrs. Todd gave a funny little laugh. " Yes 'm, old friends is always best, 'less you can catch a new one that 's fit to make an old one out of," she said, and we gave an affectionate glance at each other which Mrs. Fosdick could not have understood, being the latest comer to the house.

XIII.

POOR JOANNA.

ONE evening my ears caught a mysterious allusion which Mrs. Todd made to Shell-heap Island. It was a chilly night of cold northeasterly rain, and I made a fire for the first time in the Franklin stove in my room, and begged my two housemates to come in and keep me company. The weather had convinced Mrs. Todd that it was time to make a supply of cough-drops, and she had been bringing forth herbs from dark and dry hiding-places, until now the pungent dust and odor of them had resolved themselves into one mighty flavor of spearmint that came from a simmering caldron of syrup in the kitchen. She called it done, and well done, and had ostentatiously left it to cool, and taken her knitting-work because Mrs. Fosdick was busy with hers. They sat in the two rocking-chairs, the small woman and the large one, but now and then I could see that Mrs. Todd's thoughts remained with the cough-drops. The time of gathering herbs was nearly over, but the time of syrups and cordials had begun.

The heat of the open fire made us a little drowsy, but something in the way Mrs. Todd spoke of Shell-heap Island waked my interest. I waited to see if she would say any more, and then took a roundabout way back to the subject by saying what was first in my mind: that I wished the Green Island family were there to spend the evening with us, — Mrs. Todd's mother and her brother William.

Mrs. Todd smiled, and drummed on the arm of the rocking-chair. "Might scare William to death," she warned me; and Mrs. Fosdick mentioned her intention of going out to Green Island to stay two or three days, if this wind did n't make too much sea.

"Where is Shell-heap Island?" I ventured to ask, seizing the opportunity.

"Bears nor'east somewheres about three miles from Green Island; right off-shore, I should call it about eight miles out," said Mrs. Todd. "You never was there, dear; 't is off the thoroughfares, and a very bad place to land at best."

"I should think 't was," agreed Mrs. Fosdick, smoothing down her black silk apron. "'T is a place worth visitin' when you once get there. Some o' the old folks was kind o' fearful about it. 'T was 'counted a great place in old Indian times; you can pick up their stone tools 'most any time if you hunt about. There's a beautiful spring 'o water, too. Yes, I remember when they used to tell queer stories about Shell-heap Island. Some said 't was a great bangeing-place for the Indians, and an old chief resided there once that ruled the winds; and others said they'd always heard that once the Indians come down from up country an' left a captive there without any bo't, an' 't was too far to swim across to Black Island, so called, an' he lived there till he perished."

"I've heard say he walked the island after that, and sharp-sighted folks could see him an' lose him like one o' them citizens Cap'n Littlepage was acquainted with up to the north pole," announced Mrs. Todd grimly. "Anyway, there was Indians, — you can see their shell-heap that named the island; and I've heard myself that 't was one o' their cannibal places, but I never could believe it. There never was no cannibals on the coast 'o

Maine.   All the Indians o' these regions are
tame-looking folks."

"Sakes alive, yes!" exclaimed Mrs. Fosdick.   "Ought to see them painted savages
I 've seen when I was young out in the
South Sea Islands!   That was the time for
folks to travel, 'way back in the old whalin'
days!"

"Whalin' must have been dull for a lady,
hardly ever makin' a lively port, and not
takin' in any mixed cargoes," said Mrs.
Todd.   "I never desired to go a whalin'
v'y'ge myself."

"I used to return feelin' very slack an'
behind the times, 't is true," explained Mrs.
Fosdick, "but 't was excitin', an' we always
done extra well, and felt rich when we did
get ashore.   I liked the variety.   There,
how times have changed; how few seafarin'
families there are left!   What a lot o' queer
folks there used to be about here, anyway,
when we was young, Almiry.   Everybody's
just like everybody else, now; nobody to
laugh about, and nobody to cry about."

It seemed to me that there were peculi-
arities of character in the region of Dunnet
Landing yet, but I did not like to interrupt.

"Yes," said Mrs. Todd after a moment of

meditation, " there was certain a good many curiosities of human natur' in this neighborhood years ago. There was more energy then, and in some the energy took a singular turn. In these days the young folks is all copy-cats, 'fraid to death they won't be all just alike ; as for the old folks, they pray for the advantage o' bein' a little different."

" I ain't heard of a copy-cat this great many years," said Mrs. Fosdick, laughing ; " 't was a favorite term o' my grandmother's. No, I wa'n't thinking o' those things, but of them strange straying creatur's that used to rove the country. You don't see them now, or the ones that used to hive away in their own houses with some strange notion or other."

I thought again of Captain Littlepage, but my companions were not reminded of his name ; and there was brother William at Green Island, whom we all three knew.

" I was talking o' poor Joanna the other day. I had n't thought of her for a great while," said Mrs. Fosdick abruptly. " Mis' Brayton an' I recalled her as we sat together sewing. She was one o' your peculiar persons, wa'n't she ? Speaking of such persons," she turned to explain to me, " there was a sort of a nun or hermit person lived out there for years all alone on Shell-heap Island. Miss Joanna Todd, her name was, — a cousin o' Almiry's late husband."

I expressed my interest, but as I glanced at Mrs. Todd I saw that she was confused by sudden affectionate feeling and unmistakable desire for reticence.

" I never want to hear Joanna laughed about," she said anxiously.

" Nor I," answered Mrs. Fosdick reassuringly. " She was crossed in love, — that was all the matter to begin with; but as I look back, I can see that Joanna was one doomed from the first to fall into a melancholy. She retired from the world for good an' all, though she was a well-off woman. All she wanted was to get away from folks; she thought she was n't fit to live with anybody, and wanted to be free. Shell-heap Island come to her from her father, and first thing folks knew she 'd gone off out there to live, and left word she did n't want no company. 'T was a bad place to get to, unless the wind an' tide were just right; 't was hard work to make a landing."

" What time of year was this?" I asked.

" Very late in the summer," said Mrs.

Fosdick. " No, I never could laugh at Joanna, as some did. She set everything by
the young man, an' they were going to marry
in about a month, when he got bewitched
with a girl 'way up the bay, and married
her, and went off to Massachusetts. He
was n't well thought of, — there were those
who thought Joanna's money was what had
tempted him ; but she 'd given him her
whole heart, an' she wa'n't so young as she
had been. All her hopes were built on
marryin', an' havin' a real home and somebody to look to ; she acted just like a bird
when its nest is spoilt. The day after she
heard the news she was in dreadful woe, but
the next she came to herself very quiet, and
took the horse and wagon, and drove fourteen miles to the lawyer's, and signed a
paper givin' her half of the farm to her
brother. They never had got along very
well together, but he did n't want to sign it,
till she acted so distressed that he gave in.
Edward Todd's wife was a good woman, who
felt very bad indeed, and used every argu-
ment with Joanna ; but Joanna took a poor
old boat that had been her father's and
lo'ded in a few things, and off she put all
alone, with a good land breeze, right out to

sea. Edward Todd ran down to the beach,
an' stood there cryin' like a boy to see her
go, but she was out o' hearin'. She never
stepped foot on the mainland again long as
she lived."

"How large an island is it? How did
she manage in winter?" I asked.

"Perhaps thirty acres, rocks and all,"
answered Mrs. Todd, taking up the story
gravely. "There can't be much of it that
the salt spray don't fly over in storms. No,
't is a dreadful small place to make a world
of ; it has a different look from any of the
other islands, but there 's a sheltered cove
on the south side, with mud-flats across one
end of it at low water where there 's excellent clams, and the big shell-heap keeps
some o' the wind off a little house her father
took the trouble to build when he was a
young man. They said there was an old
house built o' logs there before that, with a
kind of natural cellar in the rock under it.
He used to stay out there days to a time,
and anchor a little sloop he had, and dig
clams to fill it, and sail up to Portland.
They said the dealers always gave him an
extra price, the clams were so noted. Joanna
used to go out and stay with him. They

were always great companions, so she knew
just what 't was out there. There was a few
sheep that belonged to her brother an' her,
but she bargained for him to come and get
them on the edge o' cold weather. Yes, she
desired him to come for the sheep; an' his
wife thought perhaps Joanna 'd return, but
he said no, an' lo'ded the bo't with warm
things an' what he thought she 'd need
through the winter. He come home with
the sheep an' left the other things by the
house, but she never so much as looked out
o' the window. She done it for a penance.
She must have wanted to see Edward by
that time."

Mrs. Fosdick was fidgeting with eagerness to speak.

"Some thought the first cold snap would
set her ashore, but she always remained,"
concluded Mrs. Todd soberly.

"Talk about the men not having any
curiosity!" exclaimed Mrs. Fosdick scornfully. "Why, the waters round Shell-heap
Island were white with sails all that fall.
'T was never called no great of a fishin'-
ground before. Many of 'em made excuse
to go ashore to get water at the spring; but
at last she spoke to a bo't-load, very digni-

fied and calm, and said that she'd like it
better if they'd make a practice of getting
water to Black Island or somewheres else
and leave her alone, except in case of accident or trouble. But there was one man
who had always set everything by her from
a boy. He'd have married her if the other
had n't come about an' spoilt his chance,
and he used to get close to the island, before
light, on his way out fishin', and throw a
little bundle 'way up the green slope front
o' the house. His sister told me she happened to see, the first time, what a pretty
choice he made o' useful things that a woman
would feel lost without. He stood off fishin', and could see them in the grass all day,
though sometimes she'd come out and walk
right by them. There was other bo'ts near,
out after mackerel. But early next morning
his present was gone. He did n't presume
too much, but once he took her a nice firkin
o' things he got up to Portland, and when
spring come he landed her a hen and chickens in a nice little coop. There was a good
many old friends had Joanna on their
minds."

"Yes," said Mrs. Todd, losing her sad
reserve in the growing sympathy of these

reminiscences. " How everybody used to notice whether there was smoke out of the chimney! The Black Island folks could see her with their spy-glass, and if they 'd ever missed getting some sign o' life they 'd have sent notice to her folks. But after the first year or two Joanna was more and more forgotten as an every-day charge. Folks lived very simple in those days, you know," she continued, as Mrs. Fosdick's knitting was taking much thought at the moment. " I expect there was always plenty of driftwood thrown up, and a poor failin' patch of spruces covered all the north side of the island, so she always had something to burn. She was very fond of workin' in the garden ashore, and that first summer she began to till the little field out there, and raised a nice parcel o' potatoes. She could fish, o' course, and there was all her clams an' lobsters. You can always live well in any wild place by the sea when you 'd starve to death up country, except 't was berry time. Joanna had berries out there, blackberries at least, and there was a few herbs in case she needed them. Mullein in great quantities and a plant o' wormwood I remember seeing once when I stayed there, long before she fled out to Shell-heap. Yes, I recall the wormwood, which is always a planted herb, so there must have been folks there before the Todds' day. A growin' bush makes the best gravestone ; I expect that wormwood always stood for somebody's solemn monument. Catnip, too, is a very endurin' herb about an old place."

" But what I want to know is what she did for other things," interrupted Mrs. Fosdick. " Almiry, what did she do for clothin' when she needed to replenish, or risin' for her bread, or the piece-bag that no woman can live long without ? "

" Or company," suggested Mrs. Todd. " Joanna was one that loved her friends. There must have been a terrible sight o' long winter evenin's that first year."

" There was her hens," suggested Mrs. Fosdick, after reviewing the melancholy situation. " She never wanted the sheep after that first season. There wa'n't no proper pasture for sheep after the June grass was past, and she ascertained the fact and could n't bear to see them suffer ; but the chickens done well. I remember sailin' by one spring afternoon, an' seein' the coops out front o' the house in the sun. How long

was it before you went out with the minister? You were the first ones that ever
really got ashore to see Joanna."

I had been reflecting upon a state of
society which admitted such personal freedom and a voluntary hermitage. There was
something mediæval in the behavior of poor
Joanna Todd under a disappointment of the
heart. The two women had drawn closer
together, and were talking on, quite unconscious of a listener.

"Poor Joanna!" said Mrs. Todd again,
and sadly shook her head as if there were
things one could not speak about.

"I called her a great fool," declared Mrs.
Fosdick, with spirit, "but I pitied her then,
and I pity her far more now. Some other
minister would have been a great help to
her, — one that preached self-forgetfulness
and doin' for others to cure our own ills;
but Parson Dimmick was a vague person,
well meanin', but very numb in his feelin's.
I don't suppose at that troubled time Joanna
could think of any way to mend her troubles
except to run off and hide."

"Mother used to say she did n't see how
Joanna lived without having nobody to do
for, getting her own meals and tending her

own poor self day in an' day out," said Mrs. Todd sorrowfully.

" There was the hens," repeated Mrs. Fosdick kindly. " I expect she soon came to makin' folks o' them. No, I never went to work to blame Joanna, as some did. She was full o' feeling, and her troubles hurt her more than she could bear. I see it all now as I could n't when I was young."

" I suppose in old times they had their shut-up convents for just such folks," said Mrs. Todd, as if she and her friend had disagreed about Joanna once, and were now in happy harmony. She seemed to speak with new openness and freedom. " Oh yes, I was only too pleased when the Reverend Mr. Dimmick invited me to go out with him. He had n't been very long in the place when Joanna left home and friends. 'T was one day that next summer after she went, and I had been married early in the spring. He felt that he ought to go out and visit her. She was a member of the church, and might wish to have him consider her spiritual state. I wa'n't so sure o' that, but I always liked Joanna, and I 'd come to be her cousin by marriage. Nathan an' I had conversed about goin' out to pay her a visit, but he got his chance to sail sooner 'n he expected. He always thought everything of her, and last time he come home, knowing nothing of her change, he brought her a beautiful coral pin from a port he 'd touched at somewheres up the Mediterranean. So I wrapped the little box in a nice piece of paper and put it in my pocket, and picked her a bunch of fresh lemon balm, and off we started."

Mrs. Fosdick laughed. " I remember hearin' about your trials on the v'y'ge," she said.

" Why, yes," continued Mrs. Todd in her company manner. " I picked her the balm, an' we started. Why, yes, Susan, the minister liked to have cost me my life that day. He would fasten the sheet, though I advised against it. He said the rope was rough an' cut his hand. There was a fresh breeze, an' he went on talking rather high flown, an' I felt some interested. All of a sudden there come up a gust, and he give a screech and stood right up and called for help, 'way out there to sea. I knocked him right over into the bottom o' the bo't, getting by to catch hold of the sheet an' untie it. He was n't but a little man; I helped him right up after the squall passed, and made a handsome apology to him, but he did act kind o' offended."

"I do think they ought not to settle them landlocked folks in parishes where they 're liable to be on the water," insisted Mrs. Fosdick. "Think of the families in our parish that was scattered all about the bay, and what a sight o' sails you `used to see, in Mr. Dimmick's day, standing across to the mainland on a pleasant Sunday morning, filled with church-going folks, all sure to want him some time or other! You could n't find no doctor that would stand up in the boat and screech if a flaw struck her."

"Old Dr. Bennett had a beautiful sail-boat, did n't he?" responded Mrs. Todd. "And how well he used to brave the weather! Mother always said that in time o' trouble that tall white sail used to look like an angel's wing comin' over the sea to them that was in pain. Well, there 's a difference in gifts. Mr. Dimmick was not without light."

" 'T was light o' the moon, then," snapped Mrs. Fosdick; "he was pompous enough, but I never could remember a single word he said. There, go on, Mis' Todd; I forget a great deal about that day you went to see poor Joanna."

"I felt she saw us coming, and knew us a great way off; yes, I seemed to feel it within me," said our friend, laying down her knitting. "I kept my seat, and took the bo't inshore without saying a word; there was a short channel that I was sure Mr. Dimmick was n't acquainted with, and the tide was very low. She never came out to warn us off nor anything, and I thought, as I hauled the bo't up on a wave and let the Reverend Mr. Dimmick step out, that it was somethin' gained to be safe ashore. There was a little smoke out o' the chimney o' Joanna's house, and it did look sort of homelike and pleasant with wild mornin'-glory vines trained up; an' there was a plot o' flowers under the front window, portulacas and things. I believe she 'd made a garden once, when she was stopping there with her father, and some things must have seeded in. It looked as if she might have gone over to the other side of the island. 'T was neat and pretty all about the house, and a lovely day in July. We walked up from the beach together very sedate, and I felt for poor Nathan's little pin to see if 't was safe in my dress pocket. All of a sudden Joanna come right to the fore door and stood there, not sayin' a word.

XIV.

THE HERMITAGE.

My companions and I had been so intent
upon the subject of the conversation that
we had not heard any one open the gate, but
at this moment, above the noise of the rain,
we heard a loud knocking. We were all
startled as we sat by the fire, and Mrs. Todd
rose hastily and went to answer the call,
leaving her rocking-chair in violent motion. Mrs. Fosdick and I heard an anxious
voice at the door speaking of a sick child,
and Mrs. Todd's kind, motherly voice inviting the messenger in: then we waited in
silence. There was a sound of heavy drop-
ping of rain from the eaves, and the distant
roar and undertone of the sea. My thoughts
flew back to the lonely woman on her outer
island; what separation from humankind
she must have felt, what terror and sadness,
even in a summer storm like this!

"You send right after the doctor if she

ain't better in half an hour," said Mrs. Todd
to her worried customer as they parted ; and
I felt a warm sense of comfort in the evident resources of even so small a neighborhood, but for the poor hermit Joanna there
was no neighbor on a winter night.

"How did she look?" demanded Mrs.
Fosdick, without preface, as our large hostess returned to the little room with a mist
about her from standing long in the wet doorway, and the sudden draught of her coming
beat out the smoke and flame from the Franklin stove. "How did poor Joanna look?"

"She was the same as ever, except I
thought she looked smaller," answered Mrs.
Todd after thinking a moment ; perhaps it
was only a last considering thought about
her patient. "Yes, she was just the same,
and looked very nice, Joanna did. I had
been married since she left home, an' she
treated me like her own folks. I expected
she 'd look strange, with her hair turned
gray in a night or somethin', but she wore
a pretty gingham dress I 'd often seen her
wear before she went away ; she must have
kept it nice for best in the afternoons. She
always had beautiful, quiet manners. I re-

member she waited till we were close to her, and then kissed me real affectionate, and inquired for Nathan before she shook hands with the minister, and then she invited us both in. 'T was the same little house her father had built him when he was a bachelor, with one livin'-room, and a little mite of a bedroom out of it where she slept, but 't was neat as a ship's cabin. There was some old chairs, an' a seat made of a long box that might have held boat tackle an' things to lock up in his fishin' days, and a good enough stove so anybody could cook and keep warm in cold weather. I went over once from home and stayed 'most a week with Joanna when we was girls, and those young happy days rose up before me. Her father was busy all day fishin' or clammin'; he was one o' the pleasantest men in the world, but Joanna's mother had the grim streak, and never knew what 't was to be happy. The first minute my eyes fell upon Joanna's face that day I saw how she had grown to look like Mis' Todd. 'T was the mother right over again."

" Oh dear me! " said Mrs. Fosdick.

" Joanna had done one thing very pretty. There was a little piece o' swamp on the island where good rushes grew plenty, and she'd gathered 'em, and braided some beautiful mats for the floor and a thick cushion for the long bunk. She'd showed a good deal of invention; you see there was a nice chance to pick up pieces o' wood and boards that drove ashore, and she'd made good use o' what she found. There was n't no clock, but she had a few dishes on a shelf, and flowers set about in shells fixed to the walls, so it did look sort of homelike, though so lonely and poor. I could n't keep the tears out o' my eyes, I felt so sad. I said to myself, I must get mother to come over an' see Joanna; the love in mother's heart would warm her, an' she might be able to advise."

"Oh no, Joanna was dreadful stern," said Mrs. Fosdick.

"We were all settin' down very proper, but Joanna would keep stealin' glances at me as if she was glad I come. She had but little to say; she was real polite an' gentle, and yet forbiddin'. The minister found it hard," confessed Mrs. Todd; "he got embarrassed, an' when he put on his authority and asked her if she felt to enjoy religion in her present situation, an' she replied that she must be excused from answerin', I thought I should fly. She might have made it easier for him; after all, he was the minister and had taken some trouble to come out, though 't was kind of cold an' unfeelin' the way he inquired. I thought he might have seen the little old Bible a-layin' on the shelf close by him, an' I wished he knew enough to just lay his hand on it an' read somethin' kind an' fatherly 'stead of accusin' her, an' then given poor Joanna his blessin' with the hope she might be led to comfort. He did offer prayer, but 't was all about hearin' the voice o' God out o' the whirl-wind ; and I thought while he was goin' on that anybody that had spent the long cold winter all alone out on Shell-heap Island knew a good deal more about those things than he did. I got so provoked I opened my eyes and stared right at him.

" She did n't take no notice, she kep' a nice respectful manner towards him, and when there come a pause she asked if he had any interest about the old Indian re-mains, and took down some queer stone gouges and hammers off of one of her shelves and showed them to him same 's if he was a boy. He remarked that he 'd like to walk over an' see the shell-heap ; so she went right to the door and pointed him the way. I see then that she'd made her some kind o' sandal-shoes out o' the fine rushes to wear on her feet; she stepped light an' nice in 'em as shoes."

Mrs. Fosdick leaned back in her rocking-chair and gave a heavy sigh.

"I did n't move at first, but I'd held out just as long as I could," said Mrs. Todd, whose voice trembled a little. "When Jo-anna returned from the door, an' I could see that man's stupid back departin' among the wild rose bushes, I just ran to her an' caught her in my arms. I was n't so big as I be now, and she was older than me, but I hugged her tight, just as if she was a child. 'Oh, Joanna dear,' I says, 'won't you come ashore an' live 'long o' me at the Landin', or go over to Green Island to mother's when winter comes? Nobody shall trouble you, an' mother finds it hard bein' alone. I can't bear to leave you here' — and I burst right out crying. I'd had my own trials, young as I was, an' she knew it. Oh, I did entreat her; yes, I entreated Joanna."

"What did she say then?" asked Mrs. Fosdick, much moved.

"She looked the same way, sad an' remote

through it all," said Mrs. Todd mournfully.
"She took hold of my hand, and we sat
down close together; 't was as if she turned
round an' made a child of me. 'I have n't
got no right to live with folks no more,' she
said. 'You must never ask me again, Almiry: I 've done the only thing I could do,
and I 've made my choice. I feel a great
comfort in your kindness, but I don't deserve
it. I have committed the unpardonable sin;
you don't understand,' says she humbly.
'I was in great wrath and trouble, and my
thoughts was so wicked towards God that I
can't expect ever to be forgiven. I have
come to know what it is to have patience,
but I have lost my hope. You must tell
those that ask how 't is with me,' she said,
' an' tell them I want to be alone.' I could n't
speak; no, there wa'n't anything I could say,
she seemed so above everything common. I
was a good deal younger then than I be
now, and I got Nathan's little coral pin out
o' my pocket and put it into her hand; and
when she saw it and I told her where it come
from, her face did really light up for a
minute, sort of bright an' pleasant. 'Nathan
an' I was always good friends; I 'm glad he
don't think hard of me,' says she. 'I want

you to have it, Almiry, an' wear it for love o'
both o' us,' and she handed it back to me.
' You give my love to Nathan, — he 's a dear
good man,' she said ; ' an' tell your mother, if
I should be sick she must n't wish I could
get well, but I want her to be the one to
come.' Then she seemed to have said all
she wanted to, as if she was done with the
world, and we sat there a few minutes longer
together. It was real sweet and quiet except
for a good many birds and the sea rollin' up
on the beach ; but at last she rose, an' I did
too, and she kissed me and held my hand in
hers a minute, as if to say good-by ; then she
turned and went right away out o' the door
and disappeared.

" The minister come back pretty soon,
and I told him I was all ready, and we
started down to the bo't. He had picked
up some round stones and things and was
carrying them in his pocket-handkerchief ;
an' he sat down amidships without making
any question, and let me take the rudder an'
work the bo't, an' made no remarks for
some time, until we sort of eased it off
speaking of the weather, an' subjects that
arose as we skirted Black Island, where two
or three families lived belongin' to the parish.

He preached next Sabbath as usual, somethin' high soundin' about the creation, and I could n't help thinkin' he might never get no further; he seemed to know no remedies, but he had a great use of words."

Mrs. Fosdick sighed again. "Hearin' you tell about Joanna brings the time right back as if 't was yesterday," she said. "Yes, she was one o' them poor things that talked about the great sin; we don't seem to hear nothing about the unpardonable sin now, but you may say 't was not uncommon then."

"I expect that if it had been in these days, such a person would be plagued to death with idle folks," continued Mrs. Todd, after a long pause. "As it was, nobody trespassed on her; all the folks about the bay respected her an' her feelings; but as time wore on, after you left here, one after another ventured to make occasion to put somethin' ashore for her if they went that way. I know mother used to go to see her sometimes, and send William over now and then with something fresh an' nice from the farm. There is a point on the sheltered side where you can lay a boat close to shore an' land anything safe on the turf out o' reach o' the water. There were one or two

others, old folks, that she would see, and
now an' then she 'd hail a passin' boat an'
ask for somethin'; and mother got her to
promise that she would make some sign to
the Black Island folks if she wanted help.
I never saw her myself to speak to after
that day."

"I expect nowadays, if such a thing happened, she 'd have gone out West to her
uncle's folks or up to Massachusetts and had
a change, an' come home good as new.   The
world 's bigger an' freer than it used to be,"
urged Mrs. Fosdick.

"No," said her friend.   " 'T is like bad
eyesight, the mind of such a person: if your
eyes don't see right there may be a remedy,
but there 's no kind of glasses to remedy the
mind.   No, Joanna was Joanna, and there
she lays on her island where she lived and
did her poor penance.   She told mother the
day she was dyin' that she always used to
want to be fetched inshore when it come to
the last; but she 'd thought it over, and
desired to be laid on the island, if 't was
thought right.   So the funeral was out
there, a Saturday afternoon in September.
'T was a pretty day, and there wa'n't hardly
a boat on the coast within twenty miles that

did n't head for Shell-heap cram-full o'
folks, an' all real respectful, same 's if she 'd
always stayed ashore and held her friends.
Some went out o' mere curiosity, I don't
doubt, — there 's always such to every
funeral; but most had real feelin', and went
purpose to show it. She 'd got most o' the
wild sparrows as tame as could be, livin' out
there so long among 'em, and one flew right
in and lit on the coffin an' begun to sing
while Mr. Dimmick was speakin'. He was
put out by it, an' acted as if he did n't know
whether to stop or go on. I may have been
prejudiced, but I wa'n't the only one thought
the poor little bird done the best of the
two."

"What became o' the man that treated
her so, did you ever hear?" asked Mrs.
Fosdick. "I know he lived up to Massachusetts for a while. Somebody who came
from the same place told me that he was in
trade there an' doin' very well, but that was
years ago."

"I never heard anything more than that;
he went to the war in one o' the early regi-
ments. No, I never heard any more of
him," answered Mrs. Todd. "Joanna was
another sort of person, and perhaps he

showed good judgment in marryin' somebody else, if only he'd behaved straightforward and manly.   He was a shifty-eyed,
coaxin' sort of man, that got what he wanted
out o' folks, an' only gave when he wanted to
buy, made friends easy and lost 'em without
knowin' the difference.   She'd had a piece
o' work tryin' to make him walk accordin' to
her right ideas, but she'd have had too much
variety ever to fall into a melancholy.   Some
is meant to be the Joannas in this world,
an' 't was her poor lot."

XV.

ON SHELL-HEAP ISLAND.

SOME time after Mrs. Fosdick's visit was over and we had returned to our former quietness, I was out sailing alone with Captain Bowden in his large boat. We were taking the crooked northeasterly channel seaward, and were well out from shore while it was still early in the afternoon. I found myself presently among some unfamiliar islands, and suddenly remembered the story of poor Joanna. There is something in the fact of a hermitage that cannot fail to touch the imagination; the recluses are a sad kindred, but they are never commonplace. Mrs. Todd had truly said that Joanna was like one of the saints in the desert; the loneliness of sorrow will forever keep alive their sad succession.

"Where is Shell-heap Island!" I asked eagerly.

"You see Shell-heap now, layin' 'way out

beyond Black Island there," answered the captain, pointing with outstretched arm as he stood, and holding the rudder with his knee.

"I should like very much to go there," said I, and the captain, without comment, changed his course a little more to the eastward and let the reef out of his mainsail.

"I don't know's we can make an easy landin' for ye," he remarked doubtfully. "May get your feet wet; bad place to land. Trouble is I ought to have brought a tagboat; but they clutch on to the water so, an' I do love to sail free. This gre't boat gets easy bothered with anything trailin'. 'T ain't breakin' much on the meetin'-house ledges; guess I can fetch in to Shell-heap."

"How long is it since Miss Joanna Todd died?" I asked, partly by way of explanation.

"Twenty-two years come September," answered the captain, after reflection. "She died the same year my oldest boy was born, an' the town house was burnt over to the Port. I did n't know but you merely wanted to hunt for some o' them Indian relics. Long's you want to see where Joanna lived — No, 't ain't breakin' over the ledges;

we 'll manage to fetch across the shoals somehow, 't is such a distance to go 'way round, and tide 's a-risin'," he ended hope-fully, and we sailed steadily on, the captain speechless with intent watching of a difficult course, until the small island with its low whitish promontory lay in full view before us under the bright afternoon sun.

The month was August, and I had seen the color of the islands change from the fresh green of June to a sunburnt brown that made them look like stone, except where the dark green of the spruces and fir balsam kept the tint that even winter storms might deepen, but not fade. The few wind-bent trees on Shell-heap Island were mostly dead and gray, but there were some low-growing bushes, and a stripe of light green ran along just above the shore, which I knew to be wild morning-glories. As we came close I could see the high stone walls of a small square field, though there were no sheep left to assail it; and below, there was a little harbor-like cove where Captain Bowden was boldly running the great boat in to seek a landing-place. There was a crooked channel of deep water which led close up against the shore.

" There, you hold fast for'ard there, an'
wait for her to lift on the wave. You 'll
make a good landin' if you 're smart ; right
on the port-hand side ! " the captain called
excitedly ; and I, standing ready with high
ambition, seized my chance and leaped over
to the grassy bank.

" I 'm beat if I ain't aground after all ! "
mourned the captain despondently.

But I could reach the bowsprit, and he
pushed with the boat-hook, while the wind
veered round a little as if on purpose and
helped with the sail ; so presently the boat
was free and began to drift out from shore.

" Used to call this p'int Joanna 's wharf
privilege, but 't has worn away in the
weather since her time. I thought one or
two bumps would n't hurt us none, — paint 's
got to be renewed, anyway, — but I never
thought she 'd tetch. I figured on shyin'
by," the captain apologized. " She 's too
gre't a boat to handle well in here; but I
used to sort of shy by in Joanna's day, an'
cast a little somethin' ashore — some apples
or a couple o' pears if I had 'em — on the
grass, where she 'd be sure to see."

I stood watching while Captain Bowden

cleverly found his way back to deeper water. "You need n't make no haste," he called to me; "I 'll keep within call. Joanna lays right up there in the far corner o' the field. There used to be a path led to the place. I always knew her well. I was out here to the funeral.

I found the path; it was touching to discover that this lonely spot was not without its pilgrims. Later generations will know less and less of Joanna herself, but there are paths trodden to the shrines of solitude the world over, — the world cannot forget them, try as it may; the feet of the young find them out because of curiosity and dim foreboding, while the old bring hearts full of remembrance. This plain anchorite had been one of those whom sorrow made too lonely to brave the sight of men, too timid to front the simple world she knew, yet valiant enough to live alone with her poor insistent human nature and the calms and passions of the sea and sky.

The birds were flying all about the field; they fluttered up out of the grass at my feet as I walked along, so tame that I liked to think they kept some happy tradition from

summer to summer of the safety of nests
and good fellowship of mankind. Poor Joanna's house was gone except the stones of
its foundations, and there was little trace of
her flower garden except a single faded sprig
of much-enduring French pinks, which a
great bee and a yellow butterfly were be-
friending together. I drank at the spring,
and thought that now and then some one
would follow me from the busy, hard-worked,
and simple-thoughted countryside of the
mainland, which lay dim and dreamlike
in the August haze, as Joanna must have
watched it many a day. There was the
world, and here was she with eternity well
begun. In the life of each of us, I said to
myself, there is a place remote and islanded,
and given to endless regret or secret happiness ; we are each the uncompanioned hermit
and recluse of an hour or a day ; we understand our fellows of the cell to whatever age
of history they may belong.

But as I stood alone on the island, in the
sea-breeze, suddenly there came a sound of
distant voices ; gay voices and laughter from
a pleasure-boat that was going seaward full
of boys and girls. I knew, as if she had

told me, that poor Joanna must have heard
the like on many and many a summer afternoon, and must have welcomed the good
cheer in spite of hopelessness and winter
weather, and all the sorrow and disappointment in the world.

XVI.

THE GREAT EXPEDITION.

MRS. TODD never by any chance gave warning over night of her great projects and adventures by sea and land. She first came to an understanding with the primal forces of nature, and never trusted to any preliminary promise of good weather, but examined the day for herself in its infancy. Then, if the stars were propitious, and the wind blew from a quarter of good inheritance whence no surprises of sea-turns or southwest sultriness might be feared, long before I was fairly awake I used to hear a rustle and knocking like a great mouse in the walls, and an impatient tread on the steep garret stairs that led to Mrs. Todd's chief place of storage. She went and came as if she had already started on her expedition with utmost haste and kept returning for something that was forgotten. When I appeared in quest of my breakfast, she would be absent-minded and sparing of speech, as if I had displeased her, and she was now, by main force of principle, holding herself back from altercation and strife of tongues.

These signs of a change became familiar to me in the course of time, and Mrs. Todd hardly noticed some plain proofs of divination one August morning when I said, without preface, that I had just seen the Beggs' best chaise go by, and that we should have to take the grocery. Mrs. Todd was alert in a moment.

"There! I might have known!" she exclaimed. "It's the 15th of August, when he goes and gets his money. He heired an annuity from an uncle o' his on his mother's side. I understood the uncle said none o' Sam Begg's wife's folks should make free with it, so after Sam's gone it'll all be past an' spent, like last summer. That's what Sam prospers on now, if you can call it prosperin'. Yes, I might have known. 'T is the 15th o' August with him, an' he gener'ly stops to dinner with a cousin's widow on the way home. Feb'uary an' August is the times. Takes him 'bout all day to go an' come."

I heard this explanation with interest.

The tone of Mrs. Todd's voice was complaining at the last.

"I like the grocery just as well as the chaise," I hastened to say, referring to a long-bodied high wagon with a canopy-top, like an attenuated four-posted bedstead on wheels, in which we sometimes journeyed. "We can put things in behind — roots and flowers and raspberries, or anything you are going after — much better than if we had the chaise."

Mrs. Todd looked stony and unwilling. "I counted upon the chaise," she said, turning her back to me, and roughly pushing back all the quiet tumblers on the cupboard shelf as if they had been impertinent. "Yes, I desired the chaise for once. I ain't goin' berryin' nor to fetch home no more wilted vegetation this year. Season 's about past, except for a poor few o' late things," she added in a milder tone. "I 'm goin' up country. No, I ain't intendin' to go berryin'. I 've been plottin' for it the past fortnight and hopin' for a good day."

"Would you like to have me go too?" I asked frankly, but not without a humble fear that I might have mistaken the purpose of this latest plan.

"Oh certain, dear!" answered my friend affectionately. "Oh no, I never thought o' any one else for comp'ny, if it 's convenient for you, long 's poor mother ain't come. I ain't nothin' like so handy with a conveyance as I be with a good bo't. Comes o' my early bringing-up. I expect we 've got to make that great high wagon do. The tires want settin' and 't is all loose-jointed, so I can hear it shackle the other side o' the ridge. We 'll put the basket in front. I ain't goin' to have it bouncin' an' twirlin' all the way. Why, I 've been makin' some nice hearts and rounds to carry."

These were signs of high festivity, and my interest deepened moment by moment.

"I 'll go down to the Beggs' and get the horse just as soon as I finish my breakfast," said I. "Then we can start whenever you are ready."

Mrs. Todd looked cloudy again. "I don't know but you look nice enough to go just as you be," she suggested doubtfully. "No, you would n't want to wear that pretty blue dress o' yourn 'way up country. 'T ain't dusty now, but it may be comin' home. No, I expect you 'd rather not wear that and the other hat."

" Oh yes. I should n't think of wearing these clothes," said I, with sudden illumination. " Why, if we 're going up country and are likely to see some of your friends, I 'll put on my blue dress, and you must wear your watch; I am not going at all if you mean to wear the big hat."

" Now you 're behavin' pretty," responded Mrs. Todd, with a gay toss of her head and a cheerful smile, as she came across the room, bringing a saucerful of wild raspberries, a pretty piece of salvage from supper-time. " I was cast down when I see you come to breakfast. I did n't think 't was just what you 'd select to wear to the reunion, where you 're goin' to meet everybody."

" What reunion do you mean? " I asked, not without amazement. " Not the Bowden Family's? I thought that was going to take place in September."

" To-day 's the day. They sent word the middle o' the week. I thought you might have heard of it. Yes, they changed the day. I been thinkin' we 'd talk it over, but you never can tell beforehand how it 's goin' to be, and 't ain't worth while to wear a day all out before it comes." Mrs. Todd gave

no place to the pleasures of anticipation, but
she spoke like the oracle that she was. " I
wish mother was here to go," she continued
sadly. " I did look for her last night, and
I couldn't keep back the tears when the
dark really fell and she wa'n't here, she does
so enjoy a great occasion. If William had
a mite o' snap an' ambition, he'd take the
lead at such a time. Mother likes variety,
and there ain't but a few nice opportunities 'round here, an' them she has to miss
'less she contrives to get ashore to me. I
do re'lly hate to go to the reunion without
mother, an' 't is a beautiful day; everybody'll be asking where she is. Once she'd
have got here anyway. Poor mother's beginnin' to feel her age."

" Why, there's your mother now ! " I exclaimed with joy, I was so glad to see the
dear old soul again. " I hear her voice at
the gate." But Mrs. Todd was out of the
door before me.

There, sure enough, stood Mrs. Blackett,
who must have left Green Island before
daylight. She had climbed the steep road
from the water-side so eagerly that she was
out of breath, and was standing by the garden fence to rest. She held an old-fashioned

brown wicker cap-basket in her hand, as
if visiting were a thing of every day, and
looked up at us as pleased and triumphant
as a child.

" Oh, what a poor, plain garden! Hardly
a flower in it except your bush o' balm! "
she said. " But you do keep your garden
neat, Almiry. Are you both well, an' goin'
up country with me? " She came a step or
two closer to meet us, with quaint polite-
ness and quite as delightful as if she were
at home. She dropped a quick little curtsey
before Mrs. Todd.

" There, mother, what a girl you be! I
am so pleased! I was just bewailin' you,"
said the daughter, with unwonted feeling.
" I was just bewailin' you, I was so disappointed, an' I kep' myself awake a good
piece o' the night scoldin' poor William. I
watched for the boat till I was ready to shed
tears yesterday, and when 't was comin'
dark I kep' making errands out to the gate
an' down the road to see if you wa'n't in the
doldrums somewhere down the bay."

" There was a head wind, as you know,"
said Mrs. Blackett, giving me the cap-basket, and holding my hand affectionately as
we walked up the clean-swept path to the

door. " I was partly ready to come, but dear William said I should be all tired out and might get cold, havin' to beat all the way in. So we give it up, and set down and spent the evenin' together. It was a little rough and windy outside, and I guess 't was better judgment; we went to bed very early and made a good start just at daylight. It 's been a lovely mornin' on the water. William thought he 'd better fetch across beyond Bird Rocks, rowin' the greater part o' the way; then we sailed from there right over to the Landin', makin' only one tack. William 'll be in again for me to-morrow, so I can come back here an' rest me over night, an' go to meetin' to-morrow, and have a nice, good visit."

" She was just havin' her breakfast," said Mrs. Todd, who had listened eagerly to the long explanation without a word of disapproval, while her face shone more and more with joy. " You just sit right down an' have a cup of tea and rest you while we make our preparations. Oh, I am so gratified to think you 've come! Yes, she was just havin' her breakfast, and we were speakin' of you. Where 's William ? "

" He went right back ; he said he expected

some schooners in about noon after bait, but
he 'll come an' have his dinner with us to-
morrow, unless it rains ; then next day.   I
laid his best things out all ready," explained
Mrs. Blackett, a little anxiously.   " This
wind will serve him nice all the way home.
Yes, I will take a cup of tea, dear, — a cup
of tea is always good ; and then I 'll rest a
minute and be all ready to start."

" I do feel condemned for havin' such
hard thoughts o' William," openly confessed
Mrs. Todd.   She stood before us so large
and serious that we both laughed and could
not find it in our hearts to convict so rueful
a culprit.   " He shall have a good dinner
to-morrow, if it can be got, and I shall be
real glad to see William," the confession
ended handsomely, while Mrs. Blackett
smiled approval and made haste to praise
the tea.   Then I hurried away to make sure
of the grocery wagon.   Whatever might
be the good of the reunion, I was going to
have the pleasure and delight of a day in
Mrs. Blackett's company, not to speak of
Mrs. Todd's.

The early morning breeze was still blowing, and the warm, sunshiny air was of
some ethereal northern sort, with a cool

freshness as if it came over new-fallen snow. The world was filled with a fragrance of fir-balsam and the faintest flavor of seaweed from the ledges, bare and brown at low tide in the little harbor. It was so still and so early that the village was but half awake. I could hear no voices but those of the birds, small and great, — the constant song sparrows, the clink of a yellow-hammer over in the woods, and the far conversation of some deliberate crows. I saw William Blackett's escaping sail already far from land, and Captain Littlepage was sitting behind his closed window as I passed by, watching for some one who never came. I tried to speak to him, but he did not see me. There was a patient look on the old man's face, as if the world were a great mistake and he had nobody with whom to speak his own language or find companionship.

XVII.

A COUNTRY ROAD.

WHATEVER doubts and anxieties I may
have had about the inconvenience of the
Beggs' high wagon for a person of Mrs.
Blackett's age and shortness, they were happily overcome by the aid of a chair and her
own valiant spirit. Mrs. Todd bestowed
great care upon seating us as if we were
taking passage by boat, but she finally pronounced that we were properly trimmed.
When we had gone only a little way up the
hill she remembered that she had left the
house door wide open, though the large key
was safe in her pocket. I offered to run
back, but my offer was met with lofty scorn,
and we lightly dismissed the matter from
our minds, until two or three miles further
on we met the doctor, and Mrs. Todd asked
him to stop and ask her nearest neighbor
to step over and close the door if the dust
seemed to blow in the afternoon.

"She 'll be there in her kitchen; she 'll hear you the minute you call; 't wont give you no delay," said Mrs. Todd to the doctor. "Yes, Mis' Dennett's right there, with the windows all open. It is n't as if my fore door opened right on the road, anyway." At which proof of composure Mrs. Blackett smiled wisely at me.

The doctor seemed delighted to see our guest; they were evidently the warmest friends, and I saw a look of affectionate confidence in their eyes. The good man left his carriage to speak to us, but as he took Mrs. Blackett's hand he held it a moment, and, as if merely from force of habit, felt her pulse as they talked; then to my delight he gave the firm old wrist a commending pat.

"You 're wearing well: good for another ten years at this rate," he assured her cheerfully, and she smiled back. "I like to keep a strict account of my old stand-bys," and he turned to me. "Don't you let Mrs. Todd overdo to-day, — old folks like her are apt to be thoughtless;" and then we all laughed, and, parting, went our ways gayly.

"I suppose he puts up with your rivalry the same as ever?" asked Mrs. Blackett.

"You and he are as friendly as ever, I see, Almiry," and Almira sagely nodded.

"He's got too many long routes now to stop to 'tend to all his door patients," she said, "especially them that takes pleasure in talkin' themselves over. The doctor and me have got to be kind of partners; he's gone a good deal, far an' wide. Looked tired, did n't he? I shall have to advise with him an' get him off for a good rest. He'll take the big boat from Rockland an' go off up to Boston an' mouse round among the other doctors, once in two or three years, and come home fresh as a boy. I guess they think consider'ble of him up there." Mrs. Todd shook the reins and reached determinedly for the whip, as if she were compelling public opinion.

Whatever energy and spirit the white horse had to begin with were soon exhausted by the steep hills and his discernment of a long expedition ahead. We toiled slowly along. Mrs. Blackett and I sat together, and Mrs. Todd sat alone in front with much majesty and the large basket of provisions. Part of the way the road was shaded by thick woods, but we also passed one farmhouse after another on the high uplands, which we all three regarded with deep interest, the house itself and the barns and garden-spots and poultry all having to suffer an inspection of the shrewdest sort. This was a highway quite new to me; in fact, most of my journeys with Mrs. Todd had been made afoot and between the roads, in open pasture-lands. My friends stopped several times for brief dooryard visits, and made so many promises of stopping again on the way home that I began to wonder how long the expedition would last. I had often noticed how warmly Mrs. Todd was greeted by her friends, but it was hardly to be compared to the feeling now shown toward Mrs. Blackett. A look of delight came to the faces of those who recognized the plain, dear old figure beside me; one revelation after another was made of the constant interest and intercourse that had linked the far island and these scattered farms into a golden chain of love and dependence.

"Now, we mustn't stop again if we can help it," insisted Mrs. Todd at last. "You'll get tired, mother, and you'll think the less o' reunions. We can visit along here any day. There, if they ain't frying doughnuts in this next house, too! These are new folks, you know, from over St. George way; they took this old Talcot farm last year. 'T is the best water on the road, and the check-rein's come undone — yes, we'd best delay a little and water the horse."

We stopped, and seeing a party of pleasure-seekers in holiday attire, the thin, anxious mistress of the farmhouse came out with wistful sympathy to hear what news we might have to give. Mrs. Blackett first spied her at the half-closed door, and asked with such cheerful directness if we were trespassing that, after a few words, she went back to her kitchen and reappeared with a plateful of doughnuts.

"Entertainment for man and beast," announced Mrs. Todd with satisfaction. "Why, we've perceived there was new doughnuts all along the road, but you're the first that has treated us."

Our new acquaintance flushed with pleasure, but said nothing.

"They're very nice; you've had good luck with 'em," pronounced Mrs. Todd. "Yes, we've observed there was doughnuts all the way along; if one house is frying all the rest is; 't is so with a great many things."

"I don't suppose likely you're goin' up to

the Bowden reunion?" asked the hostess as the white horse lifted his head and we were saying good-by.

"Why, yes," said Mrs. Blackett and Mrs. Todd and I, all together.

"I am connected with the family. Yes, I expect to be there this afternoon. I 've been lookin' forward to it," she told us eagerly.

"We shall see you there. Come and sit with us if it 's convenient," said dear Mrs. Blackett, and we drove away.

"I wonder who she was before she was married?" said Mrs. Todd, who was usually unerring in matters of genealogy. "She must have been one of that remote branch that lived down beyond Thomaston. We can find out this afternoon. I expect that the families 'll march together, or be sorted out some way. I 'm willing to own a relation that has such proper ideas of doughnuts."

"I seem to see the family looks," said Mrs. Blackett. "I wish we 'd asked her name. She 's a stranger, and I want to help make it pleasant for all such."

"She resembles Cousin Pa'lina Bowden about the forehead," said Mrs. Todd with decision.

We had just passed a piece of woodland that shaded the road, and come out to some open fields beyond, when Mrs. Todd suddenly reined in the horse as if somebody had stood on the roadside and stopped her. She even gave that quick reassuring nod of her head which was usually made to answer for a bow, but I discovered that she was looking eagerly at a tall ash-tree that grew just inside the field fence.

" I thought 't was goin' to do well," she said complacently as we went on again. " Last time I was up this way that tree was kind of drooping and discouraged. Grown trees act that way sometimes, same 's folks; then they 'll put right to it and strike their roots off into new ground and start all over again with real good courage. Ash-trees is very likely to have poor spells; they ain't got the resolution of other trees."

I listened hopefully for more; it was this peculiar wisdom that made one value Mrs. Todd's pleasant company.

" There 's sometimes a good hearty tree growin' right out of the bare rock, out o' some crack that just holds the roots;" she went on to say, " right on the pitch o' one o' them bare stony hills where you can't seem to see a wheel-barrowful o' good earth in a place, but that tree 'll keep a green top in the driest summer. You lay your ear down to the ground an' you 'll hear a little stream runnin'. Every such tree has got its own livin' spring; there 's folks made to match 'em."

I could not help turning to look at Mrs. Blackett, close beside me. Her hands were clasped placidly in their thin black woolen gloves, and she was looking at the flowery wayside as we went slowly along, with a pleased, expectant smile. I do not think she had heard a word about the trees.

" I just saw a nice plant o' elecampane growin' back there," she said presently to her daughter.

"I have n't got my mind on herbs to-day," responded Mrs. Todd, in the most matter-of-fact way. " I 'm bent on seeing folks," and she shook the reins again.

I for one had no wish to hurry, it was so pleasant in the shady roads. The woods stood close to the road on the right; on the left were narrow fields and pastures where there were as many acres of spruces and pines as there were acres of bay and juniper and huckleberry, with a little turf between.

When I thought we were in the heart of
the inland country, we reached the top of
a hill, and suddenly there lay spread out
before us a wonderful great view of well-
cleared fields that swept down to the wide
water of a bay.   Beyond this were distant
shores like another country in the midday
haze which half hid the hills beyond, and the
far-away pale blue mountains on the northern horizon.   There was a schooner with
all sails set coming down the bay from a
white village that was sprinkled on the shore,
and there were many sailboats flitting about.
It was a noble landscape, and my eyes,
which had grown used to the narrow inspection of a shaded roadside, could hardly take
it in.

"Why, it's the upper bay," said Mrs.
Todd.   "You can see 'way over into the
town of Fessenden.   Those farms 'way over
there are all in Fessenden.   Mother used to
have a sister that lived up that shore.   If
we started as early's we could on a summer
mornin', we could n't get to her place from
Green Island till late afternoon, even with
a fair, steady breeze, and you had to strike
the time just right so as to fetch up 'long o'
the tide and land near the flood.   'T was

ticklish business, an' we did n't visit back an' forth as much as mother desired. You have to go 'way down the co'st to Cold Spring Light an' round that long point, — up here 's what they call the Back Shore."

" No, we were 'most always separated, my dear sister and me, after the first year she was married," said Mrs. Blackett. " We had our little families an' plenty o' cares. We were always lookin' forward to the time we could see each other more. Now and then she 'd get out to the island for a few days while her husband 'd go fishin' ; and once he stopped with her an' two children, and made him some flakes right there and cured all his fish for winter. We did have a beautiful time together, sister an' me ; she used to look back to it long 's she lived."

" I do love to look over there where she used to live," Mrs. Blackett went on as we began to go down the hill. " It seems as if she must still be there, though she 's long been gone. She loved their farm, — she did n't see how I got so used to our island ; but somehow I was always happy from the first."

" Yes, it 's very dull to me up among those slow farms," declared Mrs. Todd.

" The snow troubles 'em in winter. They 're all besieged by winter, as you may say; 't is far better by the shore than up among such places. I never thought I should like to live up country."

" Why, just see the carriages ahead of us on the next rise! " exclaimed Mrs. Blackett. "There 's going to be a great gathering, don't you believe there is, Almiry? It has n't seemed up to now as if anybody was going but us. An' 't is such a beautiful day, with yesterday cool and pleasant to work an' get ready, I should n't wonder if everybody was there, even the slow ones like Phebe Ann Brock."

Mrs. Blackett's eyes were bright with excitement, and even Mrs. Todd showed remarkable enthusiasm. She hurried the horse and caught up with the holiday-makers ahead. " There 's all the Dep'fords goin', six in the wagon," she told us joyfully; " an' Mis' Alva Tilley's folks are now risin' the hill in their new carryall."

Mrs. Blackett pulled at the neat bow of her black bonnet - strings, and tied them again with careful precision. " I believe your bonnet 's on a little bit sideways, dear," she advised Mrs. Todd as if she were a

child; but Mrs. Todd was too much occupied to pay proper heed.   We began to feel
a new sense of gayety and of taking part
in the great occasion as we joined the little
train.

XVIII.

THE BOWDEN REUNION.

It is very rare in country life, where high days and holidays are few, that any occasion of general interest proves to be less than great. Such is the hidden fire of enthusiasm in the New England nature that, once given an outlet, it shines forth with almost volcanic light and heat. In quiet neighborhoods such inward force does not waste itself upon those petty excitements of every day that belong to cities, but when, at long intervals, the altars to patriotism, to friendship, to the ties of kindred, are reared in our familiar fields, then the fires glow, the flames come up as if from the inexhaustible burning heart of the earth; the primal fires break through the granite dust in which our souls are set. Each heart is warm and every face shines with the ancient light. Such a day as this has transfiguring powers, and easily makes friends of those who have been cold-hearted, and gives to those who are

dumb their chance to speak, and lends some
beauty to the plainest face.

"Oh, I expect I shall meet friends to-
day that I have n't seen in a long while,"
said Mrs. Blackett with deep satisfaction.
"'T will bring out a good many of the old
folks, 't is such a lovely day. I 'm always
glad not to have them disappointed."

"I guess likely the best of 'em 'll be
there," answered Mrs. Todd with gentle
humor, stealing a glance at me. "There 's
one thing certain : there 's nothing takes in
this whole neighborhood like anything re-
lated to the Bowdens. Yes, I do feel that
when you call upon the Bowdens you may
expect most families to rise up between the
Landing and the far end of the Back Cove.
Those that are n't kin by blood are kin by
marriage."

"There used to be an old story goin'
about when I was a girl," said Mrs. Blackett,
with much amusement. "There was a great
many more Bowdens then than there are
now, and the folks was all setting in meeting
a dreadful hot Sunday afternoon, and a scat-
ter-witted little bound girl came running to
the meetin'-house door all out o' breath from
somewheres in the neighborhood. ' Mis'

Bowden, Mis' Bowden!' says she. 'Your baby 's in a fit!' They used to tell that the whole congregation was up on its feet in a minute and right out into the aisles. All the Mis' Bowdens was setting right out for home; the minister stood there in the pulpit trying' to keep sober, an' all at once he burst right out laughin'. He was a very nice man, they said, and he said he 'd better give 'em the benediction, and they could hear the sermon next Sunday, so he kept it over. My mother was there, and she thought certain 't was me."

"None of our family was ever subject to fits," interrupted Mrs. Todd severely. " No, we never had fits, none of us, and 't was lucky we did n't 'way out there to Green Island. Now these folks right in front: dear sakes knows the bunches o' soothing catnip an' yarrow I 've had to favor old Mis' Evins with dryin'! You can see it right in their expressions, all them Evins folks. There, just you look up to the cross-roads, mother," she suddenly exclaimed. " See all the teams ahead of us. And oh, look down on the bay; yes, look down on the bay! See what a sight o' boats, all headin' for the Bowden place cove!"

" Oh, ain't it beautiful ! " said Mrs. Black-ett, with all the delight of a girl. She stood up in the high wagon to see everything, and when she sat down again she took fast hold of my hand.

" Had n't you better urge the horse a little, Almiry ? " she asked. " He 's had it easy as we came along, and he can rest when we get there. The others are some little ways ahead, and I don't want to lose a minute."

We watched the boats drop their sails one by one in the cove as we drove along the high land. The old Bowden house stood, low-storied and broad-roofed, in its green fields as if it were a motherly brown hen waiting for the flock that came straying toward it from every direction. The first Bowden settler had made his home there, and it was still the Bowden farm ; five gen-erations of sailors and farmers and soldiers had been its children. And presently Mrs. Blackett showed me the stone-walled bury-ing-ground that stood like a little fort on a knoll overlooking the bay, but, as she said, there were plenty of scattered Bowdens who were not laid there, — some lost at sea, and some out West, and some who died in the war ; most of the home graves were those of women.

We could see now that there were different footpaths from along shore and across
country.   In all these there were straggling
processions walking in single file, like old
illustrations of the Pilgrim's Progress.   There
was a crowd about the house as if huge bees
were swarming in the lilac bushes.   Beyond
the fields and cove a higher point of land
ran out into the bay, covered with woods
which must have kept away much of the
northwest wind in winter.   Now there was a
pleasant look of shade and shelter there for
the great family meeting.

We hurried on our way, beginning to feel
as if we were very late, and it was a great
satisfaction at last to turn out of the stony
highroad into a green lane shaded with old
apple - trees.   Mrs. Todd encouraged the
horse until he fairly pranced with gayety
as we drove round to the front of the house
on the soft turf.   There was an instant cry
of rejoicing, and two or three persons ran
toward us from the busy group.

" Why, dear Mis' Blackett! — here 's Mis'
Blackett! " I heard them say, as if it were
pleasure enough for one day to have a sight
of her.   Mrs. Todd turned to me with a
lovely look of triumph and self-forgetfulness.

An elderly man who wore the look of a prosperous sea-captain put up both arms and lifted Mrs. Blackett down from the high wagon like a child, and kissed her with hearty affection. " I was master afraid she would n't be here," he said, looking at Mrs. Todd with a face like a happy sunburnt schoolboy, while everybody crowded round to give their welcome.

"Mother 's always the queen," said Mrs. Todd. "Yes, they 'll all make everything of mother; she 'll have a lovely time to-day. I would n't have had her miss it, and there won't be a thing she 'll ever regret, except to mourn because William wa'n't here."

Mrs. Blackett having been properly escorted to the house, Mrs. Todd received her own full share of honor, and some of the men, with a simple kindness that was the soul of chivalry, waited upon us and our baskets and led away the white horse. I already knew some of Mrs. Todd's friends and kindred, and felt like an adopted Bowden in this happy moment. It seemed to be enough for any one to have arrived by the same conveyance as Mrs. Blackett, who presently had her court inside the house, while Mrs. Todd, large, hospitable, and preeminent, was the centre of a rapidly increasing crowd about the lilac bushes. Small companies were continually coming up the long green slope from the water, and nearly all the boats had come to shore. I counted three or four that were baffled by the light breeze, but before long all the Bowdens, small and great, seemed to have assembled, and we started to go up to the grove across the field.

Out of the chattering crowd of noisy children, and large-waisted women whose best black dresses fell straight to the ground in generous folds, and sunburnt men who looked as serious as if it were town-meeting day, there suddenly came silence and order. I saw the straight, soldierly little figure of a man who bore a fine resemblance to Mrs. Blackett, and who appeared to marshal us with perfect ease. He was imperative enough, but with a grand military sort of courtesy, and bore himself with solemn dignity of importance. We were sorted out according to some clear design of his own, and stood as speechless as a troop to await his orders. Even the children were ready to march together, a pretty flock, and at the last moment Mrs. Blackett and a few distinguished companions, the ministers and those who were very old, came out of the house together and took their places. We ranked by fours, and even then we made a long procession.

There was a wide path mowed for us across the field, and, as we moved along, the birds flew up out of the thick second crop of clover, and the bees hummed as if it still were June. There was a flashing of white gulls over the water where the fleet of boats rode the low waves together in the cove, swaying their small masts as if they kept time to our steps. The plash of the water could be heard faintly, yet still be heard; we might have been a company of ancient Greeks going to celebrate a victory, or to worship the god of harvests in the grove above. It was strangely moving to see this and to make part of it. The sky, the sea, have watched poor humanity at its rites so long; we were no more a New England family celebrating its own existence and simple progress; we carried the tokens and inheritance of all such households from which this had descended, and were only the latest of our line. We possessed the instincts of a far, forgotten childhood; I found myself thinking that we ought to be carrying green branches and singing as we went. So we came to the thick shaded grove still silent, and were set in our places by the straight trees that swayed together and let sunshine through here and there like a single golden leaf that flickered down, vanishing in the cool shade.

The grove was so large that the great family looked far smaller than it had in the open field; there was a thick growth of dark pines and firs with an occasional maple or oak that gave a gleam of color like a bright window in the great roof. On three sides we could see the water, shining behind the tree-trunks, and feel the cool salt breeze that began to come up with the tide just as the day reached its highest point of heat. We could see the green sunlit field we had just crossed as if we looked out at it from a dark room, and the old house and its lilacs standing placidly in the sun, and the great barn with a stockade of carriages from which two or three care-taking men who had lingered were coming across the field together. Mrs. Todd had taken off her warm gloves and looked the picture of content.

"There!" she exclaimed. "I 've always meant to have you see this place, but I never

looked for such a beautiful opportunity —
weather an' occasion both made to match.
Yes, it suits me: I don't ask no more. I
want to know if you saw mother walkin' at
the head! It choked me right up to see
mother at the head, walkin' with the ministers," and Mrs. Todd turned away to hide
the feelings she could not instantly control.

"Who was the marshal?" I hastened to
ask. "Was he an old soldier?"

"Don't he do well?" answered Mrs. Todd
with satisfaction.

"He don't often have such a chance to
show off his gifts," said Mrs. Caplin, a
friend from the Landing who had joined us.
"That 's Sant Bowden; he always takes the
lead, such days.   Good for nothing else most
o' his time; trouble is, he " —

I turned with interest to hear the worst.
Mrs. Caplin's tone was both zealous and impressive.

"Stim'lates," she explained scornfully.

"No, Santin never was in the war," said
Mrs. Todd with lofty indifference. "It was
a cause of real distress to him. He kep' en-
listin', and traveled far an' wide about here,
an' even took the bo't and went to Boston
to volunteer; but he ain't a sound man, an'

they would n't have him. They say he knows all their tactics, an' can tell all about the battle o' Waterloo well 's he can Bunker Hill. I told him once the country 'd lost a great general, an' I meant it, too."

"I expect you 're near right," said Mrs. Caplin, a little crestfallen and apologetic.

"I be right," insisted Mrs. Todd with much amiability. " 'T was most too bad to cramp him down to his peaceful trade, but he 's a most excellent shoemaker at his best, an' he always says it 's a trade that gives him time to think an' plan his manœuvres. Over to the Port they always invite him to march Decoration Day, same as the rest, an' he does look noble; he comes of soldier stock."

I had been noticing with great interest the curiously French type of face which prevailed in this rustic company. I had said to myself before that Mrs. Blackett was plainly of French descent, in both her appearance and her charming gifts, but this is not surprising when one has learned how large a proportion of the early settlers on this northern coast of New England were of Huguenot blood, and that it is the Norman Englishman, not the Saxon, who goes adventuring to a new world.

"They used to say in old times," said Mrs. Todd modestly, " that our family came of very high folks in France, and one of 'em was a great general in some o' the old wars. I sometimes think that Santin's ability has come 'way down from then. 'T ain't nothin' he 's ever acquired ; 't was born in him. I don't know 's he ever saw a fine parade, or met with those that studied up such things. He 's figured it all out an' got his papers so he knows how to aim a cannon right for William's fish-house five miles out on Green Island, or up there on Burnt Island where the signal is. He had it all over to me one day, an' I tried hard to appear interested. His life 's all in it, but he will have those poor gloomy spells come over him now an' then, an' then he has to drink."

Mrs. Caplin gave a heavy sigh.

"There 's a great many such strayaway folks, just as there is plants," continued Mrs. Todd, who was nothing if not botanical. " I know of just one sprig of laurel that grows over back here in a wild spot, an' I never could hear of no other on this coast. I had a large bunch brought me once from Massachusetts way, so I know it. This piece grows in an open spot where you 'd think 't would

do well, but it 's sort o' poor-lookin'. I 've
visited it time an' again, just to notice its
poor blooms. 'T is a real Sant Bowden, out
of its own place."

Mrs. Caplin looked bewildered and
blank. " Well, all I know is, last year he
worked out some kind of a plan so 's to
parade the county conference in platoons,
and got 'em all flustered up tryin' to sense
his ideas of a holler square," she burst forth,
" They was holler enough anyway after
ridin' 'way down from up country into the
salt air, and they 'd been treated to a sermon
on faith an' works from old Fayther Harlow
that never knows when to cease. 'T wa'n't
no time for tactics then, — they wa'n't
a-thinkin' of the church military. Sant, he
could n't do nothin' with 'em. All he thinks
of, when he sees a crowd, is how to march
'em. 'T is all very well when he don't
'tempt too much. He never did act like
other folks."

" Ain't I just been maintainin' that he
ain't like 'em ? " urged Mrs. Todd decidedly.
" Strange folks has got to have strange ways,
for what I see."

" Somebody observed once that you could
pick out the likeness of 'most every sort of

a foreigner when you looked about you in our parish," said Sister Caplin, her face brightening with sudden illumination. " I did n't see the bearin' of it then quite so plain. I always did think Mari' Harris resembled a Chinee."

"Mari' Harris was pretty as a child, I remember," said the pleasant voice of Mrs. Blackett, who, after receiving the affectionate greetings of nearly the whole company, came to join us, — to see, as she insisted, that we were out of mischief.

" Yes, Mari' was one o' them pretty little lambs that make dreadful homely old sheep," replied Mrs. Todd with energy. " Cap'n Littlepage never 'd look so disconsolate if she was any sort of a proper person to direct things. She might divert him; yes, she might divert the old gentleman, an' let him think he had his own way, 'stead o' arguing everything down to the bare bone. 'T would n't hurt her to sit down an' hear his great stories once in a while."

" The stories are very interesting," I ventured to say.

" Yes, you always catch yourself a-thinkin' what if they was all true, and he had the right of it," answered Mrs. Todd. " He 's a good sight better company, though dreamy, than such sordid creatur's as Mari' Harris."

"Live and let live," said dear old Mrs. Blackett gently. "I have n't seen the captain for a good while, now that I ain't so constant to meetin'," she added wistfully. "We always have known each other."

"Why, if it is a good pleasant day to-morrow, I 'll get William to call an' invite the capt'in to dinner. William 'll be in early so 's to pass up the street without meetin' anybody."

"There, they 're callin' out it 's time to set the tables;" said Mrs. Caplin, with great excitement.

"Here 's Cousin Sarah Jane Blackett! Well, I am pleased, certain!" exclaimed Mrs. Todd, with unaffected delight; and these kindred spirits met and parted with the promise of a good talk later on. After this there was no more time for conversation until we were seated in order at the long tables.

"I 'm one that always dreads seeing some o' the folks that I don't like, at such a time as this," announced Mrs. Todd privately to me after a season of reflection. We were

just waiting for the feast to begin. "You
would n't think such a great creatur' 's I
be could feel all over pins an' needles. I
remember, the day I promised to Nathan,
how it come over me, just 's I was feelin'
happy 's I could, that I 'd got to have an
own cousin o' his for my near relation all
the rest o' my life, an' it seemed as if die I
should. Poor Nathan saw somethin' had
crossed me, — he had very nice feelings, —
and when he asked me what 't was, I told
him. 'I never could like her myself,' said
he. 'You sha'n't be bothered, dear,' he
says ; an' 't was one o' the things that made
me set a good deal by Nathan, he did n't
make a habit of always opposin', like some
men. 'Yes,' says I, 'but think o' Thanksgivin' times an' funerals ; she 's our relation,
an' we 've got to own her.' Young folks
don't think o' those things. There she goes
now, do let 's pray her by!" said Mrs. Todd,
with an alarming transition from general
opinions to particular animosities. "I hate
her just the same as I always did; but
she 's got on a real pretty dress. I do try
to remember that she 's Nathan's cousin.
Oh dear, well; she 's gone by after all, an'
ain't seen me. I expected she 'd come

pleasantin' round just to show off an' say
afterwards she was acquainted."

This was so different from Mrs. Todd's
usual largeness of mind that I had a moment's uneasiness; but the cloud passed
quickly over her spirit, and was gone with
the offender.

There never was a more generous out-of-
door feast along the coast than the Bowden
family set forth that day. To call it a pic-
nic would make it seem trivial. The great
tables were edged with pretty oak-leaf trim-
ming, which the boys and girls made. We
brought flowers from the fence-thickets of
the great field; and out of the disorder of
flowers and provisions suddenly appeared
as orderly a scheme for the feast as the marshal had shaped for the procession. I began
to respect the Bowdens for their inheritance
of good taste and skill and a certain pleasing
gift of formality. Something made them do
all these things in a finer way than most
country people would have done them. As
I looked up and down the tables there was
a good cheer, a grave soberness that shone
with pleasure, a humble dignity of bearing.
There were some who should have sat below

the salt for lack of this good breeding; but they were not many. So, I said to myself, their ancestors may have sat in the great hall of some old French house in the Middle Ages, when battles and sieges and processions and feasts were familiar things. The ministers and Mrs. Blackett, with a few of their rank and age, were put in places of honor, and for once that I looked any other way I looked twice at Mrs. Blackett's face, serene and mindful of privilege and responsibility, the mistress by simple fitness of this great day.

Mrs. Todd looked up at the roof of green trees, and then carefully surveyed the company. "I see 'em better now they're all settin' down," she said with satisfaction. "There's old Mr. Gilbraith and his sister. I wish they were settin' with us; they're not among folks they can parley with, an' they look disappointed."

As the feast went on, the spirits of my companion steadily rose. The excitement of an unexpectedly great occasion was a subtle stimulant to her disposition, and I could see that sometimes when Mrs. Todd had seemed limited and heavily domestic, she had simply grown sluggish for lack of proper surroundings. She was not so much reminiscent now as expectant, and as alert and gay as a girl. We who were her neighbors were full of gayety, which was but the reflected light from her beaming countenance. It was not the first time that I was full of wonder at the waste of human ability in this world, as a botanist wonders at the wastefulness of nature, the thousand seeds that die, the unused provision of every sort. The reserve force of society grows more and more amazing to one's thought. More than one face among the Bowdens showed that only opportunity and stimulus were lacking, — a narrow set of circumstances had caged a fine able character and held it captive. One sees exactly the same types in a country gathering as in the most brilliant city company. You are safe to be understood if the spirit of your speech is the same for one neighbor as for the other.

XIX.

THE FEAST'S END.

THE feast was a noble feast, as has already been said. There was an elegant ingenuity displayed in the form of pies which delighted my heart. Once acknowledge that an American pie is far to be preferred to its humble ancestor, the English tart, and it is joyful to be reassured at a Bowden reunion that invention has not yet failed. Beside a delightful variety of material, the decorations went beyond all my former experience; dates and names were wrought in lines of pastry and frosting on the tops. There was even more elaborate reading matter on an excellent early-apple pie which we began to share and eat, precept upon precept. Mrs. Todd helped me generously to the whole word *Bowden*, and consumed *Reunion* herself, save an undecipherable fragment; but the most renowned essay in cookery on the tables was a model of the old Bowden house made of durable gingerbread, with all the windows and doors in the right places, and sprigs of genuine lilac set at the front. It must have been baked in sections, in one of the last of the great brick ovens, and fastened together on the morning of the day. There was a general sigh when this fell into ruin at the feast's end, and it was shared by a great part of the assembly, not without seriousness, and as if it were a pledge and token of loyalty. I met the maker of the gingerbread house, which had called up lively remembrances of a childish story. She had the gleaming eye of an enthusiast and a look of high ideals.

"I could just as well have made it all of frosted cake," she said, "but 't would n't have been the right shade; the old house, as you observe, was never painted, and I concluded that plain gingerbread would represent it best. It was n't all I expected it would be," she said sadly, as many an artist had said before her of his work.

There were speeches by the ministers; and there proved to be a historian among the Bowdens, who gave some fine anecdotes of the family history; and then appeared a poetess, whom Mrs. Todd regarded with wistful compassion and indulgence, and when the long faded garland of verses came to an appealing end, she turned to me with words of praise.

"Sounded pretty," said the generous listener. "Yes, I thought she did very well. We went to school together, an' Mary Anna had a very hard time; trouble was, her mother thought she 'd given birth to a genius, an' Mary Anna 's come to believe it herself. There, I don't know what we should have done without her; there ain't nobody else that can write poetry between here and 'way up towards Rockland; it adds a great deal at such a time. When she speaks o' those that are gone, she feels it all, and so does everybody else, but she harps too much. I 'd laid half of that away for next time, if I was Mary Anna. There comes mother to speak to her, an' old Mr. Gilbraith's sister; now she 'll be heartened right up. Mother 'll say just the right thing."

The leave - takings were as affecting as the meetings of these old friends had been. There were enough young persons at the reunion, but it is the old who really value such opportunities; as for the young, it is the habit of every day to meet their comrades,

— the time of separation has not come. To see the joy with which these elder kinsfolk and acquaintances had looked in one another's faces, and the lingering touch of their friendly hands; to see these affectionate meetings and then the reluctant partings, gave one a new idea of the isolation in which it was possible to live in that after all thinly settled region. They did not expect to see one another again very soon; the steady, hard work on the farms, the difficulty of getting from place to place, especially in winter when boats were laid up, gave double value to any occasion which could bring a large number of families together. Even funerals in this country of the pointed firs were not without their social advantages and satisfactions. I heard the words "next summer" repeated many times, though summer was still ours and all the leaves were green.

The boats began to put out from shore, and the wagons to drive away. Mrs. Blackett took me into the old house when we came back from the grove: it was her father's birthplace and early home, and she had spent much of her own childhood there with her grandmother. She spoke of those days as if they had but lately passed; in fact, I could imagine that the house looked almost exactly the same to her. I could see the brown rafters of the unfinished roof as I looked up the steep staircase, though the best room was as handsome with its good wainscoting and touch of ornament on the cornice as any old room of its day in a town.

Some of the guests who came from a distance were still sitting in the best room when we went in to take leave of the master and mistress of the house. We all said eagerly what a pleasant day it had been, and how swiftly the time had passed. Perhaps it is the great national anniversaries which our country has lately kept, and the soldiers' meetings that take place everywhere, which have made reunions of every sort the fashion. This one, at least, had been very interesting. I fancied that old feuds had been overlooked, and the old saying that blood is thicker than water had again proved itself true, though from the variety of names one argued a certain adulteration of the Bowden traits and belongings. Clannishness is an instinct of the heart, — it is more than a birthright, or a custom; and lesser rights were forgotten in the claim to a common inheritance.

We were among the very last to return

to our proper lives and lodgings. I came near to feeling like a true Bowden, and parted from certain new friends as if they were old friends; we were rich with the treasure of a new remembrance.

At last we were in the high wagon again; the old white horse had been well fed in the Bowden barn, and we drove away and soon began to climb the long hill toward the wooded ridge. The road was new to me, as roads always are, going back. Most of our companions had been full of anxious thoughts of home, — of the cows, or of young children likely to fall into disaster, — but we had no reasons for haste, and drove slowly along, talking and resting by the way. Mrs. Todd said once that she really hoped her front door had been shut on account of the dust blowing in, but added that nothing made any weight on her mind except not to forget to turn a few late mullein leaves that were drying on a newspaper in the little loft. Mrs. Blackett and I gave our word of honor that we would remind her of this heavy responsibility. The way seemed short, we had so much to talk about. We climbed hills where we could see the great bay and the islands, and then went down into shady valleys where the air began to feel like evening, cool and damp with a fragrance of wet ferns. Mrs. Todd alighted once or twice, refusing all assistance in securing some boughs of a rare shrub which she valued for its bark, though she proved incommunicative as to her reasons. We passed the house where we had been so kindly entertained with doughnuts earlier in the day, and found it closed and deserted, which was a disappointment.

" They must have stopped to tea somewheres and thought they 'd finish up the day," said Mrs. Todd. " Those that enjoyed it best 'll want to get right home so 's to think it over."

" I did n't see the woman there after all, did you? " asked Mrs. Blackett as the horse stopped to drink at the trough.

" Oh yes, I spoke with her," answered Mrs. Todd, with but scant interest or approval. " She ain't a member o' our family."

" I thought you said she resembled Cousin Pa'lina Bowden about the forehead," suggested Mrs. Blackett.

" Well, she don't," answered Mrs. Todd impatiently. " I ain't one that 's ord'narily mistaken about family likenesses, and she did n't seem to meet with friends, so I went square up to her. 'I expect you 're a Bowden by your looks,' says I. 'Yes, I take it you 're one o' the Bowdens.' 'Lor', no,' says she. 'Dennett was my maiden name, but I married a Bowden for my first husband. I thought I 'd come an' just see what was a-goin' on'!'"

Mrs. Blackett laughed heartily. "I 'm goin' to remember to tell William o' that," she said. "There, Almiry, the only thing that 's troubled me all this day is to think how William would have enjoyed it. I do so wish William had been there."

"I sort of wish he had, myself," said Mrs. Todd frankly.

"There wa'n't many old folks there, some-how," said Mrs. Blackett, with a touch of sadness in her voice. "There ain't so many to come as there used to be, I 'm aware, but I expected to see more."

"I thought they turned out pretty well, when you come to think of it; why, every-body was sayin' so an' feelin' gratified," answered Mrs. Todd hastily with pleasing unconsciousness; then I saw the quick color flash into her cheek, and presently she made some excuse to turn and steal an anxious look at her mother. Mrs. Blackett was smiling and thinking about her happy day, though she began to look a little tired. Neither of my companions was troubled by her burden of years. I hoped in my heart that I might be like them as I lived on into age, and then smiled to think that I too was no longer very young. So we always keep the same hearts, though our outer framework fails and shows the touch of time.

" 'T was pretty when they sang the hymn, was n't it?" asked Mrs. Blackett at supper-time, with real enthusiasm. "There was such a plenty o' men's voices; where I sat it did sound beautiful. I had to stop and listen when they came to the last verse."

I saw that Mrs. Todd's broad shoulders began to shake. "There was good singers there; yes, there was excellent singers," she agreed heartily, putting down her teacup, "but I chanced to drift alongside Mis' Peter Bowden o' Great Bay, an' I could n't help thinkin' if she was as far out o' town as she was out o' tune, she would n't get back in a day."

XX.

ALONG SHORE.

ONE day as I went along the shore beyond the old wharves and the newer, high-stepped fabric of the steamer landing, I saw that all the boats were beached, and the slack water period of the early afternoon prevailed. Nothing was going on, not even the most leisurely of occupations, like baiting trawls or mending nets, or repairing lobster pots; the very boats seemed to be taking an afternoon nap in the sun. I could hardly discover a distant sail as I looked seaward, except a weather-beaten lobster smack, which seemed to have been taken for a plaything by the light airs that blew about the bay. It drifted and turned about so aimlessly in the wide reach off Burnt Island, that I suspected there was nobody at the wheel, or that she might have parted her rusty anchor chain while all the crew were asleep.

I watched her for a minute or two; she was the old Miranda, owned by some of the Caplins, and I knew her by an odd shaped patch of newish duck that was set into the peak of her dingy mainsail. Her vagaries offered such an exciting subject for conversation that my heart rejoiced at the sound of a hoarse voice behind me. At that moment, before I had time to answer, I saw something large and shapeless flung from the Miranda's deck that splashed the water high against her black side, and my companion gave a satisfied chuckle. The old lobster smack's sail caught the breeze again at this moment, and she moved off down the bay. Turning, I found old Elijah Tilley, who had come softly out of his dark fish house, as if it were a burrow.

"Boy got kind o' drowsy steerin' of her; Monroe he hove him right overboard; 'wake now fast enough," explained Mr. Tilley, and we laughed together.

I was delighted, for my part, that the vicissitudes and dangers of the Miranda, in a rocky channel, should have given me this opportunity to make acquaintance with an old fisherman to whom I had never spoken. At first he had seemed to be one of those

evasive and uncomfortable persons who are
so suspicious of you that they make you
almost suspicious of yourself. Mr. Elijah
Tilley appeared to regard a stranger with
scornful indifference. You might see him
standing on the pebble beach or in a fish-
house doorway, but when you came nearer
he was gone. He was one of the small company of elderly, gaunt-shaped great fishermen whom I used to like to see leading up
a deep-laden boat by the head, as if it were
a horse, from the water's edge to the steep
slope of the pebble beach. There were four
of these large old men at the Landing, who
were the survivors of an earlier and more
vigorous generation. There was an alliance
and understanding between them, so close
that it was apparently speechless. They
gave much time to watching one another's
boats go out or come in; they lent a ready
hand at tending one another's lobster traps
in rough weather; they helped to clean the
fish, or to sliver porgies for the trawls, as if
they were in close partnership; and when a
boat came in from deep-sea fishing they were
never far out of the way, and hastened to
help carry it ashore, two by two, splashing
alongside, or holding its steady head, as if

it were a willful sea colt. As a matter of
fact no boat could help being steady and
way-wise under their instant direction and
companionship. Abel's boat and Jonathan
Bowden's boat were as distinct and experienced personalities as the men themselves,
and as inexpressive. Arguments and opinions
were unknown to the conversation of these
ancient friends; you would as soon have
expected to hear small talk in a company of
elephants as to hear old Mr. Bowden or Elijah Tilley and their two mates waste breath
upon any form of trivial gossip. They made
brief statements to one another from time
to time. As you came to know them you
wondered more and more that they should
talk at all. Speech seemed to be a light
and elegant accomplishment, and their unexpected acquaintance with its arts made them
of new value to the listener. You felt
almost as if a landmark pine should suddenly address you in regard to the weather,
or a lofty-minded old camel make a remark
as you stood respectfully near him under the
circus tent.

I often wondered a great deal about the
inner life and thought of these self-contained
old fishermen; their minds seemed to be

fixed upon nature and the elements rather
than upon any contrivances of man, like
politics or theology. My friend, Captain
Bowden, who was the nephew of the eldest
of this group, regarded them with deference ;
but he did not belong to their secret companionship, though he was neither young nor
talkative.

"They 've gone together ever since they
were boys, they know most everything about
the sea amon'st them," he told me once.
"They was always just as you see 'em now
since the memory of man."

These ancient seafarers had houses and
lands not outwardly different from other
Dunnet Landing dwellings, and two of them
were fathers of families, but their true
dwelling places were the sea, and the stony
beach that edged its familiar shore, and the
fishhouses, where much salt brine from the
mackerel kits had soaked the very timbers
into a state of brown permanence and petri-
faction. It had also affected the old fishermen's hard complexions, until one fancied
that when Death claimed them it could only
be with the aid, not of any slender modern
dart, but the good serviceable harpoon of a
seventeenth century woodcut.

Elijah Tilley was such an evasive, discouraged-looking person, heavy-headed, and stooping so that one could never look him in the face, that even after his friendly exclamation about Monroe Pennell, the lobster smack's skipper, and the sleepy boy, I did not venture at once to speak again. Mr. Tilley was carrying a small haddock in one hand, and presently shifted it to the other hand lest it might touch my skirt. I knew that my company was accepted, and we walked together a little way.

"You mean to have a good supper," I ventured to say, by way of friendliness.

"Goin' to have this 'ere haddock an' some o' my good baked potatoes; must eat to live," responded my companion with great pleasantness and open approval. I found that I had suddenly left the forbidding coast and come into a smooth little harbor of friendship.

"You ain't never been up to my place," said the old man. "Folks don't come now as they used to; no, 't ain't no use to ask folks now. My poor dear she was a great hand to draw young company."

I remembered that Mrs. Todd had once said that this old fisherman had been sore stricken and unconsoled at the death of his wife.

"I should like very much to come," said I. "Perhaps you are going to be at home later on?"

Mr. Tilley agreed, by a sober nod, and went his way bent-shouldered and with a rolling gait. There was a new patch high on the shoulder of his old waistcoat, which corresponded to the renewing of the Miranda's mainsail down the bay, and I wondered if his own fingers, clumsy with much deep-sea fishing, had set it in.

"Was there a good catch to-day?" I asked, stopping a moment. "I did n't happen to be on the shore when the boats came in."

"No; all come in pretty light," answered Mr. Tilley. "Addicks an' Bowden they done the best; Abel an' me we had but a slim fare. We went out 'arly, but not so 'arly as sometimes; looked like a poor mornin'. I got nine haddick, all small, and seven fish; the rest on 'em got more fish than haddick. Well, I don't expect they feel like bitin' every day; we l'arn to humor 'em a little, an' let 'em have their way 'bout it. These plaguey dog-fish kind of worry 'em." Mr. Tilley pronounced the last sentence with much sympathy, as if he looked upon himself as a true friend of all the haddock and codfish that lived on the fishing grounds, and so we parted.

Later in the afternoon I went along the beach again until I came to the foot of Mr. Tilley's land, and found his rough track across the cobble-stones and rocks to the field edge, where there was a heavy piece of old wreck timber, like a ship's bone, full of treenails. From this a little footpath, narrow with one man's treading, led up across the small green field that made Mr. Tilley's whole estate, except a straggling pasture that tilted on edge up the steep hillside beyond the house and road. I could hear the tinkle-tankle of a cow-bell somewhere among the spruces by which the pasture was being walked over and forested from every side; it was likely to be called the wood lot before long, but the field was unmolested. I could not see a bush or a brier anywhere within its walls, and hardly a stray pebble showed itself. This was most surprising in that country of firm ledges, and scattered stones which all the walls that industry could devise had hardly begun to clear away off the land.   In the narrow field I noticed some stout stakes, apparently planted at random in the grass and among the hills of potatoes, but carefully painted yellow and white to match the house, a neat sharp-edged little dwelling, which looked strangely modern for its owner.   I should have much sooner believed that the smart young whole-sale egg merchant of the Landing was its occupant than Mr. Tilley, since a man's house is really but his larger body, and ex-presses in a way his nature and character.

I went up the field, following the smooth little path to the side door.   As for using the front door, that was a matter of great ceremony ; the long grass grew close against the high stone step, and a snowberry bush leaned over it, top-heavy with the weight of a morning-glory vine that had managed to take what the fishermen might call a half hitch about the door-knob.   Elijah Tilley came to the side door to receive me ; he was knitting a blue yarn stocking without look-ing on, and was warmly dressed for the sea-son in a thick blue flannel shirt with white crockery buttons, a faded waistcoat and trousers heavily patched at the knees. These were not his fishing clothes. There was something delightful in the grasp of his hand, warm and clean, as if it never touched anything but the comfortable woolen yarn, instead of cold sea water and slippery fish.

" What are the painted stakes for, down in the field ? " I hastened to ask, and he came out a step or two along the path to see ; and looked at the stakes as if his attention were called to them for the first time.

" Folks laughed at me when I first bought this place an' come here to live," he explained. " They said 't wa'n't no kind of a field privilege at all ; no place to raise anything, all full o' stones. I was aware 't was good land, an' I worked some on it — odd times when I did n't have nothin' else on hand — till I cleared them loose stones all out. You never see a prettier piece than 't is now ; now did ye? Well, as for them painted marks, them 's my buoys. I struck on to some heavy rocks that did n't show none, but a plow 'd be liable to ground on 'em, an' so I ketched holt an' buoyed 'em same 's you see. They don't trouble me no more 'n if they wa'n't there."

" You have n't been to sea for nothing," I said laughing.

"One trade helps another," said Elijah with an amiable smile. "Come right in an' set down. Come in an' rest ye," he exclaimed, and led the way into his comfortable kitchen. The sunshine poured in at the two further windows, and a cat was curled up sound asleep on the table that stood between them. There was a new-looking light oilcloth of a tiled pattern on the floor, and a crockery teapot, large for a household of only one person, stood on the bright stove. I ventured to say that somebody must be a very good housekeeper.

"That's me," acknowledged the old fisherman with frankness. "There ain't nobody here but me. I try to keep things looking right, same's poor dear left 'em. You set down here in this chair, then you can look off an' see the water. None on 'em thought I was goin' to get along alone, no way, but I wa'n't goin' to have my house turned upsi' down an' all changed about; no, not to please nobody. I was the only one knew just how she liked to have things set, poor dear, an' I said I was goin' to make shift, and I have made shift. I 'd rather tough it out alone." And he sighed heavily, as if to sigh were his familiar consolation.

We were both silent for a minute; the old man looked out of the window, as if he had forgotten I was there.

"You must miss her very much?" I said at last.

"I do miss her," he answered, and sighed again. "Folks all kep' repeatin' that time would ease me, but I can't find it does. No, I miss her just the same every day."

"How long is it since she died?" I asked.

"Eight year now, come the first of October. It don't seem near so long. I've got a sister that comes and stops 'long o' me a little spell, spring an' fall, an' odd times if I send after her. I ain't near so good a hand to sew as I be to knit, and she's very quick to set everything to rights. She's a married woman with a family; her son's folks lives at home, an' I can't make no great claim on her time. But it makes me a kind' o good excuse, when I do send, to help her a little; she ain't none too well off. Poor dear always liked her, and we used to contrive our ways together. 'T is full as easy to be alone. I set here an' think it all over, an' think considerable when the weather's bad to go outside. I get so some days it feels as if poor dear might step right back into this kitchen. I keep a watchin' them doors as if she might step in to ary one. Yes, ma'am, I keep a-lookin' off an' droppin' o' my stitches; that's just how it seems. I can't git over losin' of her no way nor no how. Yes, ma'am, that's just how it seems to me."

I did not say anything, and he did not look up.

" I git feelin' so sometimes I have to lay everything by an' go out door. She was a sweet pretty creatur' long's she lived," the old man added mournfully. " There's that little rockin' chair o' her'n, I set an' notice it an' think how strange 't is a creatur' like her should be gone an' that chair be here right in its old place."

" I wish I had known her; Mrs. Todd told me about your wife one day," I said.

" You 'd have liked to come and see her; all the folks did," said poor Elijah. " She'd been so pleased to hear everything and see somebody new that took such an int'rest. She had a kind o' gift to make it pleasant for folks. I guess likely Almiry Todd told you she was a pretty woman, especially in her young days; late years, too, she kep' her looks and come to be so pleasant look-

in'." There, 't ain't so much matter, I shall
be done afore a great while. No; I sha'n't
trouble the fish a great sight more."

The old widower sat with his head bowed
over his knitting, as if he were hastily
shortening the very thread of time. The
minutes went slowly by. He stopped his
work and clasped his hands firmly together.
I saw he had forgotten his guest, and I kept
the afternoon watch with him. At last he
looked up as if but a moment had passed
of his continual loneliness.

"Yes, ma'am, I 'm one that has seen
trouble," he said, and began to knit again.

The visible tribute of his careful house-
keeping, and the clean bright room which
had once enshrined his wife, and now enshrined her memory, was very moving to
me; he had no thought for any one else or
for any other place. I began to see her myself in her home, — a delicate-looking, faded
little woman, who leaned upon his rough
strength and affectionate heart, who was
always watching for his boat out of this very
window, and who always opened the door
and welcomed him when he came home.

"I used to laugh at her, poor dear," said
Elijah, as if he read my thought. "I used to

make light of her timid notions. She used
to be fearful when I was out in bad weather
or baffled about gittin' ashore. She used to
say the time seemed long to her, but I 've
found out all about it now. I used to be
dreadful thoughtless when I was a young
man and the fish was bitin' well. I 'd stay
out late some o' them days, an' I expect
she 'd watch an' watch an' lose heart a-waitin'.
My heart alive! what a supper she 'd git,
an' be right there watchin' from the door,
with somethin' over her head if 't was cold,
waitin' to hear all about it as I come up the
field. Lord, how I think o' all them little
things!"

"This was what she called the best room;
in this way," he said presently, laying his
knitting on the table, and leading the way
across the front entry and unlocking a door,
which he threw open with an air of pride.
The best room seemed to me a much sadder
and more empty place than the kitchen; its
conventionalities lacked the simple perfection of the humbler room and failed on the
side of poor ambition; it was only when
one remembered what patient saving, and
what high respect for society in the abstract
go to such furnishing that the little parlor

was interesting at all. I could imagine the great day of certain purchases, the bewildering shops of the next large town, the aspiring anxious woman, the clumsy sea-tanned man in his best clothes, so eager to be pleased, but at ease only when they were safe back in the sail-boat again, going down the bay with their precious freight, the hoarded money all spent and nothing to think of but tiller and sail. I looked at the unworn carpet, the glass vases on the mantelpiece with their prim bunches of bleached swamp grass and dusty marsh rosemary, and I could read the history of Mrs. Tilley's best room from its very beginning.

"You see for yourself what beautiful rugs she could make; now I'm going to show you her best tea things she thought so much of," said the master of the house, opening the door of a shallow cupboard. "That's real chiny, all of it on those two shelves," he told me proudly. "I bought it all myself, when we was first married, in the port of Bordeaux. There never was one single piece of it broke until — Well, I used to say, long as she lived, there never was a piece broke, but long at the last I noticed she'd look kind o' distressed, an' I thought 't was 'count o' me boastin'. When they asked if they should use it when the folks was here to supper, time o' her funeral, I knew she 'd want to have everything nice, and I said ' certain.' Some o' the women they come runnin' to me an' called me, while they was takin' of the chiny down, an' showed me there was one o' the cups broke an' the pieces wropped in paper and pushed way back here, corner o' the shelf. They did n't want me to go an' think they done it. Poor dear! I had to put right out o' the house when I see that. I knowed in one minute how 't was. We 'd got so used to sayin' 't was all there just 's I fetched it home, an' so when she broke that cup somehow or 'nother she could n't frame no words to come an' tell me. She could n't think 't would vex me, 't was her own hurt pride. I guess there wa'n't no other secret ever lay between us."

The French cups with their gay sprigs of pink and blue, the best tumblers, an old flowered bowl and tea caddy, and a japanned waiter or two adorned the shelves. These, with a few daguerreotypes in a little square pile, had the closet to themselves, and I was conscious of much pleasure in seeing them.

One is shown over many a house in these days where the interest may be more complex, but not more definite.

"Those were her best things, poor dear," said Elijah as he locked the door again. "She told me that last summer before she was taken away that she could n't think o' anything more she wanted, there was everything in the house, an' all her rooms was furnished pretty. I was goin' over to the Port, an' inquired for errands. I used to ask her to say what she wanted, cost or no cost—she was a very reasonable woman, an' 't was the place where she done all but her extra shopping. It kind o' chilled me up when she spoke so satisfied."

"You don't go out fishing after Christmas?" I asked, as we came back to the bright kitchen.

"No; I take stiddy to my knitting after January sets in," said the old seafarer. "'T ain't worth while, fish make off into deeper water an' you can't stand no such perishin' for the sake o' what you get. I leave out a few traps in sheltered coves an' do a little lobsterin' on fair days. The young fellows braves it out, some on 'em; but, for me, I lay in my winter's yarn an' set here where 't is warm, an' knit an' take my comfort. Mother learnt me once when I was a lad; she was a beautiful knitter herself. I was laid up with a bad knee, an' she said 't would take up my time an' help her; we was a large family. They'll buy all the folks can do down here to Addicks' store. They say our Dunnet stockin's is gettin' to be celebrated up to Boston, — good quality o' wool an' even knittin' or somethin'. I've always been called a pretty hand to do nettin', but seines is master cheap to what they used to be when they was all hand worked. I change off to nettin' long towards spring, and I piece up my trawls and lines and get my fishin' stuff to rights. Lobster pots they require attention, but I make 'em up in spring weather when it's warm there in the barn. No; I ain't one o' them that likes to set an' do nothin'."

"You see the rugs, poor dear did them; she wa'n't very partial to knittin'," old Elijah went on, after he had counted his stitches. "Our rugs is beginnin' to show wear, but I can't master none o' them womanish tricks. My sister, she tinkers 'em up. She said last time she was here that she guessed they'd last my time."

"The old ones are always the prettiest," I said.

"You ain't referrin' to the braided ones now?" answered Mr. Tilley. "You see ours is braided for the most part, an' their good looks is all in the beginnin'. Poor dear used to say they made an easier floor. I go shufflin' round the house same 's if 't was a bo't, and I always used to be stubbin' up the corners o' the hooked kind. Her an' me was always havin' our jokes together same 's a boy an' girl. Outsiders never 'd know nothin' about it to see us. She had nice manners with all, but to me there was nobody so entertainin'. She 'd take off anybody's natural talk winter evenin's when we set here alone, so you 'd think 't was them a-speakin'. There, there!"

I saw that he had dropped a stitch again, and was snarling the blue yarn round his clumsy fingers. He handled it and threw it off at arm's length as if it were a cod line; and frowned impatiently, but I saw a tear shining on his cheek.

I said that I must be going, it was growing late, and asked if I might come again, and if he would take me out to the fishing grounds some day.

"Yes, come any time you want to," said my host, "'t ain't so pleasant as when poor dear was here. Oh, I did n't want to lose her an' she did n't want to go, but it had to be. Such things ain't for us to say; there's no yes an' no to it."

"You find Almiry Todd one o' the best o' women?" said Mr. Tilley as we parted. He was standing in the doorway and I had started off down the narrow green field. "No, there ain't a better hearted woman in the State o' Maine. I 've known her from a girl. She 's had the best o' mothers. You tell her I 'm liable to fetch her up a couple or three nice good mackerel early to-morrow," he said. "Now don't let it slip your mind. Poor dear, she always thought a sight o' Almiry, and she used to remind me there was nobody to fish for her; but I don't rec'lect it as I ought to. I see you drop a line yourself very handy now an' then."

We laughed together like the best of friends, and I spoke again about the fishing grounds, and confessed that I had no fancy for a southerly breeze and a ground swell.

"Nor me neither," said the old fisherman. "Nobody likes 'em, say what they may.

Poor dear was disobliged by the mere sight of a bo't. Almiry's got the best o' mothers, I expect you know; Mis' Blackett out to Green Island; and we was always plannin' to go out when summer come; but there, I could n't pick no day's weather that seemed to suit her just right. I never set out to worry her neither, 't wa'n't no kind o' use; she was so pleasant we could n't have no fret nor trouble. 'T was never 'you dear an' you darlin'' afore folks, an' 'you divil' behind the door!"

As I looked back from the lower end of the field I saw him still standing, a lonely figure in the doorway. "Poor dear," I repeated to myself half aloud; "I wonder where she is and what she knows of the little world she left. I wonder what she has been doing these eight years!"

I gave the message about the mackerel to Mrs. Todd.

"Been visitin' with 'Lijah?" she asked with interest. "I expect you had kind of a dull session; he ain't the talkin' kind; dwellin' so much long o' fish seems to make 'em lose the gift o' speech." But when I told her that Mr. Tilley had been talking to me that day, she interrupted me quickly.

"Then 't was all about his wife, an' he can't say nothin' too pleasant neither. She was modest with strangers, but there ain't one o' her old friends can ever make up her loss. For me, I don't want to go there no more. There's some folks you miss and some folks you don't, when they're gone, but there ain't hardly a day I don't think o' dear Sarah Tilley. She was always right there; yes, you knew just where to find her like a plain flower. 'Lijah's worthy enough; I do esteem 'Lijah, but he's a ploddin' man."

XXI.

THE BACKWARD VIEW.

AT last it was the time of late summer, when the house was cool and damp in the morning, and all the light seemed to come through green leaves; but at the first step out of doors the sunshine always laid a warm hand on my shoulder, and the clear, high sky seemed to lift quickly as I looked at it. There was no autumnal mist on the coast, nor any August fog; instead of these, the sea, the sky, all the long shore line and the inland hills, with every bush of bay and every fir-top, gained a deeper color and a sharper clearness. There was something shining in the air, and a kind of lustre on the water and the pasture grass, — a northern look that, except at this moment of the year, one must go far to seek. The sunshine of a northern summer was coming to its lovely end.

The days were few then at Dunnet Land-

ing, and I let each of them slip away un-
willingly as a miser spends his coins. I
wished to have one of my first weeks back
again, with those long hours when nothing
happened except the growth of herbs and
the course of the sun. Once I had not even
known where to go for a walk ; now there
were many delightful things to be done and
done again, as if I were in London. I felt
hurried and full of pleasant engagements,
and the days flew by like a handful of flowers
flung to the sea wind.

At last I had to say good-by to all my
Dunnet Landing friends, and my homelike
place in the little house, and return to the
world in which I feared to find myself a
foreigner. There may be restrictions to such
a summer's happiness, but the ease that belongs to simplicity is charming enough to
make up for whatever a simple life may
lack, and the gifts of peace are not for those
who live in the thick of battle.

I was to take the small unpunctual steamer
that went down the bay in the afternoon, and
I sat for a while by my window looking out
on the green herb garden, with regret for
company. Mrs. Todd had hardly spoken

all day except in the briefest and most disapproving way ; it was as if we were on the
edge of a quarrel. It seemed impossible to
take my departure with anything like composure. At last I heard a footstep, and
looked up to find that Mrs. Todd was standing at the door.

"I 've seen to everything now," she told
me in an unusually loud and business-like
voice. "Your trunks are on the w'arf by
this time. Cap'n Bowden he come and took
'em down himself, an' is going to see that
they 're safe aboard. Yes, I 've seen to all
your 'rangements," she repeated in a gentler
tone. "These things I 've left on the kitchen
table you 'll want to carry by hand ; the
basket need n't be returned. I guess I shall
walk over towards the Port now an' inquire
how old Mis' Edward Caplin is."

I glanced at my friend's face, and saw a
look that touched me to the heart. I had
been sorry enough before to go away.

"I guess you 'll excuse me if I ain't down
there to stand round on the w'arf and see
you go," she said, still trying to be gruff.
"Yes, I ought to go over and inquire for
Mis' Edward Caplin; it 's her third shock,
and if mother gets in on Sunday she 'll want

to know just how the old lady is." With this last word Mrs. Todd turned and left me as if with sudden thought of something she had forgotten, so that I felt sure she was coming back, but presently I heard her go out of the kitchen door and walk down the path toward the gate. I could not part so ; I ran after her to say good-by, but she shook her head and waved her hand without looking back when she heard my hurrying steps, and so went away down the street.

When I went in again the little house had suddenly grown lonely, and my room looked empty as it had the day I came. I and all my belongings had died out of it, and I knew how it would seem when Mrs. Todd came back and found her lodger gone. So we die before our own eyes ; so we see some chapters of our lives come to their natural end.

I found the little packages on the kitchen table. There was a quaint West Indian basket which I knew its owner had valued, and which I had once admired ; there was an affecting provision laid beside it for my seafaring supper, with a neatly tied bunch of southernwood and a twig of bay, and a little old leather box which held the coral pin that Nathan Todd brought home to give to poor Joanna.

There was still an hour to wait, and I went up to the hill just above the school-house and sat there thinking of things, and looking off to sea, and watching for the boat to come in sight. I could see Green Island, small and darkly wooded at that distance; below me were the houses of the village with their apple-trees and bits of garden ground. Presently, as I looked at the pastures beyond, I caught a last glimpse of Mrs. Todd herself, walking slowly in the footpath that led along, following the shore toward the Port. At such a distance one can feel the large, positive qualities that control a character. Close at hand, Mrs. Todd seemed able and warm-hearted and quite absorbed in her bustling industries, but her distant figure looked mateless and appealing, with something about it that was strangely self-possessed and mysterious. Now and then she stooped to pick something, — it might have been her favorite pennyroyal, — and at last I lost sight of her as she slowly crossed an open space on one of the higher points of land, and disappeared again behind a dark clump of juniper and the pointed firs.

As I came away on the little coastwise steamer, there was an old sea running which made the surf leap high on all the rocky shores. I stood on deck, looking back, and watched the busy gulls agree and turn, and sway together down the long slopes of air, then separate hastily and plunge into the waves. The tide was setting in, and plenty of small fish were coming with it, unconscious of the silver flashing of the great birds overhead and the quickness of their fierce beaks. The sea was full of life and spirit, the tops of the waves flew back as if they were winged like the gulls themselves, and like them had the freedom of the wind. Out in the main channel we passed a bent-shouldered old fisherman bound for the evening round among his lobster traps. He was toiling along with short oars, and the dory tossed and sank and tossed again with the steamer's waves. I saw that it was old Elijah Tilley, and though we had so long been strangers we had come to be warm friends, and I wished that he had waited for one of his mates, it was such hard work to row along shore through rough seas and tend the traps alone. As we passed I waved my hand and tried to call to him, and he looked up and answered my farewells by a solemn nod. The little town, with the tall masts of its disabled schooners in the inner bay, stood high above the flat sea for a few minutes, then it sank back into the uniformity of the coast, and became indistinguishable from the other towns that looked as if they were crumbled on the furzy-green stoniness of the shore.

The small outer islands of the bay were covered among the ledges with turf that looked as fresh as the early grass; there had been some days of rain the week before, and the darker green of the sweet-fern was scattered on all the pasture heights. It looked like the beginning of summer ashore, though the sheep, round and warm in their winter wool, betrayed the season of the year as they went feeding along the slopes in the low afternoon sunshine. Presently the wind began to blow, and we struck out seaward to double the long sheltering headland of the cape, and when I looked back again, the islands and the headland had run together and Dunnet Landing and all its coasts were lost to sight.

A DUNNET SHEPHERDESS

I

Early one morning at Dunnet Landing, as if it were still night, I waked, suddenly startled by a spirited conversation beneath my window. It was not one of Mrs. Todd's morning soliloquies; she was not addressing her plants and flowers in words of either praise or blame. Her voice was declamatory though perfectly good-humored, while the second voice, a man's, was of lower pitch and somewhat deprecating.

The sun was just above the sea, and struck straight across my room through a crack in the blind. It was a strange hour for the arrival of a guest, and still too soon for the general run of business, even in that tiny eastern haven where daybreak fisheries and early tides must often rule the day.

The man's voice suddenly declared itself to my sleepy ears. It was Mr. William Blackett's.

"Why, sister Almiry," he protested gently, "I don't need none o' your nostrums!"

"Pick me a small han'ful," she commanded. "No, no, a *small* han'ful, I said,—o' them large pennyr'yal sprigs! I go to all the trouble an' cossetin' of 'em just so as to have you ready to meet such occasions, an' last year, you may remember, you never stopped here at all the day you went up country. An' the frost come at last an' blacked it. I never saw any herb that so objected to gardin ground; might as well try to flourish mayflowers in a common front yard. There, you can come in now, an' set and eat what breakfast you 've got patience for. I 've found everything I want, an' I 'll mash 'em up an' be all ready to put 'em on."

I heard such a pleading note of appeal as the speakers went round the corner of the house, and my curiosity was so demanding, that I dressed in haste, and joined my friends a little later, with two unnoticed excuses of the beauty of the morning, and the early mail boat. William's breakfast had been slighted; he had taken his cup of tea and merely pushed back the rest on the kitchen table. He was now sitting in a helpless condition by the side window, with one of his sister's purple calico aprons pinned close about his neck. Poor William was meekly submitting to being smeared, as to his countenance, with a most pungent and unattractive lotion of pennyroyal and other green herbs which had been hastily pounded and mixed with cream in the little white stone mortar.

I had to cast two or three straightforward looks at William to reassure myself that he really looked happy and expectant in spite of his melancholy circumstances, and was not being overtaken by retribution. The brother and sister seemed to be on delightful terms with each other for once, and there was something of cheerful anticipation in their morning talk. I was reminded of Medea's anointing Jason before the great episode of the iron bulls, but to-day William really could not be going up country to see a railroad for the first time. I knew this to be one of his great schemes, but he was not fitted to appear in public, or to front an observing world of strangers. As I appeared he essayed to rise, but Mrs. Todd pushed him back into the chair.

"Set where you be till it dries on," she insisted. "Land sakes, you 'd think he 'd get over bein' a boy some time or 'nother, gettin' along in years as he is. An' you 'd think he 'd seen full enough o' fish, but once a year he has to break loose like this, an' travel off way up back o' the Bowden place—far out o' my beat, 't is—an' go a trout fishin'!"

Her tone of amused scorn was so full of challenge that William changed color even under the green streaks.

"I want some change," he said, looking at me and not at her. "'T is the prettiest little shady brook you ever saw."

"If he ever fetched home more 'n a couple o' minnies, 't would seem worth while," Mrs. Todd concluded, putting a last dab of the mysterious compound so perilously near her brother's mouth that William flushed again and was silent.

A little later I witnessed his escape, when Mrs. Todd had taken the foolish risk of going down cellar. There was a horse and wagon outside the garden fence, and presently we stood where we could see him driving up the hill with thoughtless speed. Mrs. Todd said nothing, but watched him affectionately out of sight.

"It serves to keep the mosquitoes off," she said, and a moment later it occurred to my slow mind that she spoke of the pennyroyal lotion. "I don't know sometimes but William 's kind of poetical," she continued, in her gentlest voice. "You 'd think if anything could cure him of it, 't would be the fish business."

It was only twenty minutes past six on a summer morning, but we both sat down to rest as if the activities of the day were over. Mrs. Todd rocked gently for a time, and seemed to be lost, though not poorly, like Macbeth, in her thoughts. At last she resumed relations with her actual surroundings. "I shall now put my lobsters on. They'll make us a good supper," she announced. "Then I can let the fire out for all day; give it a holiday, same 's William. You can have a little one now, nice an' hot, if you ain't got all the breakfast you want. Yes, I 'll put the lobsters on. William was very thoughtful to bring 'em over; William *is* thoughtful; if he only had a spark o' ambition, there be few could match him."

This unusual concession was afforded a sympathetic listener from the depths of the kitchen closet. Mrs. Todd was getting out her old iron lobster pot, and began to speak of prosaic affairs. I hoped that I should hear something more about her brother and their island life, and sat idly by the kitchen window looking at the morning glories that shaded it, believing that some flaw of wind might set Mrs. Todd's mind on its former course. Then it occurred to me that she had spoken about our supper rather than our dinner, and I guessed that she might have some great scheme before her for the day.

When I had loitered for some time and there was no further word about William, and at last I was conscious of receiving no attention whatever, I went away. It was something of a disappointment to find that she put no hindrance in the way of my usual morning affairs, of going up to the empty little white schoolhouse on the hill where I did my task of writing. I had been almost sure of a holiday when I discovered that Mrs. Todd was likely to take one herself; we had not been far afield to gather herbs and pleasures for many days now, but a little later she had silently vanished. I found my luncheon ready on the table in the little entry, wrapped in its shining old homespun napkin, and as if by way of special consolation, there was a stone bottle of Mrs. Todd's best spruce beer, with a long piece of cod line wound round it by which it could be lowered for coolness into the deep schoolhouse well.

I walked away with a dull supply of writing-paper and these provisions, feeling like a reluctant child who hopes to be called back at every stop. There was no relenting voice to be heard, and when I reached the schoolhouse, I found that I had left an open window and a swinging shutter the day before, and the sea wind that blew at evening had fluttered my poor sheaf of papers all about the room.

So the day did not begin very well, and I began to recognize that it was one of the days when nothing could be done without company. The truth was that my heart had gone trouting with William, but it would have been too selfish to say a word even to one's self about spoiling his day. If there is one way above another of getting so close to nature that one simply is a piece of nature, following a primeval instinct with perfect self-forgetfulness and forgetting everything except the dreamy consciousness of pleasant freedom, it is to take the course of a shady trout brook. The dark pools and the sunny shallows beckon one on; the wedge of sky between the trees on either bank, the speaking, companioning noise of the water, the amazing importance of what one is doing, and the constant sense of life and beauty make a strange transformation of the quick hours. I had a sudden memory of all this, and another, and another. I could not get myself free from "fishing and wishing."

At that moment I heard the unusual sound of wheels, and I looked past the high-growing thicket of wild-roses and straggling sumach to see the white nose and meagre shape of the Caplin horse; then I saw William sitting in the open wagon, with a small expectant smile upon his face.

"I've got two lines," he said. "I was quite a piece up the road. I thought perhaps 't was so you 'd feel like going."

There was enough excitement for most occasions in hearing William speak three sentences at once. Words seemed but vain to me at that bright moment. I stepped back from the schoolhouse window with a beating heart. The spruce-beer bottle was not yet in the well, and with that and my luncheon, and Pleasure at the helm, I went out into the happy world. The land breeze was blowing, and, as we turned away, I saw a flutter of white go past the window as I left the schoolhouse and my morning's work to their neglected fate.

II

One seldom gave way to a cruel impulse to look at an ancient seafaring William, but one felt as if he were a growing boy; I only hope that he felt much the same about me. He did not wear the fishing clothes that belonged to his seagoing life, but a strangely shaped old suit of tea-colored linen garments that might have been brought home years ago from Canton or Bombay. William had a peculiar way of giving silent assent when one spoke, but of answering your unspoken thoughts as if they reached him better than words. "I find them very easy," he said, frankly referring to the clothes. "Father had them in his old sea-chest."

The antique fashion, a quaint touch of foreign grace and even imagination about the cut were very pleasing; if ever Mr. William Blackett had faintly resembled an old beau, it was upon that day. He now appeared to feel as if everything had been explained between us, as if everything were quite understood; and we drove for some distance without finding it necessary to speak again about anything. At last, when it must have been a little past nine o'clock, he stopped the horse beside a small farmhouse, and nodded when I asked if I should get down from the wagon. "You can steer about northeast right across the pasture," he said, looking from under the eaves of his hat with an expectant smile. "I always leave the team here."

I helped to unfasten the harness, and William led the horse away to the barn. It was a poor-looking little place, and a forlorn woman looked at us through the window before she appeared at the door. I told her that Mr. Blackett and I came up from the Landing to go fishing. "He keeps a-comin', don't he?" she answered, with a funny little laugh, to which I was at a loss to find answer. When he joined us, I could not see that he took notice of her presence in any way, except to take an armful of dried salt fish from a corded stack in the back of the wagon which had been carefully covered with a piece of old sail. We had left a wake of their pungent flavor behind us all the way. I wondered what was going to become of the rest of them and some fresh lobsters which were also disclosed to view, but he laid the present gift on the doorstep without a word, and a few minutes later, when I looked back as we crossed the pasture, the fish were being carried into the house.

I could not see any signs of a trout brook until I came close upon it in the bushy pasture, and presently we struck into the low woods of straggling spruce and fir mixed into a tangle of swamp maples and alders which stretched away on either hand up and down stream. We found an open place in the pasture where some taller trees seemed to have been overlooked rather than spared. The sun was bright and hot by this time, and I sat down in the shade while William produced his lines and cut and trimmed us each a slender rod. I wondered where Mrs. Todd was spending the morning, and if later she would think that pirates had landed and captured me from the schoolhouse.

III

The brook was giving that live, persistent call to a listener that trout brooks always make; it ran with a free, swift current even here, where it crossed an apparently level piece of land. I saw two unpromising, quick barbel chase each other upstream from bank to bank as we solemnly arranged our hooks and sinkers. I felt that William's glances changed from anxiety to relief when he found that I was used to such gear; perhaps he felt that we must stay together if I could not bait my own hook, but we parted happily, full of a pleasing sense of companionship.

William had pointed me up the brook, but I chose to go down, which was only fair because it was his day, though one likes as well to follow and see where a brook goes as to find one's way to the places it comes from, and its tiny springs and headwaters, and in this case trout were not to be considered. William's only real anxiety was lest I might suffer from mosquitoes. His own complexion was still strangely impaired by its defenses, but I kept forgetting it, and looking to see if we were treading fresh pennyroyal underfoot, so efficient was Mrs. Todd's remedy. I was conscious, after we parted, and I turned to see if he were already fishing, and saw him wave his hand gallantly as he went away, that our friendship had made a great gain.

The moment that I began to fish the brook, I had a sense of its emptiness; when my bait first touched the water and went lightly down the quick stream, I knew that there was nothing to lie in wait for it. It is the same certainty that comes when one knocks at the door of an empty house, a lack of answering consciousness and of possible response; it is quite different if there is any life within. But it was a lovely brook, and I went a long way through woods and breezy open pastures, and found a forsaken house and overgrown farm, and laid up many pleasures for future joy and remembrance. At the end of the morning I came back to our meeting-place hungry and without any fish. William was already waiting, and we did not mention the matter of trout. We ate our luncheons with good appetites, and William brought our two stone bottles of spruce beer from the deep place in the brook where he had left them to cool. Then we sat awhile longer in peace and quietness on the green banks.

As for William, he looked more boyish than ever, and kept a more remote and juvenile sort of silence. Once I wondered how he had come to be so curiously wrinkled, forgetting, absent-mindedly, to recognize the effects of time. He did not expect any one else to keep up a vain show of conversation, and so I was silent as well as he. I glanced at him now and then, but I watched the leaves tossing against the sky and the red cattle moving in the pasture. "I don't know 's we need head for home. It 's early yet," he said at last, and I was as startled as if one of the gray firs had spoken.

"I guess I 'll go up-along and ask after Thankful Hight's folks," he continued. "Mother 'd like to get word;" and I nodded a pleased assent.

IV

William led the way across the pasture, and I followed with a deep sense of pleased anticipation. I do not believe that my companion had expected me to make any objection, but I knew that he was gratified by the easy way that his plans for the day were being seconded. He gave a look at the sky to see if there were any portents, but the sky was frankly blue; even the doubtful morning haze had disappeared.

We went northward along a rough, clayey road, across a bare-looking, sunburnt country full of tiresome long slopes where the sun was hot and bright, and I could not help observing the forlorn look of the farms. There was a great deal of pasture, but it looked deserted, and I wondered afresh why the people did not raise more sheep when that seemed the only possible use to make of their land. I said so to Mr. Blackett, who gave me a look of pleased surprise.

"That 's what She always maintains," he said eagerly. "She 's right about it, too; well, you 'll see!" I was glad to find myself approved, but I had not the least idea whom he meant, and waited until he felt like speaking again.

A few minutes later we drove down a steep hill and entered a large tract of dark spruce woods. It was delightful to be sheltered from the afternoon sun and when we had gone some distance in the shade, to my great pleasure William turned the horse's head toward some bars, which he let down, and I drove through into one of those narrow, still, sweet-scented by-ways which seem to be paths rather than roads. Often we had to put aside the heavy drooping branches which barred the way, and once, when a sharp twig struck William in the face, he announced with such spirit that somebody ought to go through there with an axe, that I felt unexpectedly guilty. So far as I now remember, this was William's only remark all the way through the woods to Thankful Hight's folks, but from time to time he pointed or nodded at something which I might have missed: a sleepy little owl snuggled into the bend of a branch, or a tall stalk of cardinal flowers where the sunlight came down at the edge of a small, bright piece of marsh. Many times, being used to the company of Mrs. Todd and other friends who were in the habit of talking, I came near making an idle remark to William, but I was for the most part happily preserved; to be with him only for a short time was to live on a different level, where thoughts served best because they were thoughts in common; the primary effect upon our minds of the simple things and beauties that we saw. Once when I caught sight of a lovely gay pigeon-woodpecker eyeing us curiously from a dead branch, and instinctively turned toward William, he gave an indulgent, comprehending nod which silenced me all the rest of the way. The wood-road was not a place for common noise conversation; one would interrupt the birds and all the still little beasts that belonged there. But it was mortifying to find how strong the habit of idle speech may become in one's self. One need not always be saying something in this noisy world. I grew conscious of the difference between William's usual fashion of life and mine; for him there were long days of silence in a sea-going boat, and I could believe that he and his mother usually spoke very little because they so perfectly understood each other. There was something peculiarly unresponding about their quiet island in the sea, solidly fixed into the still foundations of the world, against whose rocky shores the sea beats and calls and is unanswered.

We were quite half an hour going through the woods; the horse's feet made no sound on the brown, soft track under the dark evergreens. I thought that we should come out at last into more pastures, but there was no half-wooded strip of land at the end; the high woods grew squarely against an old stone wall and a sunshiny open field, and we came out suddenly into broad daylight that startled us and even startled the horse, who might have been napping as he walked, like an old soldier. The field sloped up to a low unpainted house that faced the east. Behind it were long, frost-whitened ledges that made the hill, with strips of green turf and bushes between. It was the wildest, most Titanic sort of pasture country up there; there was a sort of daring in putting a frail wooden house before it, though it might have the homely field and honest woods to front against. You thought of the elements and even of possible volcanoes as you looked up the stony heights. Suddenly I saw that a region of what I had thought gray stones was slowly moving, as if the sun was making my eyesight unsteady.

"There 's the sheep!" exclaimed William, pointing eagerly. "You see the sheep?" and sure enough, it was a great company of woolly backs, which seemed to have taken a mysterious protective resemblance to the ledges themselves. I could discover but little chance for pasturage on that high sunburnt ridge, but the sheep were moving steadily in a satisfied way as they fed along the slopes and hollows.

"I never have seen half so many sheep as these, all summer long!" I cried with admiration.

"There ain't so many," answered William soberly. "It 's a great sight. They do so well because they 're shepherded, but you can't beat sense into some folks."

"You mean that somebody stays and watches them?" I asked.

"She observed years ago in her readin' that they don't turn out their flocks without protection anywhere but in the State o' Maine," returned William. "First thing that put it into her mind was a little old book mother's got; she read it one time when she come out to the Island. They call it 'Shepherd o' Salisbury Plain.' 'T was n't the purpose o' the book to most, but when she read it, 'There, Mis' Blackett!' she said, 'that 's where we 've all lacked sense; our Bibles ought to have taught us that what sheep need is a shepherd.' You see most folks about here gave up sheep-raisin' years ago 'count o' the dogs. So she gave up school-teachin' and went out to tend her flock, and has shepherded ever since, an' done well."

For William, this approached an oration. He spoke with enthusiasm, and I shared the triumph of the moment. "There she is now!" he exclaimed, in a different tone, as the tall figure of a woman came following the flock and stood still on the ridge, looking toward us as if her eyes had been quick to see a strange object in the familiar emptiness of the field. William stood up in the wagon, and I thought he was going to call or wave his hand to her, but he sat down again more clumsily than if the wagon had made the familiar motion of a boat, and we drove on toward the house.

It was a most solitary place to live—a place where one might think that a life could hide itself. The thick woods were between the farm and the main road, and as one looked up and down the country, there was no other house in sight.

"Potatoes look well," announced William. "The old folks used to say that there wa'n't no better land outdoors than the Hight field."

I found myself possessed of a surprising interest in the shepherdess, who stood far away in the hill pasture with her great flock, like a figure of Millet's, high against the sky.

V

Everything about the old farmhouse was clean and orderly, as if the green dooryard were not only swept, but dusted. I saw a flock of turkeys stepping off carefully at a distance, but there was not the usual untidy flock of hens about the place to make everything look in disarray. William helped me out of the wagon as carefully as if I had been his mother, and nodded toward the open door with a reassuring look at me; but I waited until he had tied the horse and could lead the way, himself. He took off his hat just as we were going in, and stopped for a moment to smooth his thin gray hair with his hand, by which I saw that we had an affair of some ceremony. We entered an old-fashioned country kitchen, the floor scrubbed into unevenness, and the doors well polished by the touch of hands. In a large chair facing the window there sat a masterful-looking old woman with the features of a warlike Roman emperor, emphasized by a bonnet-like black cap with a band of green ribbon. Her sceptre was a palm-leaf fan.

William crossed the room toward her, and bent his head close to her ear.

"Feelin' pretty well to-day, Mis' Hight?" he asked, with all the voice his narrow chest could muster.

"No, I ain't, William. Here I have to set," she answered coldly, but she gave an inquiring glance over his shoulder at me.

"This is the young lady who is stopping with Almiry this summer," he explained, and I approached as if to give the countersign. She offered her left hand with considerable dignity, but her expression never seemed to change for the better. A moment later she said that she was pleased to meet me, and I felt as if the worst were over. William must have felt some apprehension, while I was only ignorant, as we had come across the field. Our hostess was more than disapproving, she was forbidding; but I was not long in suspecting that she felt the natural resentment of a strong energy that has been defeated by illness and made the spoil of captivity.

"Mother well as usual since you was up last year?" and William replied by a series of cheerful nods. The mention of dear Mrs. Blackett was a help to any conversation.

"Been fishin', ashore," he explained, in a somewhat conciliatory voice. "Thought you 'd like a few for winter," which explained at once the generous freight we had brought in the back of the wagon. I could see that the offering was no surprise, and that Mrs. Hight was interested.

"Well, I expect they 're good as the last," she said, but did not even approach a smile. She kept a straight, discerning eye upon me.

"Give the lady a cheer," she admonished William, who hastened to place close by her side one of the straight-backed chairs that stood against the kitchen wall. Then he lingered for a moment like a timid boy. I could see that he wore a look of resolve, but he did not ask the permission for which he evidently waited.

"You can go search for Esther," she said, at the end of a long pause that became anxious for both her guests. "Esther 'd like to see her;" and William in his pale nankeens disappeared with one light step and was off.

VI

"Don't speak too loud, it jars a person's head," directed Mrs. Hight plainly. "Clear an' distinct is what reaches me best. Any news to the Landin'?"

I was happily furnished with the particulars of a sudden death, and an engagement of marriage between a Caplin, a seafaring widower home from his voyage, and one of the younger Harrises; and now Mrs. Hight really smiled and settled herself in her chair. We exhausted one subject completely before we turned to the other. One of the returning turkeys took an unwarrantable liberty, and, mounting the doorstep, came in and walked about the kitchen without being observed by its strict owner; and the tin dipper slipped off its nail behind us and made an astonishing noise, and jar enough to reach Mrs. Hight's inner ear and make her turn her head to look at it; but we talked straight on. We came at last to understand each other upon such terms of friendship that she unbent her majestic port and complained to me as any poor old woman might of the hardships of her illness. She had already fixed various dates upon the sad certainty of the year when she had the shock, which had left her perfectly helpless except for a clumsy left hand which fanned and gestured, and settled and resettled the folds of her dress, but could do no comfortable time-shortening work.

"Yes 'm, you can feel sure I use it what I can," she said severely. "'T was a long spell before I could let Esther go forth in the mornin' till she 'd got me up an' dressed me, but now she leaves things ready overnight and I get 'em as I want 'em with my light pair o' tongs, and I feel very able about helpin' myself to what I once did. Then when Esther returns, all she has to do is to push me out here into the kitchen. Some parts o' the year Esther stays out all night, them moonlight nights when the dogs are apt to be after the sheep, but she don't use herself as hard as she once had to. She 's well able to hire somebody, Esther is, but there you can't find no hired man that wants to git up before five o'clock nowadays; 't ain't as 't was in my time. They 're liable to fall asleep, too, and them moonlight nights she 's so anxious she can't sleep, and out she goes. There 's a kind of a fold, she calls it, up there in a sheltered spot, and she sleeps up in a little shed she 's got,—built it herself for lambin' time and when the poor foolish creatur's gets hurt or anything. I 've never seen it, but she says it 's in a lovely spot and always pleasant in any weather. You see off, other side of the ridge, to the south'ard, where there 's houses. I used to think some time I 'd get up to see it again, and all them spots she lives in, but I sha'n't now. I 'm beginnin' to go back; an' 't ain't surprisin'. I 've kind of got used to disappointments," and the poor soul drew a deep sigh.

VII

It was long before we noticed the lapse of time; I not only told every circumstance known to me of recent events among the households of Mrs. Todd's neighborhood at the shore, but Mrs. Hight became more and more communicative on her part, and went carefully into the genealogical descent and personal experience of many acquaintances until between us we had pretty nearly circumnavigated the globe and reached Dunnet Landing from an opposite direction to that in which we had started. It was long before my own interest began to flag; there was a flavor of the best sort in her definite and descriptive fashion of speech. It may be only a fancy of my own that in the sound and value of many words, with their lengthened vowels and doubled cadences, there is some faint survival on the Maine coast of the sound of English speech of Chaucer's time.

At last Mrs. Thankful Hight gave a suspicious look through the window.

"Where do you suppose they be?" she asked me. "Esther must ha' been off to the far edge o' everything. I doubt William ain't been able to find her; can't he hear their bells? His hearin' all right?"

William had heard some herons that morning which were beyond the reach of my own ears, and almost beyond eyesight in the upper skies, and I told her so. I was luckily preserved by some unconscious instinct from saying that we had seen the shepherdess so near as we crossed the field. Unless she had fled faster than Atalanta, William must have been but a few minutes in reaching her immediate neighborhood. I now discovered with a quick leap of amusement and delight in my heart that I had fallen upon a serious chapter of romance. The old woman looked suspiciously at me, and I made a dash to cover with a new piece of information; but she listened with lofty indifference, and soon interrupted my eager statements.

"Ain't William been gone some considerable time?" she demanded, and then in a milder tone: "The time has re'lly flown; I do enjoy havin' company. I set here alone a sight o' long days. Sheep is dreadful fools; I expect they heard a strange step, and set right off through bush an' briar, spite of all she could do. But William might have the sense to return, 'stead o' searchin' about. I want to inquire of him about his mother. What was you goin' to say? I guess you 'll have time to relate it.

My powers of entertainment were on the ebb, but I doubled my diligence and we went on for another half-hour at least with banners flying, but still William did not reappear. Mrs. Hight frankly began to show fatigue.

"Somethin' 's happened, an' he 's stopped to help her," groaned the old lady, in the middle of what I had found to tell her about a rumor of disaffection with the minister of a town I merely knew by name in the weekly newspaper to which Mrs. Todd subscribed. "You step to the door, dear, an' look if you can't see 'em." I promptly stepped, and once outside the house I looked anxiously in the direction which William had taken.

To my astonishment I saw all the sheep so near that I wonder we had not been aware in the house of every bleat and tinkle. And there, within a stone's-throw, on the first long gray ledge that showed above the juniper, were William and the shepherdess engaged in pleasant conversation. At first I was provoked and then amused, and a thrill of sympathy warmed my whole heart. They had seen me and risen as if by magic; I had a sense of being the messenger of Fate. One could almost hear their sighs of regret as I appeared; they must have passed a lovely afternoon. I hurried into the house with the reassuring news that they were not only in sight but perfectly safe, with all the sheep.

VIII

Mrs. Hight, like myself, was spent with conversation, and had ceased even the one activity of fanning herself. I brought a desired drink of water, and happily remembered some fruit that was left from my luncheon. She revived with splendid vigor, and told me the simple history of her later years since she had been smitten in the prime of her life by the stroke of paralysis, and her husband had died and left her alone with Esther and a mortgage on their farm. There was only one field of good land, but they owned a great region of sheep pasture and a little woodland. Esther had always been laughed at for her belief in sheep-raising when one by one their neighbors were giving up their flocks, and when everything had come to the point of despair she had raised all the money and bought all the sheep she could, insisting that Maine lambs were as good as any, and that there was a straight path by sea to Boston market. And by tending her flock herself she had managed to succeed; she had made money enough to pay off the mortgage five years ago, and now what they did not spend was safe in the bank. "It has been stubborn work, day and night, summer and winter, an' now she 's beginnin' get along in years," said the old mother sadly.

"She 's tended me 'long o' the sheep, an' she 's been a good girl right along, but she ought to have been a teacher;" and Mrs. Hight sighed heavily and plied the fan again.

We heard voices, and William and Esther entered; they did not know that it was so late in the afternoon. William looked almost bold, and oddly like a happy young man rather than an ancient boy. As for Esther, she might have been Jeanne d'Arc returned to her sheep, touched with age and gray with the ashes of a great remembrance. She wore the simple look of sainthood and unfeigned devotion. My heart was moved by the sight of her plain sweet face, weatherworn and gentle in its looks, her thin figure in its close dress, and the strong hand that clasped a shepherd's staff, and I could only hold William in new reverence; this silent farmer-fisherman who knew, and he alone, the noble and patient heart that beat within her breast. I am not sure that they acknowledged even to themselves that they had always been lovers; they could not consent to anything so definite or pronounced; but they were happy in being together in the world. Esther was untouched by the fret and fury of life; she had lived in sunshine and rain among her silly sheep, and been refined instead of coarsened, while her touching patience with a ramping old mother, stung by the sense of defeat and mourning her lost activities, had given back a lovely self-possession, and habit of sweet temper. I had seen enough of old Mrs. Hight to know that nothing a sheep might do could vex a person who was used to the uncertainties and severities of her companionship.

IX

Mrs. Hight told her daughter at once that she had enjoyed a beautiful call, and got a great many new things to think of. This was said so frankly in my hearing that it gave a consciousness of high reward, and I was indeed recompensed by the grateful look in Esther's eyes. We did not speak much together, but we understood each other. For the poor old woman did not read, and could not sew or knit with her helpless hand, and they were far from any neighbors, while her spirit was as eager in age as in youth, and expected even more from a disappointing world. She had lived to see the mortgage paid and money in the bank, and Esther's success acknowledged on every hand, and there were still a few pleasures left in life. William had his mother, and Esther had hers, and they had not seen each other for a year, though Mrs. Hight had spoken of a year's making no change in William even at his age. She must have been in the far eighties herself, but of a noble courage and persistence in the world she ruled from her stiff-backed rocking-chair.

William unloaded his gift of dried fish, each one chosen with perfect care, and Esther stood by, watching him, and then she walked across the field with us beside the wagon. I believed that I was the only one who knew their happy secret, and she blushed a little as we said good-by.

"l hope you ain't goin' to feel too tired, mother's so deaf; no, I hope you won't be tired," she said kindly, speaking as if she well knew what tiredness was. We could hear the neglected sheep bleating on the hill in the next moment's silence. Then she smiled at me, a smile of noble patience, of uncomprehended sacrifice, which I can never forget. There was all the remembrance of disappointed hopes, the hardships of winter, the loneliness of single-handedness in her look, but I understood, and I love to remember her worn face and her young blue eyes.

"Good-by, William," she said gently, and William said good-by, and gave her a quick glance, but he did not turn to look back, though I did, and waved my hand as she was putting up the bars behind us. Nor did he speak again until we had passed through the dark woods and were on our way homeward by the main road. The grave yearly visit had been changed from a hope into a happy memory.

"You can see the sea from the top of her pasture hill," said William at last.

"Can you?" I asked, with surprise.

"Yes, it 's very high land; the ledges up there show very plain in clear weather from the top of our island, and there 's a high upstandin' tree that makes a landmark for the fishin' grounds." And William gave a happy sigh.

When we had nearly reached the Landing, my companion looked over into the back of the wagon and saw that the piece of sailcloth was safe, with which he had covered the dried fish. "I wish we had got some trout," he said wistfully. "They always appease Almiry, and make her feel 't was worth while to go."

I stole a glance at William Blackett. We had not seen a solitary mosquito, but there was a dark stripe across his mild face, which might have been an old scar won long ago in battle.

THE FOREIGNER

I

One evening, at the end of August, in Dunnet Landing, I heard Mrs. Todd's firm footstep crossing the small front entry outside my door, and her conventional cough which served as a herald's trumpet, or a plain New England knock, in the harmony of our fellowship.

"Oh, please come in!" I cried, for it had been so still in the house that I supposed my friend and hostess had gone to see one of her neighbors. The first cold northeasterly storm of the season was blowing hard outside. Now and then there was a dash of great raindrops and a flick of wet lilac leaves against the window, but I could hear that the sea was already stirred to its dark depths, and the great rollers were coming in heavily against the shore. One might well believe that Summer was coming to a sad end that night, in the darkness and rain and sudden access of autumnal cold. It seemed as if there must be danger offshore among the outer islands.

"Oh, there!" exclaimed Mrs. Todd, as she entered. "I know nothing ain't ever happened out to Green Island since the world began, but I always do worry about mother in these great gales. You know those tidal waves occur sometimes down to the West Indies, and I get dwellin' on 'em so I can't set still in my chair, nor knit a common row to a stocking. William might get mooning, out in his small bo't and not observe how the sea was making, an' meet with some accident. Yes, I thought I 'd come in and set with you if you wa'n't busy. No, I never feel any concern about 'em in winter 'cause then they 're prepared, and all ashore and everything snug. William ought to keep help, as I tell him; yes, he ought to keep help."

I hastened to reassure my anxious guest by saying that Elijah Tilley had told me in the afternoon when I came along the shore past the fish houses, that Johnny Bowden and the Captain were out at Green Island; he had seen them boating up the bay, and thought they must have put into Burnt Island cove, but one of the lobstermen brought word later that he saw them hauling out at Green Island as he came by, and Captain Bowden pointed ashore and shook his head to say that he did not mean to try to get in. "The old Miranda just managed it, but she will have to stay at home a day or two and put new patches in her sail," I ended, not without pride in so much circumstantial evidence.

Mrs. Todd was alert in a moment. "Then they 'll all have a very pleasant evening," she assured me, apparently dismissing all fears of tidal waves and other sea-going disasters. "I was urging Alick Bowden to go ashore some day and see mother before cold weather. He 's her own nephew; she sets a great deal by him. And Johnny 's a great chum o' William's; don't you know the first day we had Johnny out 'long of us, he took an' give William his money to keep for him that he 'd been a-savin', and William showed it to me an' was so affected I thought he was goin' to shed tears? 'T was a dollar an' eighty cents; yes, they 'll have a beautiful evenin' all together, and like 's not the sea 'll be flat as a doorstep come morning."

I had drawn a large wooden rocking-chair before the fire, and Mrs. Todd was sitting there jogging herself a little, knitting fast, and wonderfully placid of countenance. There came a fresh gust of wind and rain, and we could feel the small wooden house rock and hear it creak as if it were a ship at sea.

"Lord, hear the great breakers!" exclaimed Mrs. Todd. "How they pound!—there, there! I always run of an idea that the sea knows anger these nights and gets full o' fight. I can hear the rote o' them old black ledges way down the thoroughfare. Calls up all those stormy verses in the Book o' Psalms; David he knew how old sea-goin' folks have to quake at the heart."

I thought as I had never thought before of such anxieties. The families of sailors and coastwise adventurers by sea must always be worrying about somebody, this side of the world or the other. There was hardly one of Mrs. Todd's elder acquaintances, men or women, who had not at some time or other made a sea voyage, and there was often no news until the voyagers themselves came back to bring it.

"There's a roaring high overhead, and a roaring in the deep sea," said Mrs. Todd solemnly, "and they battle together nights like this. No, I could n't sleep; some women folks always goes right to bed an' to sleep, so 's to forget, but 't ain't my way. Well, it 's a blessin' we don't all feel alike; there 's hardly any of our folks at sea to worry about, nowadays, but I can't help my feelin's, an' I got thinking of mother all alone, if William had happened to be out lobsterin' and could n't make the cove gettin' back."

"They will have a pleasant evening," I repeated. "Captain Bowden is the best of good company."

"Mother 'll make him some pancakes for his supper, like 's not," said Mrs. Todd, clicking her knitting needles and giving a pull at her yarn. Just then the old cat pushed open the unlatched door and came straight toward her mistress's lap. She was regarded severely as she stepped about and turned on the broad expanse, and then made herself into a round cushion of fur, but was not openly admonished. There was another great blast of wind overhead, and a puff of smoke came down the chimney.

"This makes me think o' the night Mis' Cap'n Tolland died," said Mrs. Todd, half to herself. "Folks used to say these gales only blew when somebody 's a-dyin', or the devil was a-comin' for his own, but the worst man I ever knew died a real pretty mornin' in June."

"You have never told me any ghost stories," said I; and such was the gloomy weather and the influence of the night that I was instantly filled with reluctance to have this suggestion followed. I had not chosen the best of moments; just before I spoke we had begun to feel as cheerful as possible. Mrs. Todd glanced doubtfully at the cat and then at me, with a strange absent look, and I was really afraid that she was going to tell me something that would haunt my thoughts on every dark stormy night as long as I lived.

"Never mind now; tell me to-morrow by daylight, Mrs. Todd," I hastened to say, but she still looked at me full of doubt and deliberation.

"Ghost stories!" she answered. "Yes, I don't know but I 've heard a plenty of 'em first an' last. I was just sayin' to myself that this is like the night Mis' Cap'n Tolland died. 'T was the great line storm in September all of thirty, or maybe forty, year ago. I ain't one that keeps much account o' time."

"Tolland? That 's a name I have never heard in Dunnet," I said.

"Then you have n't looked well about the old part o' the buryin' ground, no'theast corner," replied Mrs. Todd. "All their women folks lies there; the sea 's got most o' the men. They were a known family o' shipmasters in early times. Mother had a mate, Ellen Tolland, that she mourns to this day; died right in her bloom with quick consumption, but the rest o' that family was all boys but one, and older than she, an' they lived hard seafarin' lives an' all died hard. They were called very smart seamen. I 've heard that when the youngest went into one o' the old shippin' houses in Boston, the head o' the firm called out to him: 'Did you say Tolland from Dunnet? That 's recommendation enough for any vessel!' There was some o' them old shipmasters as tough as iron, an' they had the name o' usin' their crews very severe, but there wa'n't a man that would n't rather sign with 'em an' take his chances, than with the slack ones that did n't know how to meet accidents."

II

There was so long a pause, and Mrs. Todd still looked so absent-minded, that I was afraid she and the cat were growing drowsy together before the fire, and I should have no reminiscences at all. The wind struck the house again, so that we both started in our chairs and Mrs. Todd gave a curious, startled look at me. The cat lifted her head and listened too, in the silence that followed, while after the wind sank we were more conscious than ever of the awful roar of the sea. The house jarred now and then, in a strange, disturbing way.

"Yes, they 'll have a beautiful evening out to the island," said Mrs. Todd again; but she did not say it gayly. I had not seen her before in her weaker moments.

"Who was Mrs. Captain Tolland?" I asked eagerly, to change the current of our thoughts.

"I never knew her maiden name; if I ever heard it, I 've gone an' forgot; 't would mean nothing to me," answered Mrs. Todd.

"She was a foreigner, an' he met with her out in the Island o' Jamaica. They said she 'd been left a widow with property. Land knows what become of it; she was French born, an' her first husband was a Portugee, or somethin'."

I kept silence now, a poor and insufficient question being worse than none.

"Cap'n John Tolland was the least smartest of any of 'em, but he was full smart enough, an' commanded a good brig at the time, in the sugar trade; he 'd taken out a cargo o' pine lumber to the islands from somewheres up the river, an' had been loadin' for home in the port o' Kingston, an' had gone ashore that afternoon for his papers, an' remained afterwards 'long of three friends o' his, all shipmasters. They was havin' their suppers together in a tavern; 't was late in the evenin' an' they was more lively than usual, an' felt boyish; and over opposite was another house full o' company, real bright and pleasant lookin', with a lot o' lights, an' they heard somebody singin' very pretty to a guitar. They wa'n't in no go-to-meetin' condition, an' one of 'em, he slapped the table an' said, 'Le' 's go over an' hear that lady sing!' an' over they all went, good honest sailors, but three sheets in the wind, and stepped in as if they was invited, an' made their bows inside the door, an' asked if they could hear the music; they were all respectable well-dressed men. They saw the woman that had the guitar, an' there was a company a-listenin', regular highbinders all of 'em; an' there was a long table all spread out with big candlesticks like little trees o' light, and a sight o' glass an' silver ware; an' part o' the men was young officers in uniform, an' the colored folks was steppin' round servin' 'em, an' they had the lady singin'. 'T was a wasteful scene, an' a loud talkin' company, an' though they was three sheets in the wind themselves there wa'n't one o' them cap'ns but had sense to perceive it. The others had pushed back their chairs, an' their decanters an' glasses was standin' thick about, an' they was teasin' the one that was singin' as if they 'd just got her in to amuse 'em. But they quieted down; one o' the young officers had beautiful manners, an' invited the four cap'ns to join 'em, very polite; 't was a kind of public house, and after they 'd all heard another song, he come to consult with 'em whether they would n't git up and dance a hornpipe or somethin' to the lady's music.

"They was all elderly men an' shipmasters, and owned property; two of 'em was church members in good standin'," continued Mrs. Todd loftily, "an' they would n't lend theirselves to no such kick-shows as that, an' spite o' bein' three sheets in the wind, as I have once observed; they waved aside the tumblers of wine the young officer was pourin' out for 'em so freehanded, and said they should rather be excused. An' when they all rose, still very digni-fied, as I 've been well informed, and made their partin' bows and was goin' out, them young sports got round 'em an' tried to prevent 'em, and they had to push an' strive considerable, but out they come. There was this Cap'n Tolland and two Cap'n Bowdens, and the fourth was my own father." (Mrs. Todd spoke slowly, as if to im-press the value of her authority.) "Two of them was very religious, upright men, but they would have their night out sometimes, all o' them old-fashioned cap'ns, when they was free of business and ready to leave port.

"An' they went back to their tavern an' got their bills paid, an' set down kind o' mad with everybody by the front windows, mistrust-ing some o' their tavern charges, like 's not, by that time, an' when they got tempered down, they watched the house over across, where the party was.

"There was a kind of a grove o' trees between the house an' the road, an' they heard the guitar a-goin' an' a-stoppin' short by turns, and pretty soon somebody began to screech, an' they saw a white dress come runnin' out through the bushes, an' tumbled over each other in their haste to offer help; an' out she come, with the guitar, cryin' into the street, and they just walked off four square with her amongst 'em, down toward the wharves where they felt more to home. They could n't make out at first what 't was she spoke,— Cap'n Lorenzo Bowden was well acquainted in Havre an' Bordeaux, an' spoke a poor quality o' French, an' she knew a little mite o' Eng-lish, but not much; and they come somehow or other to discern that she was in real distress. Her husband and her children had died o' yellow fever; they 'd all come up to Kingston from one o' the far Wind'ard Islands to get passage on a steamer to France, an' a negro had stole their money off her husband while he lay sick o' the fever, an' she had been befriended some, but the folks that knew about her had died too; it had been a dreadful run o' the fever that season, an' she fell at last to playin' an' singin' for hire, and for what money they 'd throw to her round them harbor houses.

"'T was a real hard case, an' when them cap'ns made out about it, there wa'n't one that meant to take leave without helpin' of her. They was pretty mellow, an' whatever they might lack o' prudence they more 'n made up with charity: they did n't want to see nobody abused, an' she was sort of a pretty woman, an' they stopped in the street then an' there an' drew lots who should take her aboard, bein' all bound home. An' the lot fell to Cap'n Jonathan Bowden who did act discouraged; his vessel had but small accommodations, though he could stow a big freight, an' she was a dreadful slow sailer through bein' square as a box, an' his first wife, that was livin' then, was a dreadful jealous woman. He threw himself right onto the mercy o' Cap'n Tolland."

Mrs. Todd indulged herself for a short time in a season of calm reflection.

"I always thought they 'd have done better, and more reasonable, to give her some money to pay her passage home to France, or wherever she may have wanted to go," she continued.

I nodded and looked for the rest of the story.

"Father told mother," said Mrs. Todd confidentially, "that Cap'n Jonathan Bowden an' Cap'n John Tolland had both taken a little more than usual; I would n't have you think, either, that they both was n't the best o' men, an' they was solemn as owls, and argued the matter between 'em, an' waved aside the other two when they tried to put their oars in. An' spite o' Cap'n Tolland's bein' a settled old bachelor they fixed it that he was to take the prize on his brig; she was a fast sailer, and there was a good spare cabin or two where he 'd sometimes carried passengers, but he 'd filled 'em with bags o' sugar on his own account an' was loaded very heavy beside. He said he 'd shift the sugar an' get along somehow, an' the last the other three cap'ns saw of the party was Cap'n John handing the lady into his bo't, guitar and all, an' off they all set tow'ds their ships with their men rowin' 'em in the bright moonlight down to Port Royal where the anchorage was, an' where they all lay, goin' out with the tide an' mornin' wind at break o' day. An' the others thought they heard music of the guitar, two o' the bo'ts kept well together, but it may have come from another source."

"Well; and then?" I asked eagerly after a pause. Mrs. Todd was almost laughing aloud over her knitting and nodding emphatically. We had forgotten all about the noise of the wind and sea.

"Lord bless you! he come sailing into Portland with his sugar, all in good time, an' they stopped right afore a justice o' the peace, and Cap'n John Tolland come paradin' home to Dunnet Landin' a married man. He owned one o' them thin, narrow-lookin' houses with one room each side o' the front door, and two slim black spruces spindlin' up against the front windows to make it gloomy inside. There was no horse nor cattle of course, though he owned pasture land, an' you could see rifts o' light right through the barn as you drove by. And there was a good excellent kitchen, but his sister reigned over that; she had a right to two rooms, and took the kitchen an' a bedroom that led out of it; an' bein' given no rights in the kitchen had angered the cap'n so they were n't on no kind o' speakin' terms. He preferred his old brig for comfort, but now and then, between voyages, he 'd come home for a few days, just to show he was master over his part o' the house, and show Eliza she could n't commit no trespass.

"They stayed a little while; 't was pretty spring weather, an' I used to see Cap'n John rollin' by with his arms full o' bundles from the store, lookin' as pleased and important as a boy; an' then they went right off to sea again, an' was gone a good many months. Next time he left her to live there alone, after they 'd stopped at home together some weeks, an' they said she suffered from bein' at sea, but some said that the owners would n't have a woman aboard. 'T was before father was lost on that last voyage of his, an' he and mother went up once or twice to see them. Father said there wa'n't a mite o' harm in her, but somehow or other a sight o' prejudice arose; it may have been caused by the remarks of Eliza an' her feelin's tow'ds her brother. Even my mother had no regard for Eliza Tolland. But mother asked the cap'n's wife to come with her one evenin' to a social circle that was down to the meetin'-house vestry, so she 'd get acquainted a little, an' she appeared very pretty until they started to have some singin' to the melodeon. Mari' Harris an' one o' the younger Caplin girls undertook to sing a duet, an' they sort o' flatted, an' she put her hands right up to her ears, and give a little squeal, an' went quick as could be an' give 'em the right notes, for

she could read the music like plain print, an' made 'em try it over
again. She was real willin' an' pleasant, but that did n't suit, an' she
made faces when they got it wrong. An' then there fell a dead calm,
an' we was all settin' round prim as dishes, an' my mother, that
never expects ill feelin', asked her if she would n't sing somethin',
an' up she got,—poor creatur', it all seems so different to me now,—
an' sung a lovely little song standin' in the floor; it seemed to have
something gay about it that kept a-repeatin', an' nobody could help
keepin' time, an' all of a sudden she looked round at the tables and
caught up a tin plate that somebody 'd fetched a Washin'ton pie in,
an' she begun to drum on it with her fingers like one o' them tam-
bourines, an' went right on singin' faster an' faster, and next minute
she begun to dance a little pretty dance between the verses, just as
light and pleasant as a child. You could n't help seein' how pretty 't
was; we all got to trottin' a foot, an' some o' the men clapped their
hands quite loud, a-keepin' time, 't was so catchin', an' seemed so
natural to her. There wa'n't one of 'em but enjoyed it; she just tried
to do her part, an' some urged her on, till she stopped with a little
twirl of her skirts an' went to her place again by mother. And I can
see mother now, reachin' over an' smilin' an' pattin' her hand.

"But next day there was an awful scandal goin' in the parish, an'
Mari' Harris reproached my mother to her face, an' I never wanted
to see her since, but I 've had to a good many times. I said Mis' Tolland did n't intend no impropriety,—I reminded her of David's
dancin' before the Lord; but she said such a man as David never
would have thought o' dancin' right there in the Orthodox vestry,
and she felt I spoke with irreverence.

"And next Sunday Mis' Tolland come walkin' into our meeting,
but I must say she acted like a cat in a strange garret, and went
right out down the aisle with her head in air, from the pew Deacon
Caplin had showed her into. 'T was just in the beginning of the long
prayer. I wish she 'd stayed through, whatever her reasons were.
Whether she 'd expected somethin' different, or misunderstood
some o' the pastor's remarks, or what 't was, I don't really feel able
to explain, but she kind o' declared war, at least folks thought so,
an' war 't was from that time. I see she was cryin', or had been, as
she passed by me; perhaps bein' in meetin' was what had power to
make her feel homesick and strange.

"Cap'n John Tolland was away fittin' out; that next week he come home to see her and say farewell. He was lost with his ship in the Straits of Malacca, and she lived there alone in the old house a few months longer till she died. He left her well off; 't was said he hid his money about the house and she knew where 't was. Oh, I expect you 've heard that story told over an' over twenty times, since you 've been here at the Landin'?"

"Never one word," I insisted.

"It was a good while ago," explained Mrs. Todd, with reassurance. "Yes, it all happened a great while ago."

III

At this moment, with a sudden flaw of the wind, some wet twigs outside blew against the window panes and made a noise like a distressed creature trying to get in. I started with sudden fear, and so did the cat, but Mrs. Todd knitted away and did not even look over her shoulder.

"She was a good-looking woman; yes, I always thought Mis' Tolland was good-looking, though she had, as was reasonable, a sort of foreign cast, and she spoke very broken English, no better than a child. She was always at work about her house, or settin' at a front window with her sewing; she was a beautiful hand to embroider. Sometimes, summer evenings, when the windows was open, she 'd set an' drum on her guitar, but I don't know as I ever heard her sing but once after the cap'n went away. She appeared very happy about havin' him, and took on dreadful at partin' when he was down here on the wharf, going back to Portland by boat to take ship for that last v'y'ge. He acted kind of ashamed, Cap'n John did; folks about here ain't so much accustomed to show their feelings. The whistle had blown an' they was waitin' for him to get aboard, an' he was put to it to know what to do and treated her very affectionate in spite of all impatience; but mother happened to be there and she went an' spoke, and I remember what a comfort she seemed to be. Mis' Tolland clung to her then, and she would n't give a glance after the boat when it had started, though the captain was very eager a-wavin' to her. She wanted mother to come home with her an' would n't let go her hand, and mother had just come in to stop all night with me an' had plenty o' time ashore, which did n't always happen, so they walked off together, an' 't was some considerable time before she got back.

"'I want you to neighbor with that poor lonesome creatur',' says mother to me, lookin' reproachful. 'She 's a stranger in a strange land,' says mother. 'I want you to make her have a sense that somebody feels kind to her.'

"'Why, since that time she flaunted out o' meetin', folks have felt she liked other ways better 'n our'n,' says I. I was provoked, because I 'd had a nice supper ready, an' mother 'd let it wait so long 't was spoiled. 'I hope you 'll like your supper!' I told her. I was dreadful ashamed afterward of speakin' so to mother.

"'What consequence is my supper?' says she to me; mother can be very stern,—'or your comfort or mine, beside letting a foreign person an' a stranger feel so desolate; she 's done the best a woman could do in her lonesome place, and she asks nothing of anybody except a little common kindness. Think if 't was you in a foreign land!'

"And mother set down to drink her tea, an' I set down humbled enough over by the wall to wait till she finished. An' I did think it all over, an' next day I never said nothin', but I put on my bonnet, and went to see Mis' Cap'n Tolland, if 't was only for mother's sake. 'T was about three quarters of a mile up the road here, beyond the schoolhouse. I forgot to tell you that the cap'n had bought out his sister's right at three or four times what 't was worth, to save trouble, so they 'd got clear o' her, an' I went round into the side yard sort o' friendly an' sociable, rather than stop an' deal with the knocker an' the front door. It looked so pleasant an' pretty I was glad I come; she had set a little table for supper, though 't was still early, with a white cloth on it, right out under an old apple tree close by the house. I noticed it was same as with me at home, there was only one plate. She was just coming out with a dish; you could n't see the door nor the table from the road.

"In the few weeks she 'd been there she 'd got some bloomin' pinks an' other flowers next the doorstep. Somehow it looked as if she 'd known how to make it homelike for the cap'n. She asked me to set down; she was very polite, but she looked very mournful, and I spoke of mother, an' she put down her dish and caught holt o' me with both hands an' said my mother was an angel. When I see the tears in her eyes 't was all right between us, and we were always friendly after that, and mother had us come out and make a little visit that summer; but she come a foreigner and she went a foreigner, and never was anything but a stranger among our folks. She taught me a sight o' things about herbs I never knew before nor since; she was well acquainted with the virtues o' plants. She 'd act awful secret about some things too, an' used to work charms for herself sometimes, an' some o' the neighbors told to an' fro after she died that they knew enough not to provoke her, but 't was all nonsense; 't is the believin' in such things that causes 'em to be any harm, an' so I told 'em," confided Mrs. Todd contemptuously. "That first night I stopped to tea with her she 'd cooked some eggs with some herb or other sprinkled all through, and 't was she that first led me to discern mushrooms; an' she went right down on her knees in my garden here when she saw I had my different officious herbs. Yes, 't was she that learned me the proper use o' parsley too; she was a beautiful cook."

Mrs. Todd stopped talking, and rose, putting the cat gently in the chair, while she went away to get another stick of apple-tree wood. It was not an evening when one wished to let the fire go down, and we had a splendid bank of bright coals. I had always wondered where Mrs. Todd had got such an unusual knowledge of cookery, of the varieties of mushrooms, and the use of sorrel as a vegetable, and other blessings of that sort. I had long ago learned that she could vary her omelettes like a child of France, which was indeed a surprise in Dunnet Landing.

IV

All these revelations were of the deepest interest, and I was ready with a question as soon as Mrs. Todd came in and had well settled the fire and herself and the cat again.

"I wonder why she never went back to France, after she was left alone?"

"She come here from the French islands," explained Mrs. Todd. "I asked her once about her folks, an' she said they were all dead; 't was the fever took 'em. She made this her home, lonesome as 't was; she told me she had n't been in France since she was 'so small,' and measured me off a child o' six. She 'd lived right out in the country before, so that part wa'n't unusual to her. Oh yes, there was something very strange about her, and she had n't been brought up in high circles nor nothing o' that kind. I think she 'd been really pleased to have the cap'n marry her an' give her a good home, after all she 'd passed through, and leave her free with his money an' all that. An' she got over bein' so strange-looking to me after a while, but 't was a very singular expression: she wore a fixed smile that wa'n't a smile; there wa'n't no light behind it, same 's a lamp can't shine if it ain't lit. I don't know just how to express it, 't was a sort of made countenance."

One could not help thinking of Sir Philip Sidney's phrase, "A made countenance, between simpering and smiling."

"She took it hard, havin' the captain go off on that last voyage," Mrs. Todd went on. "She said somethin' told her when they was partin' that he would never come back. He was lucky to speak a home-bound ship this side o' the Cape o' Good Hope, an' got a chance to send her a letter, an' that cheered her up. You often felt as if you was dealin' with a child's mind, for all she had so much information that other folks had n't. I was a sight younger than I be now, and she made me imagine new things, and I got interested watchin' her an' findin' out what she had to say, but you could n't get to no affectionateness with her. I used to blame me sometimes; we used to be real good comrades goin' off for an afternoon, but I never give her a kiss till the day she laid in her coffin and it come to my heart there wa'n't no one else to do it."

"And Captain Tolland died," I suggested after a while.

"Yes, the cap'n was lost," said Mrs. Todd, "and of course word did n't come for a good while after it happened. The letter come from the owners to my uncle, Cap'n Lorenzo Bowden, who was in charge of Cap'n Tolland's affairs at home, and he come right up for me an' said I must go with him, to the house. I had known what it was to be a widow, myself, for near a year, an' there was plenty o' widow women along this coast that the sea had made desolate, but I never saw a heart break as I did then.

"'T was this way: we walked together along the road, me an'

uncle Lorenzo. You know how it leads straight from just above the schoolhouse to the brook bridge, and their house was just this side o' the brook bridge on the left hand; the cellar 's there now, and a couple or three good-sized gray birches growin' in it. And when we come near enough I saw that the best room, this way, where she most never set, was all lighted up, and the curtains up so that the light shone bright down the road, and as we walked, those lights would dazzle and dazzle in my eyes, and I could hear the guitar a-goin', an' she was singin'. She heard our steps with her quick ears and come running to the door with her eyes a-shinin', an' all that set look gone out of her face, an' begun to talk French, gay as a bird, an' shook hands and behaved very pretty an' girlish, sayin' 't was her fête day. I did n't know what she meant then. And she had gone an' put a wreath o flowers on her hair an' wore a handsome gold chain that the cap'n had given her; an' there she was, poor creatur', makin' believe have a party all alone in her best room; 't was prim enough to discourage a person, with too many chairs set close to the walls, just as the cap'n's mother had left it, but she had put sort o' long garlands on the walls, droopin' very graceful, and a sight of green boughs in the corners, till it looked lovely, and all lit up with a lot o' candles."

"Oh dear!" I sighed. "Oh, Mrs. Todd, what did you do?"

"She beheld our countenances," answered Mrs. Todd solemnly. "I expect they was telling everything plain enough, but Cap'n Lorenzo spoke the sad words to her as if he had been her father; and she wavered a minute and then over she went on the floor before we could catch hold of her, and then we tried to bring her to herself and failed, and at last we carried her upstairs, an' I told uncle to run down and put out the lights, and then go fast as he could for Mrs. Begg, being very experienced in sickness, an' he so did. I got off her clothes and her poor wreath, and I cried as I done it. We both stayed there that night, and the doctor said 't was a shock when he come in the morning; he 'd been over to Black Island an' had to stay all night with a very sick child."

"You said that she lived alone some time after the news came," I reminded Mrs. Todd then.

"Oh yes, dear," answered my friend sadly, "but it wa'n't what you 'd call livin'; no, it was only dyin', though at a snail's pace. She never went out again those few months, but for a while she could manage to get about the house a little, and do what was needed, an' I never let two days go by without seein' her or hearin' from her. She never took much notice as I came an' went except to answer if I asked her anything. Mother was the one who gave her the only comfort."

"What was that?" I asked softly.

"She said that anybody in such trouble ought to see their minister, mother did, and one day she spoke to Mis' Tolland, and found that the poor soul had been believin' all the time that there were n't any priests here. We 'd come to know she was a Catholic by her beads and all, and that had set some narrow minds against her. And mother explained it just as she would to a child; and uncle Lorenzo sent word right off somewheres up river by a packet that was bound up the bay, and the first o' the week a priest come by the boat, an' uncle Lorenzo was on the wharf 'tendin' to some business, so they just come up for me, and I walked with him to show him the house. He was a kind-hearted old man; he looked so benevolent an' fatherly I could ha' stopped an' told him my own troubles; yes, I was satisfied when I first saw his face, an' when poor Mis' Tolland beheld him enter the room she went right down on her knees and clasped her hands together to him as if he 'd come to save her life, and he lifted her up and blessed her, an' I left 'em together, and slipped out into the open field and walked there in sight so if they needed to call me, and I had my own thoughts. At last I saw him at the door; he had to catch the return boat. I meant to walk back with him and offer him some supper, but he said no, and said he was comin' again if needed, and signed me to go into the house to her, and shook his head in a way that meant he understood everything. I can see him now; he walked with a cane, rather tired and feeble; I wished somebody would come along, so 's to carry him down to the shore.

"Mis' Tolland looked up at me with a new look when I went in, an' she even took hold o' my hand and kept it. He had put some oil on her forehead, but nothing anybody could do would keep her alive very long; 't was his medicine for the soul rather 'n the body. I helped her to bed, and next morning she could n't get up to dress her, and that was Monday, and she began to fail, and 't was Friday night she died." (Mrs. Todd spoke with unusual haste and lack of detail.) "Mrs. Begg and I watched with her, and made everything nice and proper, and after all the ill will there was a good number gathered to the funeral. 'T was in Reverend Mr. Bascom's day, and he done very well in his prayer, considering he could n't fill in with mentioning all the near connections by name as was his habit. He spoke very feeling about her being a stranger and twice widowed, and all he said about her being reared among the heathen was to observe that there might be roads leadin' up to the New Jerusalem from various points. I says to myself that I guessed quite a number must ha' reached there that wa'n't able to set out from Dunnet Landin'!"

Mrs. Todd gave an odd little laugh as she bent toward the fire-light to pick up a dropped stitch in her knitting, and then I heard a heartfelt sigh.

'T was most forty years ago," she said; "most everybody 's gone a'ready that was there that day."

V

Suddenly Mrs. Todd gave an energetic shrug of her shoulders, and a quick look at me, and I saw that the sails of her narrative were filled with a fresh breeze.

"Uncle Lorenzo, Cap'n Bowden that I have referred to"—

"Certainly!" I agreed with eager expectation.

"He was the one that had been left charge of Cap'n John Tol-land's affairs, and had now come to be of unforseen importance.

"Mrs. Begg an' I had stayed in the house both before an' after Mis' Tolland's decease, and she was now in haste to be gone, having affairs to call her home; but uncle come to me as the exercises was beginning, and said he thought I 'd better remain at the house while they went to the buryin' ground. I could n't understand his reasons, an' I felt disappointed, bein' as near to her as most any-body; 't was rough weather, so mother could n't get in, and did n't even hear Mis' Tolland was gone till next day. I just nodded to sat-isfy him, 't wa'n't no time to discuss anything. Uncle seemed flus-tered; he 'd gone out deep-sea fishin' the day she died, and the storm I told you of rose very sudden, so they got blown off way down the coast beyond Monhegan, and he 'd just got back in time to dress himself and come.

"I set there in the house after I 'd watched her away down the straight road far 's I could see from the door; 't was a little short walkin' funeral an' a cloudy sky, so everything looked dull an' gray, an' it crawled along all in one piece, same 's walking funerals do, an' I wondered how it ever come to the Lord's mind to let her begin down among them gay islands all heat and sun, and end up here among the rocks with a north wind blowin'. 'T was a gale that begun the afternoon before she died, and had kept blowin' off an' on ever since. I 'd thought more than once how glad I should be to get home an' out o' sound o' them black spruces a-beatin' an' scratchin' at the front windows.

"I set to work pretty soon to put the chairs back, an' set outdoors some that was borrowed, an' I went out in the kitchen, an' I made up a good fire in case somebody come an' wanted a cup o' tea; but I did n't expect any one to travel way back to the house unless 't was uncle Lorenzo. 'T was growin' so chilly that I fetched some kindlin' wood and made fires in both the fore rooms. Then I set down an' begun to feel as usual, and I got my knittin' out of a drawer. You can't be sorry for a poor creatur' that 's come to the end o' all her troubles; my only discomfort was I thought I 'd ought to feel worse at losin' her than I did; I was younger then than I be now. And as I set there, I begun to hear some long notes o' dronin' music from upstairs that chilled me to the bone."

Mrs. Todd gave a hasty glance at me.

"Quick 's I could gather me, I went right upstairs to see what 't was," she added eagerly, "an' 't was just what I might ha' known. She 'd always kept her guitar hangin' right against the wall in her room; 't was tied by a blue ribbon, and there was a window left wide open; the wind was veerin' a good deal, an' it slanted in and searched the room. The strings was jarrin' yet.

"'T was growin' pretty late in the afternoon, an' I begun to feel lonesome as I should n't now, and I was disappointed at having to stay there, the more I thought it over, but after a while I saw Cap'n Lorenzo polin' back up the road all alone, and when he come nearer I could see he had a bundle under his arm and had shifted his best black clothes for his every-day ones. I run out and put some tea into the teapot and set it back on the stove to draw an' when he come in I reached down a little jug o' spirits,—Cap'n Tolland had left his house well provisioned as if his wife was goin' to put to sea same 's himself, an' there she 'd gone an' left it. There was some cake that Mis' Begg an' I had made the day before. I thought that uncle an' me had a good right to the funeral supper, even if there wa'n't any one to join us. I was lookin' forward to my cup o' tea; 't was beautiful tea out of a green lacquered chest that I've got now."

"You must have felt very tired," said I, eagerly listening.

"I was 'most beat out, with watchin' an' tendin' and all," answered Mrs. Todd, with as much sympathy in her voice as if she were speaking of another person. "But I called out to uncle as he came in, 'Well, I expect it 's all over now, an' we 've all done what we could. I thought we 'd better have some tea or somethin' before we go home. Come right out in the kitchen, sir,' says I, never thinking but we only had to let the fires out and lock up everything safe an' eat our refreshment, an' go home.

"'I want both of us to stop here to-night,' says uncle, looking at me very important.

"'Oh, what for?' says I, kind o' fretful.

"'I've got my proper reasons,' says uncle. 'I 'll see you well satisfied, Almira. Your tongue ain't so easy-goin' as some o' the women folks, an' there 's property here to take charge of that you don't know nothin' at all about.'

"'What do you mean?' says I.

"'Cap'n Tolland acquainted me with his affairs; he had n't no sort o' confidence in nobody but me an' his wife, after he was tricked into signin' that Portland note, an' lost money. An' she did n't know nothin' about business; but what he did n't take to sea to be sunk with him he 's hid somewhere in this house. I expect Mis' Tolland may have told you where she kept things?' said uncle.

"I see he was dependin' a good deal on my answer," said Mrs. Todd, "but I had to disappoint him; no, she had never said nothin' to me.

"'Well, then, we 've got to make a search,' says he, with considerable relish; but he was all tired and worked up, and we set down to the table, an' he had somethin', an' I took my desired cup o' tea, and then I begun to feel more interested.

"'Where you goin' to look first?' says I, but he give me a short look an' made no answer, and begun to mix me a very small portion out of the jug, in another glass. I took it to please him; he said I looked tired, speakin' real fatherly, and I did feel better for it, and we set talkin' a few minutes, an' then he started for the cellar, carrying an old ship's lantern he fetched out o' the stairway an' lit.

"'What are you lookin' for, some kind of a chist?' I inquired, and he said yes. All of a sudden it come to me to ask who was the heirs; Eliza Tolland, Cap'n John's own sister, had never demeaned herself to come near the funeral, and uncle Lorenzo faced right about and begun to laugh, sort o' pleased. I thought queer of it; 't wa'n't what he 'd taken, which would be nothin' to an old weathered sailor like him.

"'Who 's the heir?' says I the second time.

"'Why, it's *you*, Almiry,' says he; and I was so took aback I set right down on the turn o' the cellar stairs.

"'Yes 't is,' said uncle Lorenzo. 'I'm glad of it too. Some thought she did n't have no sense but foreign sense, an' a poor stock o' that, but she said you was friendly to her, an' one day after she got news of Tolland's death, an' I had fetched up his will that left everything to her, she said she was goin' to make a writin', so 's you could have things after she was gone, an' she give five hundred to me for bein' executor. Square Pease fixed up the paper, an' she signed it; it 's all accordin' to law.' There, I begun to cry," said Mrs. Todd; "I could n't help it. I wished I had her back again to do somethin' for, an' to make her know I felt sisterly to her more 'n I 'd ever showed, an' it come over me 't was all too late, an I cried the more, till uncle showed impatience, an' I got up an' stumbled along down cellar with my apern to my eyes the greater part of the time.

"'I'm goin' to have a clean search,' says he; 'you hold the light.' An' I held it, and he rummaged in the arches an' under the stairs, an' over in some old closet where he reached out bottles an' stone jugs an' canted some kags an' one or two casks, an' chuckled well when he heard there was something inside,—but there wa'n't nothin' to find but things usual in a cellar, an' then the old lantern was givin' out an' we come away.

"'He spoke to me of a chist, Cap'n Tolland did,' says uncle in a whisper. 'He said a good sound chist was as safe a bank as there was, an' I beat him out of such nonsense, 'count o' fire an' other risks.' 'There's no chist in the rooms above,' says I; 'no, uncle, there ain't no sea-chist, for I 've been here long enough to see what there was to be seen.' Yet he would n't feel contented till he 'd mounted up into the toploft; 't was one o' them single, hip-roofed houses that don't give proper accommodation for a real garret, like Cap'n Littlepage's down here at the Landin'. There was broken furniture and rubbish, an' he let down a terrible sight o' dust into the front entry, but sure enough there was n't no chist. I had it all to sweep up next day.

"'He must have took it away to sea,' says I to the cap'n, an' even then he did n't want to agree, but we was both beat out. I told him where I 'd always seen Mis' Tolland get her money from, and we found much as a hundred dollars there in an old red morocco wallet. Cap'n John had been gone a good while a'ready, and she had spent what she needed. 'T was in an old desk o' his in the settin' room that we found the wallet."

"At the last minute he may have taken his money to sea," I suggested.

"Oh yes," agreed Mrs. Todd. "He did take considerable to make his venture to bring home, as was customary, an' that was drowned with him as uncle agreed; but he had other property in shipping, and a thousand dollars invested in Portland in a cordage shop, but 't was about the time shipping begun to decay, and the cordage shop failed, and in the end I wa'n't so rich as I thought I was goin' to be for those few minutes on the cellar stairs. There was an auction that accumulated something. Old Mis' Tolland, the cap'n's mother, had heired some good furniture from a sister: there was above thirty chairs in all, and they 're apt to sell well. I got over a thousand dollars when we come to settle up, and I made uncle take his five hundred; he was getting along in years and had met with losses in navigation, and he left it back to me when he died, so I had a real good lift. It all lays in the bank over to Rockland, and I draw my interest fall an' spring, with the little Mr. Todd was able to leave me; but that 's kind o' sacred money; 't was earnt and saved with the hope o' youth, an' I 'm very particular what I spend it for. Oh yes, what with ownin' my house, I 've been enabled to get along very well with prudence!" said Mrs. Todd contentedly.

"But there was the house and land," I asked,—"what became of that part of the property?"

Mrs. Todd looked into the fire, and a shadow of disapproval flitted over her face.

"Poor old uncle!" she said, "he got childish about the matter. I was hoping to sell at first, and I had an offer, but he always run of an idea that there was more money hid away, and kept wanting me to delay; an' he used to go up there all alone and search, and dig in the cellar, empty an' bleak as 't was in winter weather or any time. An' he 'd come and tell me he 'd dreamed he found gold behind a stone in the cellar wall, or somethin'. And one night we all see the light o' fire up that way, an' the whole Landin' took the road, and run to look, and the Tolland property was all in a light blaze. I expect the old gentleman had dropped fire about; he said he 'd been up there to see if everything was safe in the afternoon. As for the land, 't was so poor that everybody used to have a joke that the Tolland boys preferred to farm the sea instead. It 's 'most all grown up to bushes now, where it ain't poor water grass in the low places. There 's some upland that has a pretty view, after you cross the brook bridge. Years an' years after she died, there was some o' her flowers used to come up an' bloom in the door garden. I brought two or three that was unusual down here; they always come up and remind me of her, constant as the spring. But I never did want to fetch home that guitar, some way or 'nother; I would n't let it go at the auction, either. It was hangin' right there in the house when the fire took place. I 've got some o' her other little things scattered about the house: that picture on the mantelpiece belonged to her."

I had often wondered where such a picture had come from, and why Mrs. Todd had chosen it; it was a French print of the statue of the Empress Josephine in the Savane at old Fort Royal, in Martinique.

VI

Mrs. Todd drew her chair closer to mine; she held the cat and her knitting with one hand as she moved, but the cat was so warm and so sound asleep that she only stretched a lazy paw in spite of what must have felt like a slight earthquake. Mrs. Todd began to speak almost in a whisper.

"I ain't told you all," she continued; "no, I have n't spoken of all to but very few. The way it came was this," she said solemnly, and then stopped to listen to the wind, and sat for a moment in deferential silence, as if she waited for the wind to speak first. The cat suddenly lifted her head with quick excitement and gleaming eyes, and her mistress was leaning forward toward the fire with an arm laid on either knee, as if they were consulting the glowing coals for some augury. Mrs. Todd looked like an old prophetess as she sat there with the firelight shining on her strong face; she was posed for some great painter. The woman with the cat was as unconscious and as mysterious as any sibyl of the Sistine Chapel.

"There, that 's the last struggle o' the gale," said Mrs. Todd, nodding her head with impressive certainty and still looking into the bright embers of the fire. "You 'll see!" She gave me another quick glance, and spoke in a low tone as if we might be overheard.

"'T was such a gale as this the night Mis' Tolland died. She appeared more comfortable the first o' the evenin'; and Mrs. Begg was more spent than I, bein' older, and a beautiful nurse that was the first to see and think of everything, but perfectly quiet an' never asked a useless question. You remember her funeral when you first come to the Landing? And she consented to goin' an' havin' a good sleep while she could, and left me one o' those good little pewter lamps that burnt whale oil an' made plenty o' light in the room, but not too bright to be disturbin'.

"Poor Mis' Tolland had been distressed the night before, an' all that day, but as night come on she grew more and more easy, an' was layin' there asleep; 't was like settin' by any sleepin' person, and I had none but usual thoughts. When the wind lulled and the rain, I could hear the seas, though more distant than this, and I don' know 's I observed any other sound than what the weather made; 't was a very solemn feelin' night. I set close by the bed; there was times she looked to find somebody when she was awake. The light was on her face, so I could see her plain; there was always times when she wore a look that made her seem a stranger you 'd never set eyes on before. I did think what a world it was that her an' me should have come together so, and she have nobody but Dunnet

Landin' folks about her in her extremity. 'You 're one o' the stray ones, poor creatur',' I said. I remember those very words passin' through my mind, but I saw reason to be glad she had some comforts, and did n't lack friends at the last, though she 'd seen misery an' pain. I was glad she was quiet; all day she 'd been restless, and we could n't understand what she wanted from her French speech. We had the window open to give her air, an' now an' then a gust would strike the guitar that was on the wall and set it swinging by the blue ribbon, and soundin' as if somebody begun to play it. I come near takin' it down, but you never know what 'll fret a sick person an' put 'em on the rack, an' that guitar was one o' the few things she 'd brought with her."

I nodded assent, and Mrs. Todd spoke still lower.

"I set there close by the bed; I 'd been through a good deal for some days back, and I thought I might 's well be droppin' asleep too, bein' a quick person to wake. She looked to me as if she might last a day longer, certain, now she 'd got more comfortable, but I was real tired, an' sort o' cramped as watchers will get, an' a fretful feeling begun to creep over me such as they often do have. If you give way, there ain't no support for the sick person; they can't count on no composure o' their own. Mis' Tolland moved then, a little restless, an' I forgot me quick enough, an' begun to hum out a little part of a hymn tune just to make her feel everything was as usual an' not wake up into a poor uncertainty. All of a sudden she set right up in bed with her eyes wide open, an' I stood an' put my arm behind her; she had n't moved like that for days. And she reached out both her arms toward the door, an' I looked the way she was lookin', an' I see some body was standin' there against the dark. No, 't wa'n't Mis' Begg; 't was somebody a good deal shorter than Mis' Begg. The lamplight struck across the room between us. I could n't tell the shape, but 't was a woman's dark face lookin' right at us; 't wa'n't but an instant I could see. I felt dreadful cold, and my head begun to swim; I thought the light went out; 't wa'n't but an instant, as I say, an' when my sight come back I could n't see nothing there. I was one that did n't know what it was to faint away, no matter what happened; time was I felt above it in others, but 't was somethin' that made poor human natur' quail. I saw very plain while I could see; 't was a pleasant enough face, shaped somethin' like Mis' Tolland's, and a kind of expectin' look.

"No, I don't expect I was asleep," Mrs. Todd assured me quietly, after a moment's pause, though I had not spoken. She gave a heavy sigh before she went on. I could see that the recollection moved her in the deepest way.

"I suppose if I had n't been so spent an' quavery with long watchin', I might have kept my head an' observed much better," she added humbly; "but I see all I could bear. I did try to act calm, an' I laid Mis' Tolland down on her pillow, an' I was a-shakin' as I done it. All she did was to look up to me so satisfied and sort o' questioning, an' I looked back to her.

"'You saw her, did n't you?' she says to me, speakin' perfectly reasonable. ''T is my mother,' she says again, very feeble, but lookin' straight up at me, kind of surprised with the pleasure, and smiling as if she saw I was overcome, an' would have said more if she could, but we had hold of hands. I see then her change was comin', but I did n't call Mis' Begg, nor make no uproar. I felt calm then, an' lifted to somethin' different as I never was since. She opened her eyes just as she was goin'—

"'You saw her, did n't you?' she said the second time, an' I says, '*Yes dear, I did; you ain't never goin' to feel strange an' lonesome no more.*' An' then in a few quiet minutes 't was all over. I felt they 'd gone away together. No, I wa'n't alarmed afterward; 't was just that one moment I could n't live under, but I never called it beyond reason I should see the other watcher. I saw plain enough there was somebody there with me in the room.

VII

"'T was just such a night as this Mis' Tolland died," repeated Mrs. Todd, returning to her usual tone and leaning back comfortably in her chair as she took up her knitting. " 'T was just such a night as this. I 've told the circumstances to but very few; but I don't call it beyond reason. When folks is goin' 't is all natural, and only common things can jar upon the mind. You know plain enough there 's somethin' beyond this world; the doors stand wide open. 'There 's somethin' of us that must still live on; we 've got to join both worlds together an' live in one but for the other.' The doctor said that to me one day, an' I never could forget it; he said 't was in one o' his old doctor's books."

We sat together in silence in the warm little room; the rain dropped heavily from the eaves, and the sea still roared, but the high wind had done blowing. We heard the far complaining fog horn of a steamer up the Bay.

"There goes the Boston boat out, pretty near on time," said Mrs. Todd with satisfaction. "Sometimes these late August storms 'll sound a good deal worse than they really be. I do hate to hear the poor steamers callin' when they 're bewildered in thick nights in winter, comin' on the coast. Yes, there goes the boat; they 'll find it rough at sea, but the storm 's all over."

THE QUEEN'S TWIN

I

The coast of Maine was in former years brought so near to foreign shores by its busy fleet of ships that among the older men and women one still finds a surprising proportion of travelers. Each seaward-stretching headland with its high-set houses, each island of a single farm, has sent its spies to view many a Land of Eshcol; one may see plain, contented old faces at the windows, whose eyes have looked at far-away ports and known the splendors of the Eastern world. They shame the easy voyager of the North Atlantic and the Mediterranean; they have rounded the Cape of Good Hope and braved the angry seas of Cape Horn in small wooden ships; they have brought up their hardy boys and girls on narrow decks; they were among the last of the Northmen's children to go adventuring to unknown shores. More than this one cannot give to a young State for its enlightenment; the sea captains and the captains' wives of Maine knew something of the wide world, and never mistook their native parishes for the whole instead of a part thereof; they knew not only Thomaston and Castine and Portland, but London and Bristol and Bordeaux, and the strange-mannered harbors of the China Sea.

One September day, when I was nearly at the end of a summer spent in a village called Dunnet Landing, on the Maine coast, my friend Mrs. Todd, in whose house I lived, came home from a long, solitary stroll in the wild pastures, with an eager look as if she were just starting on a hopeful quest instead of returning. She brought a little basket with blackberries enough for supper, and held it towards me so that I could see that there were also some late and surprising raspberries sprinkled on top, but she made no comment upon her wayfaring. I could tell plainly that she had something very important to say.

"You have n't brought home a leaf of anything," I ventured to this practiced herb-gatherer. "You were saying yesterday that the witch hazel might be in bloom."

"I dare say, dear," she answered in a lofty manner; "I ain't goin' to say it was n't; I ain't much concerned either way 'bout the facts o' witch hazel. Truth is, I 've been off visitin'; there 's an old Indian footpath leadin' over towards the Back Shore through the great heron swamp that anybody can't travel over all summer. You have to seize your time some day just now, while the low ground 's summer-dried as it is to-day, and before the fall rains set in. I never thought of it till I was out o' sight o' home, and I says to myself, 'Today 's the day, certain!' and stopped along smart as I could. Yes, I 've been vis-itin'. I did get into one spot that was wet underfoot before I noticed; you wait till I get me a pair o' dry woolen stockings, in case of cold, and I 'll come an' tell ye."

Mrs. Todd disappeared. I could see that something had deeply interested her. She might have fallen in with either the sea-serpent or the lost tribes of Israel, such was her air of mystery and satisfac-tion. She had been away since just before mid-morning, and as I sat waiting by my window I saw the last red glow of autumn sunshine flare along the gray rocks of the shore and leave them cold again, and touch the far sails of some coastwise schooners so that they stood like golden houses on the sea.

I was left to wonder longer than I liked. Mrs. Todd was making an evening fire and putting things in train for supper; presently she returned, still looking warm and cheerful after her long walk.

"There 's a beautiful view from a hill over where I 've been," she told me; "yes, there's a beautiful prospect of land and sea. You would n't discern the hill from any distance, but 't is the pretty sit-uation of it that counts. I sat there a long spell, and I did wish for you. No, I did n't know a word about goin' when I set out this morn-ing" (as if I had openly reproached her!); "I only felt one o' them travelin' fits comin' on, an' I ketched up my little basket; I did n't know but I might turn and come back time for dinner. I thought it wise to set out your luncheon for you in case I did n't. Hope you had all you wanted; yes, I hope you had enough."

"Oh, yes, indeed," said I. My landlady was always peculiarly bountiful in her supplies when she left me to fare for myself, as if she made a sort of peace-offering or affectionate apology.

"You know that hill with the old house right on top, over beyond the heron swamp? You 'll excuse me for explainin'," Mrs. Todd began, "but you ain't so apt to strike inland as you be to go right along shore. You know that hill; there 's a path leadin' right over to it that you have to look sharp to find nowadays; it belonged to the up-country Indians when they had to make a carry to the landing here to get to the out' islands. I 've heard the old folks say that there used to be a place across a ledge where they 'd worn a deep track with their moccasin feet, but I never could find it. 'T is so overgrown in some places that you keep losin' the path in the bushes and findin' it as you can; but it runs pretty straight considerin' the lay o' the land, and I keep my eye on the sun and the moss that grows one side o' the tree trunks. Some brook 's been choked up and the swamp 's bigger than it used to be. Yes; I did get in deep enough, one place!"

I showed the solicitude that I felt. Mrs. Todd was no longer young, and in spite of her strong, great frame and spirited behavior, I knew that certain ills were apt to seize upon her, and would end some day by leaving her lame and ailing.

"Don't you go to worryin' about me," she insisted, "settin' still 's the only way the Evil One 'll ever get the upper hand o' me. Keep me movin' enough, an' I 'm twenty year old summer an' winter both. I don't know why 't is, but I 've never happened to mention the one I 've been to see. I don't know why I never happened to speak the name of Abby Martin, for I often give her a thought, but 't is a dreadful out-o'-the-way place where she lives, and I have n't seen her myself for three or four years. She 's a real good interesting woman, and we 're well acquainted; she 's nigher mother's age than mine, but she 's very young feeling. She made me a nice cup o' tea, and I don't know but I should have stopped all night if I could have got word to you not to worry."

Then there was a serious silence before Mrs. Todd spoke again to make a formal announcement.

"She is the Queen's Twin," and Mrs. Todd looked steadily to see how I might bear the great surprise.

"The Queen's Twin?" I repeated.

"Yes, she 's come to feel a real interest in the Queen, and anybody can see how natural 't is. They were born the very same day, and you would be astonished to see what a number o' other things have corresponded. She was speaking o' some o' the facts to me to-day, an' you 'd think she 'd never done nothing but read history. I see how earnest she was about it as I never did before. I 've often and often heard her allude to the facts, but now she 's got to be old and the hurry 's over with her work, she 's come to live a good deal in her thoughts, as folks often do, and I tell you 't is a sight o' company for her. If you want to hear about Queen Victoria, why Mis' Abby Martin 'll tell you everything. And the prospect from that hill I spoke of is as beautiful as anything in this world; 't is worth while your goin' over to see her just for that."

"When can you go again?" I demanded eagerly.

"I should say to-morrow," answered Mrs. Todd; "yes, I should say to-morrow; but I expect 't would be better to take one day to rest, in between. I considered that question as I was comin' home, but I hurried so that there wa'n't much time to think. It 's a dreadful long way to go with a horse; you have to go 'most as far as the old Bowden place an' turn off to the left, a master long, rough road, and then you have to turn right round as soon as you get there if you mean to get home before nine o'clock at night. But to strike across country from here, there 's plenty o' time in the shortest days, and you can have a good hour or two's visit beside; 't ain't but a very few miles, and it 's pretty all the way along. There used to be a few good families over there, but they 've died and scattered, so now she 's far from neighbors. There, she really cried, she was so glad to see anybody comin'. You 'll be amused to hear her talk about the Queen, but I thought twice or three times as I set there 't was about all the company she 'd got."

"Could we go day after to-morrow?" I asked eagerly.

"'T would suit me exactly," said Mrs. Todd.

II

One can never be so certain of good New England weather as in the days when a long easterly storm has blown away the warm

late-summer mists, and cooled the air so that however bright the
sunshine is by day, the nights come nearer and nearer to frostiness.
There was a cold freshness in the morning air when Mrs. Todd and
I locked the house-door behind us; we took the key of the fields into
our own hands that day, and put out across country as one puts out
to sea. When we reached the top of the ridge behind the town it
seemed as if we had anxiously passed the harbor bar and were comfortably in open sea at last.

"There, now!" proclaimed Mrs. Todd, taking a long breath, "now I
do feel safe. It 's just the weather that 's liable to bring somebody to
spend the day; I 've had a feeling of Mis' Elder Caplin from North
Point bein' close upon me ever since I waked up this mornin', an' I
did n't want to be hampered with our present plans. She 's a great
hand to visit; she 'll be spendin' the day somewhere from now till
Thanksgivin', but there 's plenty o' places at the Landin' where she
goes, an' if I ain't there she 'll just select another. I thought mother
might be in, too, 't is so pleasant; but I run up the road to look off
this mornin' before you was awake, and there was no sign o' the
boat. If they had n't started by that time they would n't start, just
as the tide is now; besides, I see a lot o' mackerel-men headin'
Green Island way, and they 'll detain William. No, we're safe now,
an' if mother should be comin' in tomorrow we 'll have all this to tell
her. She an' Mis' Abby Martin 's very old friends."

We were walking down the long pasture slopes towards the dark
woods and thickets of the low ground. They stretched away northward like an unbroken wilderness; the early mists still dulled much
of the color and made the uplands beyond look like a very far-off
country.

"It ain't so far as it looks from here," said my companion reassuringly, "but we 've got no time to spare either," and she hurried on,
leading the way with a fine sort of spirit in her step; and presently
we struck into the old Indian footpath, which could be plainly seen
across the long-unploughed turf of the pastures, and followed it
among the thick, low-growing spruces. There the ground was
smooth and brown under foot, and the thin-stemmed trees held a
dark and shadowy roof overhead. We walked a long way without
speaking; sometimes we had to push aside the branches, and sometimes we walked in a broad aisle where the trees were larger. It was

a solitary wood, birdless and beastless; there was not even a rabbit to be seen, or a crow high in air to break the silence.

"I don't believe the Queen ever saw such a lonesome trail as this," said Mrs. Todd, as if she followed the thoughts that were in my mind. Our visit to Mrs. Abby Martin seemed in some strange way to concern the high affairs of royalty. I had just been thinking of English landscapes, and of the solemn hills of Scotland with their lonely cottages and stone-walled sheepfolds, and the wandering flocks on high cloudy pastures. I had often been struck by the quick interest and familiar allusion to certain members of the royal house which one found in distant neighborhoods of New England; whether some old instincts of personal loyalty have survived all changes of time and national vicissitudes, or whether it is only that the Queen's own character and disposition have won friends for her so far away, it is impossible to tell. But to hear of a twin sister was the most surprising proof of intimacy of all, and I must confess that there was something remarkably exciting to the imagination in my morning walk. To think of being presented at Court in the usual way was for the moment quite commonplace.

III

Mrs. Todd was swinging her basket to and fro like a school-girl as she walked, and at this moment it slipped from her hand and rolled lightly along the ground as if there were nothing in it. I picked it up and gave it to her, whereupon she lifted the cover and looked in with anxiety.

"'T is only a few little things, but I don't want to lose 'em, she explained humbly. "'T was lucky you took the other basket if I was goin' to roll it round. Mis' Abby Martin complained o' lacking some pretty pink silk to finish one o' her little frames, an' I thought I'd carry her some, and I had a bunch o' gold thread that had been in a box o' mine this twenty year. I never was one to do much fancy work, but we 're all liable to be swept away by fashion. And then there is a small packet o' very choice herbs that I gave a good deal of attention to; they 'll smarten her up and give her the best of appetites, come spring. She was tellin' me that spring weather is very wiltin' an' tryin' to her, and she was beginnin' to dread it already. Mother 's just the same way; if I could prevail on mother to take some o' those remedies in good season 't would make a world o' difference, but she gets all down hill before I have a chance to hear of it, and then William comes in to tell me, sighin' and bewailin', how feeble mother is. 'Why can't you remember 'bout them good herbs that I never let her be without?' I say to him—he does provoke me so; and then off he goes, sulky enough, down to his boat. Next thing I know, she comes in to go to meetin', wantin' to speak to everybody and feelin' like a girl. Mis' Martin's case is very much the same; but she 's nobody to watch her. William 's kind o' slow-moulded; but there, any William 's better than none when you get to be Mis' Martin's age."

"Had n't she any children?" I asked.

"Quite a number," replied Mrs. Todd grandly, "but some are gone and the rest are married and settled. She never was a great hand to go about visitin'. I don't know but Mis' Martin might be called a little peculiar. Even her own folks has to make company of her; she never slips in and lives right along with the rest as if 't was at home, even in her own children's houses. I heard one o' her sons' wives say once she 'd much rather have the Queen to spend the day if she could choose between the two, but I never thought Abby was so difficult as that. I used to love to have her come; she may have been sort o' ceremonious, but very pleasant and sprightly if you had sense enough to treat her her own way. I always think she 'd know just how to live with great folks, and feel easier 'long of them an' their ways. Her son's wife 's a great driver with farm-work, boards a great tableful o' men in hayin' time, an' feels right in her element. I don't say but she 's a good woman an smart, but sort o' rough. Anybody that 's gentle-mannered an' precise like Mis' Martin would be a sort o' restraint.

"There 's all sorts o' folks in the country, same 's there is in the city," concluded Mrs. Todd gravely, and I as gravely agreed. The thick woods were behind us now, and the sun was shining clear overhead, the morning mists were gone, and a faint blue haze softened the distance; as we climbed the hill where we were to see the view, it seemed like a summer day. There was an old house on the height, facing southward,—a mere forsaken shell of an old house, with empty windows that looked like blind eyes. The frost-bitten grass grew close about it like brown fur, and there was a single crooked bough of lilac holding its green leaves close by the door.

"We 'll just have a good piece of bread-an'-butter now," said the commander of the expedition, "and then we 'll hang up the basket on some peg inside the house out o' the way o' the sheep, and have a han'some entertainment as we 're comin' back. She 'll be all through her little dinner when we get there, Mis' Martin will; but she 'll want to make us some tea, an' we must have our visit an' be startin' back pretty soon after two. I don't want to cross all that low ground again after it 's begun to grow chilly. An' it looks to me as if the clouds might begin to gather late in the afternoon."

Before us lay a splendid world of sea and shore. The autumn colors already brightened the landscape; and here and there at the edge of a dark tract of pointed firs stood a row of bright swamp-maples like scarlet flowers. The blue sea and the great tide inlets were untroubled by the lightest winds.

"Poor land, this is!" sighed Mrs. Todd as we sat down to rest on the worn doorstep. "I 've known three good hard-workin' families that come here full o' hope an' pride and tried to make something o' this farm, but it beat 'em all. There 's one small field that 's excellent for potatoes if you let half of it rest every year; but the land 's always hungry. Now, you see them little peakéd-topped spruces an' fir balsams comin' up over the hill all green an' hearty; they 've got it all their own way! Seems sometimes as if wild Natur' got jealous over a certain spot, and wanted to do just as she 'd a mind to. You 'll see here; she 'll do her own ploughin' an' harrowin' with frost an' wet, an' plant just what she wants and wait for her own crops. Man can't do nothin' with it, try as he may. I tell you those little trees means business!"

I looked down the slope, and felt as if we ourselves were likely to be surrounded and overcome if we lingered too long. There was a vigor of growth, a persistence and savagery about the sturdy little trees that put weak human nature at complete defiance. One felt a sudden pity for the men and women who had been worsted after a long fight in that lonely place; one felt a sadden fear of the unconquerable, immediate forces of Nature, as in the irresistible moment of a thunderstorm.

"I can recollect the time when folks were shy o' these woods we just come through," said Mrs. Todd seriously. "The men-folks themselves never 'd venture into 'em alone; if their cattle got strayed they 'd collect whoever they could get, and start off all together. They said a person was liable to get bewildered in there alone, and in old times folks had been lost. I expect there was considerable fear left over from the old Indian times, and the poor days o' witchcraft; anyway, I 've seen bold men act kind o' timid. Some women o' the Asa Bowden family went out one afternoon berryin' when I was a girl, and got lost and was out all night; they found 'em middle o' the mornin' next day, not half a mile from home, scared most to death, an' sayin' they 'd heard wolves and other beasts sufficient for a caravan. Poor creatur's! they 'd strayed at last into a kind of low place amongst some alders, an' one of 'em was so overset she never got over it, an' went off in a sort o' slow decline. 'T was like them victims that drowns in a foot o' water; but their minds did suffer dreadful. Some folks is born afraid of the woods and all wild places, but I must say they 've always been like home to me."

I glanced at the resolute, confident face of my companion. Life was very strong in her, as if some force of Nature were personified in this simple-hearted woman and gave her cousinship to the ancient deities. She might have walked the primeval fields of Sicily; her strong gingham skirts might at that very moment bend the slender stalks of asphodel and be fragrant with trodden thyme, instead of the brown wind-brushed grass of New England and frost-bitten goldenrod. She was a great soul, was Mrs. Todd, and I her humble follower, as we went our way to visit the Queen's Twin, leaving the bright view of the sea behind us, and descending to a lower country-side through the dry pastures and fields.

The farms all wore a look of gathering age, though the settlement was, after all, so young. The fences were already fragile, and it seemed as if the first impulse of agriculture had soon spent itself without hope of renewal. The better houses were always those that had some hold upon the riches of the sea; a house that could not harbor a fishing-boat in some neighboring inlet was far from being sure of every-day comforts. The land alone was not enough to live

upon in that stony region; it belonged by right to the forest, and to
the forest it fast returned. From the top of the hill where we had
been sitting we had seen prosperity in the dim distance, where the
land was good and the sun shone upon fat barns, and where warm-
looking houses with three or four chimneys apiece stood high on
their solid ridge above the bay.

As we drew nearer to Mrs. Martin's it was sad to see what poor
bushy fields, what thin and empty dwelling-places had been left by
those who had chosen this disappointing part of the northern country for their home. We crossed the last field and came into a narrow
rain-washed road, and Mrs. Todd looked eager and expectant and
said that we were almost at our journey's end. "I do hope Mis' Martin 'll ask you into her best room where she keeps all the Queen's
pictures. Yes, I think likely she will ask you; but 't ain't everybody
she deems worthy to visit 'em, I can tell you!" said Mrs. Todd warningly. "She 's been collectin' 'em an' cuttin' 'em out o' newspapers an'
magazines time out o' mind, and if she heard of anybody sailin' for
an English port she 'd contrive to get a little money to 'em and ask
to have the last likeness there was. She 's most covered her best-
room wall now; she keeps that room shut up sacred as a meetin'-
house! 'I won't say but I have my favorites amongst 'em,' she told
me t' other day, 'but they 're all beautiful to me as they can be!' And
she 's made some kind o' pretty little frames for 'em all—you know
there 's always a new fashion o' frames comin' round; first 't was
shell-work, and then 't was pine-cones, and bead-work 's had its
day, and now she 's much concerned with perforated cardboard
worked with silk. I tell you that best room 's a sight to see! But you
must n't look for anything elegant," continued Mrs. Todd, after a
moment's reflection. "Mis' Martin 's always been in very poor, strug-
glin' circumstances. She had ambition for her children, though they
took right after their father an' had little for themselves; she wa'n't
over an' above well married, however kind she may see fit to
speak. She 's been patient an' hard-workin' all her life, and always
high above makin' mean complaints of other folks. I expect all this
business about the Queen has buoyed her over many a shoal place
in life. Yes, you might say that Abby 'd been a slave, but there ain't
any slave but has some freedom."

IV

Presently I saw a low gray house standing on a grassy bank close to the road. The door was at the side, facing us, and a tangle of snow-berry bushes and cinnamon roses grew to the level of the window-sills. On the doorstep stood a bent-shouldered, little old woman; there was an air of welcome and of unmistakable dignity about her.

"She sees us coming," exclaimed Mrs. Todd in an excited whisper. "There, I told her I might be over this way again if the weather held good, and if I came I'd bring you. She said right off she'd take great pleasure in havin' a visit from you; I was surprised, she's usually so retirin'."

Even this reassurance did not quell a faint apprehension on our part; there was something distinctly formal in the occasion, and one felt that consciousness of inadequacy which is never easy for the humblest pride to bear. On the way I had torn my dress in an unex-pected encounter with a little thornbush, and I could now imagine how it felt to be going to Court and forgetting one's feathers or her Court train.

The Queen's Twin was oblivious of such trifles; she stood waiting with a calm look until we came near enough to take her kind hand. She was a beautiful old woman, with clear eyes and a lovely quiet-ness and genuineness of manner; there was not a trace of anything pretentious about her, or highly flown, as Mrs. Todd would say com-prehensively. Beauty in age is rare enough in women who have spent their lives in the hard work of a farmhouse; but autumn-like and withered as this woman may have looked, her features had kept, or rather gained, a great refinement. She led us into her old kitchen and gave us seats, and took one of the little straight-backed chairs herself and sat a short distance away, as if she were giving audience to an ambassador. It seemed as if we should all be stand-ing; you could not help feeling that the habits of her life were more ceremonious, but that for the moment she assumed the simplicities of the occasion.

Mrs. Todd was always Mrs. Todd, too great and self-possessed a soul for any occasion to ruffle. I admired her calmness, and presently the slow current of neighborhood talk carried one easily along; we spoke of the weather and the small adventures of the way, and then, as if I were after all not a stranger, our hostess turned almost affectionately to speak to me.

"The weather will be growing dark in London now. I expect that you 've been in London, dear?" she said.

"Oh, yes," I answered. "Only last year."

"It is a great many years since I was there, along in the forties," said Mrs. Martin. "'T was the only voyage I ever made; most of my neighbors have been great travelers. My brother was master of a vessel, and his wife usually sailed with him; but that year she had a young child more frail than the others, and she dreaded the care of it at sea. It happened that my brother got a chance for my husband to go as supercargo, being a good accountant, and came one day to urge him to take it; he was very ill-disposed to the sea, but he had met with losses, and I saw my own opportunity and persuaded them both to let me go too. In those days they did n't object to a woman's being aboard to wash and mend, the voyages were sometimes very long. And that was the way I come to see the Queen."

Mrs. Martin was looking straight in my eyes to see if I showed any genuine interest in the most interesting person in the world.

"Oh, I am very glad you saw the Queen," I hastened to say. "Mrs. Todd has told me that you and she were born the very same day."

"We were indeed, dear!" said Mrs. Martin, and she leaned back comfortably and smiled as she had not smiled before. Mrs. Todd gave a satisfied nod and glance, as if to say that things were going on as well as possible in this anxious moment.

"Yes," said Mrs. Martin again, drawing her chair a little nearer, "'t was a very remarkable thing; we were born the same day, and at exactly the same hour, after you allowed for all the difference in time. My father figured it out sea-fashion. Her Royal Majesty and I opened our eyes upon this world together; say what you may, 't is a bond between us."

Mrs. Todd assented with an air of triumph, and untied her hat-strings and threw them back over her shoulders with a gallant air.

"And I married a man by the name of Albert, just the same as she did, and all by chance, for I did n't get the news that she had an Albert too till a fortnight afterward; news was slower coming then than it is now. My first baby was a girl, and I called her Victoria after my mate; but the next one was a boy, and my husband wanted the right to name him, and took his own name and his brother Edward's, and pretty soon I saw in the paper that the little Prince o' Wales had been christened just the same. After that I made excuse to wait till I knew what she 'd named her children. I did n't want to break the chain, so I had an Alfred, and my darling Alice that I lost long before she lost hers, and there I stopped. If I 'd only had a dear daughter to stay at home with me, same 's her youngest one, I should have been so thankful! But if only one of us could have a little Beatrice, I 'm glad 't was the Queen; we 've both seen trouble, but she 's had the most care."

I asked Mrs. Martin if she lived alone all the year, and was told that she did except for a visit now and then from one of her grandchildren, "the only one that really likes to come an' stay quiet 'long o' grandma. She always says quick as she 's through her schoolin' she 's goin' to live with me all the time, but she 's very pretty an' has taking ways," said Mrs. Martin, looking both proud and wistful, "so I can tell nothing at all about it! Yes, I 've been alone most o' the time since my Albert was taken away, and that 's a great many years; he had a long time o' failing and sickness first." (Mrs. Todd's foot gave an impatient scuff on the floor.) "An' I 've always lived right here. I ain't like the Queen's Majesty, for this is the only palace I 've got," said the dear old thing, smiling again. "I 'm glad of it too, I don't like changing about, an' our stations in life are set very different. I don't require what the Queen does, but sometimes I 've thought 't was left to me to do the plain things she don't have time for. I expect she 's a beautiful housekeeper, nobody could n't have done better in her high place, and she 's been as good a mother as she 's been a queen."

"I guess she has, Abby," agreed Mrs. Todd instantly. "How was it you happened to get such a good look at her? I meant to ask you again when I was here t' other day."

"Our ship was layin' in the Thames, right there above Wapping. We was dischargin' cargo, and under orders to clear as quick as we could for Bordeaux to take on an excellent freight o' French goods," explained Mrs. Martin eagerly. "I heard that the Queen was goin' to a great review of her army, and would drive out o' her Buckin'ham Palace about ten o'clock in the mornin', and I run aft to Albert, my husband, and brother Horace where they was standin' together by the hatchway, and told 'em they must one of 'em take me. They laughed, I was in such a hurry, and said they could n't go; and I found they meant it and got sort of impatient when I began to talk, and I was 'most broken-hearted; 't was all the reason I had for makin' that hard voyage. Albert could n't help often reproachin' me, for he did so resent the sea, an' I 'd known how 't would be before we sailed; but I 'd minded nothing all the way till then, and I just crep' back to my cabin an' begun to cry. They was disappointed about their ship's cook, an' I 'd cooked for fo'c's'le an' cabin myself all the way over; 't was dreadful hard work, specially in rough weather; we 'd had head winds an' a six weeks' voyage. They 'd acted sort of ashamed o' me when I pled so to go ashore, an' that hurt my feelin's most of all. But Albert come below pretty soon; I 'd never given way so in my life, an' he begun to act frightened, and treated me gentle just as he did when we was goin' to be married, an' when I got over sobbin' he went on deck and saw Horace an' talked it over what they could do; they really had their duty to the vessel, and could n't be spared that day. Horace was real good when he understood everything, and he come an' told me I 'd more than worked my passage an' was goin' to do just as I liked now we was in port. He 'd engaged a cook, too, that was comin' aboard that mornin', and he was goin' to send the ship's carpenter with me—a nice fellow from up Thomaston way; he 'd gone to put on his ashore clothes as quick 's he could. So then I got ready, and we started off in the small boat and rowed up river. I was afraid we were too late, but the tide was setting up very strong, and we landed an' left the boat to a keeper, and I run all the way up those great streets and across a park. 'T was a great day, with sights o' folks everywhere, but 't was just as if they was nothin' but wax images to me. I kep' askin' my way an' runnin' on, with the carpenter comin' after as best he could, and just as I worked to the front o' the crowd by the palace, the gates was flung open and out she came; all prancin' horses and shinin' gold, and in a beautiful carriage there she sat, 't was a moment o' heaven to me. I saw her plain, and she looked right at me so pleasant and happy, just as if she knew there was somethin' different between us from other folks."

There was a moment when the Queen's Twin could not go on and neither of her listeners could ask a question.

"Prince Albert was sitting right beside her in the carriage," she continued. "Oh, he was a beautiful man! Yes, dear, I saw 'em both together just as I see you now, and then she was gone out o' sight in another minute, and the common crowd was all spread over the place pushin' an' cheerin'. 'T was some kind o' holiday, an' the carpenter and I got separated, an' then I found him again after I did n't think I should, an' he was all for makin' a day of it, and goin' to show me all the sights; he 'd been in London before, but I did n't want nothin' else, an' we went back through the streets down to the waterside an' took the boat. I remember I mended an old coat o' my Albert's as good as I could, sittin' on the quarter-deck in the sun all that afternoon, and 't was all as if I was livin' in a lovely dream. I don't know how to explain it, but there has n't been no friend I 've felt so near to me ever since."

One could not say much—only listen. Mrs. Todd put in a discerning question now and then, and Mrs. Martin's eyes shone brighter and brighter as she talked. What a lovely gift of imagination and true affection was in this fond old heart! I looked about the plain New England kitchen, with its wood-smoked walls and homely braided rugs on the worn floor, and all its simple furnishings. The loud-ticking clock seemed to encourage us to speak; at the other side of the room was an early newspaper portrait of Her Majesty the Queen of Great Britain and Ireland. On a shelf below were some flowers in a little glass dish, as if they were put before a shrine.

"If I could have had more to read, I should have known 'most everything about her," said Mrs. Martin wistfully. "I 've made the most of what I did have, and thought it over and over till it came clear. I sometimes seem to have her all my own, as if we 'd lived right together. I 've often walked out into the woods alone and told her what my troubles was, and it always seemed as if she told me 't was all right, an' we must have patience. I 've got her beautiful book about the Highlands, 't was dear Mis' Todd here that found out about her printing it and got a copy for me, and it 's been a treasure to my heart, just as if 't was written right to me. I always read it Sundays now, for my Sunday treat. Before that I used to have to imagine a good deal, but when I come to read her book, I knew what I expected was all true. We do think alike about so many things," said the Queen's Twin with affectionate certainty. "You see, there is something between us, being born just at the same time; 't is what they call a birthright. She 's had great tasks put upon her, being the Queen, an' mine has been the humble lot; but she 's done the best she could, nobody can say to the contrary, and there 's something between us; she 's been the great lesson I 've had to live by. She 's been everything to me. An' when she had her Jubilee, oh, how my heart was with her!"

"There, 't would n't play the part in her life it has in mine," said Mrs. Martin generously, in answer to something one of her listeners had said. "Sometimes I think, now she 's older she might like to know about us. When I think how few old friends anybody has left at our age, I suppose it may be just the same with her as it is with me; perhaps she would like to know how we came into life together. But I 've had a great advantage in seeing her, an' I can always fancy her goin' on while she don't know nothin' yet about me, except she may feel my love stayin' her heart sometimes an' not know just where it comes from. An' I dream about our being together out in some pretty fields, young as ever we was, and holdin' hands as we walk along. I 'd like to know if she ever has that dream too. I used to have days when I made believe she did know, an' was comin' to see me," confessed the speaker shyly, with a little flush on her cheeks; "and I 'd plan what I could have nice for supper, and I was n't goin' to let anybody know she was here havin' a good rest, except I 'd wish you, Almira Todd, or dear Mis' Blackett would happen in, for you 'd know just how to talk with her. You see, she likes to be up in Scotland, right out in the wild country, better than she does anywhere else."

"I 'd really love to take her out to see mother at Green Island," said Mrs. Todd with a sudden impulse.

"Oh, yes! I should love to have you," exclaimed Mrs. Martin, and then she began to speak in a lower tone. "One day I got thinkin' so about my dear Queen," she said, "an' livin' so in my thoughts, that I went to work an' got all ready for her, just as if she was really comin'. I never told this to a livin' soul before, but I feel you 'll understand. I put my best fine sheets and blankets I spun an' wove myself on the bed, and I picked some pretty flowers and put 'em all round the house, an' I worked as hard an' happy as I could all day, and had as nice a supper ready as I could get, sort of telling myself a story all the time. She was comin' an' I was goin' to see her again, an' I kep' it up until nightfall; an' when I see the dark an' it come to me I was all alone, the dream left me, an' I sat down on the doorstep an' felt all foolish an' tired. An', if you 'll believe it, I heard steps comin', an' an old cousin o' mine come wanderin' along, one I was apt to be shy of. She was n't all there, as folks used to say, but harmless enough and a kind of poor old talking body. And I went right to meet her when I first heard her call, 'stead o' hidin' as I sometimes did, an' she come in dreadful willin', an' we sat down to supper together; 't was a supper I should have had no heart to eat alone."

"I don't believe she ever had such a splendid time in her life as she did then. I heard her tell all about it afterwards," exclaimed Mrs. Todd compassionately. "There, now I hear all this it seems just as if the Queen might have known and could n't come herself, so she sent that poor old creatur' that was always in need!"

Mrs. Martin looked timidly at Mrs. Todd and then at me.

"'T was childish o' me to go an' get supper," she confessed.

"I guess you wa'n't the first one to do that," said Mrs. Todd. "No, I guess you wa'n't the first one who 's got supper that way, Abby," and then for a moment she could say no more.

Mrs. Todd and Mrs. Martin had moved their chairs a little so that they faced each other, and I, at one side, could see them both.

"No, you never told me o' that before, Abby," said Mrs. Todd gently. "Don't it show that for folks that have any fancy in 'em, such beautiful dreams is the real part o' life? But to most folks the common things that happens outside 'em is all in all."

Mrs. Martin did not appear to understand at first, strange to say, when the secret of her heart was put into words; then a glow of pleasure and comprehension shone upon her face. "Why, I believe you 're right, Almira!" she said, and turned to me.

"Would n't you like to look at my pictures of the Queen?" she asked, and we rose and went into the best room.

V

The mid-day visit seemed very short; September hours are brief to match the shortening days. The great subject was dismissed for a while after our visit to the Queen's pictures, and my companions spoke much of lesser persons until we drank the cup of tea which Mrs. Todd had foreseen. I happily remembered that the Queen herself is said to like a proper cup of tea, and this at once seemed to make her Majesty kindly join so remote and reverent a company. Mrs. Martin's thin cheeks took on a pretty color like a girl's. "Somehow I always have thought of her when I made it extra good," she said. "I 've got a real china cup that belonged to my grandmother, and I believe I shall call it hers now."

"Why don't you?" responded Mrs. Todd warmly, with a delightful smile.

Later they spoke of a promised visit which was to be made in the Indian summer to the Landing and Green Island, but I observed that Mrs. Todd presented the little parcel of dried herbs, with full directions, for a cure-all in the spring, as if there were no real chance of their meeting again first. As we looked back from the turn of the road the Queen's Twin was still standing on the doorstep watching us away, and Mrs. Todd stopped, and stood still for a moment before she waved her hand again.

"There 's one thing certain, dear," she said to me with great discernment; "it ain't as if we left her all alone!"

Then we set out upon our long way home over the hill, where we lingered in the afternoon sunshine, and through the dark woods across the heron-swamp.

WILLIAM'S WEDDING

I

The hurry of life in a large town, the constant putting aside of preference to yield to a most unsatisfactory activity, began to vex me, and one day I took the train, and only left it for the eastward-bound boat. Carlyle says somewhere that the only happiness a man ought to ask for is happiness enough to get his work done; and against this the complexity and futile ingenuity of social life seems a conspiracy. But the first salt wind from the east, the first sight of a lighthouse set boldly on its outer rock, the flash of a gull, the waiting procession of seaward-bound firs on an island, made me feel solid and definite again, instead of a poor, incoherent being. Life was resumed, and anxious living blew away as if it had not been. I could not breathe deep enough or long enough. It was a return to happiness.

The coast had still a wintry look; it was far on in May, but all the shore looked cold and sterile. One was conscious of going north as well as east, and as the day went on the sea grew colder, and all the warmer air and bracing strength and stimulus of the afternoon weather, and storage of the heat of summer, were quite gone. I was very cold and very tired when I came at evening up the lower bay, and saw the white houses of Dunnet Landing climbing the hill. They had a friendly look, these little houses, not as if they were climbing up the shore, but as if they were rather all coming down to meet a fond and weary traveler, and I could hardly wait with patience to step off the boat. It was not the usual eager company on the wharf. The coming-in of the mail-boat was the one large public event of a summer day, and I was disappointed at seeing none of my intimate friends but Johnny Bowden, who had evidently done nothing all winter but grow, so that his short sea-smitten clothes gave him a look of poverty.

Johnny's expression did not change as we greeted each other, but I suddenly felt that I had shown indifference and inconvenient delay by not coming sooner; before I could make an apology he took my small portmanteau, and walking before me in his old fashion he made straight up the hilly road toward Mrs. Todd's. Yes, he was much grown—it had never occurred to me the summer before that Johnny was likely, with the help of time and other forces, to grow into a young man; he was such a well-framed and well-settled chunk of a boy that nature seemed to have set him aside as something finished, quite satisfactory and entirely completed.

The wonderful little green garden had been enchanted away by winter. There were a few frost-bitten twigs and some thin shrubbery against the fence, but it was a most unpromising small piece of ground. My heart was beating like a lover's as I passed it on the way to the door of Mrs. Todd's house, which seemed to have become much smaller under the influence of winter weather.

"She has n't gone away?" I asked Johnny Bowden with a sudden anxiety just as we reached the doorstep.

"Gone away!" he faced me with blank astonishment—"I see her settin' by Mis' Caplin's window, the one nighest the road, about four o'clock!" And eager with suppressed news of my coming he made his entrance as if the house were a burrow.

Then on my homesick heart fell the voice of Mrs. Todd. She stopped, through what I knew to be excess of feeling, to rebuke Johnny for bringing in so much mud, and I dallied without for one moment during the ceremony; then we met again face to face.

II

"I dare say you can advise me what shapes they are going to wear. My meetin'-bunnit ain't going to do me again this year; no! I can't expect 't would do me forever," said Mrs. Todd, as soon as she could say anything. "There! do set down and tell me how you have been! We 've got a weddin' in the family, I s'pose you know?"

"A wedding!" said I, still full of excitement.

"Yes; I expect if the tide serves and the line-storm don't overtake him they 'll come in and appear out on Sunday. I should n't have concerned me about the bunnit for a month yet, nobody would notice, but havin' an occasion like this I shall show consider'ble. 'T will be an ordeal for William!"

"For *William*!" I exclaimed. "What do you mean, Mrs. Todd?"

She gave a comfortable little laugh. "Well, the Lord's seen reason at last an' removed Mis' Cap'n Hight up to the farm, an' I don't know but the weddin 's going to be this week. Esther 's had a great deal of business disposin' of her flock but she 's done extra well—the folks that owns the next place goin' up country are well off. 'T is elegant land north side o' that bleak ridge, an' one o' the boys has been Esther's right-hand man of late. She instructed him in all matters, and after she markets the early lambs he 's goin' to take the farm on halves, an' she 's give the refusal to him to buy her out within two years. She 's reserved the buryin'-lot, an' the right o' way in, an'—"

I could n't stop for details. I demanded reassurance of the central fact.

"William going to be married?" I repeated; whereat Mrs. Todd gave me a searching look that was not without scorn.

"Old Mis' Hight's funeral was a week ago Wednesday, and 't was very well attended," she assured me after a moment's pause.

"Poor thing!" said I, with a sudden vision of her helplessness and angry battle against the fate of illness; "it was very hard for her."

"I thought it was hard for Esther!" said Mrs. Todd without sentiment.

III

I had an odd feeling of strangeness: I missed the garden, and the little rooms, to which I had added a few things of my own the summer before, seemed oddly unfamiliar. It was like the hermit crab in a cold new shell,—and with the windows shut against the raw May air, and a strange silence and grayness of the sea all that first night and day of my visit, I felt as if I had after all lost my hold of that quiet life.

Mrs. Todd made the apt suggestion that city persons were prone to run themselves to death, and advised me to stay and get properly rested now that I had taken the trouble to come. She did not know how long I had been homesick for the conditions of life at the Landing the autumn before—it was natural enough to feel a little unsupported by compelling incidents on my return.

Some one has said that one never leaves a place, or arrives at one, until the next day! But on the second morning I woke with the familiar feeling of interest and ease, and the bright May sun was streaming in, while I could hear Mrs. Todd's heavy footsteps pounding about in the other part of the house as if something were going to happen. There was the first golden robin singing somewhere close to the house, and a lovely aspect of spring now, and I looked at the garden to see that in the warm night some of its treasures had grown a hand's breadth; the determined spikes of yellow daffies stood tall against the doorsteps, and the bloodroot was unfolding leaf and flower. The belated spring which I had left behind farther south had overtaken me on this northern coast. I even saw a presumptuous dandelion in the garden border.

It is difficult to report the great events of New England; expression is so slight, and those few words which escape us in moments of deep feeling look but meagre on the printed page. One has to assume too much of the dramatic fervor as one reads; but as I came out of my room at breakfast-time I met Mrs. Todd face to face, and when she said to me, "This weather 'll bring William in after her; 't is their happy day!" I felt something take possession of me which ought to communicate itself to the least sympathetic reader of this cold page. It is written for those who have a Dunnet Landing of their own: who either kindly share this with its writer, or possess another.

"I ain't seen his comin' sail yet; he 'll be likely to dodge round among the islands so he 'll be the less observed," continued Mrs. Todd. You can get a dory up the bay, even a clean new painted one, if you know as how, keepin' it against the high land." She stepped to the door and looked off to sea as she spoke. I could see her eye follow the gray shores to and fro, and then a bright light spread over her calm face. "There he comes, and he 's striking right in across the open bay like a man!" she said with splendid approval. "See, there he comes! Yes, there 's William, and he 's bent his new sail."

I looked too, and saw the fleck of white no larger than a gull's wing yet, but present to her eager vision.

I was going to France for the whole long summer that year, and the more I thought of such an absence from those simple scenes the more dear and delightful they became. Santa Teresa says that the true proficiency of the soul is not in much thinking, but in much loving, and sometimes I believed that I had never found love in its simplicity as I had found it at Dunnet Landing in the various hearts of Mrs. Blackett and Mrs. Todd and William. It is only because one came to know them, these three, loving and wise and true, in their own habitations. Their counterparts are in every village in the world, thank heaven, and the gift to one's life is only in its discernment. I had only lived in Dunnet until the usual distractions and artifices of the world were no longer in control, and I saw these simple natures clear. "The happiness of life is in its recognitions. It seems that we are not ignorant of those truths, and even that we believe them; but we are so little accustomed to think of them, they are so strange to us—"

"Well now, deary me!" said Mrs. Todd, breaking into exclamation; "I 've got to fly round—I thought he 'd have to beat; he can't sail far on that tack, and he won't be in for a good hour yet—I expect he 's made every arrangement, but he said he should n't go up after Esther unless the weather was good and I declare it did look doubtful this morning."

I remembered Esther's weather-worn face. She was like a Frenchwoman who had spent her life in the fields. I remembered her pleasant look, her childlike eyes, and thought of the astonishment of joy she would feel now in being taken care of and tenderly sheltered from wind and weather after all these years. They were going to be young again now, she and William, to forget work and care in the spring weather. I could hardly wait for the boat to come to land, I was so eager to see his happy face.

"Cake an' wine I 'm goin' to set 'em out!" said Mrs. Todd. "They won't stop to set down for an ordered meal, they 'll want to get right

out home quick 's they can. Yes, I 'll give 'em some cake an' wine—
I 've got a rare plum-cake from my best receipt, and a bottle o' wine
that the old Cap'n Denton of all give me, one of two, the day I was
married, one we had and one we saved, and I 've never touched it
till now. He said there wa'n't none like it in the State o' Maine."

It was a day of waiting, that day of spring; the May weather was
as expectant as our fond hearts, and one could see the grass grow
green hour by hour. The warm air was full of birds, there was a glow
of light on the sea instead of the cold shining of chilly weather
which had lingered late. There was a look on Mrs. Todd's face which
I saw once and could not meet again. She was in her highest mood.
Then I went out early for a walk, and when I came back we sat in
different rooms for the most part. There was such a thrill in the air
that our only conversation was in her most abrupt and incisive
manner. She was knitting, I believe, and as for me I dallied with a
book. I heard her walking to and fro, and the door being wide open
now, she went out and paced the front walk to the gate as if she
walked a quarter-deck.

It is very solemn to sit waiting for the great events of life—most
of us have done it again and again—to be expectant of life or expectant of death gives one the same feeling.

But at the last Mrs. Todd came quickly back from the gate, and
standing in the sunshine at the door, she beckoned me as if she
were a sibyl.

"I thought you comprehended everything the day you was up
there," she added with a little more patience in her tone, but I felt
that she thought I had lost instead of gained since we parted the
autumn before.

"William's made this pretext o' goin' fishin' for the last time. 'T
would n't done to take notice, 't would scared him to death! but
there never was nobody took less comfort out o' forty years courtin'.
No, he won't have to make no further pretexts," said Mrs. Todd,
with an air of triumph.

"Did you know where he was going that day?" I asked with a sudden burst of admiration at such discernment.

"I did!" replied Mrs. Todd grandly.

"Oh! but that pennyroyal lotion," I indignantly protested, remem-
bering that under pretext of mosquitoes she had besmeared the

poor lover in an awful way—why, it was outrageous! Medea could not have been more conscious of high ultimate purposes.

"Darlin'," said Mrs. Todd, in the excitement of my arrival and the great concerns of marriage, "he 's got a beautiful shaped face, and they pison him very unusual—you would n't have had him present himself to his lady all lop-sided with a mosquito-bite? Once when we was young I rode up with him, and they set upon him in concert the minute we entered the woods!" She stood before me reproachfully, and I was conscious of deserved rebuke. "Yes, you 've come just in the nick of time to advise me about a bunnit. They say large bows on top is liable to be worn."

IV

The period of waiting was one of direct contrast to these high moments of recognition. The very slowness of the morning hours wasted that sense of excitement with which we had begun the day. Mrs. Todd came down from the mount where her face had shone so bright, to the cares of common life, and some acquaintances from Black Island for whom she had little natural preference or liking came, bringing a poor, sickly child to get medical advice. They were noisy women with harsh, clamorous voices, and they stayed a long time. I heard the clink of teacups, however, and could detect no impatience in the tones of Mrs. Todd's voice; but when they were at last going away, she did not linger unduly over her leave-taking, and returned to me to explain that they were people she had never liked, and they had made an excuse of a friendly visit to save their doctor's bill; but she pitied the poor little child, and knew beside that the doctor was away.

"I had to give 'em the remedies right out," she told me; "they would n't have bought a cent's worth o' drugs down to the store for that dwindlin' thing. She needed feedin' up, and I don't expect she gets milk enough; they 're great buttermakers down to Black Island, 't is excellent pasturage, but they use no milk themselves, and their butter is heavy laden with salt to make weight, so that you 'd think all their ideas come down from Sodom."

She was very indignant and very wistful about the pale little girl. "I wish they 'd let me kept her," she said. "I kind of advised it, and her eyes was so wishful in that pinched face when she heard me, so that I could see what was the matter with her, but they said she wa'n't prepared. Prepared!" And Mrs. Todd snuffed like an offended war-horse, and departed; but I could hear her still grumbling and talking to herself in high dudgeon an hour afterward.

At the end of that time her arch enemy, Mari' Harris, appeared at the side-door with a gingham handkerchief over her head. She was always on hand for the news, and made some formal excuse for her presence,—she wished to borrow the weekly paper. Captain Littlepage, whose housekeeper she was, had taken it from the post-office in the morning, but had forgotten, being of failing memory, what he had done with it.

"How is the poor old gentleman?" asked Mrs. Todd with solicitude, ignoring the present errand of Maria and all her concerns.

I had spoken the evening before of intended visits to Captain Littlepage and Elijah Tilley, and I now heard Mrs. Todd repeating my inquiries and intentions, and fending off with unusual volubility of her own the curious questions that were sure to come. But at last Maria Harris secured an opportunity and boldly inquired if she had not seen William ashore early that morning.

"I don't say he was n't," replied Mrs. Todd; "Thu'sday 's a very usual day with him to come ashore."

"He was all dressed up," insisted Maria—she really had no sense of propriety. "I did n't know but they was going to be married?"

Mrs. Todd did not reply. I recognized from the sounds that reached me that she had retired to the fastnesses of the kitchen-closet and was clattering the tins.

"I expect they 'll marry soon anyway," continued the visitor.

"I expect they will if they want to," answered Mrs. Todd. "I don't know nothin' 't all about it; that 's what folks say." And presently the gingham handkerchief retreated past my window.

"I routed her, horse and foot," said Mrs. Todd proudly, coming at once to stand at my door. "Who 's coming now?" as two figures passed inward bound to the kitchen.

They were Mrs. Begg and Johnny Bowden's mother, who were favorites, and were received with Mrs. Todd's usual civilities. Then one of the Mrs. Caplins came with a cup in hand to borrow yeast.

On one pretext or another nearly all our acquaintances came to satisfy themselves of the facts, and see what Mrs. Todd would impart about the wedding. But she firmly avoided the subject through the length of every call and errand, and answered the final leading question of each curious guest with her non-committal phrase, "I don't know nothin' 't all about it; that 's what folks say."

She had just repeated this for the fourth or fifth time and shut the door upon the last comers, when we met in the little front entry. Mrs. Todd was not in a bad temper, but highly amused. "I 've been havin' all sorts o' social privileges, you may have observed. They did n't seem to consider that if they could only hold out till afternoon they 'd know as much as I did. There wa'n't but one o' the whole sixteen that showed real interest, the rest demeaned themselves to ask out o' cheap curiosity; no, there wa'n't but one showed any real feelin'."

"Miss Maria Harris you mean?" and Mrs. Todd laughed.

"Certain, dear," she agreed, "how you do understand poor human natur'!"

A short distance down the hilly street stood a narrow house that was newly painted white. It blinded one's eyes to catch the reflection of the sun. It was the house of the minister, and a wagon had just stopped before it; a man was helping a woman to alight, and they stood side by side for a moment, while Johnny Bowden appeared as if by magic, and climbed to the wagon-seat. Then they went into the house and shut the door. Mrs. Todd and I stood close together and watched; the tears were running down her cheeks. I watched Johnny Bowden, who made light of so great a moment by so handling the whip that the old white Caplin horse started up from time to time and was inexorably stopped as if he had some idea of running away. There was something in the back of the wagon which now and then claimed the boy's attention; he leaned over as if there were something very precious left in his charge; perhaps it was only Esther's little trunk going to its new home.

At last the door of the parsonage opened, and two figures came out. The minister followed them and stood in the doorway, delaying them with parting words; he could not have thought it was a time for admonition.

"He 's all alone; his wife 's up to Portland to her sister's," said

Mrs. Todd aloud, in a matter-of-fact voice. "She 's a nice woman, but she might ha' talked too much. There! see, they 're comin' here. I did n't know how 't would be. Yes, they 're comin' up to see us before they go home. I declare, if William ain't lookin' just like a king!"

Mrs. Todd took one step forward, and we stood and waited. The happy pair came walking up the street, Johnny Bowden driving ahead. I heard a plaintive little cry from time to time to which in the excitement of the moment I had not stopped to listen; but when William and Esther had come and shaken hands with Mrs. Todd and then with me, all in silence, Esther stepped quickly to the back of the wagon, and unfastening some cords returned to us carrying a little white lamb. She gave a shy glance at William as she fondled it and held it to her heart, and then, still silent, we went into the house together. The lamb had stopped bleating. It was lovely to see Esther carry it in her arms.

When we got into the house, all the repression of Mrs. Todd's usual manner was swept away by her flood of feeling. She took Esther's thin figure, lamb and all, to her heart and held her there, kissing her as she might have kissed a child, and then held out her hand to William and they gave each other the kiss of peace. This was so moving, so tender, so free from their usual fetters of self-consciousness, that Esther and I could not help giving each other a happy glance of comprehension. I never saw a young bride half so touching in her happiness as Esther was that day of her wedding. We took the cake and wine of the marriage feast together, always in silence, like a true sacrament, and then to my astonishment I found that sympathy and public interest in so great an occasion were going to have their way. I shrank from the thought of William's possible sufferings, but he welcomed both the first group of neighbors and the last with heartiness; and when at last they had gone, for there were thoughtless loiterers in Dunnet Landing, I made ready with eager zeal and walked with William and Esther to the waterside. It was only a little way, and kind faces nodded reassuringly from the windows, while kind voices spoke from the doors. Esther carried the lamb on one arm; she had found time to tell me that its mother had died that morning and she could not bring herself to the thought of leaving it behind. She kept the other hand on William's arm until we reached the landing. Then he shook hands with me, and looked me full in the face to be sure I understood how happy he was, and stepping into the boat held out his arms to Esther—at last she was his own.

I watched him make a nest for the lamb out of an old sea-cloak at Esther's feet, and then he wrapped her own shawl round her shoulders, and finding a pin in the lapel of his Sunday coat he pinned it for her. She looked at him fondly while he did this, and then glanced up at us, a pretty, girlish color brightening her cheeks.

We stood there together and watched them go far out into the bay. The sunshine of the May day was low now, but there was a steady breeze, and the boat moved well.

"Mother 'll be watching for them," said Mrs. Todd. "Yes, mother 'll be watching all day, and waiting. She 'll be so happy to have Esther come."

We went home together up the hill, and Mrs. Todd said nothing more; but we held each other's hand all the way.